The
Cock's
Spur

ALSO BY CHARLES F. PRICE

Hiwassee: A Novel of the Civil War
Freedom's Altar

The Cock's Spur

by Charles F. Price

John F. Blair, Publisher *Winston-Salem, North Carolina*

Published by John F. Blair, Publisher

*The paper in this book meets the guidelines
for permanence and durability of the
Committee on Production Guidelines for
Book Longevity of the Council on
Library Resources.*

Library of Congress Cataloging-in-Publication Data

Price, Charles F., 1938–
The cock's spur / by Charles F. Price.
p.   cm.
ISBN 0-89587-230-7 (alk. paper)
1. North Carolina—Fiction. 2. Distilling, Illicit—Fiction. 3. Race relations—
Fiction. 4. Mountain life—Fiction. 5. Cockfighting—Fiction. I. Title.

PS3566.R445 C6 2000
813'.54—dc21
00-057954

*Illustration on dust jacket and pages ii and iii © Marian Bantjes
Design by Debra Long Hampton*

For Ruth
Again, and always

Part I

Dreams of Flight

CHAPTER 1

March 1880

*S*ylvester was his given name. When he was a sprout his pap used to call him Syl, but he bore his pap many a grievance, and once he got his size he swore never again to use the ill name Oliver Price, that fool, had fixed on him. So he called himself Ves instead.

Nineteen years of age, long and gangly, Adam's apple protruding like a walnut, Ves Price lay sprawled drowsing under a shebang of yellow birch bark at the edge of a ravine way up Tusquittee Creek nearly behind the peak of Piney Top, waiting for the mash to ferment. He rested mostly in shade but also amid spots and strips of light because of the way the sunshine streamed in between the pieces of bark lashed with withes to the roof of the shebang. Beneath him was a bed of fragrant spruce boughs, and under his head for a pillow were his shoes and his suit of good clothes rolled up in a ball and tied with twine. Next to him lay Rehoboam Bolt's old iron Winchester.

Laurel and ivy choked the ravine, where ran the little stream that some hundred yards below joined a branch, which wound through woods of still-leafless chestnut, oak and tulip poplar and at last emptied into the main creek down in the smoke-hazed valley. Before him on the far side of the drainage rose the Tusquittees, rank on rank of round-headed peaks, the nearest a velvety gray spotted as if from rust by the crowns of maples coming into bud, the rest wearing shades of blue that got lighter the farther off they stood, till the last range looked so faint it might have been a cloud and not a mountain at all.

The still-house sat in the throat of the ravine not ten steps from where Ves lay, but it was nonetheless unseen, so cleverly had Rehoboam Bolt teased out the branches of the ivy and laurel, so intricate had been his interweaving of creeper and cut branches of balsam. Higher up was the tub-mill, where they ground the corn after sprouting it; it was made of such rude stuff it more resembled some natural outcrop of rotten rock than anything from the hand of man. Nor would the furnace of the still-house, when lit, give out more than the merest thread of nearly transparent gray smoke, thanks to Rehoboam's skill in laying the fire and the care with which he and Jared Nutbush tended the embers, keeping them hot enough to cook the mash but not so hot they would flare and smolder. There would be only that thin line of smoke and the slight shimmer of heat in the air above it to suggest there was anything in that ravine beyond a lot of brush and clutter.

What *was* there wasn't just the blockade Ves and Rehoboam and Jared had gone partners on; there also awaited Ves's future in life. Ves had resolved to win himself a stake selling blockade—a stake the likes of which he could never earn cobbling shoes and farming on shares, no matter how earnestly he toiled. He was quits with all of that. Let his pap spend his days bent over shoe lasts pecking away with a peg hammer, then waste every evening following the hind end of a borrowed mule up and down the furrows of somebody else's field. Let his pap groan and sweat and burst his blood vessels from strain. Ves would marry Becky Curtis and live on the money he fetched selling moonshine—and on her dowry, too, which he reckoned to be considerable. They would flourish and prosper while Oliver Price went on wearing himself out in labor worse than any nigger.

Already Rehoboam and Jared and Ves had made a run of singling, which they had put through a thumping-chest and prodded some with lye and buckeye pods and a dash of pepper and ginger, to give it a bite and make it bead up convincingly. Most of this run Rehoboam and Jared had carried down to Hayesville in ten-gallon kegs on a mule sledge last evening to sell; they were due back anytime now with the sacks of shelled corn they'd gotten for the next run. Till they returned it was Ves's job to tend the mash, which was now in its seventh day of fermenting and might at any time turn to beer ready for the still.

Ves rose from the shebang and crept in crisp sunlight down the ravine to the still-house, a shanty irregularly roofed with a few loose planks. Here the mash was steeping in several large barrels that Rehoboam Bolt had buried in the ground up to the top hoops, the better to keep them hid. Hard by, a trough made of split lengths of poplar came down crookedly from upstream and took an elbow turn into the top of the big barrel enclosing the worm, atop the furnace of mortared rock. Save for the beer itself, all was in readiness for the stilling. Ves opened a barrel of mash and gazed in, frowning. This was a delicate time, and Ves was nervous as to whether he could recognize the signs.

Ree had told him how the bubbling mash would sound when it was ready—like rain on a roof, or pork frying in the pan—and how it would taste—sour as all hell, and like to knock you dead if you sampled more than a dab of it. Ree had also taught him how to get the still working. But Ree hoped to return before there was any need for Ves to undertake that, because stilling was Ree's specialty. He'd been blockading ten years, and when he wished he could make the smoothest, most limpid and powerful sugar liquor anywhere around—although on these last two occasions he'd elected to still the singlings, rather than to take the time to work the doublings and so get out the water and worst oils. Nor had the Revenue ever come near him. Still, Ves hoped Ree would soon arrive. Ves had never done a whole run by himself, had only made one run partially with Ree coaxing him, and he'd been so nervous then that he couldn't remember a thing about it now.

Also he felt skittish on account of what he planned for later on. It was a large thing he had in mind to do. Once he got his money from that run of blockade he would go down to the Curtis place and call out sweet young Becky and tender her his heart. He might take as much as twenty-five dollars as his share of the eighty gallons—after the cost of the corn and the tribute Ree must set aside for Webb Darling, the king of that region, were deducted. He thought that if Becky favored him maybe she would go away with him right off, right the evening of this very day, so that before the sun came up again he might lie with her, as he'd dreamt every hour since coming into Clay County four years ago to stay. That was when he set eyes not on the gawky snot-nosed gal-child he'd ignored on his first trip up, but on a divine being ten years older than he remembered her, a woman now, all filled out bosomy and willowy, a heap of lustrous brown hair piled high, her flesh as fair as ivory.

Ves took a dipper and lifted out a little of the mash and tasted it. It was sour enough to make a pig squeal, as Ree had said it would be when it turned. Maybe *had* turned; maybe it was ready. But then again maybe it wasn't. Ves stood irresolute. But after a time he convinced himself the mash could go awhile longer. He arrived at this conclusion because he was afraid of starting the stilling only to somehow mess it up, although he couldn't admit that fear to himself. Hoping for the best, he replaced the lid of the mash barrel, then stood and checked the position of the sun, which was two hands' breadth above the eastern horizon. It was a brilliant sky that heralded the coming spring, blue as periwinkle, with just a scud of low clouds off to the northwest drawing patchy shadows after it across the face of the hills. Nervously Ves licked his lips; it was past time for Ree and Jared to come climbing back, and he was worried; but then he remembered that the mule drawing all that corn would slow them down. Returning to the shebang, he pulled up a fern and, squatting there, commenced plucking off its leaves one by one.

He'd first set eyes on Becky Curtis when he was six and she was eleven, when he came up with his pap to visit the Curtises; but at such a time of life a boy is apt to pay small heed to any female, no matter how fetching her grin or how bright her eyes of brownish gold, like the pebbles at the bottom of a clear pool lit by the sun. He'd spent all his time cavorting around the Curtis house with the Cartman boys, chasing calves to ride, snaring toads and garter snakes, trying to get the swinging bridge undulant enough to pitch somebody in the river. But in the time since, Ves's sap had risen and Becky had blossomed like the rose of Sharon, and even though she was twenty-one to Ves's fifteen when next he saw her, he wanted her so fiercely his heart throbbed like a sparrow's whenever he beheld her.

Normally Ves cherished few notions not applying entirely to himself, and it was true that when he conceived of Becky it was often to contemplate the joys of the flesh that might be his, were she to couple with him. Yet there was something more to what he felt than this. He could not name the thing or even guess its nature, but all the same he felt it, and he knew the innocent soul of Becky had inspired it. Because of it Ves sometimes pondered buying Becky a dress or singing her a song, not in the low hope that a dress or a tune might tempt her to give herself to him at last but simply for the pleasure of seeing her done up in fresh gingham or smiling at his melody.

Now at twenty-five Becky was the last of Judge Madison Curtis's girls left unmarried. Regrettably she was something of a spinster, not because of any ill looks or awkward ways or disagreeable traits but on account of having a brother, old Andy Curtis, who on occasion acted rude and strange—so strange that most fellows who might've offered themselves as beaux were shy of him. Andy had dashed the contents of a milk pitcher over one would-be swain—meaning no ill, he'd explained, but trying to drown a small person he'd seen squatting on the fellow's hat brim. Another he'd run off by raving poems at him. A third he'd pursued around the yard brandishing a black-snake he swore was a coachwhip. One suitor he greeted at the front door wearing a wreath of laurel branches on his brow. But Ves had known Andy Curtis most of his life, and Andy's quirks were nothing new to him, Andy having always been peculiar. Ves doubted Andy would light into him, sane or no. Ves's obstacle was Tom Carter, damn his soul.

Having stripped the fern, Ves got up and stood musing. Then on impulse he left the shebang and took the weedy path up out of the ravine to where a big gnarly red oak stood leaning, dry patches of last year's leaves still clinging to it. This was the lookout. He shinnied barefoot up the shaggy trunk to the first crotch, which gave him a long broad view down the slope. Settling there, he squinted this way and that along the part of the mountainside where he knew the dim trail came zigzagging up underneath the laurel and galax. Sure enough he glimpsed a stir in the tops of the brush halfway down the pitch, maybe as much as a half-mile off. Although he thought it was Ree and Jared coming up at last—was in fact certain of it—still there was always a chance it was the Revenue instead. So he slid down from the oak and descended to the shebang and took up Rehoboam's Winchester. Opening the action partway, he looked in to confirm that a shell lay in the chamber. Then he sat on the edge of the ravine with the rifle across his knees and waited.

To himself he bitterly spoke that name again—Tom Carter. Tom came of a long line of Methodist preachers from over by the Pinelog, and by repute there were even Quakers in his background, too. With so much religion running in his veins how could Tom escape being tedious? He was a pious soul, one of those lofty ones who when a good thing happened would render conspicuous praise to God and when misfortune occurred would just as loudly thank Him for the wisdom and humility to be gained from a setback, the Divine Will being unknowable. Faith so showy and outspoken struck Ves as the hypocrisy of the Pharisees and turned his stomach with disgust. Yet Tom Carter's righteousness was much admired, and, furthermore, when his pap passed on, he would possess his own farm of a hundred acres of cropland and fifty of timber, and so Andy Curtis for all his strangeness looked on Tom with favor. And Tom fancied Becky Curtis as much as did Ves himself. Ves was shrewd enough to calculate that when the time came to choose a spouse for Becky, loony old Andy would cast her lot with Holy Tom before he would with Ves, who despite his upright pap and God-fearing people had earned a notorious name, in addition to being six years younger than the woman he craved.

So it was elopement or nothing. After elopement might come all the slippery delights of the flesh at last. Hence his plan. This was what Ves pondered as he impatiently waited for Ree and Jared and the mule to climb the trail—or, less likely, for the Revenue to spring out at him. He felt a need to ease his nerves. Presently, laying aside the Winchester, he fetched the tin flask from his clothes bundle, and uncorking the one demijohn of the run that they'd kept back, he poured the flask full. In the grip of his sudden thirst he took a single greedy swallow. It went down easy if a little oily, but then it stung him so his eyes teared up, and after that it set his belly afire. He felt scorched as if with sunburn, and tiny sparks danced before his eyes.

He shuddered, and then he grinned. It was the bumblings sure enough; he supposed folks would call it White Mule, Forty-Rod or Bust-Head. It would positively send a body flying.

⚬❧

Ree was a Melungeon, dark as any nigger or Ay-rab but with the pale eyes of his mysterious kind, who some surmised sprang from a lost tribe of Israel or maybe Portuguese sailors somehow cast away on the highlands. He had a wild mop of black hair that stuck out from under his hat in thick ringlets. He came up the trail leading the mule, and at the edge of the ravine he stopped and sniffed the air, and his face got even blacker, and his eyes snapped with temper. "Hit's ready," he declared, nodding toward the mash barrels. "Why ain't you a-cooking hit?"

Ves laid the Winchester down and shrugged and dug in the ground with his big toe; after his swig of corn he felt a little slow. "I was fixing to," he murmured. "Directly. Till I heard you-all a-coming."

Down the trail a ways, Jared Nutbush peered anxiously at Ves around the loaded sledge and the rump of the mule. In exasperation Ree glared, and the look on his face made Ves recall hearing how Ree had once killed a miller back in Hancock County, Tennessee, where he was from—shot him down with a Remington pistol for grinding Ree's grain too coarse and then sassing him. Ves knew Ree had gone partners with him against his better judgment. Anybody nineteen years old that hadn't yet made brush whiskey couldn't be much of a man, Ree had sneered. It was Jared, Ves's boyhood chum, who'd talked Ree into it—Jared's people had been moonshining as long as anybody in the Hiwassee Valley could remember. But Ves had been timid and slow to learn and had made a number of blunders, and now he could see that Ree was tired of putting up with him. Ruefully it occurred to Ves that his scheme of making a stake blockading might be shorter of life than he'd counted on.

Ree threw up his hands. "Get that corn off," he growled at Ves. "And then load up the sledge with the slops. Take the slops down to your pa." He turned and crossed to the still, swearing and stripping off his coat. By the buried mash barrels he rounded on Ves again and snapped, "Feed the mule first."

For some reason Ree admired Ves's pap—maybe on account of their both serving in the same brigade of the old Army of Tennessee. Often Ree tried to do Oliver Price favors, most of which Oliver managed politely to decline, since Oliver, a temperance man all his life, didn't approve of blockading. Yet aside from this they were friendly in a distant sort of way, and now that Ves had earned Ree's displeasure he partly counted on Ree's liking for his pap to keep Ree from chasing him off. Ves needed that stake.

Ree didn't know that Oliver had spurned his last gift of slops. A few days back Ree had sent Ves down with a load, but Oliver had refused it, saying his mast-fed hogs made firmer lard than slop-fed ones and gave meat that was tastier and more delicate. Oliver was so trusting he didn't suspect Ves of blockading with Ree. Ves told his pap Ree had paid him fifty cents to make the delivery, after they'd met by chance in the woods; Oliver thought Ves was hiring out to a farmer over by Hickory Stand. Ves had dumped that whole load of slops in the Hiwassee rather than risking Ree's ire by telling him the truth. He guessed he'd do the same today, once he got far enough away from camp. Yet he knew that he could not long play that game, for it was only a matter of time before Ree and his pap spoke together and found him out. But Ves was used to slithering free of such dilemmas; it was a skill he'd counted on his whole life, having been always more sly than wise.

Grudgingly Ree passed Ves his twenty-five dollars. Then while Ree and Jared commenced stilling Ves changed into his good suit and put on the patent-leather high-button shoes he'd made for himself to celebrate the great occasion he imagined was to come.

Ves set off down the branch with the sledge load of slops. The nearer drew the moment when he would stand before Becky Curtis and make his proffer, the more uneasy he became, so now and then as he walked beside the sledge holding the reins of the mule he resorted to his flask and liberally sampled it. Around him the day soon grew agreeably mellow, and presently Ves felt himself equal to any conceivable challenge or emergency, up to and including winning the hand of his beloved Becky. A merry mood came over him, so that he spoke nonsense to the mule and then berated the beast in fun for failing to answer him in kind.

At the fork of the branch and the Tusquittee—a spot where the water ran quick enough to go frothing over the rocks—he checked the mule and, overturning the barrels one by one, dumped the slops into the current. Concealing the empty barrels in a nearby laurel slick, he mounted the sledge and, after taking another drink, rode the rest of the way down the Tusquittee, giving the mule its head. Knowing its way from habit, the mule plodded steadily on. Ves lay on his back on the bed of the sledge, his hands cupped behind his head and the reins loose over one arm, lazily watching the clouds change shape and slowly drift across the sky. Once he saw several turkey buzzards circling high up. Another time he heard the shrill of a hawk but did not glimpse it. Bees hummed. He thought of Becky, of her brown-gold eyes. He drowsed; he dreamt; Becky took him tenderly by the hand—he felt her soft palm cupping his, as real as anything. Then he awoke and was sorry to find himself alone, after having had her so close and familiar. He sat up bemused, then after a moment fetched the flask, uncorked it and swallowed another dram. When he replaced the cork the flask was nearly empty.

It was not that he and Becky had an understanding. In fact Ves had never in his life spoken a private word to Becky on this enormous matter. Indeed he'd spoken precious little to her on any subject whatsoever. Nor had there ever been much chance. Never were they alone together—always her brother or her nephews or the mulatto Hamby McFee or Oliver Price or somebody had been about. It was possible this would've made no difference; in her presence his tongue always grew thick and stupid and his hands and feet felt three sizes too large. Mostly this was because Becky hexed him with her charms, but also it reflected a certain discomfort Ves had forever felt among the Curtises, a sense of being slightly out of place even while given ready welcome.

At all times Ves was aware he had the run of the Curtis farm only by sufferance, on account of deeds done long ago that caused his pap and Andy Curtis to hold one another equal. When all was said and done it had to be conceded that Curtises were quality and Prices weren't, and this was in nowise forgotten, not by any party on either side. A Price did not presume on a Curtis. So Ves had worshiped Becky in solitude and with the fewest of words and from afar. Yes, he was aware how great a gulf he must leap, the cobbler's son longing to possess the planter's daughter. Yet his ardor was such that he was sure she must've felt the sear of it the same as he. On occasion their looks had mildly met, he thought. Also he was certain she had smiled on him once, exclusively, two years ago in the fall, when he was helping Andy cut river cane. And they had talked, he and Becky. One time they talked about whether trolls lived under bridges, and another time they talked about the doctrine of infant baptism, and the third time they talked about her chestnut pony, Lauralee.

Riding along to the jolt of the sledge and pondering his thoughts, Ves from time to time caught sight of certain early wildflowers that captured his fancy, and soon the happy notion came to gather a nosegay to give to Becky. From a piece of woods he plucked some purple violets that were just now poking their heads out of the dead leaves. From a rocky bank he took some dwarf irises and a hank of trailing arbutus whose tiny white blossoms were newly opened. From a clearing in the forest he picked dandelion. Because of the whiskey he also chose some weeds and nettles and plumes of sedge without knowing it. All these collections he laid on the bed of the sledge next to him, a mass of many hues, if somewhat irregular looks.

Untended, the mule would've gone trudging on to Hayesville, but where Peckerwood Branch came into the creek Ves got him turned aside toward the Curtis place. In doing so he felt a certain numbness in his fingers and toes, and his head commenced to swim. Also his vision had gone shimmery, and he suffered a mild headache. It didn't occur to him that it was the lightning working, for he'd drunk his flask all unintended. By an effort of will he went on, lightly slapping the hindquarters of the mule with the reins, affectionately cussing it. Leaving the Tusquittee, he steered among the sycamores along the bank of the Peckerwood, and then coming into open country, he passed under the Double Knobs by way of Downings Creek.

Along here lay the Shuford farm, old Pete and Liza's place, and it was Ves's poor luck that eighteen-year-old Katie Shuford was swinging on the gate as he drew near the lane. Ves was forced to admit that Katie looked as fetching today as a yearling colt, her black hair all a-fly and her green eyes dancing. Her smock of burlap hung loose and inviting, so when she leaned at him from the gate, which she did now, her could see her two teats dangling, each with its pink nipple like a Maytime dogwood bud. Had he not been on an errand of such gravity Ves would've dallied; in recent times he and Katie had gone mingling up many a holler and hayloft. But he was on a mission of love, and Katie was naught to him but an appeasement of the loins.

Katie shone with delight. "Why, Ves Price," she cried, having spied the bouquet by him on the sledge, "you've brung me flowers." Dropping off the gate, she advanced to grasp up what she thought to be her trophy of devotion.

But quickly Ves held up a hand. "No, I ain't. Fact is, this here's my token to another." The light died in Katie's face, and tears rose to make her eyes glimmer. "I'm sorry for it," Ves hastened to say. He hated it when a female wept; because of him many a one had done so, yet he'd never got used to the sight of it.

"Ves Price, I ought to snatch you bald-headed," Katie declared. Stooping, she picked up a stone out of the road and flung it at him. It struck his forehead with a noise so sharp his skull might've been a dry gourd hanging from a limb. It hurt like fury and made Ves see about a million stars. He spoke to the mule and started off, Katie following, cussing at him and pitching stone after stone. One hit him in the back; the others bounced off the sledge or the rear end of the mule. He left her in the bend of the road hollering.

Near the place where the Curtises' lane cut off the wagon road Ves guided the mule on to the grassy edge of a meadow shaded by a stand of pine. Tethering the mule to a fence corner, he turned aside, not noticing that the knot he'd tied in his drunken state came loose almost at once, when the mule first pulled at it. Finally now Ves felt utterly calm in the face of the mighty thing that awaited. In what he conceived to be serene composure he patted the dust from his clothes and with his handkerchief wiped the dirt from his patent-leather shoes. Wetting his fingertips, he smoothed down his cowlicky hair. He opened his trousers and lavishly pissed. Then he took up the bouquet and started confidently forward. He was unconcerned when he found himself walking not in the lane at all but stumbling amid weeds in the ditch beside it; gravely he climbed out and stood picking beggar-lice off his pants, thinking of his mam, how she'd loved him; he hoped Becky's love would be akin to that—a devotion that never questioned nor repined.

Comforted by the memory of his mam Ves went on slowly down the lane—he seemed to be wading—to the turnaround at the end, in front of the big white frame house with its double gallery. A varnished black buggy with a leather hood was parked in the turnaround; the sorrel gelding hitched to it turned its head inquiringly to look at Ves, showing its white blaze. The horse appeared familiar, but for the moment Ves couldn't place it. *Why*, he dully thought, *they've got company*. He hesitated, uncertain; it might not be fitting to come courting at such a time. He glanced about to observe who'd arrived, but all he saw were the gelding and the buggy in the turnaround and old Andy Curtis rocking on the lower gallery of the house, wearing a collarless shirt and carpet slippers, a big book open in his lap, and a long ways off in the cornfield Hamby McFee plying a hoe. Ves recovered his resolve and went unsteadily up the walkway between the boxwoods; he would approach old Andy and inquire after precious Becky.

Andy was reading out loud—to himself, to an imaginary audience, maybe to all outdoors. "Almost five thousand years agone," he intoned, "there were pilgrims walking to the Celestial City, as these two honest persons are: and Beelzebub, Apollyon, and Legion, with their companions, perceiving by the path that the pilgrims made, that their way to the city lay through this town of Vanity, they contrived there to set up a fair; a fair wherein should be sold all sorts of vanity, and that it should last all year long."

At the foot of the steps Ves stood swaying, holding his flowers before him in both hands, but Andy never took any notice. He read solemnly on: "Therefore at this fair are all merchandise sold, as houses, lands, trades, places, honors, preferments, titles, countries, kingdoms, lusts, pleasures, and delights of all sorts, as whores, bawds, wives, husbands, children, masters, servants, lives, blood, bodies, souls, silver, gold, pearls, precious stones . . ."

Ves blinked in befuddlement as the river of words without meaning flowed over him. His headache was worse—it pounded in his temples like the beat of a drum—and now his stomach gave a heave of nausea. Big dollops of sweat suddenly drenched him. He opened his mouth to address Andy, but no speech came forth; he seemed to have lost the power of utterance, as if his tongue was bee-stung and swollen up. Andy, his little square-lensed spectacles pinching his nose, kept reading in a flat voice, making no sense at all as far as Ves could tell: "Here are to be seen, too, and that for nothing, thefts, murders, adulteries, false swearers . . ." Ves reeled, felt faint. Then nearby he heard the sparkle of Becky's laugh.

She came around the corner of the barn arm in arm with Tom Carter. The sight of Becky in all her glory—she wore a white shirt-waist as pure as her soul, and her bounty of hair shone brightly in the sun, like so much spun copper—stunned him so that for an instant the odious presence of Tom Carter failed to register. He stared in admiration as Andy read on and on—"As in other fairs of less moment, there are the several rows and streets, under their proper names, where such and such wares are vended and several such vanities sold." Then, afire with love, Ves got his tongue to stir at last and spoke Becky's name and advanced between the boxwoods holding out the bouquet. The look of horror on Becky's face stopped him even before Tom Carter pushed between them and laid a hand on Ves's breast. Not till then did it come to Ves who Tom was, that the gelding belonged to Tom. He glared in scorn at Tom while Becky gaped.

Living with a brother who had been losing his mind for the better part of a year had accustomed Becky Curtis to many a peculiar, if not repugnant, sight, but none was so unseemly as the one Ves Price now presented. Ves reached around Tom Carter to offer her his flowers, so drunk he could hardly stand. A great knot was on his brow, from which so much blood had poured that his face and suit coat were soaking with it. His trousers were smeared with mash slops and sodden with piss, and worst of all his fly was unbuttoned so that his thing hung out thick-necked from its hairy thicket, bent slightly to one side like a great blind worm. Nor had Becky ever smelt such a stink as Ves gave off. Covering her face, she turned away; Ves made as if to follow her, but Tom shoved him back, and Ves lost his balance and fell. He could hear Andy still reading on the gallery as he sought to rise. On his hands and knees he started gathering up the flowers he had dropped. Then he commenced to puke.

Of course the mule Ves had so laxly tethered wandered off. Hamby McFee discovered it next day in the Hiwassee bottom, where the sledge had fetched up between an ash tree and a big boulder. Hamby recognized the mule and the sledge as belonging to Rehoboam Bolt and went to Ree's seeking to return them. But by then Ree and Jared Nutbush had been taken up by the Revenue, who, while watching the streams for evidence of moonshining, had observed the mash slops Ves dumped and eventually found the empty barrels hid in the laurel. Following the branch, they'd come on the still-house while Ree and Jared were charcoaling the latest run of blockade. Though Ves was the cause of their capture neither Ree nor Jared condemned him to the Revenue; such was blockaders' honor. They went away to the government penitentiary in faraway Auburn, New York, without any utterance whatsoever. In their absence Webb Darling the moonshiner king looked after their families.

Ves cleaned himself up in the creek the best he could, then made his way to the Shuford farm and hid in the corncrib till night, when he pitched pebbles at Katie's window, hoping to entice her out to give him comfort. It developed that Katie was in a forgiving mood; they sported away the hours till dawn.

This continued a great while afterward, a year or so, till Jared Nutbush, of all people, took up with Katie after coming home from the penitentiary.

CHAPTER 2

July 1880

*A*t the end of the row of half-grown tobacco plants Rebecca Curtis entered the welcome shade of the sycamore and put aside her basket of crushed hornworms. Reveling in the coolness, she sank down on the cushion of moss that grew between the exposed roots of the tree. Tucking her legs underneath, she lay back against the rough bole and rested, blinking into the dazzling sun on the field before her. In the noontime glare the leaves of the plants in their long files shone as if polished, and in the distance the foothills stood behind a pearly membrane of haze that promised a thunderstorm later in a day that would grow even hotter. In the next field Hamby McFee was topping the early crop, and nearer at hand her nephews the two Cartman brothers were suckering and worming the late one, as Rebecca had been doing till the need for rest overtook her.

She watched the nearly identical bend of the backs of the Cartmans as they moved crouching from plant to plant, and she saw the dark patches of sweat under the arms and between the shoulders of their shirts of rough Chilhowee cloth. Farther on, Hamby, wearing his broad-brimmed straw hat, was expertly wielding a knife whose blade now and then blinked in the light like a semaphore. To defy convention, as was his wont, Hamby had stripped to the waist, and in the sun his muscled torso gave off a bronze radiance. She ought to speak to him about that, reprove him, as she'd learned she so often must, but just now she was too fagged out to confront him and beat back his touchy pride. She sighed; she smelt her own sour armpits, her soiled clothes, the ironlike odor of the heat, the acrid stink of the mashed worms in the basket.

Papa had always burnt the hornworms, she recalled. He had a notion that mashing them didn't necessarily suffice, and from that concern of his Rebecca in her girlhood had imagined that maybe, like salamanders, they could grow back the parts you crushed or, like snakes, their mates would come to search them out and so infest the crop again and again. Rebecca when she was small used to tend the fires. She remembered the greasy white smoke and the bitter odor of the burning worms, how they hissed in the heart of the fire.

Dragging the kerchief from her head, she used it to wipe dirty sweat off her face and neck. In the shade the air felt cool on the damp curls of her hair, flattened by the kerchief. She removed the bulky canvas gloves covered with the green slime of the pinched worms and laid them down. Then she sat turning her hands front and back before her, ruefully observing the yellow calluses on her palms, the dirt-rimmed and broken nails, the scabbed knuckles. *Lordy*, she inwardly lamented, dropping the hands into her lap, *what a beauty I be*. She tipped her head back against the shaggy trunk. Her spine ached. Her fingers and forearms hurt from mashing the hundreds of worms. She wanted to sleep. She was tired beyond expression.

As she rested, her gaze wandered up the grassy slope beyond the early field to the manse on its commanding height amid its crescent of magnolias and apple trees and Spanish oaks. The sight of it inspired in her a kind of reverie. It felt strange to her that the house yet stood while so many of the people who'd built it and lived and striven in it had long since passed on. How peculiar it seemed—they who'd lived were gone, yet the house, which was a dead thing, remained. Or was it dead after all? Did a house have a sort of life, a memory of deeds done in it? Did it remember Papa and Mama? All her departed kin? Sometimes she thought so. Sometimes in her bedroom by night she thought she heard a familiar footfall, a certain laugh for years unuttered, the murmur of a dear voice long ago stilled.

In the near field the Cartmans came to the end of their rows and commenced the next in absolute uncanny concert, as if they were as twinned in action as they'd pretended to be in blood for as long as Rebecca could remember. In smooth motions that were mirror images the brothers plucked the worms and their eggs from the undersides of the leaves, peeled off the sucker shoots, primed each plant by tearing away the bottom growth, which otherwise would ripen only into low-grade lugs. Despite the infestation it was a good hearty crop, the best in years.

Last winter, when Brother Andy wasn't ailing yet, he and Hamby and the Cartmans and Brother Andy's friend Oliver Price and Mr. Price's older boys had cleared a section of field and burnt the cut trees and brush on it in a big bonfire, which Brother said would add rich ashes to the soil and kill any seeds or sprouts that might compete. Before the cold weather broke they'd sowed there and covered the seedbeds with long sheets of muslin firmly pegged down; then, by the end of spring, when the seedlings were well up, they'd transplanted them to the part of the field where the Cartmans now worked.

Today those dozens and dozens of plants waxed strong and lustrous, row on plentiful row, needing only the constant worming and suckering—and, in a week or two hence, Hamby's topping to keep them from tasseling—in order to ripen for the fall lay-by.

It was good that the work required no guiding hand such as Brother Andy had provided while still in health. Now that he was sickly and the crop well planted and thriving, each of them pretty much knew what must be done next, and as the seasons changed they sweated away at every succeeding task in its due turn with no more of Brother's oversight than an occasional round he might make of the fields and maybe a halting word he might dispense to exhort them. And lately even this had ceased. They did miss his steady presence, but loyally they worked on.

In time, as mild bedevilments vexed them one by one, the others had begun to turn to Rebecca to ask of her the little things they might've once asked of Brother Andy—how best to combat the tobacco fly, what remedy might soothe hands worn and torn—as if they sensed that the wisdom they admired and relied on, that was failing in him, had passed somehow into her, perhaps by magic or through blood or the spirit. Rebecca had been surprised to find such a duty devolving on her and for weeks now had resisted it with all her might, for she felt wholly unsuited to fill any inch of Brother Andy's large place.

Now, while she leaned against her tree, Brother himself appeared on the upper gallery of the house across the way, as if her very thoughts had summoned him. He was still wearing his cotton nightgown, and below its hem she could see his skinny ankles gleaming bone-white. He put forth both hands and laid them on the gallery railing and stood looking down into the tobacco fields. She saw his head revolve slowly this way and that as he studied the broad acres of bottom land.

So serene, so composed did he appear—the grand seigneur surveying his domain—that Rebecca could hardly credit her memory of the night before, when at bedtime she'd peeked into his room to check on him and in horror found him gone. With the help of the Cartmans she'd mounted an anxious search in the black of night, to find him at last sitting on the bank of the river by the near end of the swinging bridge, his union suit mud-smeared and covered with burrs, his feet dangling in the water while he sang "Sally Had a Wooden Leg." *Lordy,* Rebecca repeated, this time with a despairing wag of the head. Poor Brother—once so particular, so polite, so presentable, no hair out of place, groomed tidy as a house cat, every thread of clothing in perfect order, every unseemly function of the flesh so deftly concealed with powders and toilet waters and sweet lotions that you thought him incapable of the low necessities all others had to bear. Andrew J. Curtis, veteran of war, county commissioner, scientific farmer, deacon of the church, teacher of many a Sunday school—the only kin near at hand to her, whom she'd worshiped from girlhood. There he sat sodden with dew, splashing his feet in the river, the seat of his underwear filled with his excrement, singing a low song.

He looked all right this morning, gazing over his cropland in that composed and proprietary way. But she'd learned of late how quickly he could loosen his moorings, and she dwelt now in a constant state of worry lest in some moment of her inattention he might slip off, as he'd done a dozen times or more already, and maybe wander into calamity and do himself some hurt.

But these days it was hard for Rebecca to concentrate for long on any one of the host of woes that beleaguered her. If Brother was quiet there was always some issue of propriety that Nephew Jimmy Cartman would feel obliged to raise. Jimmy was the self-appointed guardian of the Curtises' virtue. For some time now he'd been sending a series of glowering looks Hamby's way, deploring the mulatto's naked torso;

now his outrage finally overtook him, and he came marching toward Rebecca across the sunlit rows, holding his head cocked to the side and his mouth set purselike, as he always did when he was fixing to deliver a pronouncement. Behind him his younger brother—Andy's namesake—never once glanced up but went squatting on down the row, plucking off worms and suckers; despite their sameness in other ways he had little of Jimmy's capacity for moral judgment. Rebecca's unwanted duty loomed. *Why come a-pestering me?* she wailed to herself as she watched Jimmy approach. *Why do they all come?*

Besides, it was unaccountable to Rebecca how Jimmy, so wild and gay in boyhood, had attained such sanctimony in but twenty-odd short years. Jimmy was pious. Jimmy spoke to God and God spoke to him, and apparently God was in the habit of sharing with Jimmy His opinions about the shortcomings of every mortal on the upper Hiwassee. Or at least Jimmy behaved so and seemed to believe. Now he stopped at the edge of the ring of shade around Rebecca and commenced his harangue.

"Things have come to a sorry pass," he intoned, "with McFee parading around half-nekkid in front of a white woman, showing no decent respect." He'd tied a rag about his head to protect his prematurely balding dome from the sun; while he stood there lecturing her Rebecca thought how absurd he looked, fervently expounding on right conduct and all the while resembling some heathen redskin.

"Why, what d'you reckon the folk coming by are apt to think?" Jimmy earnestly went on. "Seeing you countenance the sight of that nigger's nekkidness, thinking maybe you like it, or maybe even thinking something worse, who knows? One night some of those old boys'll come over here and lynch McFee for the liberties he takes."

He stopped to take a breath that was scornful in itself, then noticed Brother on the gallery of the house and seemed to decide— since he was about the business of correction—that he might as well denounce Andy, too, for the chase he'd led them on the night before.

"And also I bet afore long somebody at the county court'll decide to call a jury and declare Uncle Andy insane—which he is—and send him off to the asylum where he belongs."

Why bother me? Rebecca wearily thought. *I don't have the slightest notion what to do. Brother Andy when in his right mind would know; Papa would know; Mama would know. But I don't.* Yet she also recognized they had no one to turn to but she. Andy was lost to them; no one else of the clan remained who was in a position to help; Hamby, though he functioned now as manager of the farm in all but name, could not be consulted in large matters by either Cartman without loss of face because he was colored—and anyway, Hamby so relished whatever mischief he could stir up that it would have been idle for Jimmy to approach him. So yes, maidenly Rebecca at twenty-five was what the Curtises had come down to. In her small person glimmered the very last spark of the sovereignty of James Madison Curtis her departed father, to whom so many had been beholden for so long.

She pondered this awhile. Moments ago she'd thought to upbraid Hamby for exposing his body; now that Jimmy was offended for the same cause she recoiled from siding with him. In a sudden spurt of ire she blurted, "I declare, one time or another, I've seen every man on this place in his birthday suit, and that includes Hamby McFee, and it includes you, too, Jimmy Cartman. And I don't know about decent or indecent, but as far as Hamby goes I only know it's hot as a stove lid out here, and he's working harder than any of us and deserves what ease he can get. And where your uncle Andy's concerned you ought to remind yourself he's been sickly of late and don't mean to be doing shameful things." In her asperity she even shook a finger at him. "I tell you, Jimmy Cartman, you need you some charity, you do."

Indignantly Jimmy drew himself up. "I've got charity," he insisted. "But appearances count."

"Beware you don't become a whited sepulcher," Rebecca shot back, and then went on to recite the words of Jesus that the evangelist Matthew quotes, about how a whited sepulcher appears beautiful outwardly but within houses dead men's bones and all corruption. Rebecca had the words of the Bible as much by heart as Jimmy did. Not for nothing had she attended—albeit grudgingly—the family devotionals Papa held every evening of her childhood, when the passages of Holy Writ were reverently read out.

"You misuse the Scriptures to your own ends, Aunt Becky," Jimmy argued, as if she'd taken unfair advantage. In his estimation he was of course no hypocrite at all; he only put on the garment of righteousness to do the work of the Lord among men, as any good Christian ought. Jimmy believed he was Christlike and humble—he pronounced it "umble"—but Rebecca thought him entirely puffed up with the awful sin of pride.

She drew in air and blew it out. Her tirade surprised her; like Sarah her mama she did have a temper but usually held it to a fault. Yet today she was too giddy with fatigue to put up with Jimmy's piety, and she realized that blessing him out for once had proved salutary, had buoyed her mood. Even so, she no more wished to argue further with him than she wanted to wrangle with Hamby McFee, so she shooed Jimmy off with an impatient wave of a hand. Frowning his reproach, he turned to leave, holding his head at that same disobliged angle. As he went she called sharply after him, "You see you treat your uncle Andy with the respect due him. He's a good man and has got sick through no fault of his own. Just now he can't help himself. You'll treat him kindly, or you'll answer to me."

She saw the nape of his neck color red and drew from the sight a small satisfaction. Rebecca did not often invoke her seniority of five years and more over her nephews, but when she did they tended to defer, as Jimmy did now, remembering how she'd mothered them after her mama passed and before their great-aunt Granny Cartman took them in.

A little revived by the exchange, Rebecca got groaning to her feet and pressed the flats of her hands into the small of her back and commenced to bend and stretch to unkink all her cramps and strains. She took up the basket, noting with disgust that some of the worms in it weren't dead after all but lay wetly squirming amid the mashed ones. Their rank smell rose to her nostrils. Grimacing, she left the shade and entered the field at the head of the row she must work next. Before bending to it she glanced once more to the gallery, and when she did Brother spied her at last. Even at the distance she saw the ready flash of his smile. It seemed to be his old smile. Happily, airily, he waved, and she hoped his cloud of confusion had lifted for the day and would remain in abeyance and let him see her and know her for who she was and to remember the times of their lives. Thinking sadly how much she loved him, she raised a hand and waved back.

Presently the toilers heard the rumble and grind of a wagon on the gravel of the drive and looked up to see Oliver Price's old red Studebaker descending on them, drawn by his two mules Shadrach and Meshach; Abednego was a notorious goat of his. Mr. Price's younguns were jammed in the bed so thickly that their heads resembled a pretty patch of black-eyed Susans. Asserting the right she'd long claimed, Miz Henslee was driving. Mr. Price was her second husband, but he insisted on calling her by the widow's name she'd borne when he made her his. Handling a span of mules was but one of her many practical talents. Mr. Price freely confessed that Miz Henslee wore the pants in the family, and he was glad of it, for it relieved him of many a worrisome obligation. Perched on the box beside her he robustly brandished his cane, hollering out, "Hidy! Hidy thar!"

Miz Henslee checked the mules, set the brake, wound the reins around the brake handle with practiced ease. Like so many mallards scuttling off a riverbank into water, the least of the younguns swept over the sides of the wagon and scattered to every quarter. The older ones—Miz Henslee's Jim and Caledonia and Ellen, and Mr. Price's fourteen-year-old James Littleton (the rascal Ves hadn't come, thank the Lord)—hung back surveying the progress of the work and guessing how much of what remained they'd be expected to do. Mr. Price dismounted and went limping to help Miz Henslee down as gallantly as if the two were still sweethearts, instead of an old couple thirteen long years wed.

Miz Henslee came toting a hamper that had a tantalizing look. The pair of them left the turnaround and advanced to the edge of the early field, where Mr. Price greeted Hamby with an exuberant wring of the hand, steered him by the elbow across the rows to Rebecca, who stood among the plants smiling and waiting. Mr. Price peered into Rebecca's basket and gave a whistle of wonder. "You-all surely got yourselves a plague of hornworms. Where's that flock of turkeys? A turkey'll eat a mess of worms."

"When it come to hornworms," Hamby explained, shrugging into his shirt at last, "them turkeys all on strike. They downriver a ways dining on grasshoppers. Whole mess of 'hoppers swarming down there. Two times I been down, drive them turkeys back, and soon as I do, off they goes downriver again to eat they goddamn 'hoppers."

"Hush up your cussing with the younguns about," Rebecca admonished him, but laughingly. Nephew Jimmy, having recovered his zeal and certain as always that bad behavior was never corrected by any display of mirth, scowled in disapproval. Hamby of course ignored him, even made a point of pulling defiantly lower over his eyes the brim of the straw hat he always refused to doff in the presence of any person, of whatever hue or station.

"With this multitude of mine," Mr. Price announced, "we'll make short work of them worms without no turkeys about atall." For years it had been his custom to help with the Curtises' tobacco crop when his shoemaking business in Hayesville permitted. "But," he asserted by way of qualification, "we must break bread first. Ain't that so, Miz Henslee?"

"We fetched some eats," she nodded, setting the hamper in the shade of the sycamore. She was a handsome and rosy woman in her forties. Her bounty of yellow-brown hair starting to turn gray was done up nicely in back with a long-tailed bow of scarlet ribbon. She had hazel eyes that smiled all the time. She named out the treats she'd brought: "Cracklins and side meat, deviled eggs, peaches, figs, cornbread. Cool cider to drink."

"Here, here now," Mr. Price broke in, rushing to extract his toddler Rachel from the mudhole into which she'd just pitched headlong. Under the sycamore Miz Henslee was busy laying out the food and took no visible account of such upsets; clearly it was Mr. Price's part to mind them. Setting his drenched tot on dry land, Mr. Price patted ineffectively at her ruined smock just as ten-year-old Freddy tried to yank out the tail feathers of a Curtis goose. "Leave that critter alone!" Mr. Price commanded with a wave of his cane. Then of course the goose gave a hiss of fury and took a bite of Freddy's arm, and Mr. Price's mission changed from discipline to comfort.

Meantime, Rebecca dispatched Andy Cartman to run up to the house and bring Brother out. But no sooner had the lad set off than Brother obligingly emerged on the main gallery of the house and began to make his way down. As Brother came, Mr. Price, consoling Freddy, spied six-year-old Lillian nearby eating a fat hornworm. He deserted the bawling boy to relieve her of it. "We'll have better'n that to eat here directly," he promised. Presently some of the younguns fell to eating, and the commotion waned sufficiently for Mr. Price to take thought of the troubles of the day. Bringing Freddy by the hand, he approached Rebecca, eyeing sadly the thin hobbling figure of Andy Curtis. "Tell me, sugarplum, how is he?"

As Rebecca answered she saw him squint and wrinkle up his nose, as he did whenever a powerful sorrow took him. Though he'd known war and bad times, these hadn't hardened him; maybe instead they'd sharpened his capacity for pity; he'd kept an affinity for the suffering of others that was so acute it was painful to see. As she talked Mr. Price watched his old comrade coming along in his slow and tottery way; tears started in the corners of his eyes till with the back of a fist he stopped them.

Presently under their watchful gaze Brother Andy drew near. Rebecca was mortified to see how he appeared. He'd shaved one half of his face but not the other; something had diverted his attention while he plied the razor, and he'd forgot to finish. In a whispery voice he said a mild hello to one and all. His thinning brunet hair was neatly combed, but regrettably bits of yellow matter clung in his mustache, and a bead of snot pulsed in one nostril; he wore the white shirt Rebecca had only yesterday washed and starched for him, yet the front of it was smeared with what looked like tomato catsup and egg yolk; his trousers were torn and grimy, and from their odor you could tell he'd moved his bowels again and failed to wipe his bottom. Benevolently he smiled, took Mr. Price's proffered hand, patted the heads of some of the swarming younguns. With a pleasant expression he glanced about, but when his eye met hers Rebecca saw it was as dead as the glass orb in the head of a stuffed bobcat.

"I want to thank you-all for coming," Brother Andy said now in a stronger voice. "There can be no better benefit to the people of this community than to provide and maintain a system of first-class roads, by which we may efficiently carry to market the bounty of our land. If you honor me with your vote you may rest assured that I will undertake this much-needed reform with the greatest promptitude and will brook no undue impediment or delay." Very gravely he bowed and once more thanked them, then turned and started up the hill toward the house, clasping his hands behind him. As he went he seemed to scan with special attention the rising ground before him, as if by mishap he'd dropped some small item he'd long treasured and was hoping to find it.

While they ate in the shade of the sycamore, the haze over the hills slowly thickened till the summits melted into it, leaving a scant irregular outline only faintly darker than the haze itself. In the distance thunder bumped with a noise like someone dragging a heavy suitcase down a stairway. "Be a-storming after a while," Mr. Price allowed. Indeed the coppery smell of imminent rain already tinged the air. Reluctantly they rose and ventured out. The sear of the midday sun was diffused by the haze into a sourceless web of light that burned exposed skin no matter which way one turned. Hamby resumed his topping, while the Cartmans and Mr. Price's oldest and Miz Henslee and Rebecca all suckered and wormed. Mr. Price lounged against the sycamore incompetently supervising the tots, who darted about in wild abandon, oblivious of his reprimands and entreaties.

Rebecca and Miz Henslee worked the same row. At the end of it they stopped to ease their backs and dry their sweat with their kerchiefs. Because of the embarrassment Andy had caused her Rebecca was in a prickly state. She fancied her brother. He was the oldest, the one she'd adored all her life for his mild ways and for what she conceived was his power to endure hard times with grace; Jack and Howell had died before she was eight, and she hardly remembered them enough to miss them. Furthermore Andy had been the closest thing to a papa she'd had in the longest time, and he owned the best heart of any man living. But now, due to his fits, she was put out with him nearly to death. The spectacle he'd made of himself last night and now today had degraded him and Rebecca both. All of a sudden she threw down her basket, spilling a mass of hornworms between the rows, crying, "I feel harder against him, more and more every time."

She never spoke of her trials with Andy to anyone outside the family. But today she felt all her fences were down, and in the past Miz Henslee had shown herself a sympathetic spirit. Now she looked Rebecca steadily in the eye with perfect understanding and said, "I know."

Grimly Rebecca wound the wet kerchief over her head once more, drew it tight, knotted it. "I even feel hard against him when he ain't addled, on account of waiting for him to have another fit." She pulled off the gloves, slung them violently away, put her rough hands to her face as if to hide it for shame. "He's such a tender soul when his head's clear, and there I am being snappish and mean, poisoning what little good he can get between spells."

Miz Henslee reached out a hand and fondly tucked a stray wet curl of Rebecca's under the edge of her kerchief. "Putting up with any man atall's a torment. Sick or well, however he be. A woman's a slave to a man the same as any nigra used to be. I don't know why the Book of Genesis makes so much of man having to earn his bread by the sweat of his brow, after the Fall. Seems to me a woman can match any man when it comes to sweat, and mostly outdo him. And on top of that bear the pains of childbirth"—here she made an ironical face— "which the Lord in His wisdom has made the lot of woman, too."

Rebecca's eye took on a hard vindictive glint. "God favors the male," she declared.

"Yes, it seems so. But Becky, look how sorely burdened you are, away beyond the normal."

Rebecca was astonished, for to her Miz Henslee's life seemed far more afflicted than her own. Wanly she smiled. "I've not been much tried, not next to you."

"No, I mean it," Miz Henslee insisted. "I've got a good man that cherishes me. I've got a whole crowd of sprouts about me that I can care for. It's what I always wanted. This is my dream come true. 'Tain't a trial, 'tis a blessing." Speaking of it made her eyes brighten in a way that Rebecca couldn't help envying.

In contrast Rebecca could not recall a time when chores and duties had not eaten her own spirit from the edges inward. Forever she was washing excrement out of bedsheets, boiling Jerusalem oak and pine root to make worming syrup, laying off rows of stony dirt with a bull-tongue plow behind an ox with manure smeared all over its behind, holding the brows of puking boys, helping birth colts and calves, cooking hydrangea to make poultices for boils, hoeing, castrating calves, milking, picking off head lice, churning, lancing pustules, pounding May apple into a powder to cure constipation, bathing Brother's slack white flesh over and over in the tin tub while he searched himself for signs of the cancer and pox he was now convinced he'd somehow contracted.

"I ain't all by myself like you," Miz Henslee was saying. "Why, I've got Mr. Price and the ones of his that are near grown, and my own. I've got more help than I can stir with a stick. But look at you. Your sisters are all married off, or in the tomb, bless 'em. Your pa and ma, your brothers, everyone dead save Andy."

Rebecca nodded while from beyond the mountains came another faraway thump and murmur of thunder. It was true. Starting when she was but a child, she'd tended Mama and Papa in their decline, then reared the Cartmans, her dead sister's boys, whom her folks had kindly but unwisely taken in to raise. And after Mama went to her reward she'd been alone except for what guidance Grandma Cartman could provide—whose teaching, Rebecca suspected, was the root of Nephew Jimmy's tiresome evangelism, Grandma Cartman being famously saved and holy.

Now to her shock and very much against her will misery swept over her, and Rebecca began to weep. Again she covered her eyes with her hands; they reeked of mashed worms. "Lately," she burst out, "he's took a notion that somebody—maybe even me—has made off with all his wealth. He spends hours in the study going through his stock and bond certificates, giving me suspicious looks. Half the time he don't even know me—or if he does he thinks I'm his enemy." She shivered, hesitated for fear of demeaning herself, then went on in an eager rush, wanting to be truly understood even if it did demean her. "He thinks he's diseased, thinks he's got all manner of awful contagions. Fiddles with his body, with his manly part, looking for sores and cankers and rashes. All of a sudden I can't keep him away from any kind of filth. The other day I found him in the summer kitchen picking through a bowl of stool like he was looking for sweetmeats."

She sobbed, wiping her nose with the back of a smelly hand. "Now he's taken to wandering off of a night. Daytimes, too. To go where, to do what, I don't know. He just goes. It's like he's looking for something—his sense, maybe, or who he used to be. I'm scared to death some accident'll befall him. Or that a friend or neighbor will see him, and he'll be revealed and disgraced. God forgive me, I've had to lash him down to keep him. One night I even slept in the same bed with him, tied his leg to mine. But I can't watch him every second. Why, he got out last night, and it took me and Nephew Jimmy more'n two hours to round him up again, and me worried sick the whole time."

Miz Henslee wasn't fazed; likely she'd seen far worse, as hardships aplenty were her portion. She put her arms about Rebecca, drew her close, gently patted the back of her head; sobbing against Miz Henslee's bosom, Rebecca smelt—even through a nose swollen with crying—a faint bite of the lye soap still left in Miz Henslee's shirtwaist from its last washing and the sour scent of her sweaty hair and, stronger than any, an essence Rebecca knew must be Miz Henslee's own, her very aura, a cool breath such as caves exhale, redolent of dark earth and old stones. "I know, I know," Miz Henslee crooned. "He's getting worse all the time. He'll need more and more from you. And you're at the end of yourself, ain't you, sweetheart?"

Yes, Rebecca thought without saying it aloud. Every day brought its new abomination that she must rectify. Above all, Brother must be coddled, tended, shielded from harm, secreted away when necessary, kept clean. Yet when she searched inside herself for the wherewithal to persevere in the work, all she found was a void born of exhaustion and dead hopes. What of *her?* What of the dreams *she* might cherish? All the while she lavished care on Andy time was inexorably passing; she was growing steadily older; her beauty—which was once the prize so many young men of the valley had avidly sought—was fading, coarsening, drying up. The sun had bleached swatches of her hair an unlovely russet; there were nets of fine sun-grins around her eyes; she even felt the slow parching of her neglected privates. Already she knew people spoke of her as a hopeless spinster and condemned it as a pity. And it seemed to her that they were right, that Rebecca Curtis was one more ugly, peckish, shriveled-up old maid.

Miz Henslee held her at arm's-length and leveled a deep look at her. "Mr. Carter's anxious to help. Wants to wed you. Wants to share your load."

Bless his heart, it was so. Doggedly Tom had paid court, never flagging or failing. True, he was as boring as a slab of rock and plain as a mud fence, but he offered a considerable boundary of land and a good deal of timber and herds of livestock that he owned outright or would one day inherit. Thanks be, he'd set his cap for Rebecca and gave no time at all to the many ambitious lasses of the county who coveted his goods, if not his indifferent looks and bland ways. "Yes," she said, drying her tears with the tail of her apron. "Yes, I know.

He's a gift. But how can I marry? Brother needs me, needs me worse every day."

Miz Henslee bit her lips into a flat impatient line. "Mr. Carter's all the choice you've got anymore," she declared. "After him you can expect naught but rascals to come calling, scoundrelly fellows with their minds set on sly and naughty things."

Stung, Rebecca shook herself loose and moved a step or two away among the plants and stood rubbing the places on her arms where Miz Henslee had held her. But despite being offended she saw that Miz Henslee was right; low men would pursue her, thinking the unfed yearnings of her flesh would make her yield to them. Still it angered her to see that glimpse of an ugly future. "Tom Carter ain't my idea of an answered prayer," she stiffly said, then wondered at once why she'd spoken such a cruel thing.

"Maybe not," replied Miz Henslee. "Maybe Mr. Price wasn't any answer to mine. Not at first. But in time he came to be." She nodded. "It happens. It happened to me."

Rebecca stood reflecting. It *was* almost a miracle that Tom looked past the hardening shell of her and into the well of her heart; most persistently he wanted her for his wife. Not that she fancied him much; it was almost more than she could do to keep awake while he droned on about fertilizers and the uses of weirs and the principles of hog droving and the perverse habits of hoop snakes. Nor was she under any illusion that a life with Tom would be free of its own woes, for she knew how any kind of life was beset. At least if she took up with Tom she'd trim down the number and size of the things that beleaguered her. Tom seemed a harmless fellow, even if she did disapprove of how he parted his thick auburn hair down the middle like a salesman of cheap encyclopedias, and even if she did detest his nasty habit of dipping snuff. Her rage petered out, and she dropped her head sideways and smiled at Miz Henslee, half in apology and half in affection. "Maybe," she said, still not convinced, "I could come to like him."

"You bet you could," said Miz Henslee.

They resumed working then, bending along the rows as the haze darkened over the hills and the thunder drew nearer out of the south. But even as she tried to accustom herself to the notion of taking a husband in Tom Carter, Rebecca could not help thinking how much Brother needed her in his sickness, needed her just as Mama and Papa had in their dotage, as the Cartman boys had when young, as her own sister Polly had in dying of a stillbirth.

She held dear so many images of the past—of herself as a child, straddling Brother's neck as he ran through the bottom-land rye holding her by the ankles, how his hair under her chin smelt of Macassar oil, how his laugh sounded, how as she bounced up and down with his running she would loudly hum, then laugh to hear the way each bounce would interrupt the hum with a silly sound, *yuh-yuh-yuh*. She remembered Andy presenting her the pony Lauralee when she was twelve, Andy reading to her the wonderful adventures of King Arthur and the Knights of the Round Table while the fire on the library hearth cozily whined and popped, Andy holding her by the hand at Mama's funeral, Andy making her a set of stilts out of rhododendron trunks so she could go pacing abroad lofty and heronlike, looking down imperially on pullets and pups and shoats, which stared back amazed as she glided past.

Andy was the last male to carry the Curtis name, and he was childless, and now he was going feeble in his reason; after him the Curtis name would flicker out like a lamp whose oil has burnt away. Was Rebecca not then the steward? Was it not her duty to carry on the honor of the line?

She stopped and stood at the end of the row, drenched with sweat, her gloves covered with the muck of the worms. The fond memories of Brother faded; the woes of today rose again. Sourly she recalled every wasted body she'd ever tended. *All I've done*, she thought, *is help others live their lives, while my own life went to seed.* Rebecca Curtis was a field of waste, all grown up rank in weeds and briars and brush. And in spite of the slaving and nursing she'd doled out to others, those she'd helped had soon died anyway, or lost their wits, or like the Cartmans never ceased to suck at her substance. She must make an end to that. But she must follow the path of duty, too, the path marked out for her by Papa, Mama, her dead brothers, poor dear Andy. But how? How?

CHAPTER 3

October 1880

Crossing the yard of swept dirt, Hamby passed the spirit tree covered with bottles of brown and green and indigo blue and went on beyond it to Gouger's pen. Made of dried creeper vine, the pen sat on the hard-packed ground in a crazy quilt of light that the sun coming through the colored glass of the bottles had laid down. In the pen Gouger rounded on him while the hen shrank back in dread; the patterns of bottle light—luminous spots of amber and jade and sapphire—moved over Gouger and the hen, changing form and size and even awakening the tints of a peafowl's tail in the gusts of chaff Gouger's wings whipped up.

Hunkering, Hamby unlatched the gate of the pen and took hold of Gouger with both hands and lifted him out. Carefully—mindful of Gouger's sharpened spurs—he undid the tether and took Gouger by the legs with one hand and with the other slid him gently but firmly into the crook of his left arm, then released the wiry legs into the grip of the left hand to keep him fast. Gouger's neck feathers bristled, and in a rage he twisted his head to glare up at Hamby with his fierce red eye. Harshly, imperiously, he crowed. Hamby bent to him and blew his breath over Gouger's head, and Gouger quieted.

Hamby hefted Gouger while the hen fussed alone in the pen and then in another moment forgot her alarm and commenced scratching idly at the dirt with her yellow foot. *Four, four and a half pound,* Hamby judged; Gouger had put on weight in the six months since he was last in the pit. Against Hamby's side Gouger felt lean as an otter and twisty as a snake, except for the great meaty bulge of his breast. Hamby watched in approval as the blood rose in Gouger's bobbed comb and made it glow as if it were a sliver of ruby laid on edge along the top of his head. Presently Hamby latched the gate of the pen with the hen in it and stood and reached in his pocket and one by one fed Gouger several small pieces of middlin meat lightly rolled in gunpowder. Gouger wolfed them down and looked sharply about for more.

What breed he was Hamby couldn't have guessed. The glossy black of his head shaded lighter down his neck, first to tobacco brown, then to rust, then to the hue of a ripe pumpkin; he had hackle feathers pale as cream; elsewhere he was speckled like a piebald horse, save for his wings and tail, which were cinnamon and tipped with the same black that was on his head. His breastbone was a good straight one, and he carried himself in a wide-set knock-kneed way that gave him a stubborn balance. Some who'd seen him in the pit said he had Sumatra in him; others claimed he was Earl of Derby or some kind of Roundhead or even an old Accheet out of faraway India. But those boys were all ignorant and were just using names they'd heard. Nor did Hamby care. Whatever Gouger's bloodline he was the fightingest damn chicken in all of Clay County. Ever since his stag year, when Hamby first started pitting him in hack fights up and down the river, he'd killed or whipped upwards of a hundred of the best roosters going—shufflers, cutters, big old shakes as mean as sin, it didn't matter to Gouger.

Hamby blew again on Gouger's head and spoke in confiding fashion as he carried him around the corner of the cabin toward the stable, where the jenny waited. "We going to tear us up some chickens today, ain't we?" he said. Gouger's narrow head weaved and dodged and jerked sharply back, as if he understood and agreed; his red eye burned. He stretched out his neck and crowed again with his grating cry. The pullets were high-stepping hither and yon in the side yard, and now Hamby leaned down and held Gouger out so he could peck one on the head; he struck like a timber rattler, and the pullet fled under the porch with an indignant burble. Greedily Gouger gobbled the piece of wattle he'd ripped off.

It would be Gouger's last time in the pit. He was four now, blind in one eye, stiff and sore from dozens of old wounds. Around his chest and under his wings his many scars shone livid where feathers would no longer grow. He was close to the end and seemed to know it; sometimes now Hamby would find him standing motionless by his pen at the length of his tether, gazing off into the distance in a way that seemed melancholy. Yet he was still dead game. From long experience Gouger knew the signs of a coming fight—being fetched up from his pen, untied, fed the middlin meat, encouraged to peck at the pullets, toted around the corner of the cabin to the stable fence— and now under Hamby's arm he began to shake with a terrible fury and anticipation. Hamby even fancied he could feel Gouger's small brave spirit flexing like a muscle, like some great heart beating. Gouger had maybe two more full days of fighting left in him—say, ten or twelve fights all told. Then if he lived he'd be a brood cock. But meantime Hamby meant to see if Gouger couldn't summon up grit enough to lick Rollin Livingood's old shake, a Georgia Shawlneck famous as a cutter, name of Slingshot, reputed to be the champion cock of the country around Hanging Dog.

In Hamby's pocket were eight dollars in silver and pennies, a trove he'd amassed over several weeks from the profit on his last corn crop and from the wage the Curtises paid him. By betting on Gouger he aimed to parlay that eight dollars into enough of a stake to free himself from the valley of the Hiwassee, of which he'd grown weary. He'd done it before—won a great pot on Gouger's grit. He'd done it plenty of times, but then due to the temptations that came over him whenever he got flush, he'd always squandered the funds on women and drink and gambling. This time he meant to hold true to his resolve. Yes, improbably, his whole fate was riding on one beat-up, old, half-blind rooster long past his prime, and Hamby supposed the odds were against them both. Already he could taste in his mouth the ashes of failure and sense the fading of his dream. Yet in a peculiar way he felt he owed Gouger this wild cast of fortune—Gouger who time and time and time again had so valiantly offered himself up to death on Hamby's account.

Hamby did not really wish to escape the valley altogether. On the contrary the Hiwassee was the best of all the homes he'd known, and he fancied it more than he'd admit out loud. But lately the discomfort of living in the place had come to irk him beyond what he wanted to bear. He was weary. In his youth he'd been afire with hate of every white and of every black and finally of his own person, because he thought that as a high yellow he had no place in the world. In time his stepdaddy Daniel McFee made him see the place he did have, and the Curtises gathered him in as close as kin, despite the ill temper and saucy mouth he perversely kept about him, as if to hold them at a distance. Through the years Hamby had repaid them with loyalty and much hard toil, though he covered it over with cussing and smart-alecky talk, which to his aggravation they all forgave and even grew to enjoy.

But now his stepdaddy was fourteen years in the grave, and most of the Curtises he'd cared anything about were gone as well—old Judge Madison and Sarah his wife, two of the boys dead in the war, all the girls but lonesome Miss Becky married or passed on. And then there was Andy. Why, Andy Curtis was slipping deeper day by day into what seemed lunacy, so that Hamby—goddamnit all!—Hamby must manage the Curtis place while his own farm on Downings Creek went steadily to rack and ruin. Hamby was sick of it—sick of minding Curtises, especially Curtises that were weak, dogged by worries, crazy, leached out. They were but the pitiful remnants of a formerly mighty tribe; they were the last withered leaves sprung from a tree once great but now slowly dying. If he kept on tending them, he'd come to believe, he'd be no better than the slave he was in his boyhood, when the Curtises had owned him body and soul.

It tired Hamby to see the old ones wither and fade; it tired him to watch those who came after the old ones rise up—Ves Price and the Cartman brothers and Webb Darling and all such sorry ilk. Hamby didn't want to stand by looking on while Andy Curtis—who was as decent as a white man could likely be—came to the finish that he must. Nor did he wish to give of himself any longer in causes not his own, for a race he only partway belonged to, for a family that wasn't even his.

No, Hamby was weary to the bone; he was fed up; above all he was angry. He needed to drain all this off somehow and replenish his strength. He thought if he went someplace else—someplace new, perhaps a city like Asheville or Atlanta or Knoxville—it might refresh him, and then maybe he would wax strong enough one day to come back to the home of his heart and find what was left of it and see if it still offered him a nest as before. Could he do it? God knew. It was all up to Gouger now.

He'd saddled the jenny and tied her to the top rail of the fence by the stable. Now as he approached with Gouger the jenny eyed the two of them unhappily. Hamby reckoned she was recalling the several instances in the past when Gouger had got dissatisfied with her gait or the pace of travel or had some other such grievance and had given her a fearful flogging. So Hamby laid a hand on her halter and uttered sentiments of reassurance into her ear, at the same time holding Gouger safely back as he kept viciously shooting out his neck, hoping to snatch himself a hunk of donkey hide.

Then Hamby drew a coiled length of braided leather from the saddlebag, passed an end of it into one of the brass-rimmed tie-holds on the old McClellan saddle and drew the cord through. Where the ends met he made two turns around one of Gouger's legs and knotted the double line. That would give Gouger four feet or so of slack, so if he got bored riding in back of the saddle on the roll of burlap he could get up on Hamby's shoulder and survey the passing scene like the royalty he believed himself to be. Now once more Hamby blew his breath on Gouger. Then he raised him up and set him behind the cantle, while the jenny looked around at them with rue and misgiving.

In the pasture the old stallion Tom stood watching the preparations. When Hamby finished and was fixing to mount, Tom nickered and as always came slowly over to the fence, with every step giving a heavy nod of his head, which was frost-white now with age. A milky film covered both Tom's eyes. His nether lip pendulously dangled, giving him an unwarranted air of idiocy. Flies swarmed over him. Silver hairs in multitudes dulled his coat, once so bright and satiny a bay it seemed to give off its own light. "You, Tom," Hamby said to him, stepping up on the jenny. He reined her close by the fence and reached out and touched Tom's muzzle, and Tom grunted and blew two jets of steam from his nostrils into the damp morning air, then stood patiently by the fence watching as Hamby started the jenny down the lane, Gouger behind him savagely flapping his wings and crowing.

⌒

Hamby followed the creek downstream past maples molted of all their foliage and Spanish oaks still wearing masses of sere brown and bent-over weeping willows shedding the last of their yellowed leaves into the water like coins sparsely spent. Underfoot the dry mast crackled and crunched like popcorn. As the sun rose toward the low zenith of the season the line of shade along the edge of the woods to Hamby's left withdrew, leaving behind a grassy space of dewy wetness which then began to smoke as the warmth of new sunlight dried it. The air smelt of Indian summer with cold to follow close behind. The curling drifts of mist rising on the sides of the mountains looked to Hamby like the plumes on the helmets of the old-timey knights that Daniel his stepdaddy used to tell him about.

Where the creek flowed into the Hiwassee Hamby took the path that ran along the river to Jackrabbit Mountain. In another twenty minutes or so he saw the marker Eli Abernathy had told him about—a dead standing pine that had turned red—and here he diverged and entered the woods at the mountain's foot. Making his way through fern and bracken turning yellow and gold, Hamby heard a commotion up ahead. He guided the jenny toward it, while behind him on the cantle Gouger, sensing the immediacy of a fight, began again to beat his wings and squall.

In a moment Hamby broke into the clearing, where several whites crouched around a cockpit they'd outlined in the red dirt with a sharp stick. They smoked or chewed and passed a bottle of blockade while

45

they waited. Nearby in the undergrowth and tethered at safe distances from one another were a number of fighting cocks, all at full cry. Off to one side a small campfire smoldered. The ring of pale faces lifted and turned Hamby's way. One fellow Hamby didn't know—he was slender and knobby-shouldered and had a nose like a potato left too long in the cellar and pale hair as lank as corn silk—swore and laughed and blew his nose between his fingers in distaste at the sight of him; Hamby knew he'd better keep this peckerwood under watch. As always Mose Sullivan bobbed his head hello. Luke Truly and Cecil Dobbs just squatted there by the pit staring. Eli Abernathy had the bottle; he stood and spat sideways and took a swig and said, "Well, here's the nigger and his murdering chicken."

Luke Truly turned red as a shined apple. "*Now* where in hell's this damn Livingood?" he wanted to know. "I want to see the old bird that's going to take the nigger down."

"Shit," Hamby said with an air of good cheer. "Why, I already down, being as I ain't even a *whole* nigger, but only a *half* of one." He dismounted and tied the jenny to the trunk of a young locust tree, while Gouger flared and screeched on the saddle. Then he turned to Truly with a not-unpleasant nod. "While you," he added, "you a whole entire son of a bitch and can't do a goddamn thing about it."

After speaking so, Hamby stood loose by the jenny, ready to move, but Truly lost some of his color thinking of the razor Hamby always carried and of the five-shooting Colt's Police Model he knew Hamby sometimes stuck in the pocket of his britches; Truly had no more to say. Even the peckerwood looked uncertain. One by one the others glanced off someplace else, and then after a time Hamby felt he could relax. He went and sat on a stump slightly apart from the others and lit his pipe and smoked. Of course nobody offered him any of the blockade, but he had some of his own in a little tin bottle he always toted, and now he lightly sampled it.

After a time the peckerwood, who now seemed intrigued by

Hamby, got up and ambled across and stood before him grinning. "Where I come from," he said, "a coon with a mouth as loose as yourn would've did a rope dance afore now." His eyes were the green of the scum on a pond of dead water and were hooded by heavy lids that made him appear in need of slumber.

Hamby settled a mild look on him. "You *ain't* where you come from. You where *I* come from."

The peckerwood's bloated lids blinked. "Damn," he said. He glanced sideways at the others, who avoided his eyes, then back to Hamby. "Shit, you boys around here let a goddamn nig go on sassing this way at a white man?" Nobody answered him. He scuffed at the ground with the toe of a brogan and ran his thumbs up and down inside his galluses. Then he shrugged. "Hellfire, I got four dollars says my old Arkansas Traveler can whup that ugly-looking rooster of yourn all hollow."

"Done," Hamby agreed. He laid down his flask and got to his feet and crossed to where the jenny stood drowsing. Gouger lashed his wings, ruffled his feathers, drew out his neck, hoarsely crowed. Hamby undid the tether and lifted Gouger down, brought him close, once more blew his breath over the darting imperial head.

The Traveler was pea-colored and had blue wings and tail. He looked to have good power and spring in the legs, and Hamby approved of the way he strutted and glared about in contempt, arching his long neck. He had a red eye as ferocious as Gouger's own and was plump, but with muscle only. The Travelers were good shufflers and cutters and were utterly without fear, and Hamby expected this one to give a good account of himself, just as they all did. Abernathy weighed the birds, and the Traveler went to pecking at his arm, while Gouger for a change rested thoughtful and quiet. After hefting them both Abernathy raised the Traveler and said to Hamby, "This-un's got near half a pound on ye."

Hamby waved a dismissing hand. "Let it go." He took Gouger

back, blew on Gouger's head and went past the dying campfire to kneel at the edge of the pit. He set Gouger down and let him get his feet firm under him on the bare dirt. The peckerwood fetched the Traveler from Abernathy and walked around the pit and squatted opposite Hamby, holding the Traveler down on the ground with both hands. He was still grinning, and the grin showed the stumps of his rotted teeth. The Traveler scrabbled at the dirt with his ocher talons. Still in the grip of his eerie calm, Gouger looked on in a disinterested way that was all the more remarkable for his previous agitation. Once more Hamby sensed in the old warrior the strange brooding melancholy he'd seen come over him by his pen in the cabin yard.

Abernathy took his place on the rim of the pit and leaned in, hands spread on his knees. "Bill 'em," he said.

Reached out head to head into the middle of the pit, the birds eyed one another, then in a flash went to pecking and hacking. You could hear the clatter of their beaks like swords crossing. The Traveler slashed at Gouger's throat and tore off a pinch of feathers, and Gouger, his ruminations ended, went for the Traveler's eye but missed and opened a gash along one side of his head. "Shit-fire," the peckerwood blurted in dismay, drawing the Traveler quickly back. He bent and used his tongue to lick the cut on the bird's head.

When the peckerwood was done Abernathy made a roundabout gesture and said, "Pit 'em."

But a split second before Abernathy spoke, the peckerwood let the Traveler go, and he came across the pit like a whirlwind blowing grit and dust behind him and came down shuffling on Gouger and made as if to cut him but instead drove a spur through the web of flesh between the thumb and forefinger of Hamby's left hand, where it was still folded around Gouger's body. Hamby swore, snatched Gouger off, stood, slung his hand so the blood spattered wide, some of it hissing in the embers of the fire. The peckerwood retrieved the

Traveler, turned his head aside, spat, gazed up at Hamby out of his sleep-lidded eyes and offered his smirk. "Sorry. Sometimes this old bird just turns so ill he gets a-loose from me."

While Gouger trembled under his right arm Hamby sucked at his wound. "Yeah," he said. Drawing a handkerchief from his back pocket, he wrapped it around the bloody hand. Gouger cocked his head this way and that, as if already looking for an angle of attack. Again the peckerwood spat.

Hamby knelt again and set Gouger before him and turned him loose at once, and the two cocks met at the center of the pit pounding one another with their wings. They ascended as if along some unseen vertical wire and seemed for an instant to hang suspended in space while they drove their spurs with the thrashing of their wings. Tufts of feathers fluttered down, and as Hamby rose and backed away a spray of blood finely sprinkled him. When the birds plunged back to earth Gouger came down hung; the Traveler had sunk a spur in him that wouldn't come out.

Abernathy pointed, told Hamby, "Handle him," and Hamby entered the pit and took hold of the Traveler's hung leg. It was his responsibility, for if the opponent came in to handle he might slyly manipulate the spur so as to kill the enemy bird. Gouger lay panting with his wings spread in the dirt while Hamby drew the spur out; Hamby thought Gouger still wore that look of wistful melancholy. The cut wasn't deep; Hamby scooped up some soil and rubbed it in. Then he pitted Gouger again and stepped away, and the instant he did Gouger sprang and slashed the Traveler deep under one wing, and the Traveler sagged and dropped and then lay motionless except for his head, which jerked to and fro, still trying to peck. Gouger had severed a nerve, and the Traveler was paralyzed except for his head. Lying there, he kept trying to peck Gouger, and Hamby watched him full of admiration. Gouger whipped his wings, shot out his neck, in a harsh voice cock-a-doodle-dooed his victory. The peckerwood stooped down cussing and grasped the Traveler by his neck while he was still trying to peck Gouger and whirled him around in a circle and wrenched off his head. He tossed the head and body separately into the underbrush, and after it landed the body kept flopping and trying to get up.

Hamby gathered Gouger and carried him to where the jenny was hitched and lashed him again to the saddle. Bending down, he grasped another handful of dirt and put it on the place where Gouger had got hung and then pressed his thumbs there to slow the bleeding. Gouger's eye avidly watched him. Under his thumbs he felt the beating of Gouger's heart. "All right," he said to Gouger. "All right." He drew out his clasp knife, opened it with his teeth, cut off half of a hackle feather and laid it longways on the cut till the seepage wet it enough to hold it. When he was satisfied with Gouger's condition he put away his knife and turned and came back to the pit, where he stood adjusting the handkerchief wrapped around his hurt hand. Inquiringly he bent his head at the peckerwood. "Four dollar you be owing me," he said.

"Hell," the peckerwood laughed, "I ain't giving no money over to no damn nigger as puffed up and smart-alecky as you. You want four dollars, go and shit 'em out your own self."

With a flat smile Hamby considered him. "If you'd cheat a part of a nigger, I wonder what you'd do to a whole one?"

"Part or whole, makes no difference to me," sneered the peckerwood. "A coon's a coon in my book. I don't know why these here boys didn't take you off and stretch your neck a long time ago. And maybe light a fire under your shiny ass while they was at it."

Hamby smiled. "These old boys, they know what it take to necktie me. It *take* something. Up to now ain't nobody had that much to give."

Abernathy stepped between them. "Colored or not," he admonished the peckerwood, "you ort to pay up. His chicken beat yourn fair and square."

As the referee Abernathy had to try and protect the integrity of the fight, no matter how he felt about Hamby's entitlements or lack of them. But Mose Sullivan was under no such compulsion, and so Hamby was gratified when Mose spoke out and said to the peckerwood, "Give the man his bet. He may be a darky but he suits us."

As Hamby might've expected, Luke Truly and Cecil Dobbs said naught but stood warily by, darting edgewise looks in his direction to see if he aimed to make another fuss of the sort he sometimes did, which was getting harder and harder for a white man with any sand to ignore.

The peckerwood wagged his head, and a light of pure malice kindled in the scum-green eyes. "No, sir," he drawled, "I ain't a-paying."

Hearing this, Hamby gave himself over to pondering whether he could teach the peckerwood the lesson he deserved without inflaming Abernathy and the others and ending up twirling by his neck at the end of a rope after all. Hamby was a special case. He enjoyed the sanction of the Curtises; nobody in the valley was rougher yet more fair; many a white owed him an obligation. He'd earned a kind of grudging respect, but he and the whites always understood without saying it that the respect was conditional. Times past, Hamby had licked the tar out of bad white men and made the county like it, especially when the fuss was forced on him. But it was a fine line he trod, a line that the whites got to draw but a black man, even Hamby, always had to guess at. If he shamed a white unduly—any white— he'd pay with his life. Also this peckerwood was an outlander and didn't understand how Hamby stood. If he went home—wherever that was—proclaiming how much the men along the Hiwassee loved their coons, how could any white in Clay County ever hold up his head again? The prospect might be enough to move, or even erase, that line Hamby was trying to walk. So in the end he chose to be wise and await a more propitious moment to act in his own behalf; he only nodded to the peckerwood and turned off in a disappointed way toward his stump, while the fellow sniggered at his back through that ugly potato nose of his.

Still Livingood had not arrived. Impatiently Mose Sullivan unstrung his watch and consulted it. Livingood was over an hour late. Time hung heavy. The whites complained of the delay, cussed, passed the bottle, boasted, whittled, spat; Hamby squatted on his stump a ways off smoking his pipe and now and then sipping from his bottle. The peckerwood told a naughty story. Then Luke Truly spoke up and said they should start with the chickens on hand and mentioned he had a Claret he'd like to pit against Eli Abernathy's Roundhead. When the bets were placed Hamby put two dollars on Abernathy's bird because every Roundhead he'd ever seen was fast as hell, though sometimes their courage did fail them. Dobbs took duty as referee. The whites crowded eagerly around the pit—Hamby never moved— but almost at once they came away moaning in disgust; the Claret had shown his hackles and run from Eli's bird, and Truly'd had to kill him. Everybody including Hamby hated a cowardly rooster and felt bad for Truly for having got one. But Hamby won his wager.

Next Dobbs matched his two-year-old Red Brown against an Old English the peckerwood had brought. Out of principle Hamby laid his bet on the Red Brown, although that Old English looked damn strong, straight-legged, head slim as a lizard's, his bill coming over just so, long-necked and showing a big broad breast. He was mighty handsome, too, with his black front and gold neck and body of brownish red as bright as a polished cuspidor. While they were fixing to pit the birds Hamby finally got up from his stump and sidled over to

Mose Sullivan and inquired, "Who this stranger talk so nasty?"

Mose eyed the peckerwood kneeling at the pit, holding the Old English out to bill the Red Brown. He rubbed his stubbly chin. "Why, I reckon I never did hear a name. But I believe he's kin somehow to Truly. Cousin to Truly's wife, I think I heard. Truly says he's a Missionary Baptist. Comes from someplace down in South Ca'lina." The men pitted the birds, which came together with a noise like somebody slapping a pair of overstuffed cushions smartly to. Mose frowned and spat. "That feller's a right ill-un, ain't he? Even for a Missionary Baptist."

Hamby thought it best to offer no opinion on the matter. Instead he asked, "Where he staying at?"

The Old English and the Red Brown thrashed violently in the pit; Abernathy bent in, watching them closely. Pinfeathers lazily floated in the cloud of red dust the birds lashed up. The peckerwood exhorted the Old English with a stream of fervent cussing.

Mose waited a beat or two before replying; he set a shrewd look on Hamby and seemed almost to smile but then did not; instead he shifted his chaw and turned his attention back to the pit. "Why, he's a-stopping over at Truly's by the foot of Low Gap," he finally said, then added by way of calculated specificity, "a-sleeping in that old corncrib—you know, by the sweet gum." Hamby knew the place; he was obliged; he nodded but said no more.

In the pit the birds got hung, and Dobbs told the peckerwood to handle, which he did. Then they went at it again. They fought for ten, twelve minutes straight without either one gaining an advantage. By then both were near done. Abernathy scratched a drag-pit in the dirt off to one side, and Dobbs and the peckerwood moved over there to rest and then pit them again, while at the main pit Mose Sullivan matched his War-Horse against the Roundhead of Abernathy's that had chased off Luke Truly's cowardly Claret. Hamby laid a bet on the Roundhead again and won when the Roundhead broke one of the War-Horse's legs and then got on top of him and speared him. Then while Hamby was counting his gains—he'd got forty-two dollars up to now—Rollin Livingood finally appeared.

He was riding a big roan stallion, which he checked at the edge of the clearing. For a time he sat in his saddle watching the desultory scuffle in the drag-pit between Dobbs's bird and the peckerwood's Old English. Hamby recognized him on account of the raspberry-colored birthmark that stained one whole side of his face, which he'd often heard described. Livingood was large, fleshy but not fat; he wore a smile that stopped just short of self-satisfaction but from a distance appeared congenial; he showed an air of settled confidence. Two men on mules joined him. One, Hamby noted with mild shock, looked to be a full-blooded Cherokee. Before him on the pommel this Indian was holding a cage made of withes with a cock in it— surely the deadly Slingshot. Hamby couldn't make out the size or shape of the rooster. "Them old birds is about done in," Livingood remarked of the ones in the drag-pit.

But no sooner had he spoken than the bedraggled Red Brown, whipped near to death, suddenly by a miracle drew on some heretofore untapped well of rage and surged up with a roar of wings and commenced to slicing that peckerwood's chicken all to pieces. In another five seconds it was over. Hamby'd won again. The peckerwood swore. Cecil Dobbs knelt to examine the bloody Red Brown where he lay shivering in the dirt of the drag-pit. He laid a hand on the bird and kept his hand there awhile and then wrung his neck.

"That chicken was game as hell," Livingood declared, dismounting to hitch the roan to a dogwood shrub. Abernathy stepped up and shook hands with him, and one by one the others followed suit. Except for the peckerwood they all showed the shy but resentful air of men in the presence of a fame they envy and suspect is undeserved;

the peckerwood, while he touched flesh the same as the others, also gave Livingood a good hard look that Hamby approved of in spite of himself. Not reckoning himself part of any such ceremony, Hamby leaned his back against the jenny and fussed with the handkerchief on his wounded hand, waiting for them to get done; but Livingood glimpsed him there and turned partway in his direction and fixed on him a hard little eye as black as a cinder. He didn't approach Hamby but said, "Heard of you," and gave Hamby a short nod.

"Heard of *you*," Hamby replied, and just a smidgen of—what was it, respect?—sparked inside him like a tiny new star. The jenny was leaning against him to counterbalance his weight, and from her saddle Gouger playfully pecked at the brim of Hamby's hat. Still holding his distance, Livingood next focused a considerable study on Gouger himself. In the meantime his own cock commenced to crow and bang its wings against the sides of the cage the Indian was holding; the Shawlneck's cry had a piercing tone like the blast of a trumpet.

Now Livingood swung his attention back to the others. He jerked a thumb at the Cherokee. "This here's my handler, name of Longrunner." Nobody spoke, nor did any man stir; it was Livingood's affair if he wished to let a red nigger handle his own bird, a thing none of them would ever have considered. For his part the Indian sat his mule seeming to consider without any judgment at all the line of autumn-colored trees opposite. He was darker than Hamby, but the color had a ruddy light to it that made him seem dimly to shine, a little like the way the glare of the sun comes through a pall of smoke. In another second or two he slowly swiveled his head to look at Hamby, and they abided awhile that way, looking. "The other's my brother-in-law," Livingood was saying with a wave of his hand, leaving it to the man himself to supply his name.

"Petrie," the man said.

Slingshot, when Longrunner fetched him out, looked to be just an ordinary pecked-up old chicken, except scrawnier than normal; he was rangy as a granddaddy-longlegs and by his first appearance seemed to own no more strength than such a harmless creature. A murmur of amazement passed through the group as the fellows regarded this thin and bedraggled fowl that improbably owned such a dire reputation. But under Livingood's tolerant smile Hamby drew near, examined Slingshot by eye and hand and concluded that although the Shawlneck was surely light—no more than three and a quarter pounds, he judged—his legs, if dainty looking, were in fact as strong and supple as a deer's, his thighs strung with slim muscle like wires. The breast was narrow but long and straight. The bird himself had a lackadaisical manner that inspired small confidence, but Hamby, who believed roosters were generally a good deal smarter than most folk thought, wondered if the lazy demeanor wasn't a blind to fool the gullible. He stepped back impressed and, thinking of Gouger, touched by a cold finger-end of fear.

First they pitted Abernathy's Roundhead against the Shawlneck. Although the Roundhead had already proved its mettle twice, Hamby was sufficiently intrigued by what he'd seen to place his money on Livingood's bird, and it wasn't long till he saw his intuition rewarded. As soon as Longrunner pitted that ragged old bird he fluffed up something terrific, seemed to swell before the eyes of the astonished watchers into another kind of cock altogether, larger, implacably fierce, one that hungered for the blood of all that lived. He killed the Roundhead on his second pass, and Hamby collected. He collected again when the Shawlneck disposed of a Butcher that Luke Truly offered up. He won a third time when the Shawlneck crippled a Dominecker-looking chicken of Mose Sullivan's. After Mose's bird was dispatched Hamby held two hundred and forty-seven dollars. Then Livingood looked at him with those cinder-black eyes, his birthmark reddening, and said, "I'd like to fight that-un of yourn now."

Hamby counted out all his money, every last dime, and said to Abernathy, who was holding the bets, "This all go on my bird." Having witnessed the ferocity of the Shawlneck, Hamby knew Gouger could not prevail. He could see in Abernathy's face that Abernathy knew it, too. But if Gouger was old and tired and cut by that damn Arkansas Traveler, his fighting heart was as great now as ever. And even as Abernathy took Hamby's money Gouger commenced to crowing and lashing his wings on the jenny's saddle, eager to light into whatever he might meet. Hamby knew he owed it to Gouger to give him a last great chance, owed him that and more. What was Hamby's wish to escape the tribulations of the valley compared to paying off a debt the size of the one he owed Gouger?

Longrunner hunkered beside the pit smearing dirt on Slingshot's few cuts, while Livingood stood by meting out to Hamby his complacent smile; the brother-in-law Petrie sat on the ground nearby smoking a cigar. Hamby could see the Shawlneck wasn't even winded. Exuberantly he stuck out his neck and shrieked; he switched his head sharply one way and another taking in the sights, looking for his next victim. Without a doubt he was the meanest chicken Hamby'd ever seen. He sighed. Then crossing to the jenny, he unfastened the tether and brought Gouger down, blew on his head, gently fitted him into the curve of his arm.

Under the dim light of a new moon Hamby crept up the weedy path and stopped by a fence corner to get his bearings. Before him between dark looming mountains he saw the notch of Low Gap with multitudes of stars glimmering in the sky behind it. Beyond the fence corner the path bent to the right around a field of dead cornstalks and ran up toward the cabin. The house showed no light. On his hands and knees Hamby eased past the corner of the fence and then stopped again to peer closely across the yard. As his eyes got used to the pattern of shadows an uneven shape began to emerge from the faintly silvered night; soon he made it out for a sweet gum tree with a corncrib set next to it. Slowly he crawled forward, hoping the dogs of Truly's, which he'd hunted with many and many a time, would recognize his scent and wouldn't rouse and betray him.

Gaining the sill of the crib at last, he reached quickly in and grasped a forearm as thin and stiff as a broom handle and twisted it counter-clockwise till the peckerwood came up off his bed of cobs with a howl. "I come for my four dollar," Hamby said.

CHAPTER 4

December 1880

*P*ieces were falling out of time and out of the world. When they fell they left holes behind in the places where they'd been. Each hole was an opening to somewhere. The pieces had been falling out for quite some time, so there were a great many holes now. And altogether the holes looked as mazy as a honeycomb. Through these he could travel like a mole in its tunnel—but much easier than a mole, smoother. Taking any opening, he could emerge anyplace. Then all was different; the light fell a different way. Sometimes after arriving he could peer back and see whence he'd come. On other occasions his starting point was a mystery, or he forgot having started at all.

She covered her ears with her hands and told him to stop his shouting. As always he wondered why She had authority over him, for he seemed to recall that he possessed standing of a sort. But if he did She failed to respect it. Continually She found new reasons to berate him. Who was She? Why was She at him night and day? Besides, he knew he was making no utterance such as She was resenting; what She heard was the voice of the cancer screaming in his bowels.

He supposed She stemmed from his sin. Maybe God had sent her to begin his punishment, to start what would later grow worse. She would pick and nag at him till the Time Came. When the Time Came the men would take him away in manacles and shut him in a dungeon, where he would languish till the cancer ate through him and he perished in the dark and damp. With a washrag She wiped drool from his mouth and chin. This act caused him to move his bowels where he sat. She burst into tears. Again She begged him to cease his yelling. "I'm not yelling," he said between the shrieks of his cancer.

If he had not sinned so gravely he would not be required to suffer her tyranny. This was the way of Providence. Do wrong, and wrong shall be done to you. And his was a fearful wrong. He couldn't remember what wrong it was; he only knew it had been so bad it was beyond redemption. God wouldn't save him; God would only punish him. She scrubbed at his bottom with the sponge while he crouched naked on hands and knees in the tub. As She washed him his nether part stiffened and poked its head down into the water. She averted her eyes and began to cry again. He handled himself. Then he thought of the French pox he was pretty sure had infected him, along with the cancer. How strange that he should have the pox. He'd not known any woman in years. Without doubt it was another penalty of God's. God could give disease where a cause was lacking. It was a kind of miracle.

Later he was walking in the garden. Papa was hoeing. Papa looked up as he approached. *I'm ashamed of you,* Papa said, leaning on the old braid hoe.

I'm sorry, he confessed.

But Papa only repeated he was ashamed, then went back to hoeing. It was the sin that stood between them.

Mama came out of the root cellar, her apron full of onions and sweet potatoes. *I'm ashamed of you,* she said. He wished he knew what he'd done. Even if it was beyond correction, he thought it would help to know.

The cancer began to speak again, and soon She came running and besought him to stop. He tried to explain about the voice of the cancer, but he only heard himself bleating and blaring like a goat. He was so aggravated by this that he smote himself on the side of his head with the heel of his own hand and toppled over half-swooning. He lay between the furrows of the garden gazing up at the dry blue of the sky. She stood over him holding her hands on her ears and asking him please to be still and remember She loved him.

He chose a hole and slipped into it. Everything was smothered in a pale smoke that had a tinge of yellow in it. The smoke smelt like eggs gone bad. They were all in a row abreast as they trotted. The file-closers were at their backs. He was saying, *Guide center. Close up the line, close up the line.* He heard a rattling noise.

She helped him to his feet. She drew his arm across her shoulders and started him toward the house. "Remember," She was saying, "I love you." He thought She said this to throw him off his guard so She could gain some advantage. His feet dragged.

In the smoke before him a flock of small lights flickered. The lights made a noise like a heavy cough. The red flag up ahead dropped. Next to him a man seemed to do a frantic dance. The man's arm came off at the root and went sailing in a spray of blood. The name of the man came. J. C. Calton. From Wilkes County. Enlisted while the regiment was at Greeneville, Tennessee. Fondly he shook his head. Old J. C.

He sat rocking on the lower gallery wearing his Sunday best. The man with his hair parted down the middle was visiting her. He and She were in the swing at the other end of the gallery. They held hands. They glided back and forth in the swing. They talked. The cancer was quiet now.

He entered another hole. Where he came out a dark woman embraced him. He felt her firm body against his. Her hair was black and coarse like the pelt of a bear. She whispered in his ear, held his face between her hands. He knew her name but could not say it. She kissed his mouth, and now he remembered the tangy taste of her, a little like that of roast lamb. She did not seem to be ashamed of him. He hoped that when the Time Came, she would be by him. He slept.

As they rocked in the swing Tom Carter softly held Rebecca's hand upturned in one of his own, and with the forefinger of his other hand he pityingly traced little lines and circles on her horny palm, the sight of which struck him to the quick. Once her hand had been as tender as a rose petal; now when he raised it to kiss it the harshness scraped his lips. It smelt faintly of cooking grease, and the fingertips were withered from scalding wash water. He felt sorry for her—for what that hand revealed—but because of his reticent nature he didn't know how to remark about it.

So instead he commented—unnecessarily—that Andy had fallen asleep yonder in the wicker armchair. Surely Andy's sleep was a comfort not only to himself but to those around him and so was worthy of some notice, yet belatedly Tom realized there was small need of his mentioning it now, since Andy's snores rumbling across the gallery proclaimed his slumber to one and all. Tom sighed; he knew one of his faults was a habit of too often pointing out the obvious. He guessed how tiresome this must be to others, but he could never seem to stop speaking out in such a way.

Thankfully Rebecca was tolerant. She nodded, gave a wistful smile. "Poor Brother," she said distantly. "Can't sleep of a night, and most days now he's either ailing"—that was what she called his fits—"or dozed off, one or t'other."

While they swayed he gazed long at her. He studied the familiar lines of her face, the proud brow, the small sprig of nose, her mama's strong chin. *So fair she is,* he thought. But he saw, too, how worn down she'd got. There were maroon circles under her eyes, and the whites were finely laced with filaments of red. Tiredness crimped her mouth. Strands of white were mixed in the hair at her temples. He wished to rescue her, to ask her again to marry him, but he knew from much past experience what her answer would be. *Brother needs me,* she would insist. *There ain't nobody else to tend him,* she would say. Sometimes she would add, *I'm used up, Friend Tom. You need to find you somebody fresh.*

She'd say that with her wry small laugh. She never lost that way of seeing things, saucy and bittersweet. In Rebecca's eyes the condition she was in was not so much tragic as absurd. Tom often suspected she saw the whole world in that fashion, as a mistake that was as funny as it was sad. Maybe she was right, too. Maybe all Creation was comically askew; oftentimes, like now, Tom felt ridiculous enough himself. But he couldn't say anything about that either; he was either tongue-tied about great matters or babbling like a fool about trivial ones. If only he could get the hang of civil discourse.

But he couldn't. So he brought up the subject of what kind of winter they might expect. "The woolly worm had a good deal of black on him this year," he observed with an air of astuteness. "But then the squirrels were all late gathering nuts, and there was less holly and dogwood this year than normal. So the signs don't agree." The sound of his own words wearied him. He wished he were brighter. He wished he'd gone to the Hicksville Academy like Rebecca. "And it's been a mild December," he plodded on, hating himself.

Again Rebecca smiled. How kind she was! How patient with his slow ways. But then without warning she said a thing that took him up short, said it while gazing sorrowfully across at Andy: "I can't decide if a human's a high type of beast or a low type of angel."

Tom wondered if such a question might flirt with heresy, yet he dared not raise any reproof; he didn't want to get Rebecca provoked with him. He thought awhile, ran the tip of his tongue uncertainly over his lips. Then the notion of redemption came to him, and he remarked, "Ain't we one or t'other at different times, depending on whether we're saved or not?"

She made a gesture of impatience. "I don't mean that. I mean, what's a man's nature? Look at Brother. He passes from angel to beast and back again as easy as changing his coat. They're both him. But then again the beast ain't him atall. Yet he's got it in him."

Anxiously Tom rubbed his chin. "Seems to me you're a-studying it too deep. He's just addled, is all. You can't make out nothing about it."

"Yes, I know," she sighed. "I expect he's going mad, and sure enough there's no sense to a madman. But even so, I know him— *know* him, know him heart and soul for mostly an angel. That he has such a beast in him, too, just scares me to death." She paused, gave Tom a sidelong and questioning look. "If *he* does maybe we all do."

Inwardly Tom recoiled. He believed man was made in the image of God and, while subject to sin, was still only a little lower than the angels. To think mortals might be no more than brutes smacked of blasphemy or, even worse, of unbelief. Was Rebecca veering along the edge of the Abyss? Tom scowled. "Preacher wouldn't like to hear you carry on so."

As soon as he uttered the thought Tom knew he'd put his foot wrong; a flare of temper darkened Rebecca's cheeks, and her eyes flashed fire. "One thing you better get straight, Tom Carter," she snapped. "I'm just about finished on religion. My whole family believed. Belief was poured down my gullet all the time I was growing up. And what good did it do any of us? Dead and poor and crazy and used-up like we are? No, sir. We're in the world, and the world's hard, and faith's got no place in it."

Tom stirred in discomfort. "I wish you wouldn't talk thataway. You know you don't mean it."

Rebecca pulled a sour face. "Right this minute I do. I can't say how I'll feel come Sunday."

She's just tired, Tom thought. *Worn out with cares.* He felt a surge of pity for her. "The Lord'll give you strength," he said, patting her hand.

She didn't seem to hear him; instead she appeared to take grave thought. Then abruptly she declared, "I don't know how long I can keep on caring for Brother." She looked down and away, as if she could not bear to speak the idea with Andy under her eye.

Here was a bolt from the blue. Tom felt an upwelling of hope. With his feet he stopped the motion of the swing, the better to ponder what she'd said. She could mean but one thing, that she was thinking of putting Andy away. At last. After a year and more of anguished sacrifice. He ransacked his brain to find arguments that would draw her out, tempt her to follow the notion to its end. But he might as well consult a rock in the road. The only expression he could coax out of himself was, "It's been hard, I know."

"He's been more like my papa than my brother," Rebecca said with a wan expression. Tears filled her eyes, and her nose began to run. "Some thought he wasn't strong the way a man ought to be. I don't know. He seemed strong to me. I knew what scared him, but I saw him go beyond that time and time again. He'd take a run at anything, no matter how much he dreaded it." She wiped her nose with the back of a hand.

"And he was something few men are," she kept on. "He was gentle. A gentle man is scarce as hen's teeth—present company excepted, of course." Eagerly Tom nodded; he hoped he was gentle, but mainly he just wanted her to go on. "All those years, Brother was strong and gentle to me, like my papa. So when he commenced to fail I wanted to be strong and gentle back. Wanted to give him what he gave me. But now . . ." The tears ran over, and she sat shivering with sobs. Awkwardly Tom stroked her hand. The hand was hot in his grasp and as dry as a chip of wood.

Tom wanted to feel sorrow for Andy's plight, wanted to share Rebecca's guilty pain. He'd known the Curtises all his life, and their troubles should be partly his as well. But he was too borne up by anticipation to entertain such somber notions. So he had to pretend to sympathy and cover up his pleasure. Again he petted her hand. "I'm sorry. I'm real sorry," he crooned.

"A body commences all full of spunk. You believe you can handle anything," Rebecca mused, still looking down. "And for a time you can. You can do good, you can serve. But then it saps you. Wears you out. Thins the blood. Your spirit just shrinks down to nothing." She took a handkerchief from the wrist of her blouse and blew her nose with a ringing honk like a man. "But still I can't help feeling it's puny of me to falter. I feel like a weakling. I ought to be up to it, no matter how hard it seems. I tell myself Brother never gave up, not while he had his sense."

Tom nodded mutely. Yes, it was too bad what had come to pass. But nonetheless Tom was more than ready to load Andy into the buggy right this minute and hustle him off to the asylum in Raleigh or Morganton, one or the other. "You done all you could," he decided to say. "You done more'n anybody had a right to expect." It was several more words than he'd thought he had in him when he opened his mouth, and he was agreeably surprised.

"No," she replied, "I ain't done enough. But then a person *can't* do enough, can they? We can't ever pay the whole of the debt we owe." Anxiously Tom nodded. "Anyway I'm thinking on what to do," she said. "I'm going over to Franklin next Tuesday and talk to Kope Elias." Elias was the Curtises' lawyer; now Tom saw with despair that what Rebecca had in mind would take time—alas, much time. "Will you go with me?" she asked.

"Of course," he said, not without a certain glumness. But at bottom he still felt sanguine. The day he'd dreamt of was coming—it seemed certain now—and so he must be content to await it with calm. He kicked the swing into motion again. Continually he patted her rough hand.

True to her unchanging habit, old Mrs. Hemphill came by on her way home from divine services at Hayesville Methodist. It was Mrs. Hemphill's self-chosen duty to stop at the Curtis place each Sabbath noon to pay the respects of the faithful to Andy, their stricken lay leader. But Rebecca knew the real purpose of the visits was to allow Mrs. Hemphill to examine Andy on a weekly basis for signs of advancing derangement. Then any indecency he might happen to commit could be gleefully reported not only to the congregants but to the inhabitants of the whole valley, so that all might gossip and deplore and affect pity while secretly savoring every delectable detail of Andy's failing.

Rebecca saw this as a threat to what was left of Andy's honor and the good name of the family. Let Mrs. Hemphill's black phaeton descend the drive, as it did now, drawn by her chestnut mare, one of her mob of oafish grandsons at the reins, and Rebecca would coil like a copperhead ready to strike. Of course as a saved soul Tom Carter took Mrs. Hemphill at her own measure and always gave her fulsome greeting. And at those moments Rebecca, her teeth on edge, wondered how she could have ever entertained the idea of marrying such a fool as Tom was showing himself to be.

Happily till now Andy had managed not to offend Mrs. Hemphill in any really appalling way. The worst he'd done was loudly break wind while she prayed over him; Rebecca assumed even that small misdeed had sent its thrill of horror and delight up and down the country. On other occasions he'd picked his nose and appeared to talk in tongues, or at least in some language none of his hearers could understand. He'd spoken a good deal about having lost all his money and about cancer but mercifully hadn't mentioned the French pox. Mostly he just sat drumming his fingers on the arms of his chair, beating time to a tune only he could hear. The truth was that so far he'd proved something of a disappointment to Mrs. Hemphill and the many who eagerly awaited her bulletins.

Yet the old lady remained full of hope. So now as she mounted to the gallery in a brisk rustle of black taffeta, she failed for a moment to conceal how much it annoyed her to find Andy modestly and quietly asleep. But she was too formidable to let such a setback vex her for long. Grandly she took a seat in the extra chair and announced she'd drink some hot tea, doubtless in the hope Andy would offer up some revilement in due time. In a vengeful mood Rebecca brought her a piece of brown betty along with the tea; it was in her mind how the Savior said returning kindness for evil heaped coals of fire on the heads of the ungodly.

Mrs. Hemphill might have stayed all day had Captain Irish Bill Moore not come trotting down the lane on his big brown stallion Crockett an hour or so after she arrived. She was in the act of chiding Rebecca and Tom for shirking Sabbath worship. Till today Tom had never once missed a service in his life; all he could do was hang his head and say he'd done it for love and out of care for Andy. But

Rebecca, a notorious slacker in this regard, argued back; if the Most High insisted on placing His own adoration over a calling of mercy such as she owed Brother, then He was a mighty selfish God and would do better to mind the teachings of His Son, who'd blessed the merciful.

Mrs. Hemphill paled at the sacrilege Rebecca had put forth—Tom, too, gaped in shock—but the approach of Captain Moore averted the reprimand the old lady was fixing to deliver. The Captain was a freethinker and enough of a scamp that she dared not remain in any spot he occupied, lest she herself suffer a blot. This being an even more pressing need than rebuking a backslider, she rose to go. Captain Moore tipped his hat to her as he came up the steps; she swept royally down unheeding, mounted to her phaeton and was gone.

After greeting Rebecca and Tom the captain went to Andy and knelt by him; he rested a hand on Andy's knee. He said nothing, only crouched there gazing into Andy's face as he slept. By habit the captain was a great talker, a spinner of fantastic tales, a whimsical and elfish man given to jokes and pranks. He was famous for riding Crockett at full tilt around the Hayesville square, bending down on the run to snatch his hat from the ground. He loved to tell how his wife Miss Hattie Gash had rejected him again and again over years of courting, till he wore her down with his persistence. He carried with him everywhere a letter she'd written him during the war, which he often read aloud at public gatherings, much to Miss Hattie's embarrassment: "I received your letter last week and consider it due you that I should make some reply, though I must confess I am at a loss to know what to say. I fear from the tenor of your letter that you have misconstrued some parts of my conduct towards you and have thus been led to write and expect a more favorable reply than I shall be able to make. I have known you a long while and have respected you and regarded you as a friend and I still wish you to regard me as one, but nothing more. My age forbids my being more to you, or any one else. I hope what I have said will be sufficient and that I have not said more than was required." It was, he guffawed, a devil of a letter for a fellow to get who was off fighting for hearth, home and sweetheart. Winning Miss Hattie's hand at last, he avowed, was the bravest act of his life.

So when he came to see Andy and fell so grave and quiet, Rebecca always found the change unsettling. He and Andy were pards of long standing; the captain had commanded young Howell Curtis's cavalry troop in the war and so was one living link to the brother Andy and Rebecca had lost a long time ago in Tennessee. And during the dismal days of Reconstruction Andy and Captain Moore together had fended off conquerors and carpetbaggers and scalawags alike. All this history fused them, and with the captain kneeling there by the chair grasping Brother Andy's knee Rebecca could feel the force of the old times like the power of a lodestone to draw metal; it wanted to bring Brother out, but strong as it was, it couldn't. The captain could only kneel searching Andy's sleeping face in the vain hope Brother might awaken and know him. But even as Andy continued serenely to doze Rebecca had the odd conviction that he knew the captain was by him, that in some way he felt the force of the past, that they communed after all; she wept to feel this. Tom held her fast by the hand.

In time Captain Moore stood; he turned, kissed Rebecca's hand, bade them good-bye in a voice that had an unaccustomed tremor in it, though his eye was dry. In the turnaround he gathered Crockett's reins and stood to the saddle. Then with powerful thrusts of his hindquarters Crockett carried the captain up the gravel drive and out of sight.

❦

Late in the afternoon Andy awoke, and as soon as he set his eye on Tom and Rebecca opposite, it was clear that in his sleep he had somehow slid back into his former self. "I feel right swimmy-headed," Andy declared in a blurred voice. He yawned, stretched, gave out a sheepish grin, as if he'd only drifted off in the midst of a conversation instead of gone roaming in the swamps of his lunacy.

To Tom in his desolation it seemed a poor coincidence. Andy was sitting there as sane as ever a man could be. Sure, he looked a fright—his face showed ugly lumps from sleeping, his hair stuck out every which way. But look how lively his regard, how rosy his countenance! Rebecca saw it, too, saw it clearer than Tom; delight flooded her like a lamp turned up. At the same time Tom sensed her resolution of but hours ago starting to melt. How could she think of shutting Andy away in the asylum when—though there was appreciably less and less of him with every day that passed—in times like now he was her old admired and beloved brother?

"Why, if it ain't the turtledoves," Andy familiarly chaffed them. He looked interestedly about him, as if all were new, then got up and shrugged off the shawl Rebecca had spread around him, folded it, laid it aside with the remark that the day was warm for the beginning of winter. With a firm tread he crossed the gallery to them. Tom got to his feet, and they shook hands. Andy's sturdy grip squeezed painfully together all the little bones of Tom's hand, and Tom was sorry to see that Andy's eyes were as clear as a running brook. "Good to see you, Brother Carter," said Andy. Tom mumbled some rejoinder and resumed his seat, mired in a disappointment he dared not show. "Sister!" Andy cried, turning to Rebecca. "Why, you look plumb give out." Rebecca didn't—couldn't—answer; she bounded up with a squeal and threw herself into Andy's arms.

Tom was glad, too, of course. What sort of a blackguard would he be if he weren't? Andy had been a friend—no, more than a friend. He'd been someone you could pattern yourself after, if you had it in mind to be a certain kind of man, level of head, modest in manner, charitable, churchly, true. He'd held Andy Curtis always before him as a guide of good deportment and worthy thought. So now it was not without rue and remorse that Tom wished Andy sick again, as he most fervently, ignobly did. Tom was burning in the fires of his longing; he was on edge from swearing off the snuff Rebecca hated. Perhaps the Lord would excuse him his selfish dudgeon. He tried to tell himself he must accede to God's will, however heaven might manifest it. He tried, but he failed.

They talked awhile about things of no importance. Tom could excel at that. He could, that is, once he gained mastery over his feelings. When he did he spun a long yarn about an old three-legged painter that had preyed on his lambs last fall, that he'd never seen except for its peculiar tracks. For a story about an invisible cat it lasted a creditable spell. Then he and Rebecca decided to go strolling by the river, and Andy drew his wicker chair to the edge of the gallery, where the light of the December evening would strike him from behind.

He sat watching Tom and Rebecca in the distance, two specks afloat on the brown grass of the riverbank, Rebecca's white mantua gleaming like a beacon. A latticework of winter-bare trees arched over them, finely black against the flat yellows and tans of the pastures that rose in low folds beyond them on the far bank. In the distance the hills over by Jackrabbit drew an uneven line of china blue from east to west; then, farthest off of all, he could just make out the broad peak of Brasstown Bald and its clinging family of lower mountains, their profiles of eggshell gray along the bottom of the sky.

Although here in the valley a sloping light came from a clear sky, along the horizon many flat clouds with undersides the color of slate lay stacked as close as the scales on a fish. They were full of rough weather, but from long experience Andy knew they would pass around.

Forty-one years—except in wartime—the high valley of the Hiwassee had held him in its bosom, wafted over him its gentle weathers, soaked him in its warmth. Winter storms would usually divide about its bulwark of mountains and pass on to visit snowy blasts on lands north, south and beyond, while in the valley itself the sun would smile as it did today and tender breezes would blow, as if the Almighty held the place in the cup of His saving hand. Papa, he remembered, used to say the valley was a fallen bit of Paradise.

Papa. A vision of Papa came—his rugged head, his wiry frame, the outsized hands—and with it arrived a vague apprehension that made Andy restive. He shifted in his chair. He seemed to remember something recent, something to do with Papa. And with Mama, too; Mama carried onions and sweet potatoes in her apron. But what was it they'd said? And how could it be recent, when they'd both been so long in the grave? Andy found it puzzling. He spied another hole and ducked into it.

In the dusk Tom and Rebecca came up from the river. They paused between the two bare tobacco fields—the crop was curing in the barn now—and watched while the sun slipped slowly behind the range. Rebecca remarked how it limned the shapes of the trees edging the far ridge lines in a way reminiscent of drawings she'd seen in the Chinese style, in a book in Papa's study. Tom—who knew little of art—dumbly assented. This evening Rebecca's pleasure was his torture; all he could think of was how Andy had rallied so inconveniently and how Rebecca was all a-sparkle now with renewed hope for his recovery. Yet Tom remained awake to his duty. He commented on the bite in the air, now that the day was nearly gone; he took her under his arm to warm her; soberly and in edifying manner he related how the name of the mountains—Tusquittee—was a Cherokee word meaning "the Rafters," how in their ignorance the savages thought the mountains held up the sky, as rafters held up a roof; then he remembered with a pang of humiliation that it was Rebecca herself who'd told him that. He blushed and fell silent. They moved toward the house through the last of the pewter-colored light.

Approaching the manse between the rows of boxwoods, they saw that the gallery was empty and the parlor lamp was burning. "I reckon Brother got cold and went indoors," Rebecca said. They climbed the stairs to the gallery, and Rebecca went to the door and peeped in through the sidelight. Andy's clothes lay in a heap on the entryway floor. But Andy himself was nowhere to be found—not in the house, not in the outbuildings, not anywhere on the grounds.

Half that night they searched for him. Not till nearly three o'clock in the morning did they finally come upon him walking purposefully along the wagon road toward Murphy, entirely naked except for a pair of Hersome gaiters and an old flat-brimmed hat of Madison Curtis's.

Part II

Castle Keep

CHAPTER 5

June 1881

*I*n his stone fort on top of Pot Rock Bald, Webb Darling decided it was time to see about the nigger. Carrying his ram's horn, he went to the point of the mountain and stood on the rim with the blue-green valley spread out far below him and blew a long note that echoed back and forth off the hills roundabout. Then, cradling the horn in his arm, he waited for the echoes to fade, and while he waited he ran a proud eye over his domain, for he was king of the whole of it, as far as he could see, from the Nantahalas and Chunky Gal on his left all the way up the rumpled spine of the Tusquittees to the high place he stood on. In all that country no blockader could say him nay, especially not any nigger.

A film of kitchen smoke lay over the valley, and beneath it he could see as if through a fogged lens the broad patchwork of field and pasture, the ribbons of road twisting hither and yon, the tiny farmsteads, the many bands of timber. Under the layer of smoke it all wore a coat of dim light, as if faintly glowing of its own accord, like foxfire but in daytime. The high tops rimmed the valley, row on row of them receding westward with the new sun on them, fading by distance from olive green to violet to topaz, plumes of morning vapor rising out of every cove and holler. Yes, it was a kingly realm, and Webb Darling would never risk losing any smallest part of it, which was why he must see to the errand he had in mind before another sun came up.

The answering cry of a horn floated up from the south, somewhere by Piney Top; it was Rehoboam Bolt's old army bugle; Ree was back from prison, thank God. In another moment the Long Branch horn sounded from the foot of the Valley River range on the right. Darling couldn't help but smile, to hear his power so promptly confirmed. The power was still heady and new. It had flowed to him only last winter—after the Revenue fetched Bill Berong the moonshiner king of north Georgia—and he savored it. The horn was the voice of that power. He put it to his lips and blew two short acknowledging blasts. Then, sweeping a last fond gaze over the valley and its crimped brim of mountains, he turned back.

The woman fixed him a breakfast of fatback and pone and inkblack coffee, which he consumed sitting in a cane chair on the roof of the fort looking out at the peaks and crags over the parapet made of split logs spiked flat sides–to. The parapet stood breast high, and he'd augured holes in it every ten or twelve feet to shoot through, if matters ever came to that. Tendrils of vine had wound about it, and wolfsmilk was growing on one part of it and monkshood on another, all in the two months since he and the others had finished the fort. Creeper was advancing over the stone of the bald from the dwarf oak and hawthorn and from the masses of hazelnut and raspberry growing close about. *Beat back the wilderness as you will*, he thought. *It'll always reclaim itself.* He wasn't king of that, at least. The notion made him chuckle—he possessed a quirk of irony—but if his power did have limits, still he held what was his absolutely and without appeal. Let nature take *its* course; Webb Darling would take *his.*

He'd heard the nigger had killed one or two, so after breakfast he disassembled, cleaned and oiled his Richards-conversion Colt's army pistol and loaded it with five cartridges, the noses of whose bullets he'd notched with a knife. Next he took up his trusty Henry repeater, which he'd carried when he rode with bushwhacker Kirk the Union partisan. He cleaned it, too, and then twisted open the head of the magazine and shoved in fifteen shiny brass shells. He'd toted that gun both in the Rebellion and in the Holden war on the Ku Kluxers, yet now it was doing service against the government he'd once defended and in behalf of the White Caps he used to chase. Again he smiled. Well, he'd fought the Rebels out of principle—believing in Union, hating the slavers—and he'd gone after the Ku Klux because Kirk had said to, and Kirk was his old chief. Today he was at odds with a government that had gone so corrupt it would deny a blockader his natural calling and set up niggers as the equal of whites. Nor was he alone. In these parts almost every blockader was a White Cap also; the two kept the world in balance.

Yet he wouldn't have denied any biddable coon a role in that world. More than a few blacks were cooking liquor and paying him tribute all through these hills. Of course any such nig must know his place and keep to it. When he did, Webb Darling would defend him to the last; Webb would shed blood, even his own, for a loyal darky, who was after all a jewel beyond price. Loyalty was the gift of the race, just as arrogance was its new curse. And White-Capping answered for the arrogant.

By the time he finished with the Henry it was midday and the roof had grown hot, so Darling climbed down and stowed his weaponry inside the fort and meandered across the yard of bare rock to the pens where he kept his roosters. There he fed them out of a poke he kept. He gave them bits of raw beef and a mix of cracked corn, calf manure and rabbit pellets, along with tufts of bluestem grass he'd pulled out by the roots down the mountain to make up for the green they couldn't get on the bare floor of the bald. They ate with a ferocious ardor, and for a time he hunkered on his hams watching them in approval. He liked to think something lived in him that was close to their savagery, something that wanted to cut down every foe. It had been some time since he'd fought them, and he felt a sudden yearning for the pit. He thought that after tonight he'd take the best ones down the Tusquittee and see if he couldn't find a derby or arrange a hack fight.

Next he went up the ravine to his garden and looked over his corn and his beans and sweet potatoes, his okra and peas and cabbage—a larder fit for a monarch indeed. He looked into his hogpens and his sheepfold, checked on the cows in the high stomp. Nobody, Revenue or otherwise, could starve out Fort Darling, nor thirst it out either, on account of its own spring that spilled a sluice of bright water between two leaning stones. Webb never tired of walking the bounds of his stronghold; lofty and snug and secure as it was, it filled him with a settled comfort.

Above the spring he came upon his brother sitting on a rock whittling the small figure of a bear out of a block of laurel wood; his brass-framed Winchester lay next to him. "I want you to come along tonight," Webb said. The brother chewed and spat and nodded but spoke no reply. Webb left him whittling there at nearly the top of the kingdom, in the center of a grand powder-blue space that only the domed summit of Tusquittee Bald in the east surmounted.

Returning by way of the ravine, Darling went past the fort to the stable beyond it. He heard a distant boom of thunder and reckoned it was going to rain. In the stable yard he gave the mule a nose bag of oats. Once he started down tonight he'd need the mule at its best. If its mood was right and its belly full it could walk the edge of a razor, and the trail down the mountain offered a pretty good resemblance to a razor, only it was crooked as a mare's hind leg. Darling muttered to the mule awhile in hopes of cajoling it into a decent temper. Once more he quietly laughed. How royal and dangerous would he look if it pitched him off into a rock patch?

The thunder came again, and he looked southwest over the tops of the trees to see banks of cloud whose heads shone gold in the light and whose purple-black bellies dragged translucent curtains of gray rain after them. He hoped it would be done raining before he started down; the way was hard enough dry. After a last soothing word to the mule he headed back. The metallic smell of the rain to come freshened in his nose. The first breeze blew over the bald, and the millions of leaves in the woods all turned up their pale undersides and trembled; the whole forest stirred, gave forth a long hiss.

When he got to the fort he mounted to the roof again to watch the storm approach. It blotted out the sun and then came up the darkened valley in a slanted wall the color of a catbird, pushing ahead of it a long line of dust where the first of the rain pounded the dry growth. The chill of its wind smote him; its thunder crackled overhead. Here and there in its dark mass luminous veins of lightning flared. The air felt charged. Fat drops of water stung him. Darling loved it, opened his arms to it, took it into himself.

Hightower and Mozingo came in from their lookouts, and Darling's brother brought down his whittling and his rifle, and while the rain lashed at the roof they all waited in the damp main room of the fort, bathed in the greenish radiance the open windows let in.

Now and then a flicker of lightning would sear the dark, and peals of thunder would jar them. Webb fetched his fiddle of spruce and curly maple, which had a snake's rattle in it to improve the tone; he scraped out several melodies while the younguns played mumbletypeg and jackstraws on the floor of packed dirt, stopping now and then to sing the words of the songs they knew. The woman, who was afraid of storms, came in and sat silent in a corner, her hands wrapped up tight in her apron. The pullets paced about chortling and pecking. Mozingo fell asleep, sprawled snoring in his chair, his rifle across his lap. The brother whittled. The roof leaked in a number of places, and soon puddles formed in the low parts of the floor. The bluetick hound drowsed on the hearth, coiled up head to tail.

It rained a long time, and finally Darling laid down his fiddle and called the younguns to him, so as to pass the time telling them an instructive tale. "My pappy," he began, speaking in the lofty way he often did when smitten by his own grandeur, "was a man of some learning, and once he told me how in olden times the king was the one who looked after the common folk. Although a noble, too, the king kept the low-downers safe from the other nobles that would despoil them. Now when I first heard this I had no notion I'd ever be a king myself. But when I became one the notion of a king such as my pappy talked of appealed to me. It was the kind of a king I wanted to be, a king whose duty was to the simple folk, white and colored alike, who were loyal. I'd be loyal to them, and they'd be loyal to me, you see."

They nodded.

"Now my pappy also explained how hard it was to be a king. You couldn't just reign kindly. Every realm had its enemies inside and out. Even a kinsman could be an assassin. Kings had to watch out for treason. Sometimes the king must act harshly to save the kingdom and the good work he could do, and to set an example to others who might be tempted to betray him. Many kings, my pappy said, had to commit such acts and afterward felt regret despite the necessity. My pappy said this was the tragedy of being a king."

He gave a small shrug. He removed his hat and showed them the small brass pin shaped like a crown that he wore on the front of it as a sign of his rule, which he'd bought at a jeweler's shop in Murphy. "Now I'm the king and must go and do an act like that, to keep the people loyal. It'll be harsh, and already I regret it. But it's got to be done. For it's the king's power that keeps us all safe." He extended his hands in supplication. "I want you-all to pray for me now as I go down to wield the scepter. Pray that I'll be granted the grace to do the act not in rage but in pity."

In the last year he'd felt at first hand the tragedy of kingship his pappy had described. But eventually he'd found a way past it. He'd seen that doing the act in a blaze of revenge led only to worse and worse extremes. Since he was a moderate soul at heart, the trick was to do every act in cold blood, to regard it as a chore that was disagreeable but necessary, like cutting the sac that lets out the guts of a slaughtered hog. This was his method now.

The rain stopped late in the afternoon, and they emerged from the fort into a world that dripped and steamed and was covered in clouds that the sunset had turned a dewy amber. Darling stuck his pistol in the waistband of his trousers and held the Henry raked over one shoulder. The brother had his Winchester. In the bright mist the two of them crossed to the stable. Hightower and Mozingo were staying back to keep watch at the fort, lest the Revenue spring a surprise assault. Webb saddled the mule, trying to appease it with mellow talk. The brother caught up his dapple-gray in the corral. Webb booted the Henry under the stirrup fender. Next he passed into the back of the stable, where he kept his tools. He soon returned carrying his double-bit ax. He stuck the ax by the haft into the carbine socket of the old army saddle and tied a rag around the blade to blunt its edge, so he wouldn't cut himself as he rode.

They started down off the bald through the stunted growth, and soon they were in the bigger woods of beech and sugar maple and yellow birch lower down. The brother rode bareback, using a length of plowline for a rein; he balanced his Winchester across his thighs; his regalia was in a drawstring sack hung around his neck. As they went they heard the drumming of woodpeckers, the chirps of ground squirrels warning of their approach. Swarms of gnats tormented them. The switchbacks of the path took them in and out of shadow and a waning light that was soft and wistful. On all sides and over them the leaves shed water like the rain itself and breathed a mossy fragrance. Fog lingered among the trees and gave everything the sickly tint of peach pulp, as if they'd all taken jaundice, man and beast alike. Blue jays scolded them overhead.

Because the downpour had eroded runnels in the trail that exposed many a loose rock, the mule and the brother's horse picked their way with care; continually Webb spoke in reassuring fashion to the mule, who so far seemed confident, if not wholly superior. As dusk came they entered the head of the cove that drained down Compass Creek to the main Tusquittee, and so descended through the familiar foot-slope forest of poplar, oak and hickory. They heard the rush of the stream, the soft roar of a nearby waterfall; soon the creek itself was flowing beside them, its banks red with fire pink and bee balm. Fern grew thick here; flowering laurel hung in damp clumps that soaked them as they passed. A skunk had sprayed somewhere close by; its fetor burned in their noses.

It was dark when they arrived at the mouth of the creek and found Ree Bolt and the man from Long Branch waiting in a stand of shumake by the Tusquittee, where the path down from Pot Rock Bald met the wagon road to Hayesville. The damp woods around them twinkled with the tiny lights of fireflies. Ree had brought his Sharps carbine and the other a shotgun. Darling didn't know the one with the shotgun and so grew wary and questioned him for a time, till he'd satisfied himself Abner Mullinax was indeed in bed with rheumatism and had sent a cousin instead. Once he'd established that, they mounted and set off down the Tusquittee, then up Greasy Creek past the Double Knobs and over the bottom land to the river, avoiding the farmsteads.

At the river they turned southwest and followed it downstream toward the mouth of Downings Creek. As they went a full moon rose and cast over them a glint so pure they could see their shadows on the ground. The surface of the river looked like a wrinkled strip of tin; they smelt its musky odor. Dogs barked in the distance.

At Downings Creek they turned north and east, away from the Hiwassee. They rode past Hamby McFee's and the Shuford place, and a mile or so farther they drew rein in a brake of cedars at the edge of a farm. While Webb sat the mule and watched the unlighted house, Ree Bolt and the brother and the Mullinax cousin dismounted to don their regalia; in a moment they changed from mortal men to demons in horned hoods and gowns marked with hex signs. But Webb would not change his guise. Webb would present himself as he was, as the king come to do a harsh but just act. Webb was terrible enough in himself. He unwrapped the rag from the head of the ax.

Hamby didn't hear the noise that woke him, only what seemed its echo dwindling away in the night. The echo had a crackle in it suggesting a gunshot. For a time he lay waiting for it to repeat, but it did not. He thought perhaps some aggravated farmer had fired at a fox raiding his chicken house. But as he listened he heard only the piping of tree frogs and a distant growl of thunder. Maybe it wasn't a shot; maybe it was thunder he'd heard; it had rained earlier. Soon again he slept.

Next morning he hitched the steer to the cart and drove around to the edge of his potato patch, where last spring he'd left the wooden-toothed drag harrow he owned in common with Lige Dollar. Lige had sent word he aimed to make a second crop of corn this year, and he had a field that needed breaking up. Hamby found the harrow by a fence corner, half-hidden in a bank of wet morning glory. He man-handled the awkward thing into the bed of the cart and then climbed in and spoke sharply to the steer. Slowly he trundled out the farm lane to the road. Bearing right, he followed the road half a mile to the muddy turnout that led up the creek to Lige's.

The first thing he noticed was how torn up the turnout was; several horses and a mule had passed that way coming and going, and not so long back either. Yet nothing lay ahead that could justify that much traffic. There was only Lige's cabin, and while Lige owned a mule he had no horse at all. This gave Hamby pause. Lige was one hard nigger, and he spent a good deal of time up the Tusquittee with some folk Hamby knew were mighty rough; he was blockading with Darling the moonshiner king. Hamby had made some blockade himself awhile back, when Bill Berong was still the king, and he understood what could transpire when that business went wrong. Hamby felt a chill of foreboding and wished he'd brought his pistol. Nevertheless he slapped the steer's back with the reins and went rattling on up the path, past the cedar brake to the cabin of squared logs.

Some years ago Lige had built a post-and-rail fence around his place, but afterwards he neglected it till much of it fell down. Now it was just a mass of honeysuckle and trumpet creeper, except for the place where the gate used to be. Hamby drove through the gap and stopped the steer in the bare dooryard. When he saw Lige's headless body in the yard he put his hands on the splashboard and dropped his gaze and for some time made no further move, just stood there in the cart looking off to the side, till presently the steer turned its head curiously back at him. After a time he got down and went and stood over it and saw that it had been shot four or five times with different kinds of guns. That was the shooting he'd heard in the night. They were killing him while Hamby slept.

The head lay on the door log of the cabin. Shoved in the mouth was a piece of paper rolled into a cylinder. Hamby drew out the paper and opened it. It was smeared with blood. "INFORMER," it said. Hamby folded the paper and put it in his pocket. He stared a long while at the face, as if he meant to commit it to memory. While he watched he heard a noise in the trees above him and knew the buzzards and ravens had come and were peering eagerly down. He stood then and turned; dozens of them waited overhead, the buzzards with their wings spread out like dark capes. Now truly he wanted his five-shooter.

The morning was hot, and already the part of Lige that had been shot was swelling and turning waxy black, and the flies were working at it; the buzzards would soon have their way with it, too, unless Hamby took steps before going into Hayesville to tell the sheriff. So grasping it by the legs, Hamby dragged that part into the cabin and laid it on the cot and covered it with the Jacob's-ladder quilt a woman of Lige's had once made. Stripping off a pillowcase, Hamby rolled the head in it and placed it on the bed next to the rest. Then he shuttered up all the windows and closed the door and left.

Lige Dollar never had any use for religion—often he'd said if Jesus came back to earth not a church in the world would recognize Him—so the AME folk wanted naught to do with any funeral. Nor did Lige have living kin that Hamby knew of. So when Sheriff Cherry finished with his investigation and released the body, Hamby decided he'd do the burying himself, at Lige's place. He passed the word, and at the appointed time ten or twelve fellows showed up to help with the digging and to send Lige off in proper style. All were colored but three—Webb Darling and a pair of his rowdies.

The sheriff had found no evidence to show who'd done the murder, but everybody knew Darling was the one. It turned out Lige had informed to the Revenue on a white man named Bullock, a blockader who'd been stilling at a place Lige considered too close to his own setup near the head of Fires Creek. Lige and Bullock were both beholden to Darling, and Darling could hardly be the king of the Tusquittees if one of his folk could give another to the government without paying the cost. Some even said that Lige had been a Revenue Dog for years, that he'd put a slew of blockaders in prison, that the Revenue collector of North Carolina paid him a regular wage. Darling could not have held still for that.

Hamby understood it all. Lige had knowingly played a risky game, and Darling had done what he must. Regrettably Lige had come up short, like many a nigger before him. It was the way the world worked. But to Hamby the manner of a man's death was even more important than the reason it came about. This belief went way back, back to his grandmam that he hardly recalled, who said she came from a great tribe of Africa. There wasn't much about her that he could bring to mind, but one thing in particular he did remember. She'd said her tribe thought dying was but the last part of living and was the best blessing one received—but only if those who remained could give the body honor. No honor could be conferred if the body suffered desecration. Violating it broke the sacred spell of afterlife. To tear the flesh and break the bones was to set the spirit loose between the worlds, a booger and a haint, neither quick nor dead.

Hamby was too levelheaded to embrace altogether any such nigger superstition, but he did agree that anybody who played a man's part deserved a man's end, deserved to go to his Maker with respect. It was wrong to degrade him, even for the purpose of setting an example that others inclined to treachery might heed. One gunshot to the temple would've been right. What Darling did was as wrong as anything could ever be, and it was in Hamby's head to put it right.

But when Darling approached him at the grave he drew in turtlelike, the way he always did whenever a white he didn't trust—which was any white at all—came near; in this way none could ever guess even the merest wish of his heart. "I'm obliged to you for taking care of this," Darling said with a nod toward the plain pine box. "Since he was one of mine, by rights I ought to've had it done."

Hamby watched him, shrugged, rejoined, "Lige was my friend."

The two who'd come with Darling lounged against the wall of the cabin, looking on. One was a queer shade of reddish black and had shaggy hair that stuck out from under his hat; soon it came to Hamby that this was the Melungeon Ree Bolt, newly home from the pen, older, bonier, most likely meaner. The other was younger by some years, slight and rangy; he slid his looks narrowly from side to side, as a white man does when outnumbered by coloreds.

Darling nodded. He removed his hat and dried his brow with a handkerchief. Hamby noticed the hat had a little brass doohickey in front resembling a crown. Darling's hair grew close to his head, kinked and thick-knit like a bed of moss; so blond was it that it looked almost white. He had a yellow mustache curled up at the ends, which made him look amused whether he was or not. His eyes were as clear as skim-ice and had the same delicate blue in them that you sometimes see in mother-of-pearl; his lashes were long and luxuriant like a woman's, and he used them to the same effect a woman might, dropping and raising them almost coyly. He had a scatter of fine freckles over the bridge of his nose. He put away his handkerchief, fished in his pants pocket and held up two silver dollars. "Still I'm grateful. This is for your trouble."

Hamby took the coins without the least hesitation and held them down by his leg in his fist while Darling went on. "It's too bad about Lige. In some ways he was as fine a darky as I ever knew. But then it was hard for him to be constant, wasn't it? Somehow he just never took root. We need to be true to something, don't we? We can't just jump at everything that passes. We must be loyal to some single thing. Loyalty's the key of life." Sadly he shook his head, sighed, fluttered his long lashes. "I'll miss him. He used to tell the funniest stories."

In Hamby's fist the coins grew warm and sweaty; he felt their milled edges against his palm. Darling brightened and began to laugh. "I remember one he told. This boy went to his daddy and said, 'I fancy that gal Mary Anne Jones and am thinking of marrying her,' and his daddy said, 'You can't marry her. She's your cousin.' So sometime later the boy came in and said, 'I like that gal Jenny Smith and am thinking of marrying her,' and his daddy said, 'You can't marry her. She's your cousin.' A little while later the boy came back and said, 'I'm a-favoring that gal Libby Brown and am thinking of marrying her,' and his daddy said, 'You can't marry her. She's your cousin.' And his mama spoke up and said to the boy, 'Don't pay no attention to him. He ain't no kin to you.' "

Clutching the coins, Hamby joined him in laughter. Then it was time to pray over Lige. They all uncovered, and Darling stepped up to the lip of the grave and held his hat over his heart and said, "Lord God Almighty, ruler of heaven and earth, we offer up to you this day the soul of Elijah Dollar, who was a true and honest nigger and in no way deserved the cruel manner of his taking off. Soothe his hurts and give his soul comfort, we pray Thee. And at the Last Judgment draw him to your bosom and grant him the life everlasting. In the holy name of Jesus our Savior, amen."

They all repeated the amen, then took up the shovels and commenced to fill the grave. Hamby slipped the two dollars into the watch pocket of his vest and made to join them. But again Darling approached, bade him set his shovel down, took him aside under a buckeye tree. "I've got some mighty fine roosters I'd like to fight," Darling told him. "I know you're a good chicken man. Have you got a cock you can fight?"

"My best-un got killed last year," Hamby replied. "Ain't got no more 'cept a pair of little old stags ain't ready for the pit yet."

Darling frowned. "That's too bad. Yes, I heard about your bird, how that old Shawlneck of Livingood's got him." He drew a rueful face and repeated, "Too bad. We could've made a good match. But I reckon I can get Livingood to give me a match."

"I expect so," Hamby said. He watched Darling, heard the rattle and thump of the dirt on the lid of the coffin behind him, saw Darling's lashes demurely fall and rise. Darling's breath smelt pleasantly of peach brandy. "Tell you what," Hamby said then. "I see if I can't get me a good-un here directly. I know a man might let me have a rooster or two. Take me awhile to train it up right. But maybe we make us a match one of these days after all."

Darling beamed, showing his perfect teeth. "Good, good. I hope you can get your birds. Nobody white or colored's better'n McFee in a hack fight, is what I've heard—though I think I've got a cock or two can whip whatever you put in the pit. Anyway, however it turns out, it'll be something to see." He touched the brim of his hat and went to his mule and pulled himself to the saddle. "When you're fixed," he said, "send me word." Ree Bolt and the other one mounted and came to flank him; Ree as he sat his dun horse bent a smoky look down at Hamby that might've meant a lot or nothing at all.

"Yessir," Hamby replied.

They put their mounts into the lane and through the gate, and he watched them down the way and around the curve out of sight. Yes, he had the time. He couldn't leave the valley anyhow, for he'd lost all his money, and besides, no matter how it annoyed him, Andy

Curtis and Miss Becky needed him to run the farm; he didn't see any way to avoid that without feeling smaller than he preferred to. Now Webb Darling had given him another reason to stay, and to Hamby it was just about the best reason there could be. He crossed to the privy and opened the door and took the two dollars out of his vest pocket and dropped them down the hole. Then he came back to the grave to join the others, picked up his shovel and drove the blade of it deep into the mound of black dirt.

CHAPTER 6

July 1881

*E*very time one of his stratagems got away from him—which was more often than he liked to admit—Ves Price was in the habit of climbing the hill above the Curtis place and sitting on a favored flat quartz rock above a blowdown, where he had a fine view of the old house and the broad valley in its cup of mountains.

The deadfall—a tangle of old scaly trunks and branches all covered with a mottled white crust of dried rosin—had cleared a hole in what used to be unbroken forest and opened a prospect over the bottom. The space was open to the sun and smelt tartly of the hot pines, and the carpet of red needles underfoot gave off a warm scent that was similar to that of the pines but also subtly different, just as the notes of a chord of music are both related and apart. The clearing and its smells were his balm. Whenever he came here he always brought with him some burnt nerve or defeated hope or spoilt plot that needed soothing, and never had the spot disobliged him.

Just now he was footsore and weary from plodding the better part of three days and thirty-odd miles all the way home from Duke's Creek down in Georgia, where he'd gone in hopes of panning himself a fortune in gold. He'd heard they used to get gold there in the old days—placer mining, they called it, nuggets big as your fist. He'd stolen one of Miz Henslee's saucepans and toted it the whole way to the head of the Hiwassee in the country where the High Shoals and the Spoilcane met, then on even past the canyons of the Chattahoochee, to the bogs in the valley there in White County by Yonah Mountain, where they used to get the gold.

Ves had got naught for his ten days of hardship but the stink of the stagnant bogs and the songs of a horde of bullfrogs to torment his sleep and as many cottonmouths in those damn old ponds as you could shake a stick at and at least a million skeeters feasting on him day and night. And not a grain nor a dab of gold. Nary a speck nor a fleck.

It seemed more than a misfortune; it seemed unjust. He'd shown a commendable ambition, had put himself to a good deal of trouble, had indeed worked harder in worse conditions than ever before in his life, yet unfairly Providence had weighed down the scales against him. His enterprise had not been rewarded, though many—his silly pap foremost among them—had often assured him it would be if he exerted himself. Now he'd lost Miz Henslee's saucepan in a sinkhole and was suffering an awful dread of her wrath to come, which he suspected to be worse even than that of the Lord Himself, whenever He descended in glory on the Last Day.

Feeling sorry for himself, he sat on his rock picking apart an old pine cone while the breeze stirred the woods around him and wafted to him the tangy perfumes. Below, the tin roof of the Curtis house sent a rectangular glint of light straight up at him, so he had to shift his position on the rock to keep from being blinded. He hadn't seen

Becky today. He didn't even consider it necessary any longer to see her; just being so close to her was enough. Together with the peace of his little clearing in the pines, the closeness of Becky Curtis helped ease whatever hurts he had. And as always when he thought of Becky he thought also of his late mam, who'd loved him in the same way he knew Becky could, if only she'd be willing.

His first memory was of his mam holding him on her lap. He remembered how when she sang her bosom would hum against the ear he'd laid warm against her. The hum would be answered in his head and in his stomach in a low and lulling way that made him feel safe and drowsy. Her arms would be clasped about him gently rocking him. She smelt strongly of wood smoke, and the memory of that smell was so clear and so valuable to him that after he grew up, whenever he smelt the smoke of a poplar fire, he always thought with sorrow of his lost mam. But to his regret he could never bring to mind a single one of those songs she'd sung while holding him to her bosom.

He recalled reclining on a quilt under a tree, while beyond him in a slanted field she jerked and pushed at a plow drawn by a bony ox. He recalled following her along fresh-turned rows of red earth dropping seeds where she told him. He recalled the sight of her on her knees by a creek beating the wash against a stone with a battling stick. He recalled the clicking whir of her spinning wheel at night and the clang of her gourd banjo and the motion her arm made as she sewed. His mam was the only one to love him. All others had slighted him and found fault. Even Becky had shunned him, though he couldn't find it in his heart to blame her; he'd made a mistake, he'd scared and maybe even revolted her, but all unwittingly. And how could she know that? Tom Carter, the son of a bitch, had poisoned her against him. Left to herself, Ves was sure, Becky would've come to fancy him after all. Ves knew that it was a vain hope now. His chance at Becky, if ever there'd been one, was gone. But still he lingered nearby, if only to draw into himself some faint whiff or breath of her that might rise to him and awaken notions of his mam and of a love equal to his mam's that Becky might've felt, had fate not been so harsh.

As he mulled these reveries Ves was amazed when all at once a shadow fell over him. He looked up to see a man standing next to him wearing a broad gray hat and a black frock coat of wool with satin lapels and tan corduroy britches stuffed into a pair of high boots. This was a gent Ves did not know, nor could he imagine how the fellow had come by him, much less why. He had a shaggy mustache that was sort of a brindle color and a little goatish tuft of rusty hair sprouting from his chin. "Hidy," he said.

"Hidy," Ves replied, shading his eyes with his hand. "You come up mighty quiet."

The stranger nodded, then with both hands he hiked up the front of his pants and took a seat on the rock beside Ves, then when the glare from the Curtises' roof struck him he moved off the rock and sat on the carpet of pine needles instead. "You gonna get chiggers," Ves warned him, looking closely at his boots to note how expensive they were.

"I've had 'em, and will again," said the stranger with an air of indifference. He drew a twist of Star of Virginia from an inside coat pocket and held it out. "Chaw?"

"Don't mind if I do," said Ves. He tore off a chunk and put it in his cheek. "How come you to climb this hill?"

The stranger sat chewing. He looked out over the valley from under the brim of his big hat but appeared to take no interest in what he saw. "Made it my business to," he finally said. Ves couldn't see his eyes to find their color or what they might imply, for he'd slitted them against the sun.

"How come?" Ves wanted to know. The hairs on the backs of his arms were standing up, and he felt a sink in his scrotum, as he did when in the presence of what he conceived was danger. He didn't care for this rangy jasper in his plainsman's sombrero and fancy boots, the way he'd appeared out of nowhere in Ves's most secret spot, his flat and nasal voice that sounded bored even as a thin wire of hard intent ran through it, his offhand manner of casual negligence, the wisp of hair on his chin, the motion of his big jaw as it chewed.

"Wanted to get you alone so's we could talk." The stranger turned his head aside and spat and turned back to gaze again across the valley he didn't seem to see.

Ves was afraid of him. Who wouldn't be? He was such a long-legged cuss with so much of a snake's slyness, so much of its noiseless slither, such a cold presence. But even so, despite his fear, Ves was getting irked. Whoever he was, the bastard was trespassing on Ves's private retreat and had upset his tender mood. "What we got to talk about?" he demanded. "Why, I don't even know who in hell you are."

"Name's Richbourg," the fellow declared. Again he leaned and spat to the side.

Ves took a sideways spit of his own, then gave a snort to suggest he was braver than he felt. "Well, Mr. By-God Richbourg, I ask you again, what in hell you want?"

"Tucker Richbourg," amplified the gent. "Tuck for short. Special deputy collector of revenue, out of Towns County, Georgia." He laid his forearms on his knees, so his long white hands hung from his knobby wrists expectant but unmoving, like implements suspended from pegs on a barn wall, waiting to be put to use.

Ves was astounded, thunderstruck. Ves reeled. Never in all his life had he spoken face to face with any agent of the hated Revenue, and now that he was doing it—innocently unaware till this very moment—all he could think of was what would happen to him should somebody glimpse him doing it. He gagged on his chaw; he coughed it out; he made as if to rise and flee, lest the worst occur and his name be carried up to Pot Rock Bald within the hour and handed to Webb Darling, who would condemn him just as old Lige Dollar had got condemned. But before Ves got halfway up, Richbourg stopped him with a single word. That word was *money*.

"Thirty dollars," he said. "Every month."

Ves resumed his seat.

To give proof Richbourg took from the side pocket of his coat three gold eagles, which he reached over and laid one by one—how agreeably they clinked!—on the flat top of the rock where Ves sat. Ves looked at the coins, two showing a Liberty head wearing a coronet and the other an image of the bird the coin was named for. Ves pondered. Around the valley he could hire himself out doing farm work for two bits a day if he was fortunate—which he usually wasn't—and make himself fifteen dollars in a month. Or he could lay hold of twice that by striking whatever bargain Deputy Revenue Collector Tuck Richbourg had in mind.

Ves had an inkling what that was. Having lost Lige Dollar, the Revenue needed themselves one good spy. Without such they had to rely on luck, thrashing around in the brush, hoping to run upon a still by happenstance. Most every soul around the Tusquittee knew where all the stills were and even knew how to get to Webb Darling's fort on top of Pot Rock Bald. But not a one of them was about to tell the Revenue any damn thing at all, for they were all blockaders themselves or kin to some, nor would they even piss on a Revenue if his heart were afire. Besides, nobody wanted to have his head chopped off like old Lige. "That's good money," Ves remarked, still gazing on the three coins shining on the rock beside him. "But it wouldn't do me much good if I was dead."

Richbourg took the point. He nodded, leaned, spat. "That coon tried to work out a private spite. Tattled on a fellow aiming to cut down competition. Stepped out of line, Lige did. When you're out of line you're conspicuous. That's why the king spotted him." Richbourg touched Ves with a flick of a glance. "Lesson is, keep to your own good hole, do your job and no harm'll come."

"Easy for you to say," Ves pointed out. *Thirty dollars a month*, he was thinking. Hell, at that rate, he could fetch nearly two hundred in six months, more than enough to pay his way out of the valley of the Hiwassee for good. And six months would be just about right. For in fact he wasn't ready just yet to go. Becky still held him captive. Even knowing he'd lost her, still he couldn't yet stand to tear himself away; he couldn't give up being close enough to breathe her aura, to taste the elixir of her spirit on the air, sometimes to glimpse her precious self in the distance with the light in her hair. But surely in six months' time he could wean himself. Surely by then his wounds would heal. He turned to the deputy. "How come you to pick me anyways?"

Richbourg seemed almost to smile behind his mustache. "Word is, you're dumb as a cord of firewood"—Ves was hurt and offended to hear this—"but I've been watching you quite a spell now, and although I agree you're dumb I also think you've got a low sort of cunning that we could use. And you're greedy as hell. That helps."

Ves bristled. "I ain't dumb."

"You ain't?" Now Richbourg laughed; his laugh sounded like a dry stick breaking. "How about pouring them slops in the creek last year and hiding the barrels in them laurel woollies, that led us to Ree Bolt and that Nutbush?"

Ves hung his head and blushed. Well, he'd been in love. If he'd had his proper wits about him he'd never have done such a deed. But there it was; it marked him. He sighed. At least Richbourg had said he was cunning. But then he wondered why his cunning was low and not high. He frowned. "You got such a bad opinion of me, why you ready to pay me thirty dollars a month to turn in my friends and neighbors?"

"'Cause I know you'll do it," the deputy replied.

And he was right. For thirty dollars a month Ves would tell on his own pap—him for sure—or on Miz Henslee or Hamby McFee or his stepbrother Jim or any mortal alive. What ties had he to anyone? Save for Becky his only obligation was to himself. And even Becky was becoming a wraith that soon must drop away. It was only Ves that mattered. And he was cunning; Richbourg himself had said it. He was cunning enough to play the game and keep from getting killed. He picked up the three eagles.

⤸

Ves was crossing the bridge at Sanderson Ford with a pole over his shoulder that had his goods tied in a budget on the end of it when Captain Irish Bill Moore came trotting down the Tusquittee road on that big-shouldered brown stud of his. The captain drew abreast and reined Crockett back to a walk and cried in his voice that rang like a cymbal, "It's young Mr. Price, ain't it—Oliver's oldest?"

Ves allowed he was. Ves called him sir. Like everybody else in that district he felt obliged to treat the captain outwardly with respect, for he was a hero of war and by far the most prosperous man between Buck Creek and the Snowbirds. But in his heart Ves begrudged giving Moore any due at all, just as he did anybody he thought undeserving of such good fortune as they had—especially if what they enjoyed was better than he could get. And what the captain had was so much greater than Ves's poor portion that it towered like Babel. Envy fed on Ves's vitals.

But Moore had no notion of Ves's spite; as he went along he appeared to engage in considered thought, cocked his head aside, buried a ruminating hand in his long beard, which had the hue of molasses. Crockett snorted and set his bit chains rattling, rolled a speculative black eye Ves's way. The captain took note of Ves's stick with its poke of goods. "May I inquire," he said then in his bright tone, "whether you're arriving or departing?"

"I'm headed home," Ves replied somewhat shortly. Grand the captain might be, noble his very name, but it was still none of his damn business how Ves came and went.

"You've been on a journey then," Moore concluded.

In surly fashion Ves confirmed it.

The captain withdrew his hand from the depths of his beard and used it to twist the end of the beard into a point. "Was it far?"

Clearly the old man meant to quiz Ves till he got the news he wanted, so Ves stopped in the middle of the bridge and looked to him and confessed, "I was down to the gold country in Georgia, by Duke's Creek."

"Ah, gold," the captain knowingly smiled. A mist of nostalgia seemed to settle over him as he contemplated far-off times and the follies he'd chased. He drew rein and brought Crockett to a stand; the big horse bent his huge neck, one hoof pawing impatiently at the bridge timbers. "Yes, gold," Moore went on. "In my boyhood I myself panned many a stream in that region. Like others I wished to make one great raise." He crossed his hands on the pommel of his saddle and sighed. "It's the curse of youth."

The hell it is, Ves thought. He preferred not to let the captain go any farther along that path; old men were always forswearing the fevers of the young that wouldn't burn in themselves anymore, making it sound like a virtue or an advantage that their fires were out. To prevent such maundering Ves spoke his own question, "Did you find any?"

"Gold?" Old Moore chuckled and shook his head. "No, son. Nobody ever does."

Ves shrugged. "I heard some did."

"Not in our time," the captain assured him. He gathered his reins, touched Crockett's flanks with his spurs. They crossed the bridge and started up the road toward Hayesville on its hill. "So you hoped to make your fortune," the captain mused.

"I did," said Ves. He was wary; it seemed queer how old Moore was probing at the very matter of treasure, as if he somehow surmised Ves had just made a pact with Tuck Richbourg to lay hands on some in a fashion most would find wrongful. For the second time that day the hairs on Ves's arms stood up. Could the captain know? *How* could he know?

"A man's fortune is never what he expects it to be," old Moore said. "Whatever he gets, *that's* his fortune. Doesn't matter what he wanted or how much he wanted it or how he strove to get it. He just gets what comes. And if he's a wise man he sees it for his fortune. He takes what comes. Accepts it as his due. Looks for no other." He cut his eyes down at Ves, but Ves looked away, having no desire to hear yet more counsel that young men ought to be satisfied with little, so old rich ones could get more.

"I know what you're thinking," the captain went on. "I'm a wealthy man, and I own a great farm and beautiful wide lands, field and brook and hill, crops, timber, a fine house. 'Listen to him,' you're saying to yourself. 'That old bastard, he's rich and I'm poor, and he's telling me not to try and grasp at riches.' But you're wrong, son. I'll tell you what my fortune was. It was coming home from war and getting Miss Hattie Gash to be my wedded wife."

Again the captain glanced down, and again Ves looked away. "I'd lost everything," old Moore went on. "My health was broke, hateful Yankees were trying to confiscate what few goods I had left, I was whipped to a nubbin like every other raggedy Rebel in all of Dixie, my faith was gone, my hopes blasted, my very ass was dragging after me over the ground. But Miss Hattie took me. When I had naught to offer her she took me. That was my fortune."

Again he stopped Crockett, yet this time he didn't put his eyes on Ves but on the buildings of the town ahead of them. "I don't care how it looks to you, son," he said. "But I'm telling you, what's come to me since that day ain't my fortune atall. It's just the trimmings of life, that goes as easy as it comes. I know how hard it is to go lacking. I've had nothing—had less than you, if you'll believe it. So I know what has value and what don't. And I could lose all I own tomorrow and never turn a hair, for I've got Miss Hattie."

Bullshit, thought Ves. *Bull Shit.* Still it spooked him how old Moore had taken it into his head to lecture him in this way; it was as if the captain had lurked unseen in the woods on the hill above the Curtis place, peering and listening as Ves and Tuck Richbourg laid their plans. Hell, come to think of it, Richbourg himself had seemed like a bewitchment, appearing out of nowhere, conjured from the ether. All of a sudden Ves felt himself at the convergence of powers beyond his ken. Maybe some unearthly force had delivered Tuck Richbourg to tempt him to do evil and then sent Captain Irish Bill to warn him of the fruits of wrong. Maybe what he faced was a choice posed him by Hell or by Heaven, there was no knowing which. Ves drew a shaky breath. Under his feet all Creation shifted by a slight but still measurable distance.

CHAPTER 7

August 1881

*B*efore leaving, Hamby crossed to the fence where the stallion Tom stood with his grizzled jaw resting on the top rail, as if the weight of his big skull were too great for his neck to hold. But as Hamby came to him Tom rumbled a greeting and lifted that heavy head, reached out his saggy lips to nuzzle the palm Hamby extended. The old horse gave off the same sad yet compliant air Hamby had noticed in him more and more since spring; Tom seemed to know that not much else was ever going to happen to him and to have decided that such a fate was better than some. It made Hamby think of how Gouger used to stand silently by his pen, lost in seeming melancholy, as if he'd guessed his own end. He thought how much he missed Gouger. He dug his fingers into Tom's forelock, scratched the roots of the nearly hairless ears. "You, Tom," he said.

It would take a day and a half on the jenny to get to Hanging

Dog, so Hamby had collected some rations—side meat, boiled eggs, a pone of cornbread, an onion, a couple of apples, a piece of a cherry cobbler Miss Becky had baked for him, a canteen of water and another of blockade. There wasn't an eating place or an inn anywhere between his farm and Grape Creek that would serve the likes of him, so he must tote his own rations and the feed for the jenny and camp out on the way one night going and one coming. The whole business was a lot of trouble to go to and would take him away from the Curtises—and from his own ground—just as the harvest drew nigh. But it was a thing Hamby reckoned he had to do, no matter its inconvenience. He hadn't told Miss Becky what this was, nor had she asked about it; it was sufficient to her that Hamby said the errand was vital. She'd assured him she and Andy and the Cartmans could manage, and no doubt faithful Tom Carter could be counted on to help.

As he saddled the jenny while the old stallion watched resignedly from the fence, Hamby felt a twinge of foreboding. There were tales a body could hear about Rollin Livingood—that he'd been Cyclops of a Ku Klux den in Rutherford County a few years back, that he and his brother-in-law Petrie had been convicted of Kluxing and served terms in the pen at Auburn, New York, along with Randolph Shotwell and thirty or so other nigger-haters. Some even said he'd hanged a darky or two with his own hands, and it was sure he'd given a whipping to many another. His was reputation enough to inspire in Hamby such a mix of hate and dread and contempt that it was going to be hard to offer himself to Livingood in congenial fashion. Yet to consummate his scheme he must. And despite his stew of feelings he knew he'd manage to do it in the end; he'd amassed a lifetime's practice holding up to whites whatever mask he had to, so as to hide what lived in his heart. But always—as now—it sickened him.

Hamby slung his two pokes of rations and feed over the pommel, one to each side. Ducking his head through the straps of the canteens, he hung them right and left from his shoulders. He stood then to the stirrup and mounted. So small was the jenny and so long the leathers that his bare feet nearly touched the ground, yet as always she took his weight with but a single groan of complaint, the prelude to a tolerance whose limit she had not reached in five long years of carrying him. From the fence Tom looked patiently on; Hamby turned and spoke him a good-bye; Tom slowly blinked his long white lashes in what looked like reply. Hamby clucked to the jenny, shook her one rein of old rope. They went past the spirit tree and out of the yard and turned right on the road. The sun was just clearing the crowns of the Nantahalas behind him, and Hamby felt the scorch of it on his back, abnormally hot for the hour; it would be a searing day.

Yes, Livingood bore an ill name. Yet when they'd met at the Jackrabbit hack fight he'd seemed to give Hamby a good regard. Also the Cherokee Longrunner, his handler, was evidence that in Livingood's view a man's skill could sometimes trump his color. Moreover, word was that Livingood had forsworn the Ku Klux when he came to Cherokee County to live after getting out of prison and had refused to have any truck whatsoever with Webb Darling and his White Caps. Maybe, as happened to some men, jail had changed Livingood for the better.

Anyhow the life Hamby lived had lent him a pretty fine sense of which whites were deadly and which few were more or less benign— though of course the best of them would turn on you in the worst of circumstances. This sense, which had never yet misled him, hinted that Livingood, despite his vile past, was less of a threat now than most. If Hamby didn't believe that, he wouldn't have conceived this queer scheme of his at all. Still, before starting out, on the off chance his instinct might have failed him for the first time, Hamby had loaded his stepdaddy's old .36-caliber Colt's five-shooting pistol and put it in his waistband under his coat. He also kept his ivory-handled straight razor ready in a hip pocket of his jeans.

In the growing heat the jenny bore him plodding along Downings Creek to the bridge of the Murphy wagon road, then west around a ridge and past the wooded headland that was one shaggy flank of Carroll Mountain. By the time the day was hottest they were in the broad green bottom land near Sweetwater; Hamby let the jenny graze in a clover field shaded by weeping willows. Later in the cool of evening they moved on down the Hiwassee past Mission and Peachtree. Near sunset Hamby camped by the roadside for the night; the town of Murphy was but a mile or two ahead. He reclined on a blanket and ate his supper, listening in contentment to the quiet sounds of evening—the river's flow, the rattle of the crickets, jar flies whirring, the last songs of meadowlarks and mockingbirds. Bullbats wheeled against the dimming sky. A stately heron waded in the shallows, so near at hand it seemed to dare him to disturb it. To the north he watched a line of shadow gradually climb the slopes of Fain Mountain and the more distant Snowbirds till at last it reached and dimmed out the points of twilight that had lingered on the highest knobs. He was a little wary underneath his calm, but he was also as confident as his experience would let him be. Tomorrow would tell the tale.

An old colored man at Grape Creek told him how to get to Livingood's, and when he reached the turnout the nigger had described—a weedy lane that went looping off through a wood between zigzags of worm fencing—he found Longrunner sitting by the path on a fallen beech log braiding thongs of leather into what might become a horse halter. Hamby couldn't tell if

Longrunner was standing some sort of guard for Livingood or had just decided to sit down by the fence corner and go to braiding because it suited him. Longrunner didn't look up when Hamby steered the jenny to him. "Hidy," Hamby said. Longrunner touched him with a dark look, then bent his attention silently back to the work of his hands. This high-hat manner annoyed Hamby. "You a ugly-natured cuss," he declared. Longrunner seemed not to hear. Hamby got down from the jenny and hunkered in front of him and remarked, "I said hidy, you sulled-up son of a bitch."

The Cherokee allowed himself a small and narrow smile. "What you after?" he inquired. "You got you another bird you want that old Shawlneck to kill?"

Hamby felt a flare of anger on Gouger's account but quickly mastered it in the name of larger things. He was inclined to give the surly Indian the go-by and climb back on the jenny and follow the lane on up to Livingood's, but then something he couldn't name held him, something about Longrunner that he wished to plumb or measure. He made no reply to the slur; instead he fetched his pipe from his breast pocket and put it in his teeth and sucked on it empty, letting the stillness settle in between them; he could wait out any damn Cherokee at all.

He was mildly vexed by his rude reception because at Jackrabbit he'd got the idea Longrunner approved of him. But he was also accustomed to swallowing much disrespect he hadn't earned, which could come from any quarter without warning; he could abide it if he must. He watched Longrunner's hands working nimbly at the thongs. The stem and bowl of the pipe whistled as Hamby sucked. The jenny cropped the wayside grass; hummingbirds buzzed in the honeysuckle on the fence; somewhere off in the woods a hawk whistled. Presently Hamby sat all the way down cross-legged in the lane and filled his pipe and lit it; he sat a long while smoking. When he'd smoked it nearly down he finally said, "I come to see Livingood."

Longrunner tilted his head and stared at Hamby as if he'd only just discovered him sitting there. "The man's got a first name and a mister in front of that, for a nigger to use."

Hamby snorted. "Is that so? Well, then, what a goddamn smart-alecky rag-headed red-dick *Injun* be calling him?"

Longrunner said naught by way of reply. He sent a glance at Hamby that soon slid off him to the side, as if to show he found Hamby unworthy of interest. Then he stood up slowly from his log and laid the unfinished halter over one shoulder and turned up the path. He moved smooth and high-jointed, like a painter. "Well," he said, "come on ahead if you're a-coming." Hamby hadn't learned a thing and rued the time he'd wasted trying to puzzle out the redskin. Scowling, he followed, leading the jenny by her rein of rope.

Livingood's place was a saddlebag cabin of chinked and daubed logs shingled with cedar shakes held in place by flat stones. A cracked chimney of sticks and mud leaned precariously out from one end of it. The house stood on the crest of a low hill in the scant shade of an old black walnut, and the lane led up to it over bare ground past a dozen or so pens with chickens in and around them. All about stood the hardwood forest. As they came up, a pair of black-and-tan hounds dashed out from behind the house baying and howling till Longrunner told them to hush; they lay down at once under the walnut, satisfied to observe events rather than comment on them.

Following Longrunner up the path, Hamby glanced into the pens one by one, and although he was not conversant with all the breeds, he thought he recognized the downy plumage and small wings and tail of a Langhan—or maybe he was a Brahma—and a skinny long-necked bird that might have been a Malayan. He saw one with a white crest he guessed was a Sultan, maybe a black-and-white Houdan, a pair of Whitehackles, some Red Wheels. But most were just cross-bred shotgun fowl of every hue and size. Last of all and nearest the house was the Shawlneck's pen. Here Hamby stopped and knelt to peer into the scrawny bird's avid little eye. "Get too close," Longrunner warned, "he take off you goddamn nose."

Hamby didn't need the reminder. Slingshot glared back at him with fierce little twists of his head, as if testing the acuity of each eye in turn. "You a mean-un," Hamby told him. The Shawlneck squawked and flogged his wings as if to confirm the remark.

Hamby rose then and led the jenny across the dooryard to a shed and tied her there to an iron ring set in the wall of milled planks. When he started toward the dogtrot Longrunner spoke up sharply, saying, "Such as you goes round back."

Hamby stopped and turned to him. He'd expected this and was ready for it. He'd do what he ought, even if it meant the misfiring of his plot. Besides he figured if Livingood had once been the sort to hang a saucy nigger, acting saucy now would put him to a useful test. "No," Hamby said, "that won't do. It cut me down too damn short."

Longrunner set his jaw and placed his hands on his hips. The hands were huge; each looked the size of Hamby's head. He drew a breath that swelled out his chest like a hogshead of tobacco. "You goes round back or you goes home," he declared, darkening. "That's the two things you can do."

"I reckon I can do one other thing," Hamby replied. He readied himself to start, although he doubted he was any match for the Chero-kee. He was calculating whether to try and shoot Longrunner with his stepdaddy's pistol or cut him with the razor when who but Rollin Livingood himself should step out of the cabin to the dogtrot, then advance into the dooryard. Hamby turned to challenge him, too, but Livingood bobbed his head somewhat agreeably; his birthmark took the sun in a shade of purple-red as bright as springtime phlox. He wore a dingy undershirt; the braces of his duck trousers dangled by his knees. His face betrayed no emotion at all, but still Hamby got a sense he was in a mood to listen. On impulse Hamby told him straight out, "I got a proposition."

Longrunner started toward Hamby, but Livingood lifted one languid hand, and this was sufficient to bring up the Indian short. There was a dirt daubers' nest under the eaves of the cabin, and in the silence that followed, Hamby heard the dry hum of the wasps. Then Livingood stirred. "As a general rule," he said to Hamby while Longrunner stood by scowling, "I hate any nigger and won't do no business with one." He rubbed at his birthmark as if it itched him, then bent aside and spat. Casually he drew up his braces and shrugged into them one after the other, as if the act conferred on him the formal mien he thought fit for the occasion. "But I do take niggers one at the time," he added. And just that quick Hamby knew Livingood had made up his mind, that he was ready to do business even with so low a darky. Hamby returned him a nod.

So commenced the parley. Livingood settled on the doorstone, while Hamby crouched on his hams before him in the yard; Longrunner withdrew, placed himself with the two hounds in the patchy shade of the walnut tree, resumed his braiding as if there had been no fuss at all. "I be needing money," Hamby explained, as he'd rehearsed for days. "Like to get it fighting roosters. I good at that, but I ain't got no chicken." He paused, thinking briefly of Gouger, as he was sure Livingood also was, then pressed ahead. "You breed good birds, some say the best. What if you was to rent me a couple stags near ready to pit, or lend 'em, and me go to fighting 'em? On shares, I mean. Then we both make us some cash."

Livingood appeared to take thought, and since this was a promising sign Hamby chose to wait him out, rather than to push on with his argument. Livingood was a minute or more at his figuring before he spoke. "What share?"

Hamby squinted, as if he'd never before essayed such a calculation. After a suitable delay he offered, "A half."

Livingood scoffed at that, and his little cinder-black eyes sharpened. "Half, hell. A quarter. It's *my* birds. Shit-fire, I had the cost of breeding 'em, training 'em, keeping 'em." Vigorously he shook his head. "A quarter's plenty for any nigger. It's a quarter or nothing."

Of course a quarter was as much as Hamby had figured all along, but for Livingood's benefit he put on a show of disappointment. "All right," he murmured, looking off sideways, feigning to be disconsolate. "A quarter it is."

"You get a bird of mine killed," Livingood went on, "you pay me ten dollars extra."

Now it was time for Hamby to scoff. "Shit, like you just said, *you* done trained the goddamn things. If they no damn good 'tain't *my* fault. Hell, 'fore I pit 'em to suit me, I got to train out the bad habits *you* put in." He bit a corner of his lip, tugged at the lobe of one ear. "I lose one," he said after a moment, "I give you two-fifty."

Livingood let out a thin and scornful laugh. "Two-fifty, hell," he countered. "Five."

"Three," said Hamby.

Livingood shrugged. "Four."

"Three-fifty."

They went down among the pens then to look over the prospects. Livingood said although he'd done some pure breeding and even line breeding he'd come to think crossing them was best; a cross-bred rooster, he insisted, would whip an inbred anytime. His preference was to mate a shuffling gamecock to a good hen, and lately he'd commenced crossing shufflers with single-strokers from up north and had got a kind of Roundhead-looking bird that was mean as sin and would cut like hell. None of this meant much to Hamby, who'd never done more than pitch some old rooster out in the yard with a flock of hens to see what would happen. He'd heard tell of Baltimore Top-Knots and Kelsos and Mugs and Irish Grays and White Piles but wouldn't know a one of them if it sidled up and pecked him on the ass.

Yet he did like two of the birds Livingood showed him. All of them were fine—lively, strong, bright of hue, not a spot of lice anywhere on them. But one that drew Hamby's look had the tint of a late apricot, except for wings and tail of silky black; Livingood had bobbed the tail. This one boasted a wicked set of spurs and a gold eye that darted in a violent way that to Hamby bespoke much grit. Livingood called this one Pile-Driver, on account of how hard the bird could pound in those spurs with his heavy wings. The other one Hamby noted was a cream-colored chicken with red eyes and long yellow legs and a head speckled black and gray. He was stout—about four pounds, Hamby guessed—and his breast was broad, but his neck looked nearly as long as a gander's. He was double-nosed, like most of Livingood's fowl. "That's Buttermilk," Livingood said.

Hamby put Pile-Driver and Buttermilk each in a wicker cage that Livingood was loaning him and lashed them to the rear skirts of the old McClellan saddle; the jenny, remembering Gouger's floggings, watched him in dismay. Now that their business was done Livingood bantered no further, nor did he offer to shake Hamby's hand; he simply touched a finger to the brim of his hat and turned and went back through the dogtrot into the cabin and left Hamby in the yard with Longrunner, who'd come out from under his walnut tree, still braiding his halter. Hamby swung up and took his rein, and when the jenny started down the lane Longrunner started, too, walking alongside and keeping on with his braiding. "You a fortunate nigger," Longrunner remarked. Only for the second time he permitted himself that nearly unseen smile.

Cocking a glance at him, Hamby concluded he'd solved the riddle of the Cherokee after all. Longrunner's purpose was to try the mettle of any who came, to see if they merited Livingood's time. If they did, Longrunner was content. Now as they followed the path down through the woods neither spoke, but Hamby felt as if they'd come to share an understanding of a sort, although it was also true he could never have put into words what in hell it was. Side by side he and Longrunner went down to the wagon road, where Longrunner stopped and resumed a place on the beech log by the fence corner, where he'd been when Hamby first appeared; he sat there braiding as before. Hamby gave him a nod, turned the jenny to the left and headed home.

The next day was a Sunday, and church bells were ringing in the distance as Hamby came up Downings Creek and took the turnout to his place and rode past the spirit tree into his dooryard, the two cocks screeching and whipping their wings against the sides of their cages, the jenny cringing at their every onset. Hamby was weary, sick of the birds' racket, pleased to be home. But no sooner had he drawn rein than he had a feeling some large matter was amiss; puzzled, he sat the jenny and scanned the yard, the house, the near fields. Nothing appeared out of place; naught was missing. A breeze stirred the boughs of the two elms overhead; a wren on the roof peak wove its oversized song; a cluster of butterflies cooling themselves on a spot of damp earth nearby languidly hopped and fluttered. All was peace save for the far clang of the bells. Then with a bolt of shock in the pit of his gut he glimpsed it—in the pasture old Tom was down.

Hamby dismounted, left the jenny and the protesting chickens in the yard, ran to the fence, scrambled over it, waded through dewy knee-high grass that sopped his trouser legs. Tom lay on his side. He rolled a milky eye at Hamby, and just as Hamby knelt by him he let out a great sigh that sounded as if all the pains and woes of his twenty-odd years were coming out of him at last; Hamby put his hand on Tom, felt that long outrush of breath. Tom lingered awhile after that; he lay shallowly panting, his eyes shut behind their silver lashes. Hamby took the big head over his lap and sat waving off the flies. Sometime later Tom passed. So easily did he go that Hamby missed it; he simply looked down after a while and saw that Tom was gone.

Hamby sat in the grass with the heavy head lying still across his lap. Tom had been his stepdaddy's horse; it was Tom that old Daniel McFee was riding when he was shot down many a year ago, just a few rods farther along the very road passing by Hamby's. Nigger though he was—a whole nigger, not a half of one like Hamby—slave that he'd been, old Daniel had died that night to save the Curtises, whom he'd called family even if they were white, even if they'd once owned him the same as they'd owned a barrel or a hammer or a scythe. Tom had bound Hamby to all that—to his stepdaddy, to his mama, to the Curtises of old, to those hard but large days. Now, in losing Tom, Hamby felt he was losing all the rest, too. And if he lost that, he wondered what he'd have.

Later, after he stabled and fed the jenny and set the roosters in the shade, Hamby got a shovel and returned to the pasture and commenced to dig. It was going to take a long time because Tom was a big horse and because Hamby was tired already from his trip and would need long rests between spells of digging. He'd just turned his first chunk of earth when Jimmy and Andy Cartman came by in the Curtises' carryall on their way home from church. They halted in the road and sat and took in the scene for a time while Hamby worked. Then in a little while they steered into the yard, got down, shucked off their Sunday coats, fetched shovels from the shed, joined him. It was the Sabbath, and for Jimmy at least what they did was a sin. But Tom had meant as much to the Cartmans in their way as he had to

Hamby in his, and together they toiled on as daylight faded, as night came slowly down.

ᓚᘏ

That same afternoon when Mrs. Hemphill made her regular Sunday visit to the Curtis home, she discovered the grounds aswarm with rowdy children. Oliver Price, Miz Henslee and Tom Carter were in the parlor enjoying a repast of lemonade and Indian pudding Rebecca had served them. Mrs. Hemphill could not help but feel chagrined that Tom and the Prices had got in ahead of her, but despite the fact they'd stolen her thunder she made an effort to be congenial.

As Tom and Mr. Price stood to receive her she spied the poor shell of Andy Curtis sitting in a corner in a slat-backed rocker with a checkered shawl over his lap, nodding and smiling and taking notice like a sane man for a change. While as a lady of quality she was relieved to think he might keep his wits today and not commit one of his untoward acts, she was also sorry to think there'd be nothing unbecoming for her to witness and report abroad. Frankly she was disappointed that so far, in contrast to the tales she'd heard, nothing truly abhorrent had ever transpired in her expectant presence.

This apart, her duty of Christian charity remained to be performed. She took a seat in the painted Hitchcock chair opposite the settee where Tom and the Prices were. Rebecca poured lemonade and brought another bowl of pudding. They chatted pleasantly of church matters, weather, the state of the harvest, the advent of the seven-year locust, the old reel-footed bear that some in the valley were hunting, the absence of moral tone in the world, the ineffable workings of the Trinity. Andy even ventured a few remarks about advanced methods of cultivation that did not sound out of place or in any way the ravings of the lunatic Mrs. Hemphill knew him to be. Rebecca of course was all smiles to see her brother doing so well. And as always when Rebecca beamed, Tom Carter shone back her joy like a reflection in a mirror; in fact it occurred secretly to Mrs. Hemphill that Tom was indeed more like a mirror than a man.

After three-quarters of an hour Mrs. Hemphill was thinking it was time to depart; there were limits to dutiful dedication when it offered so scant a reward. She announced her intention, and the men sprang to their feet—rather eagerly, she darkly suspicioned. She gathered up her reticule and parasol and turned to Andy to bid him farewell but stopped curiously when Andy inquired, "Ma'am, I'm wondering, do you remember a man named John Harrolson, who ran the Mining and Nitre Bureau for the South during the war?"

Mrs. Hemphill doubted whether it was altogether proper to be discussing nitre in mixed company. But she did know the name. "Yes," she nodded a bit tentatively, "I believe I do."

"I've just recalled some lines of poetry we army boys used to recite, about Harrolson and his work," Andy smiled.

So now the poor fool is going to declaim, Mrs. Hemphill thought in superior fashion. No doubt he wanted to speak some sentimental doggerel about tenting in the field far from home, about longing for fireside and loved ones. In his idiocy he was dwelling on the distant days of wartime. She pretended an interest and sat again, wearing a forbearing smile, supposing good manners required it. But just as he began to speak she remembered about the nitre and began to frown in apprehension.

> "John Harrolson! John Harrolson!
> You are a wretched creature.
> You've added to this bloody war
> A new and awful feature.
> You'd have us think while every man
> Is bound to be a fighter,
> That ladies, bless the dears,
> Should save their pee for nitre.

"John Harrolson! John Harrolson!
Where did you get the notion
To send your barrel round the town
To gather up the lotion?
We thought the girls had work enough
Making shirts and kissing,
But you have put the pretty dears
To patriotic pissing.

"John Harrolson! John Harrolson!
Do pray invent a neater
And somewhat more modest mode
Of making your saltpetre;
But 'tis an awful idea, John,
Gunpowdery and cranky,
That when a lady lifts her skirts
She's killing off a Yankee!"

Later in the day Captain Moore stopped by. Oliver Price, outdoors pretending to supervise his mob of younguns, related the offense Andy had committed that had so outraged Mrs. Hemphill.
Inside, the captain found Rebecca prostrate on the settee, Miz Henslee
applying wet cloths to her brow, Tom sitting by her helplessly a-fret.
Mercifully they'd shut Andy away in his room; Tom said he thought
Andy was asleep. Pulling a chair close, the captain took Rebecca's
hand and gave her some words of comfort, and then they all prayed.
Presently Rebecca felt better and sat up. "Every time his mind comes
back I think it might be for good," she explained, dabbing at her eyes
with a handkerchief. "But I know it's not the truth. It comes back less
and less. And when it's gone it's always worse."

Sometime since, the county court had made Captain Moore
Andy's legal guardian, from a finding not of insanity but of advanc-

ing decrepitude. So the captain was in a position to know that Rebecca and Tom had been to seek counsel from lawyer Kope Elias in Franklin. He inquired what they'd learned. Elias, said Rebecca, had recommended Andy be examined by an eminent doctor of his acquaintance in Asheville, who knew the diseases of the brain and could give advice on the right course of treatment.

But even as she spoke Rebecca knew what must eventually be done. No doctor was going to pronounce Andy sane or curable. What was left of him that was worthy of her old affection was now so spotty and so elusive that she could no longer recall how it used to fit together with all his other parts to make him whole. And even the few good pieces of him left were winking out now one by one, like blown candles.

"What hurts worst," she told the captain, "is his honor's gone. All that's left is flesh that does whatever it will. How can I keep him here, like a varmint in its cage, to revolt folk with its antics?" She caught the captain by an arm. "If he knew," she sobbed, "he'd want it done with. Wouldn't he?"

CHAPTER 8

September 1881

*V*es Price was making a happy discovery. The same low qualities that had branded him a rascal and a byword all his life now began to shape him into the best informer the revenue collectors of North Carolina and Georgia had ever employed.

Never before had Ves felt the exhilaration that comes when all one's powers meet. Hitherto whatever force he mustered had issued forth as faint as a ghost's breath, to dissipate in air—yes, he could admit it now that he'd come into his glory. He saw why so much misfortune had befallen him in the past. He saw that what he'd needed all along was a challenge great enough to call up his every base talent at once, so each one could lend its body and might to the whole; he realized men won rank and goods when they met the work they were meant to do. Ves was meant to be a Revenue Dog. How could he not excel at duties that drew on all his worst assets?

The ordinary spy played Judas on occasion, while generally holding true to certain loyalties. He wouldn't inform on kin save for grave cause; he wouldn't give up any pard or pal. Though he took the Revenue's money and did such of its bidding as suited him, he never forgot that the Revenue was a thing foreign to him and to his folk and to the way of life of the place where he lived. He served the Revenue in small part; he offered to it just as much as would return him what he deemed a fit reward. Those he sacrificed were the scraps and leavings of the community, fellows so mean that nobody—not even the king—would take their part. And never for fear of death would he divulge the whereabouts and doings of the king himself.

But because of his crass character Ves Price was free of any such piddling scruples. It didn't matter a damn to him if the Revenue was an outside power imposed unfairly on an ancient way of life; to him it was just a paymaster more reliable than most. Nor did he finely discriminate as to whom he'd turn over; he'd inform on anybody and do it in job lots. Nor did he dread the goddamn king, for Webb Darling could have no reason to suspect him; ironically the names of rogue, scoundrel and slacker that Ves had earned and once detested were now transformed into an advantage, since Darling would never think a jasper as chuckleheaded as Ves Price could play that deadly game.

The dangers didn't daunt Ves. It wasn't that he was brave; not even Ves with all his boasting would've advanced a notion so preposterous. But he was sly, and thanks to this quality he thought he could successfully act the turncoat long enough to win his fortune, elude Webb Darling's ax and so escape the valley with his head yet on his shoulders and his purse full to bursting, as in his dream.

Nor would the task even consume the time he'd thought at first it might. Instead of the six months he'd counted on, it now appeared he could wind up his affairs in less than three. Wonderfully there were bonuses to be earned; on top of Ves's wage of thirty a month,

Deputy Collector Richbourg was ready to pay five dollars for every still the Revenue cut down on Ves's say-so. With such an incentive before him Ves could put away a host of stillers; hell, he might even put away Webb Darling himself. Yes, he'd make his stake in ninety days. Ninety days and Ves Price would be gone among the delights of the wide world.

Thanks to Ves's guidance the Revenue destroyed twelve of the county's best and most venerable stills in his first month of service, which made sixty dollars' worth of bonuses that Ves could pocket. Ves gave them all up—Bender's on the Rattlesnake, Frost's on Wolf Ridge, Gaitskill's at the top of Matlock Creek, Streeter's on the Rockhouse, Scott's on the little branch that fed Hurricane Creek. This was the very heart and soul of Webb Darling's kingdom. The only ones he spared—perhaps out of guilt and contrition, perhaps only to display his newfound power to bless or curse—were Ree Bolt and Jared Nutbush.

Ves worked for Tuck Richbourg, whose boss was the revenue collector of Georgia, a man named Clark. But since so much moonshining occurred in the wilderness between the two states, J. J. Mott the North Carolina collector also had an interest in the region; he helped fund the work of the Georgia deputies and sometimes sent his own officers to cooperate with Clark's. General Raum, the commissioner of the Revenue up in Washington, kept after Mott and Clark to wind up the blockading in the border counties. Raum liked his people to stage grand raids by big posses through the country, in the style of Sherman's March. That September he ordered Clark and Mott to take a force into the Tusquittees to clean out Webb Darling.

The first Ves knew of this was when the little black messenger came to fetch him. Ordinarily Ves communicated with Richbourg by letter, addressing it to the name of George Washington Cornett, an old uncle by marriage in Gilmer County who'd long since died;

Richbourg called himself Cornett and kept a post office box in that name at the village of Hiawassee just across the Georgia line. When he needed to, Richbourg would write to Ves pretending to be the dead uncle. He used the messenger only when matters were urgent, so when the boy knocked at the rear door of Ves's pap's cobbler shop in Hayesville, Ves knew something large was in the offing.

The following day Ves took his mule and rode the twelve miles upriver into Georgia to a place near Shady Grove, where he and Richbourg always met when they had to speak man to man. The spot was in a stand of beech and sugar maple on a ridge above Bearmeat Creek. On the east the long stony crown of Hightower Bald just barely topped the nearer hills; perhaps because he was engaged in deeds of treachery Ves thought that bald resembled the head of a giant taking a suspicious peek at him over the profile of hills, as if the giant were a spy the same as Ves but maybe served another, grander purpose.

At nightfall Richbourg came up the creek on his dun horse. He dismounted and seated himself on a cushion of moss under an old maple. For a time he sat working his chaw, meting out his air of threat while Ves impatiently fretted. In Richbourg's attitude Ves thought he read a hint of something that went beyond the deputy's normal reticence, as if Richbourg wanted to delay the talk, perhaps in hopes some option might offer itself other than the one he'd come to present. Ves waited him out sucking on the stem of a blade of grass, wondering if Richbourg was harboring doubts; maybe despite the success Ves had enjoyed Richbourg still was wary of him, still rated him low in brains and judgment. The notion peeved Ves, but only a little. He'd been low-rated so much in his life that at this late date he could muster only so much indignation. Finally Richbourg spoke. "We're going to do a raid on Fort Darling," he said.

"Good," Ves applauded. The news tickled him. Why, if he could be instrumental in catching the king himself, who knew what bonuses might come, what fame? Broadly and eagerly he grinned. "I can tell you the best way to get there," he declared with confidence. When he was blockading on his own he'd gone up Pot Rock Bald more than once, and he well remembered the path and all its markers.

"Hell," Richbourg retorted with a sarcastic turn of mouth, "we know how to get up the goddamn mountain. What we don't know is how the fort's set up."

Nor did Ves know, for Webb Darling had built his fort since Ves ceased blockading. Before, Darling had used no more than a cabin and a camp of lean-tos; the fort had come after Bill Berong got arrested and Darling in his vanity concluded he ought to have something to prove his kingship. Mentally Ves thrashed about for an idea. "I could find out, talk to some fellows," he mused. As soon as he heard Richbourg's snapped-stick laugh he realized how foolish that had sounded.

"Sure," Richbourg scoffed. "You ask around. See how long your ass stays in one piece."

Ves scowled. "Then how can we do it?"

Richbourg paused as if savoring a tasty morsel. For the first time he looked straight at Ves from under the brim of his big hat. "*You're to do it,*" he said with what Ves considered undue relish. Just that quickly Richbourg's previous reluctance was gone; it was as if he'd made up his mind that the amusement to be got from putting Ves in such a fix was worth whatever risk might ensue.

Ves was aghast. "Me? *Me?*"

Richbourg nodded. "You. Go up there yourself and scout the place out and bring me the word. Come back with a sketch of the layout, tell me how many men he's got, show me the weak points, all that. Then our posse'll go and snatch him."

Ves gaped; his ears took fire in terror. Clearly there'd been some blunder. When he mastered his voice he undertook to explain a manifest truth that Richbourg unaccountably seemed to have forgot. "That ain't *my* job. My job's to tell you-all things, and *you-all* go and do them." He waved his hands before him to ward off the absurdity of the thought Richbourg had so mistakenly advanced. "*I* don't do 'em," he added, in case Richbourg still didn't understand. Suddenly he was ready to embrace the concept of his own ineptitude, the very thought of which had insulted him but a moment before. "Why," he stammered, "why, I wouldn't know how to do such as that. I wouldn't do it right. They'd suspect me. They'd catch on to me."

Richbourg tipped his head. "It's possible," he acknowledged. He looked as if the prospect were a pleasant one to him. But he still had his duty to perform, and as always before in their negotiations he knew how to concentrate Ves's mind and muster his courage. "They's twenty dollars' bonus in it," he said.

This fact spun Ves's mind like a fortune's wheel. He pondered, took counsel both of his doubts and his ambition, listened to his head, plumbed his heart. Could he do it? Could he go into Fort Darling on some convincing pretext and comport himself so coolly that none would suspect him? Was twenty dollars a rich enough prize to warrant putting himself in such jeopardy? Ves placed his virtues on the scales to weigh up whether his greed was heavier than his fear.

Just ahead, where the path took a turn around a lichen-covered boulder with clusters of fern growing on its top, a man carrying a carbine stepped out and barred Ves's way. The sight of him nearly gave Ves a seizure, so sudden was his advent and so fierce his look. He had a chin-beard as bristly as a bramble patch and as black as sin, and his little agate eyes twinkled in an ugly way beneath brows so shaggy they grew together over his nose and curled up at the ends nearly to his temples; he seemed about the size of the rock he'd sprung from. His gun was an old seven-shot Spencer that shone like silver from good keeping. "I believe you've missed your trail, neighbor," this man remarked. He smiled; he seemed amiable. But that Spencer didn't. Its muzzle came level at the height of Ves's belly, and Ves saw that its hammer was cocked.

"No, no," Ves babbled. "I'm going right, this is right, I'm on my way to see the king." He nodded briskly in the vain hope that his enthusiasm might prompt a nod in return.

"Are you now?" The big man laughed a large laugh that brought an echo off the face of the surrounding woods. "Well, let me tell you, neighbor. Folk don't come to see the king on their own notion. *He* sees *them*. And he only does that when it suits him and *where* it suits him." He made a prodding motion with the nose of the repeater. "Now, if you know what's good for you, you'll get on back down this hill."

Ves was sorely tempted to take this advice and spare himself the ordeal that impended. But once more he brought to mind an image of the twenty dollars awaiting him and drew from it the will to persist. "Well, sir," he explained, pretending earnestness, "I aim to commence a-stilling, and a fellow that wants to do such must get the permission of the king and fix a tribute. That's what I mean to do." He thought he'd kept his voice steady enough; he thought he'd managed to gaze the fellow frankly in the eye; he thought he'd concealed the fact his heart was pounding fit to bust.

Evidently he had. To Ves's relief the big man lifted the snout of the Spencer away from him and let down the hammer with his thumb and set the butt of the piece on his hipbone and stood in the path stroking his beard in thought. He asked Ves's name, and Ves told it. Then the man regarded him with renewed interest, inquiring, "You Oliver Price's boy?" Ves said so, and the man nodded. He took off his slouch hat, scratched an itch in his scalp, replaced the headgear;

so old and greasy was his hat that its hole breathed an air that made Ves's stomach roll over. "Old Price, he's a damn good man. I voted for him when he ran for coroner sometime back," said the guard. "But he's a teetotaler and don't cotton to making no brush liquor. Does he know what you're up to?"

"No, sir, he don't," Ves replied somewhat more stoutly. It felt good just now to tell a truth, no matter how minute; also it always eased his temper to disparage his pap. "He don't hold with me, nor me with him."

"That's too bad," the man remarked. "There ought not be such a shadow falling between a man and his boy."

Evidently the jasper considered himself a ponderer of large themes. Now Ves's mood changed from dread to impatience; he hadn't come all this way at the risk of his life just to hear a lecture on how he ought to get along with his goddamn pap. "Can I go on up?" he hastily cut in.

For all his hard looks the fellow seemed hurt to have his good intentions so rudely shut off, but he stood aside with a shrug and let Ves pass, and Ves went on up between banks of laurel toward the top.

Now a queer thing happened. As Ves encountered two more armed sentinels and they led him toward the rocky crest of the bald where the fort stood, all his powers lapsed or got addled, so he could make no sense at all of anything he heard or looked at. He knew he should note the fort's features, its strong points and weaknesses, yet somehow everything about the place melted into a blur; the surrounding terrain might have been tropical forest or even an expanse of water, for all Ves could tell. When people spoke to him it seemed they did so in a foreign dialect, and when he answered he had no notion what he said; his tongue flopped in his mouth like a trout in the bottom of a boat. His earlier resolve was utterly gone; fear had driven it out of him. He quailed; his back teeth began to grind and rattle; his mouth felt parched. He cared no longer about completing the mission he'd embarked on. To hell with the goddamn mission. Now he wanted only to survive the damn thing, get through it any old way he could, escape back down this mountain to safety—no matter the loss of twenty dollars' bounty, no matter if Tuck Richbourg got the tidings he needed, no matter what.

Despite these misgivings he found himself in a dim room on the ground floor of the fort before he knew it. The space smelt of damp rock and mildew, and although the windows were unshuttered and looked out on a sunshiny day, the place had a lingering chill that went to the very ends of Ves's bones. He stood shivering. Before him in the gloom floated a narrow face topped by a close-grown mat of too-blond hair that Ves recognized with another bolt of nausea belonged to the king himself. The light was so faint that Ves couldn't make out the finer features of the king's countenance, but he did see how Darling smiled in a crooked way as he lounged back in his chair and folded his hands on the table he sat behind. "Well, I declare," Darling said in mocking fashion, "if it isn't the slop-dumper." He turned his head and remarked to one of his minions standing by, "We ought to get Bolt and Nutbush up here. Let 'em pay this-un back for all that time in the pen they had to do on his account."

Darling and the minion laughed, and Ves heard others in the room laughing, too. He couldn't see them—he didn't dare peer around, for you no more took your eyes off Webb Darling than you would a mad bull—but he could smell their cloying odors of grimy clothes and wood smoke and old sweat and tobacco and gun oil. He blinked in hopes of seeing more clearly, and although his vision did sharpen a bit he still felt he peered at the scene as if through a pane of dirty glass. And as he replied it seemed to him that an awful gap loomed between his thoughts and the words he spoke, a gap he feared was so great it would betray him. "You know I'm sorry for that," he reminded Darling as firmly as he could, remembering how the king admired men that spoke right up. "I came to you before, admitted I'd made a mistake. And you agreed to overlook it, to let me go a-stilling on my own."

Indulgently the king nodded, blinking his long lashes. "I did indeed, for I'm a tolerant and forgiving man." He placed one hand over his heart, as if to bless himself for his virtues. Then the hand fell away, and a glint of malice came into his eye. "But that was while Bolt and Nutbush were still in the pen." His smile widened. "Now that they're out I doubt they feel as much Christian charity toward you as I do." Again the round of low laughter circled among the unseen men.

A mosquito whined in Ves's ear; he whisked it away with a wave of his hand. His brain whirled; he trembled; his voice nearly failed him. But in a fever of self-preservation he managed an observation he thought might touch Darling's pride: "I reckon them two'll do as *you* say, however they feel."

The king leaned forward in his chair to consider his clasped hands on the tabletop. He seemed favorably impressed by Ves's remark. "Yes," he agreed, "you're right. I'd hardly be king if men failed to respect my will." He took a breath, shrugged. "Even so, I hesitate to take you on again."

"How come?" Ves eagerly wanted to know. Maybe Darling would indeed reject him; maybe it would all be over in another minute; maybe Ves would soon be free to withdraw to his home and sleep snug and safe in his own bed this very night, the dangers of the day forgotten. He felt groggy and near to swooning; the blood pounded in the veins of his head.

"Because," said the king, "you're a heedless and negligent fellow, you take no care, you pay no mind. I've excused the slop-dumping, but last year when you stilled for me you showed no initiative. You were a lick-and-a-promise fellow, didn't give a damn. A good block-ader works hard. When it's done right it's the hardest toil there is. But *you* wouldn't work. You wouldn't break a sweat. No sir, you'd hardly bestir yourself atall. You weren't worth a pinch of owl shit to me *or* yourself. You made no profit to speak of for either of us."

Still, though he delivered himself of these condemning words, the king showed no ire; he sighed in a semblance of resignation. Ves could see Darling better now as his eyesight adjusted to the murk. The king licked at his straw-colored mustache, plucked at the end of his freckled nose. On the table where he sat were the remnants of a meal of liver mush and potatoes, over which several flies were crawl-ing. A hound slept on the floor beside him. Darling folded his hands again, rotated his thumbs before him and sat a second or two watch-ing them go round and round. Then he said, "The Revenue has got mighty lively of late and cut down some of the best of my stills. I reckon they've got themselves one good Dog." Ves didn't know whether to be flattered or to drop dead from fright. But to his vast relief the king went on without showing a shred of suspicion. "Last year they got Bill Berong, and just awhile back they took in Hutsell Amarine over in Tennessee, and they even got old Redmond." Lewis Redmond, Ves knew, was a famous king of South Carolina. "Next," mused Darling, "they'll be coming after me, for I'm the last of the kings."

He fixed his cold eye of cerulean blue on Ves. "I need to count on every man. I can't afford to have anybody around me who's weak of spirit or shy on grit. If I do then the Revenue will come at 'em, work on 'em, turn 'em against me." His smile went bleak and bitter; he leaned back again in his chair and watched Ves closely from un-der his gold lashes. "You *do* see my problem, don't you, slop-dumper?"

Ves understood. Vigorously he nodded. The logic of the king

was indisputable; Ves was a risk. He was even turning to go when to his dismay Darling spoke on, in what seemed a more reasonable vein than before. "But it's the duty of a king to provide for those that depend on him, isn't it? A good king returns loyalty for loyalty. You're a pretty bad bet, slop-dumper. I don't know if you've got any loyalty in you atall—probably not. But you've come to me with respect and begged my blessing. You've repented your past errors. Maybe you've changed for the better, and maybe you haven't, I don't know. Time will show, won't it?"

He looked narrowly up at Ves and batted his eyes coquettishly, for all the world like a bashful woman. "But I wouldn't want to be a king," he said, each word sounding like it was chiseled out of ice, "if I couldn't put my trust in others." Emptily he smiled. "I'm a hopeful soul and a lenient man. I want to think the best of everyone. So I'm going to put my trust in you."

He stood then and faced Ves across the table. In the faint light his pale eyes seemed luminous and without any color. "But you don't want to disappoint me, slop-dumper. You don't want to repay my trust with carelessness or woolgathering, and surely not with any outright treachery. For I'll be watching you. I'll see what you're up to. You do me wrong, you can be certain I'll know it—know it the same day it happens. And I can promise you'll be a dead man before the next sun rises." Again he dropped his lashes, as if he were a girl flirting at a dance. "And not dead only," he sweetly added, "for we'll work on you awhile, before we let you pass on." Then he reached out a hand to reassure Ves and gave his upper arm a friendly squeeze. "I've no choice, you see. A king must be firm, no matter the clemency of his heart. It's the cross I bear. It's the pain of wearing the crown."

They settled the details quickly then. Ves's still—no more than half a barrel turned over a soap kettle with a worm in it—would yield maybe fifteen gallons a week. He could sell the dew at a dollar a gallon, but in the first weeks over half his earnings would go for meal and the cost of the worm, and the king would get a fifth of what remained. Ves would be fortunate if he cleared twenty dollars in a month, an amount so small he was sure it would arouse the king's doubts. But Darling assumed Ves meant to make blockade mainly for his own use and saw nothing unusual in the trifling amount.

Presently Ves was winding his way down Pot Rock Bald on rubbery legs, hardly willing to believe he'd escaped with his whole hide. He felt like he'd come too close to a furnace and got scorched—he had that same sense of cold that seared and heat that froze—and his limbs were all brittle, as if they'd pop in two at a wrong touch. Halfway down the mountain he veered into some hemlocks and puked up his sock heels. While he lay there a long time panting and whimpering he watched a number of nuthatches on the trunks of the nearby trees; now and then they curiously cocked their little heads at him. Ves wished he were a nuthatch scuttling up and down a tree.

When he got home Ves took a piece of ruled paper and a stub of pencil and sketched out a plan of Fort Darling that bore no conceivable relation to the actual place he'd been. This was because he kept no memory of the fort at all; his panic had scoured it right out of his head. Instead he conjured from his fevered imagination a stronghold of bastions, towers, battlements, moats, glacis, sally ports, secret entrances, tunnels, stables, kitchens, drawbridges, sentinel posts—anything that came to mind he thought a lord in his castle might need. He even drew a flag decorated with a skull and crossbones flying over the gatehouse. On a second page he made up a number—seven seemed plausible—and said this was how many men Webb Darling commanded.

What did he care? He'd done his part. *He* wouldn't be assaulting the place. He'd seen the elephant; the image of Ves's demise had flared in the blue of Webb Darling's eyes. He was through; he was finished as a Revenue Dog; he meant to draw his bounty and his wage and light out for parts unknown, the sooner the better. It cut no figure with him if, thanks to his fanciful rendering of the fort and its garrison, Tuck Richbourg and a lot of Revenue scum got into a ruction with the king. It didn't make a damn to him if they all got killed, Revenue and blockaders alike. To hell with the lot of them.

He put the map and a note demanding his pay in an envelope and directed it to George Washington Cornett in Hiawassee. While he waited for the funds he busied himself getting his plunder together for his departure. What a grim surprise it was, then, before dawn four days later, just into October, when Tuck Richbourg with a twenty-man posse of officers at his back pounded on Ves's door and announced Ves must guide the attack on Fort Darling, which was to be mounted that selfsame afternoon.

CHAPTER 9

October 1881

*T*hey rode the Pinckney Rollins mail stage over the Nantahalas and through the Cowees and Balsams to the railhead at Pigeon Ford near Waynesville. As always at the start of autumn the light came sharply from a new part of the sky; overnight the earth seemed to have tilted a fraction off its ordinary axis, as if intentionally to catch that light from a lower and brighter angle. The light itself had the clarity of fine crystal and was hot as a burning-glass in the sun, yet in shade one felt a chill. In the clear air every leaf of every tree on the mountains surrounding them stood crisply revealed—red if sourwood or oak, purple if sweet gum, yellow if maple or poplar, brown if chestnut, tattered gold if locust, dark wedges of spruce set like dragon's teeth along the spines of the ridges.

From the railhead they took the train up the wide valley of the Big Pigeon, thence between rows of parti-colored hills along Hominy Creek, eventually to the French Broad River and the new iron bridge that crossed it at Asheville. As the train approached its foot their chaperon Captain Moore explained to Rebecca how the iron bridge had replaced an old log affair that had long served the town, from which not a few folk had got pitched in the river, due to its lack of railings. Now the metal trusses of the new span alarmingly clanged as the cars bore them over; below, the wrinkled surface of the brown river moved with such slow uniformity it made Rebecca imagine a long panel of canvas, cleverly painted to resemble a river, drawn beneath her from right to left by unseen hands, for some hidden and possibly malicious purpose. She reckoned it was a measure of her disquiet over Brother Andy's fate that she glimpsed such unlikely harbingers in such commonplace sights.

Andy had been quiet the whole trip. Either he'd slept or he'd sat wordlessly gazing at the landscape sliding past, flicking his fingers on his lap in time to the beat of his secret melodies. Rebecca didn't know if Brother understood what was in store; she'd told him they were going to see a doctor but doubted whether he took the news in; at the time he'd been pawing through his bank books and bond papers in his endless search for evidence of the embezzlements he was convinced were impoverishing him and in which he more and more suspected Rebecca was complicit. If he did understand, Rebecca guessed he probably welcomed the prospect of medical attention for his host of imagined ailments.

At any rate he seemed content. He sat passively while the uneven rooftops of hilly Asheville swam before them, distorted by the wavy windowpanes and by the blown steam of the locomotive. To Rebecca, who'd never traveled so far, the place was nothing like the great city she'd imagined; instead it looked smoke-dimmed, mean, dismal, forlorn. She felt foreboding at the sight of it, which, added to the queer turn the look of the river had given her, sent a low shiver of dread all through her. By her side Tom Carter, impervious to all possibly sinister signs, felt compelled to offer up the uninteresting fact that Asheville contained nearly three thousand souls, an increase of three or four hundred since the arrival of the railroad the year before. God alone knew how he'd come by these tidings. Rebecca made a humming noise and gave him a tight smile, her unfailing response now whenever Tom grew tedious, which lately seemed to be happening more and more often.

They disembarked at a small board-and-batten depot at the foot of South Main Street and hailed a hack, which carried them up to their lodgings over a road that was partly macadamized and partly brick but mostly dirt with an overlay of dust the consistency of talc, which settled at once into every seam and wrinkle of one's clothes. A skein of telegraph wires held up by big two-span poles made an oppressive tangle overhead. In the rear seat Andy gaped and gawked; Captain Moore sat beside him with an arm clasped companionably about his shoulders. Rebecca wondered if Brother remembered coming to Asheville on an autumn day fourteen years ago, to seek the help of his old commander Colonel David Coleman, the eminent attorney, in his trouble with scalawags. Andy had been a hero that day, taking on the task of saving the family from ruin. Now look at him. Rebecca sighed. Even if Brother had kept his wits, probably Asheville was so much changed that naught remained of the village it had been at war's end, when Brother came here to do his great and good thing. And of course little enough remained of Andy himself, poor wretch.

They took rooms at the Eagle Hotel, a hostelry of some repute near the top of South Main just below the public square, a spot lawyer Elias had told them would be convenient to Dr. Kester's. Indeed next morning when they took the mule-drawn omnibus to the doctor's they were agreeably surprised to find it a distance of but a few short blocks that they might have easily walked. The house, a two-story whitewashed frame, stood in a little patch of woods between a weedy lane pretentiously called Aston Street and Patton Avenue, after Patton & Summey's famous brick store, situated hard by. The avenue, lined with storefronts some of which were still under construction, was rapidly becoming the town's main commercial way. In fact not far beyond the doctor's house stood a large white building used by the Eagle Hotel as overflow quarters, while on the far side of it, Rebecca noted with distaste, a rough-looking saloon seemed to be doing a great business even at such an early hour.

On the grounds of the doctor's house was a small structure of yellow clapboard roofed with chestnut boarding. There was an open door at the end facing the road, before which a number of Negroes were queued. It turned out this was Dr. Kester's office and apothecary, and the blacks were waiting to pick up prescriptions for their employers. "The niggers won't call it a drugstore," the doctor laughed as, summoned by one of the coloreds, he came forth to greet them. "No, they believe they must be elevated and refined. So in trying to say apothecary shop they say shot-i-carry-pop." His laugh was shrill and thin and ended by petering out into a kind of wheeze, as if he suffered from a shortness of breath. Politely they chortled, then followed him up a flagstone walk bordered with pansies.

In the entryway of the house they made their introductions. Rebecca found Dr. Kester congenial and obliging but somehow lacking in gravity; he was like his laugh, jovial but vague and windy and too soon understood, his purposes too apt to dwindle out before their time. Sitting in the parlor, he spoke affectionately of lawyer Elias, made a special effort to put Brother at his ease, comfortably conversed with Tom and Captain Moore. And all the time Rebecca gazed at him wholly disapproving, especially of the oily strings of hair he'd combed sideways over his bald head; she'd never known a man who did that who was any account at all. Andy sat faintly smiling, as if he knew a mischievous story that he dared not tell, and when Dr. Kester announced he'd like to keep Andy overnight to make his examination and report his findings, Brother brightened like a child promised a special play-pretty. So it was decided. They shook hands all around. On her way out Rebecca went to Andy and hugged him and kissed his cheek. He gazed down at her, and miraculously the veil of his madness briefly rose. "I love you, Sis," he said. She hurried out, weeping.

That afternoon to ease her distractions Rebecca went shopping with Tom at Rankin and Pulliam's mercantile. Captain Moore excused himself to take the airs, he said, but wandered off in what Rebecca thought was the direction of that saloon she'd noticed from the doctor's. In the mercantile she bought a pair of ready-made work shirts for Hamby, a pocket testament for Jimmy Cartman and a clasp knife for the less devout of the brothers, a cameo brooch for Grandma Cartman, a cravat of black silk for Andy. Each new item in its box she passed to Tom for him to tote. The cravat she bought almost in defiance, as if she were daring Tom to point out the obvious, that Brother might soon be in no position whatever to wear such a fancy article. In between purchases she kept bursting into tears, and at every instance of this Tom would wince and set about juggling his stack of boxes tied with twine, so as to free a hand and give her a clumsy pat of comfort.

She was robbing him, he insisted. If only he had his papers about him he could prove it. One day soon She would reduce him to pauperism, and he would wander the byways homeless and despised, no better than a tramp. Or the Time would Come, and functionaries would appear to drag him off to the poorhouse. All because of her thievery.

"Why do you think she wants to steal from you?" the man asked, drawing his palm over the top of his shiny head. "If she robs you doesn't she rob herself, too?"

"Oh," he said, "She doesn't wish to steal, She just can't help herself. Except for embezzling She's right good to me. I expect She even loves me. Though She does act bossy and irritable at times." He squirmed in his seat. "I've got to do my morning job."

The man ushered him to a small room that had a big porcelain bowl set against one wall with a round wooden seat on it and water in it and a box fixed to the wall above it with a chain hanging down. The round seat reminded him of a privy hole, so when the man left he took down his trousers and sat on the seat and did his business, not bothering to wipe. Standing up, he eyed the dangling chain from several angles, then tentatively reached out and pulled it to see what would happen, only to jump back in alarm when water gushed loudly in the throat of the bowl and swept away his turds. He was annoyed; now he couldn't pick through the stool to locate the signs of the cancer. From his innards the cancer began to howl.

The man came and took him back to the chairs, and they sat. The cancer kept on hallooing. The man said he must quit carrying on so. Between the cancer's wails he explained it was the disease, not him. "I'm a doctor," said the man. He pointed to a framed paper on the wall that he said proved it. The cancer quit screaming. He remembered now. She'd said they were going to see a doctor. He grew hopeful. A doctor might have the power to cure the cancer and the pox, too.

In the war on his way back to duty after a furlough he'd gone to a hospital in Atlanta to see a sick messmate. Jasper Bowers, it was; Jasper was down with the measles. He remembered that—Jasper Bowers of old Company E, down with the measles that ended by killing him. There were some cases of the French pox in that hospital. One was covered all over with spots like a leopard, only the spots were rose-colored and made him look like some altogether new species that somehow combined the traits of pied cats and humans. One had a face festering with huge pus-filled blisters and spotted with black scabs, till you could hardly tell it was a face at all. The legs of another were ulcerated to the bone.

His worst fear and deepest revulsion had come from seeing that. What a blessing it would be if the doctor could ward off such calamities! Yet he recalled what he'd heard was done to effect a cure for the syphilis—cauterizing; blistering; dosings of mercury, black wash, corrosive sublimate, lunar caustic, potassium iodide, calomel, quinine. And even if he were freed of the pox, the cancer would yet remain, consuming his insides, now and then hooting out its hate and rage. He'd never heard of anyone overcoming a cancer. Nor did he know what treatments might be applied; likely they were worse than the ones used against the pox. All he understood was what befell when a cancer took root.

His ailments were a judgment on him, he said.

"Why so?" asked the doctor—if he *was* a doctor.

"For my transgressions," he replied.

"Do you mean God has judged you?"

He nodded.

"What is your guilt?"

He laughed knowingly but made no reply, for his guilt was that he lived, lived while the others who were better than he were dead. Even if he were truly going mad—and he thought he was, thought the Time was Coming—he'd held on to wits enough to know that every breath he took was an offense against the past, that he was unfit to stand on the ground of home.

He spoke no more. Off to his right the fabric of the world parted and a path opened to him, and though needful of the doctor he was drawn into it anyway, for the truth was he doubted the doctor could do him any good. Passing through, he felt curious and expectant. Where he came out the dark woman waited. The sight of her calmed him—her rough black pelt of unbound hair, her fawn's eyes, her smile. He lay back. She soaped his hair, rinsed it, dried it with a rough towel. *I'm resting now*, she told him. *It's over and I'm resting. You can rest, too. Then we'll be resting together for all time.* She kissed him, gave him her meaty flavor.

Another hole opened up and sucked him all unwilling into the maze, while behind him the dark woman cried out his name. He emerged in Papa's library. All about him stood shelves full of leather-bound volumes whose backs were lettered in gold leaf. As always the space felt cozy and secure; it smelt agreeably of dust and mold and old leather. A shaft of sunlight streamed in through the window. Motes floated in the light, doing a stately dance. He drew down a book, sat, paged idly through it. He heard a peeping noise like that of a newborn chick. Then they came, the varmints that hid in the shelves behind the books. *Peep, peep,* they said. They were about the size of mice but stood on their hind legs and were shaped like men. They scampered about. One stood on his knee and gazed wisely up at him.

Are you God? Andy asked.

The following morning the doctor showed them into a parlor covered in mauve wallpaper vertically striped with teal, which, in combination with the closed shutters and the green trim of the windows and crown molding, made the darkest and most disagreeable room Rebecca had ever been in. In gilt frames hung a number of oil portraits of dour-looking men all sharing with Dr. Kester the same long nose with a bump in the middle, though none of whom showed any sign of his evident good nature. They sat, Rebecca and Tom on a sofa, Captain Moore in an armchair, the doctor on a folding camp stool he fetched specially for the purpose, as if it were an implement of his practice. Andy was not present; he was resting, the doctor explained.

Into their anxious faces he pleasantly beamed. "It's my duty to inform you," he began, "that in my considered opinion Mr. Curtis suffers from moral insanity and that his case is entirely hopeless."

The happy sparkle of his eyes, his cheerful smile, the chirp of his voice, the brisk nod of his bald dome with its few strands of hair plastered over—all these had led them to expect good news. Now that he'd inexplicably given them the worst instead, they sat stunned. There was no way to reconcile his gratified air with the black import of his words. White-faced, unwilling to trust the evidence of his own ears, Captain Moore leaned at the doctor and begged him please to repeat himself.

"Moral insanity," Dr. Kester piped. "A hopeless case."

The captain sank back into his cushions, staring in disbelief. Rebecca was possessed by a rage that nearly blinded her; violently she began to shake. Tom glanced in confusion from the doctor to Rebecca and back again.

Impossibly Dr. Kester went on in his sunny and confiding way. "Insanity," he said, "is a generic term we apply to certain morbid mental conditions produced by a defect or disease of the brain. One we designate congenital insanity, and under this heading fall both the idiot and the cretin."

He darted affable looks at the three of them, his smile widening; incredibly he seemed to hope they would smile back. *Idiot?* Rebecca thought in cold horror. *Cretin?* Were these the words to describe her poor Andy?

"Obviously in these cases we have to deal with a brain condition fixed by pathological circumstances under which the patient came into the world," Dr. Kester was saying, "or that supervened before full cerebral activity could be developed." He spread his hands in a narrow gesture, seeming to denote a small concession. "It will be seen of course that the insanity of Mr. Curtis is not of this type."

Despite a whiff of relief that blew faintly through her, Rebecca was still trembling head to foot. "What are you saying?" she demanded, then instantly regretted her wavering voice, induced by shock, which made her sound frightened rather than furious, her true state. Then it struck her that the wrong was not so much what the doctor said but how he *was*, in his ghastly complacency and merriment. So she amended her question at once and cried in firmer guise, "What are you *doing?*"

But her plea failed to discompose the doctor. Again he gave a series of ready nods; again he smiled. "Mr. Curtis's insanity is not congenital but acquired. By this we refer to an incidence of disease which renders insane a brain which, prior to the onset, was in a congenitally perfect state. The disease in turn may obtrude as a result of one or more of several causes."

Captain Moore had recovered his composure sufficiently to inquire, "Such as?"

Dr. Kester shrugged; the points of his little shoulders popped up and down as if he were trying out a pair of unseen fairy wings. "Oh, traumatic causes," he said. "Or injuries. Nervous diseases such as epilepsy, hysteria or locomotor ataxia. Tumors and cancers of the brain. Morbid conditions of the general system implicating the brain, such as consumption, rheumatism, gout, syphilis. Also the effects of evolutional periods concurrently affecting the brain—puberty, adolescence, utero-gestation, old age."

Rebecca shuddered on the sofa. Why was he speaking of the maladies of children and women and old men and the dissolute and low-down, of diseases from which Brother had never suffered, of the hated and unmentionable pox? Again in near-frenzy she shrilled, "*What are you doing?*"

In a sprightly and awful vein the doctor supplied a sort of answer. "None of these conditions explains the morbid action of the brain we find in Mr. Curtis, however. Instead we must look to what are called idiopathic causes, which affect the tissues yet are difficult if not impossible to trace. In contradistinction to physical causes, much of idiopathic morbid action is due to overexcitation of the brain, often rising from *moral* causes—grief, anxiety, domestic complications, disappointment, terror, sorrow or joy, religious or political excitement, sexual obsessions, unduly prolonged study."

Tom Carter thought he saw a chance to contribute. He gave Captain Moore an earnest and confirming look, then remarked, "Well, Andy always *did* work right hard." This startled the captain into a fierce blush of embarrassment. Just then Rebecca wanted to kill Tom Carter with some heavy instrument. But she must kill the doctor first. She opened her mouth to speak a reprimand, but his breezy recital had now resumed.

"Moral insanity is not so readily recognized as when we see insanity proceed directly from a deterioration of brain structure. To the most superficial observer the deformed head of the idiot is a coarsely material condition. But when mental aberration follows on mental excitement, men are prone to regard it as a derangement of function rather than of structure. Yet it has been shown that the moral causes may be the producers of physical cerebral disease."

At the doctor's every use of the word *moral* Rebecca blanched. Who'd been more moral than Brother? Who more Christlike? Whose morals had been stronger, loftier, more enduring, harder tested? What right did this chirping creature with his threads of hair pasted over his skull have to hint that Andy's morals were somehow rotted, corrupt? But brightly, inexorably, Dr. Kester pressed on.

"Among the moral causes," he explained, "overexcitation of the intellectual function is not by any means such a prolific cause of brain disease as *undue emotion.*" He raised a hand to capture their special attention. To signify the importance of what he meant to say next, he allowed his smile to fade, his nods to cease, his oriole's chatter to give way to somber tones more appropriate to the topic. "In the case of moral insanity it is not work," he declared, "but *worry* that kills the brain. When both are combined—as in the case of your Mr. Curtis— the result is often rapid."

Rebecca was incredulous. "Brother's lost his mind because he *feels* too much?" she exclaimed. "Because he *worries?*" But even as she blurted her doubt she recognized in the doctor's litany of causes of agitation of the brain several that she knew did sorely vex Andy. Grief was one, over his brothers lost in a war he felt he'd unworthily survived, over Papa and Mama, over what he felt was his failure to measure up to the standard of courage and high conduct they'd set. Anxiety, too, for he was bedeviled by the notion he hadn't provided for the family as he should and so pushed himself hard—and against his nature—to succeed in farming and business and politics. Domestic complications? Yes, Brother was a widower forever in mourning for his dear dead wife Salina; he was childless; and now the care he needed in his decline was blighting the life of his last unmarried sister, whom he cherished. There was more. Disappointment? Surely. Terror? Sorrow? By all means. A throng of woes fed on him. Rebecca's head reeled; she felt feverish; she caught her breath with a ragged sob. *Poor Brother.*

So offended by now was Captain Moore at Dr. Kester's heedless manner that he spoke to him hissing through gritted teeth like a mean old gander. "You say a cure's impossible."

The doctor nodded, passed a caressing hand over his dome to smooth his few hairs. "Quite. Mr. Curtis suffers from acute idiopathic melancholia, evidenced by a simple depression of feeling with delusions and occasional mania or delirium. Often a case of this sort depends on the removal—or the persistence—of the morbid congestion. Then there may be a recovery, or there may be a further and permanent advance of the disease. I'm afraid in Mr. Curtis's case relief cannot be obtained. Consequently the changes in the cells of the brain occasioned by morbid action will be followed by lesions of other brain structures, which in their turn will cause yet more important pathological conditions affecting the general system. These will then render recovery impossible. Death is the only possible outcome."

Captain Moore bit his lower lip and sent out his gander's hiss once more. "How soon?"

"Perhaps a year," answered Dr. Kester. "Perhaps ten years, or five. Perhaps less. No one can say."

"And his care?"

"There can be no question of the family"—he bowed his head toward Rebecca—"of you, Miss Curtis, caring for him at home. He must go to the asylum. Naturally I will be pleased to arrange it."

Rebecca detested the doctor—what could lawyer Elias have been thinking, to recommend so vile a man?—but now she found herself believing absolutely that despite his odious deportment Dr. Kester had spoken the truth. After all, he'd said no more than Rebecca herself had perceived many times when Brother disgraced himself. Andy was sick in his mind, irreversibly sick, sick unto death, although death might wait a long time to claim him. How many years he would continue to eke out an existence while his madness slowly took him was anyone's dreary guess. In the meantime all his admired grace and dignity would decay. What would remain? A squirming bag of brittle bones with no more sense than a bat. She knew she could not watch that come about. Nor could she wait for as long as it all might take. She thought of the cravat she'd bought. Suddenly with tears blurring her eyes she stood. As good manners required, Tom and Captain

Moore and the doctor bolted to their feet with her; the doctor, reverting to his former good cheer, stood expectantly blinking, wreathed in smiles, ready to accept in all humility their grateful thanks. "Bring me my brother," Rebecca said.

When Dr. Kester led him downstairs Brother shot anxious glances from side to side. In waking he'd lost his bearings and forgot where he was. His eyes were pouchy from sleep; the wrinkles of a pillowcase were printed pinkly on his cheek; the hair on one side of his head stood comically up. But the looks he sent about him were wild. He seemed both like a little boy rousted too early from bed and like the madman the doctor had pronounced him to be. Feeling a burst of affection, Rebecca went to him, smoothed the rebellious hair, stood on tiptoe, planted a kiss on the end of his nose. At once his agitation ceased. He greeted the others. Drowsily he smiled. "I had good dreams," he reported.

While Captain Moore took Brother outside for a walk, Rebecca, swallowing her dislike, remained behind to work out with Dr. Kester the details of the commitment and to prepare the papers, some of which must be carried on to lawyer Elias in Franklin to be executed. While they worked at a small round table by a window, Tom Carter waited on the sofa with his hat balanced on his knees, looking acutely on, worrying that the doctor might somehow take advantage of his betrothed—as if, Rebecca sourly reflected, Tom were shrewd enough to spy such a stratagem should Dr. Kester attempt it, or to know what to do about it if he did.

In Franklin, while Tom and Captain Moore ambled about the square, Rebecca and Andy stopped at the office of lawyer Elias, who'd handled the affairs of the Curtises since war's end, when he and Brother Andy and Mr. Price had stood together against the scalawags trying to dispossess the family. By now he was an old and trusted friend. When he saw Andy's condition lawyer Elias was deeply moved. Andy recognized him, eagerly shook his hand, spoke of times past, then abruptly subsided into a stupor. Lawyer Elias sat gazing at him in dumb anguish, like a kicked dog heretofore coddled. Rebecca knew Elias to be a practical man—a man of affairs and of little feeling—and the sight of his upset touched her. Intruding on the moment, for they must soon be on their way, she recounted what Dr. Kester had said, laying on the desk between them the papers to be completed and signed.

Lawyer Elias shook his head, as if he wanted to deny what he saw and heard and now had to do. "I can hardly take it in. Must I now set in motion the train of events that will forever immure my oldest companion in an asylum for the insane?" He scowled. "I confess, in sending you to Dr. Kester I thought he would pronounce Andy sane but troubled, that he would prescribe rest, medicines, perhaps a change of scene. But this . . . this . . ." He pinched the top of his nose between his fingers. "Forgive me," he begged of Rebecca. "I fear I'm overcome."

Just then Brother stirred. His empty gaze filled with light. He rose, came around the corner of the desk to lay a hand on Elias's shoulder. "Don't worry," he said. "We'll beat 'em. The right's on our side." Gently he smiled down on lawyer Elias, rocked him with his grasp by way of consolation.

On the way home at last, when the mail stage had come through the Nantahalas by way of Winding Stair Gap and was rounding a shoulder of Chunky Gal that offered a view west across the valley of the Hiwassee, Brother asked the driver to halt for a moment. Despite a pressing schedule the driver did so, for he'd grown somewhat fond of this big, smiling, shambling fellow so sweetly addled in the head.

While the others watched, Andy got down from the tonneau and went to the verge of the drop-off. Rebecca had suffered a bad coughing fit of late, and in her side was a touch of what felt like pleurisy; thus worn down and afflicted she grew unduly alarmed, lest Brother throw himself into the void from despair. Then she saw how easily he stood. Below spread the great bowl of the valley rimmed with mountains, all mottled with the dazzling hues of the season. Above, the sky was scrubbed clean, so blue it seemed to ache with its own purity. Andy lifted his head. He smelt the cool breath the valley sent up to him.

CHAPTER 10

October 1881

*W*ebb Darling was feeding his roosters when he heard the first
of the horns. He straightened, cocked an ear, stood a moment without moving, his open poke of scratch feed and table scraps balanced
in the palm of a hand. Around him the roosters, impatient for their
eats, clucked and squawked, batted their wings, pecked at their teth-
ers. But despite their commotion he heard again the long tapering
tenor note, drawn thin as a wire across the distance, and knew it for
the horn of the Fires Creek rim.

He moved then, twisted the neck of his poke into a knot, turned,
trotted across the bare rock of the bald toward the fort; behind him
one by one the cocks broke into squalls of complaint to see the meal
so rudely interrupted and whisked away. The king was but a few steps
from the door of the fort when the brother came out carrying his
Winchester in one hand and a bitten half of a boiled egg in the other,

his jaw grinding sideways, bits of egg caught in his beard. Another horn sounded, out of the south and west this time—likely Shearer's Creek or Pigpen Knob. Almost at the same time came the brassy cry of Ree Bolt's bugle from the foot of Piney Top. The brother popped the last of the egg into his mouth and spoke, blowing a spray of yellow crumbs: "Fight or skedaddle?"

"Let's see the size of 'em," Darling said. He wanted to fight—he'd give anything to hand the Revenue a licking they'd never forget—but it was wiser to learn how many were coming and by what ways before he made the choice. The prospect of a ruckus roused him, and he couldn't help giving out a laugh of excitement. He moved past the brother, entered the dark room, tossed the poke on the table, fetched up his pistol belt from the back of a chair and buckled it around him. Drawing the Colt's, he put it on half-cock and, slanting it upward against the dim light from the window, rotated the cylinder to check the loads, then reseated it in its oiled scabbard. He caught up his field glasses from the whipsawed plank that served as a mantelpiece. He was bending to grasp the Henry from where it leaned against the fireplace when yet another horn faintly blew. Taking up the rifle by the barrel and looping the lanyard of the field glasses over his head, he came to rejoin the brother by the doorstone. "Which way?"

The brother jabbed the muzzle of his Winchester to the left. "Compass Creek, or Matlock's. Coming up by way of Dead Line Ridge, looks like." So that bunch was nearer than Pigpen or Shearer's, either one. "They's enough of them so's they split up," the brother said. "Two batches, most likely. One by Fires Creek, t'other thisaway." Far down the valley a gun softly popped, and an echo mellowly answered back. The brother swallowed the last of his egg. "Skedaddle, I say."

Darling brayed another laugh, but this one was scornful. "*You'd* say." He whirled; quick and nimble as a monkey he scuttled up the ladder to the roof of the fort and advanced to the front parapet, where he planted his elbows on the coping and leveled the field glasses down the valley. While he twisted the little knurled disk to focus the glasses at their longest range, two more shots floated up, each twinned with its vaguer echo.

He looked to his right, toward the foot slopes of the Valley River Mountains. In the eyepieces the faraway hills sprang shockingly close, offering up their brilliant warp and woof of autumn. Tracking downward, Darling saw a puff of smoke blossom in the lower woods and start to rise. Some moonshiner pecking away, God bless him. Lower still he could make out a line of tiny black specks winding across a field of stumps on the south side of Wolf Ridge, where he knew Irish Bill Moore had once done some timbering. Against the tilted square of green the specks looked smaller than ants—than mites even. Smaller yet were the black stumps, scattered fine as iron filings. Now he heard the sound of the shot whose smoke he'd seen seconds before. From the line of specks another flower of smoke formed and drifted, another distant boom sounded, another echo lazily came. Darling smiled. The brother was right, or at least half right. One crowd was coming up Fires Creek.

He hurried to the south wall and peered down Dead Line Ridge. The way the land lay, he couldn't see into the drainages of Matlock Creek or Compass Creek, but awhile ago some moonshiner had kindled a signal fire on the top of the ridge itself. He hadn't noticed it till now, intent as he'd been on his chickens; he could see the glow of it among the red and gold of the trees like a single live coal in banked ashes, its line of smoke standing straight up in the still air for a mile or more before layering out flat in a long paling streamer. Damn Hightower and Mozingo for not reporting it. Darling leaned over the coping, shouted down, "Get the woman and the younguns out by the back way!"

The brother squinted doubtfully up. "Are we a-fighting?"

Two routes of attack. One team was nearer than the other, probably because the way up Dead Line was harder. They'd come one bunch at a time, not all together—unless the party in the lead waited to link up with the other, which they wouldn't do because the alarm had been raised and the whole country was astir and they must make what haste they could. So he'd be able to meet them in turn. He had five hands now; more soon would be coming in answer to the horns. He had walls to fight behind; the Revenue would be in the open. Again he laughed the laugh of exaltation, "Hell, yes, we're fighting." He brandished the rifle. "Go ahead now, get the others down." The brother slumped, swore. He was lazy; to him a scrimmage looked too much like work on a hot Indian summer day. But nonetheless he ducked inside, and presently Darling heard him call the woman by name below.

Webb was delighted they were coming. The two wings were likely even more of a posse than had gone against Lewis Redmond, more than it had taken to bring in Bill Berong. And Redmond and Berong were legends. Such a force confirmed Darling's rank; he was the last of the kings, and the best. Till now they'd not dared try conclusions with him. They were sparing no effort or expense, were using their wiliest tactics. Darling felt himself swell with significance. What king's castle had not withstood a siege by his enemies? What monarch had not called to his side his faithful retainers, defended the realm with grit and blood? He was grateful; he gave thanks to God and the Revenue; he blared out another happy laugh; he leaned over the parapet and yelled a yodeling war whoop; then as its echo came weirdly back he jacked the loading lever of the Henry and fired a shot of pure exuberance into the bright air overhead.

Mozingo and Hightower came jogging down the paths from their posts higher up. They stopped when Darling hailed them. "You see that goddamn signal smoke yonways?"

Each turned and gazed, turned slowly back. "Hell," shouted Mozingo, "we figured it for natural. It lightened over thataway last night."

Darling shook a fist at them. "Sons of bitches. When this is done I'll have the both of you by the balls." The way they hung their heads struck him as amusing. "Where's Redmane and Nutbush?" he demanded, choking back his laugh.

"Down to the still," Hightower hollered back.

Darling stuck the Henry under one arm and shouted down between his two hands, "Go and get 'em. Take 'em down the cove to the head of Compass. Make sure they've got their guns. Some of the Revenue's coming up that way an hour from now, maybe two. Lay yourselves a good ambuscade in there amongst the laurel. When they come up, light into 'em. Hold 'em long as you can. Soon as some more of the boys come up I'll send 'em along."

Supposing themselves shriven of their sins, they waved in acknowledgment, then turned down the trail that led under Dead Line; the forest closed behind them.

The brother emerged from the fort, then the woman with the younguns strung out behind her, so she and they resembled a goose with her goslings trailing obediently along. The woman and the bigger younguns carried rations. None looked up to find the king; none so much as raised a hand either in greeting or farewell. Darling watched them pass through the fringe of low growth and up along the saddle that connected Pot Rock to Tusquittee Bald. If worst came to worst they could escape down the backside of the big bald into the watershed of Tuni Creek, and so to the Nantahala.

But there'd be slim need of that, he figured. Let the goddamn Revenue come coursing up these steeps and throw themselves at Fort Darling; he'd bloody their noses for them. Then what a king he'd be!

He mused. What was greater than a king? Maybe an emperor was. Yes, he'd give the Revenue a good sound whipping, and then he'd be the emperor. All hail! Before the emperor every menial would bend his knee. He descended the ladder, propped the Henry at the doorjamb, went inside to fetch his fiddle. He came out with the fiddle and bow in one fist, dragging a splint-bottomed chair behind him with the other. He took the chair out to the point of the bald, where the vista opened vastly on a huge vault of sky and on all the tinted hills, their flanks dotted now with the smoke of shooting like scattered cottonwood down. Amid the racket of horns and gunfire he tucked the fiddle under his chin and began to play.

In a little while Ree Bolt, red as a penny and blowing like a race-horse from the heart-bursting climb, broke out of the woods cradling his Sharps carbine in the bend of an arm; he was wild of eye, and his shirt and the waist of his trousers were soaked with sweat. Darling sat him down on the doorstone with a demijohn of cherry bounce to let him recover himself and ease the cramps in his legs. Presently Abner Mullinax arrived from Long Branch, together with a cousin and the nephew who'd gone with Webb that time to fix Lige Dollar. Before an hour was up six more had come, three of whom Darling dispatched down by Dead Line to Hightower and Mozingo, as he'd promised.

So when the head of the posse turned up the last bend of the main trail, Darling had himself an army of seven, not counting the ones on the Compass. Ree was on the roof with Darling and the Mullinax nephew and two of the late-comers, a fellow called Grainger from the Rockhouse and Billy Wetmore of the Perry Creek Wetmores. Darling posted Grainger and the Mullinax nephew along the north parapet, which guarded the fort's strongest approach, a narrow scree of shale that sloped like frosting on a bad cake along the rim of a cliff that dropped a hundred feet or more into a pit of darkness the sun never lit; nobody but a goat figured to come up that way, so two ought to be able to watch it. Webb stationed himself, Ree, Wetmore and the Mullinax cousin along the east wall opposite the mouth of the main trail, where he figured the attack might start; the Revenue would want to hold down the garrison with sniper fire from in front, while flanking parties worked their way around to hit the west and south faces of the fort. To either side of the trail's mouth, behind big layered boulders of granite covered with yellowing fern, waited Abner Mullinax and a man name of Jonas, from down the Rattlesnake.

Webb was watching through his field glasses when the column rounded the last turn of the trail and started up toward the fort. In front came a rangy cuss chalky with dust and wearing a broad-brimmed hat and high boots, a rifle strapped over one shoulder. Darling recognized him at once. "Richbourg," he said to Ree.

Sitting with his back to the wall with the demijohn by him, Ree made a snorting noise. "Longest prick they got."

But Darling didn't laugh, for Tuck Richbourg was doing a peculiar thing, and it intrigued him to see it. Richbourg had hold of another man by an arm and with violent jerks was yanking him up the path behind him. The fellow he was dragging dug in his heels and grabbed at every bush and bough he passed, holding back as hard as Richbourg was hauling him up. Queerly he was wearing a flour sack over his head with holes cut in it to see through, only with every jerk Richbourg gave him the eye holes got wrenched out of line and made him blind, so he kept stumbling and partway falling while he grabbed at the hood with his free hand, trying to twist it back so he could see. Now Darling did laugh. He handed the glasses to Ree. "Have a look at that."

Ree rose, turned, knelt, rested the glasses on the top of the wall and peered. When he passed the glasses back he said, "You know who that is Richbourg's got?"

Darling raised the glasses again and looked. "No, who?"

Ree tilted the demijohn on the bend of his elbow and greedily drank, lowered it, licked his lips, hugged the stoneware against him. "Ves Price is who. See that patch on his britches, the red-un? That's his patch and his britches—and his ass I mean to shoot."

Webb studied the skinny fellow struggling in Richbourg's grasp and nodded. "He's the Dog." A part of him had known it all along, known it the day Ves came to him so solicitously begging. But another part—elevated and generous, kingly—had prevailed on him then, and he'd given the poor fool a chance at redemption, which it turned out he hadn't deserved. Sadly Darling shook his head. *The slop-dumper*, he thought. *Shit.* "Wearing a goddamn hood," he sneered, "hoping we won't know him." In contempt he watched Ves writhe and hang back. "He don't appear to be much of a willing recruit, does he?" Then he grinned. "Let's show him we *do* know him."

He laid aside the field glasses and took up the Henry, chambered a round, settled the barrel of black steel on the rim of the wall. He flipped up the vertical leaf of the sight, raised the little notched horizontal band with his thumb, set the sight for two hundred yards and drew a bead on the rebellious figure in Richbourg's grasp. Then he remembered his plan of battle. Mullinax and Jonas were his skirmishers; he daren't shoot yet; it was up to them to begin the attack, while the force on the parapet held fire till it came clear what they faced, at which point they could open up with maximum effect. He ought not break his own rules; that way led to anarchy. Too bad. He consoled himself with the thought that kings must exercise forbearance and self-denial for the good of the land; it was one of the costs of rule. Anyhow the slop-dumper's time would come. One large benefit of being a king was that more often than not one could accurately predict the future of one's enemies. He lowered the hammer.

He didn't have long to wait. One after another the posse men, in a snaky line led by Richbourg and Ves Price in his absurd flour-sack hood, came nearer and nearer up the narrow way. As he looked on, Darling grew puzzled. After gaining the last turn why hadn't some of them flanked off? If they had a guide why in hell were they all blundering in on the fort from the front, as if they didn't know how it lay? Maybe the slop-dumper was no better a guide than he was a blockader. Six of the posse were in view, bent this way and that on the zigzagging trail, when Abner Mullinax and the man Jonas from the Rattlesnake drew down on them. Their volley racketed along the path, divided the crooked file. Some broke one way and some the other; Ves in his hood cringed, dove behind a hemlock; Tuck Richbourg never moved, stood firm in the path, unslung his rifle and raised it to his shoulder as casually as at a target shoot.

When Richbourg fired, a gout of dust spewed out of the rock Abner Mullinax was hiding behind, and way up on the parapet Webb Darling heard the ricochet go past his ear like a mad hornet. He grinned across at Ree, pulled a face of mock horror. Killed by a bullet on the bounce—that would've been a joke, a mean end indeed for the king. Mullinax and Jonas—was that his first or his last name?—both fired at Richbourg, and two spurts of earth jumped out of the ground a few yards behind him. Darling twisted his head aside and spat. *To hell with the rules*, he thought. *Make 'em, break 'em.* Leaning into the wall, he drew back the hammer of the Henry and set Richbourg into the **V** of his sight, and the Henry stroked his shoulder with its sweet recoil. But in the half-second between his aiming and his shot Richbourg dodged behind the same hemlock Ves Price had chosen. In the lull that followed the shooting Darling thought he heard the two of them back there cussing and arguing.

They traded shots with the posse for a few minutes, no harm

being done on either side that Darling could see. Somewhat disappointed at himself for violating his own rule of tactics, Darling let Jonas and Mullinax do most of the shooting, while he and Ree Bolt scouted. Presently Ree touched his arm and pointed off to the left. When Webb glanced that way he saw a rifle-toting man darting bent-over across a space between two big mossy rocks. Behind him came another. And another. Finally they were flanking. But no! Darling gazed in wonder as the dark shapes plunged on through the bracken. They were rounding the northeast corner and going on.

"Hellfire!" he exclaimed to Ree. "They're going for the north wall." He shook his head, thinking of the shaley rim, the dark abyss of the cliff. "Don't they know that's our strongest side?" He whistled up Wetmore and the Mullinax cousin, and he and Ree led them across the roof to the high north parapet, where Grainger and the Mullinax nephew were even now leaning far out over the wall and firing across at the rim of the cliff, where the first posse man had already appeared. In chagrin Darling saw their shots strike high; you'd think a hillbilly would know how to shoot downhill. "Aim low, goddamnit!" he yelled. "Shoot for their kneecaps!"

There were two on the shaley rim now and two more—Richbourg and the slop-dumper—twenty paces or so behind, just now breaking out of the thickets of hawthorn and hazelnut. Darling saw Richbourg stop, glance about him, stiffen, consult a piece of paper he held, then turn and strike the slop-dumper with his fist. Ves Price in his hood toppled back into the bushes, which opened up to receive him, then closed over him as if providentially to hide his shame.

By then one of the agents on the rim had got hit and was lying on a crust of shale that slipped and commenced to move, sliding toward the edge. The other one managed to stretch out flat and catch him by a wrist and hold on, but then the shale under him broke free, too, and began to go. Richbourg was firing up at the fort and at first didn't see what was happening. When he did he dropped his gun and started to dash to help, then saw it wasn't possible; that whole bank of shale was either already sliding or bound to go at the merest touch. With his free hand the shot one scratched at the rotten rock slipping and tilting underneath him, but there was no purchase to be got in all that moving mass. His pard held on to him, but as the slide bore them both toward the verge the pard saw his own end yawning before him, so he opened his grasp and let the first one go and latched on to the broken stump of an old spruce sticking up just at hand. He clung to that stump while the avalanche poured past him with a dry rattling noise like the rustle of so many dead bones. And through the cloud of white dust it roiled up they all saw the shot one curl over the edge and drop out of sight.

Soon after that the Revenue pulled back and left. But it was too early to celebrate. For some time now there'd been a steady crackle of gunfire down toward Compass Creek, where Mozingo and the rest were holding off the other wing of attack. So when Richbourg's half of the posse withdrew, Darling took Ree Bolt and Abner Mullinax and hurried down the cove to reinforce that flank. As it turned out they needn't have rushed; by the time they arrived at the ambush site the Revenue had retreated there as well. Proudly Hightower and Mozingo turned toward Darling, smiling at their prowess, awaiting his thanks; and Darling put the snout of his pistol against Mozingo's forehead and shot him dead. Then to Hightower he said, "Keep a closer watch next time."

Afterwards Darling and Ree Bolt sat down in the main room of the fort to discuss the fate of the Dog. Webb wanted to act at once, that very night. "Let's go down and do him up like we did the nigger."

But Ree wagged his head no. "I ain't degrading his pappy. That Oliver Price, he's a white man, a Christian if there ever was one. Hell, we served together. It's Ves that's lower'n vomick. Oliver, why he never done nobody no hurt. We can't take his boy afore his own eyes, his eldest, in front of his woman and all them younguns." Again Ree shook his head. "I couldn't live with it."

It was news to Webb that anything was too hard for Ree Bolt. The notion made him go to studying—which in itself was a measure of his regard for the big Melungeon.

"I say let some time pass," continued Ree. "A few weeks. Let the hooraw over this here raid die down. Everybody'll know Ves is the Dog, that he guided 'em up here. The whole county'll be watching. They'll *expect* us to close him out, the Revenue and the sheriff both. He dies, they'll be on us like a hen on a beetle. So I say wait. Bide our time. Get him later, on the road, in the woods, off in some field. Meantime think how he'll suffer, a-waiting on it."

Darling considered. He liked that last part. While he sat thinking, the woman and the younguns and the brother came traipsing in from their refuge up on the high bald. "All right," he said to Ree, then by turns went to hugging the kids lined up solemnly before him.

After his disheartening trip to Asheville with the Curtises and Tom Carter, Captain Moore was wrapped in melancholy to think his friend Andy must go to the asylum. So he fetched his Yankee drum and drumsticks from the attic, as he did whenever his spirits sank low, sat himself down on the arcaded gallery of his fine four-gabled house overlooking the wide Tusquittee bottom and the hills beyond, then commenced to tap out the various army calls he remembered— "The General," "Drill Call," "Tattoo," "The Long Roll."

Although he had been a cavalryman for most of the war and so had got used to obeying only trumpet calls, at the outbreak he'd been a second lieutenant in the Nineteenth North Carolina Infantry; ever since, he'd been partial to the voice of the infantry drum. The drum gave measure to the unmeasurable, order to the chaos of battle. Somehow it wove men together and made them all part of the same rhythm; when it spoke the organs of the body resonated back; the drumbeat was to the march or the assault what the heartbeat was to the flesh.

He'd picked up this particular drum on the field of Chickamauga, at the end of that glorious first day, when the Sixty-fifth Cavalry had held off the Yanks before Reed's Sawmill; the drum was lying next to a pitiful dead drummer boy who looked no more than twelve. He'd shipped it home to Miss Hattie, and she'd kept it for him till the surrender, even while she was spurning his overtures of love. She gave him back the drum eight years before she gave him herself.

He thought it right handsome for a drum, if maybe somewhat gaudy. It was painted a glossy dark blue and had a gold eagle on the front of it holding a curly banner in its beak that said "14TH OHIO INFANTRY." For its chest the eagle had a shield marked with the Stars and Stripes. The wings of the eagle were spread, and its talons held bolts of lightning and sheaves of arrows, and in back of all that was a kind of yellow sunburst. Upon finishing the army calls, the captain played the beat of one of his favorite songs of the war, "Nellie Bly," and sang the words with his cracked voice. Then, tapping out the time on the drum, he commenced whistling some of the liveliest tunes he used to hear the fife-and-drum corps play—"Carry Me Back," "Liverpool Horsepipe," "Jefferson and Liberty," "Garryowen."

The regiment was never the same after Chickamauga, where they'd tasted fame under Nathan Bedford Forrest. Soon after that fight the authorities sent the Sixty-fifth off to the area around Knoxville— young Howell Curtis was killed in a skirmish there—and into such hard times they soon bled away to a puny remnant, not from battle but from Toryism and desertion. So for the most part the captain's had not been the sublime war many old heroes recalled. For every Chickamauga there'd been a dozen dirty little outpost fights, a hundred ambushes, a thousand skirmishes with enemies one never saw. What he remembered most were the scared faces of his boys, longing for home. He was proud of his service, but the pride he had was a sad one.

While he drummed he also grieved for Andy Curtis, scarred by war himself, scarred, too, by the hard peace—scarred not in his body but in his heart, his mind. It seemed to the captain that some people— Andy was one—lived too near the next world to bear the cruelty of this one. Such were already mostly saints, or maybe angels. God knew them better than He knew the brutish run of mankind, and they knew Him better than they could ever know the mortals that caused their torments in this life. It would be a blessing, the captain reflected, should the Lord carry Andy away before the year was out. That was where Andy belonged, there in Paradise with his papa, his mama, his brothers Howell and Jack and his lost sisters Betty and Polly. Captain Moore would pray for that to come to pass.

Awhile longer he sat rattling the drum and whistling his remembered melodies—"Sweet Evelina," "Dixie," "Annie of the Vale," "Home, Sweet Home." He ceased only when he heard the clatter of many hooves on the road just above his boundary of land. Earlier he and his best hired man had been back behind the barn at the spot he called the Jack Holler, standing his jackass to a mare of Green Haigler's, when a cavalcade of armed riders passed by on the road going up the Tusquittee. He'd come around the house to see what they were about and had recognized the deputy revenue collector from Towns County—the one that wore the big hat—at the head of the column. So he knew another raid was under way to try and run out the blockaders that infested the hills.

He'd seen many such go up and come down, for the road past his house was the chief way into the fastnesses. While finishing with Haigler's mare he'd heard gunfire somewhere way up in the range.

That wasn't unusual either; the moonshiners always popped away at the Revenue, but rarely did they do any hurt. So now the captain was surprised when he spied the same party who'd gone up so briskly that morning coming down again past his gate all hangdog and raggedy, one of their number lashed head-down and bloody over the back of his horse.

Setting aside his drum, the captain stood solemnly to attention and rendered a salute, the back of his hand to the brim of his hat in the best Confederate style. It wasn't *his* government, and never would be; Irish Bill Moore was A Good Old Rebel, as in the song. But a fallen enemy was an enemy no more. The dead who died for duty deserved respect, whatever cause they served. He held the salute as the file of riders passed by. The agent in the broad hat was the last one in the column, riding a dun gelding; he glanced toward the gallery, saw the captain's salute, nodded, bowed low over his saddle horn, swept his sombrero off and away with a fine flourish and stayed bareheaded all the way out of sight. The captain dropped his hand, resumed his seat, once more took up his drum and sticks.

Awhile later Miss Hattie and the younguns came back from town in the buggy, and the captain helped unload their parcels and carry them inside. Then he took thought of the weeds he'd noticed growing along his fence by the roadside and got his shears and went out to trim them, when who should he find leaning on his gate but Ves Price, looking as if he'd got pulled through a threshing machine. Cuts and scrapes covered him; blood was matted in his hair; he wore rags and tatters; one eye had swollen shut; his bottom lip was split in two places. Woefully he regarded Captain Moore with his one good eye. "Can I please have a drink of water?" he pled.

The captain took Ves by the hand, led him like an invalid to the well, sat him gently down. While he pumped a pail of water the captain looked Ves over and remarked, "It appears misfortune has beset you, son."

Very slowly Ves bent to the side, spat out a molar, sat back against the well probing with his tongue the place where the tooth had been. "I reckon," he said.

Captain Moore set the pail down, took the dipper and broke the surface of the water with its rounded cup, raised the dipper to Ves's lips. Painfully Ves drank. Even the movement of his Adam's apple seemed to hurt him. "What happened to you, son?" the captain asked.

Ves wouldn't look at him. Instead he sat staring down at the ragged grass that grew around the well; he watched a black beetle go crawling by. "Can't tell," he said.

"Matter of honor, eh?"

Ves shrugged. "You might say."

The captain was a charitable man, but he didn't believe that. Ves took another dipper of water. The captain knelt, drew out a handkerchief, dipped it in the pail and began to blot and soothe Ves's many wounds.

"I'm obliged," Ves told him, looking up and then quickly away.

The captain worked tenderly on. "Ever make that fortune we talked of?"

"No, sir."

"Ever think on what I told you that day, about what a man's fortune is?"

"No, sir," Ves said. "Not till now." Every time the captain's damp cloth touched him Ves would very gently push back against it, the way a cat will do when you pet it.

Part III

The Cockpit

CHAPTER 11

November 1881

*N*o sooner had Hamby got Buttermilk and Pile-Driver home than they commenced to molt, which made them unfit for fighting or even for any sort of heavy conditioning. They looked mighty dilapidated with their old feathers falling out in swatches and the green ones growing in, taking so much of their blood their colors paled down to a wan and milky semblance that but dimly recalled their former glory. Scrawny and near-naked, they tottered listlessly around the yard. They hardly appeared the fighters their proud bloodlines proclaimed them to be; a wormy pullet seemed more fierce. But Hamby knew they'd revive. He fed them well—middlin meat with gunpowder, pork, beef, calf manure, oats, the seeds of sunflowers. Frequently he moved their pens and tethering spots from one place to another around the grassy edge of the yard, so they could always get fresh green, and he gave them lettuce and cabbage leaves to eat.

Even had the stags been fit, nobody pitted chickens in molting

season, so in the meantime Hamby helped the Curtises get their tobacco crop in the barn and then cut and stacked his own, which he'd
planted later than they had. Looking over the yield, he figured to get
no more than seven or eight hogsheads, which was hardly worth the
effort; the more he did for the goddamn Curtises the less he did for
himself. Nonetheless he plowed the Curtises' bottom land and sowed
it for wheat and oats; earlier he'd planted hay and rye in some of the
corn lands. He cut the cane and made syrup. When he had time he
planted turnips, collards, mustard and cabbages in his own garden
plot beyond the pasture where Tom used to be. Then he pegged his
tobacco and hung it on laths in the Curtises' barn to cure, as was his
right.

Working for the Curtises was harder of late than usual. Whenever he was there he had to put up with prissy Jimmy Cartman hec-
toring him about this and that—how he behaved, what he wore or
failed to wear, how he was uppity and cussed, whether he was going
to accept Jesus as his Lord and Savior and get redeemed. Hamby
could argue back and bluster, but he daren't give in to his wish to
knock Jimmy winding, for Jimmy was a Curtis, and the Curtises were
Hamby's—what? employers? household? kin? Whatever they were,
Jimmy partook of it, and because of that Hamby must forbear. Also
Jimmy was the sort of white who'd make sure a nigger—or any part
of a nigger—paid dearly for the least trespass on him. And while
Hamby could look after himself he disliked extra trouble; ordinary
trouble was worrisome enough.

He longed for the coming of the chicken-fighting season so he
could pit his birds and square up his account with Webb Darling and
then pull stakes and leave behind him all his woes, especially Jimmy's
scolding—but not, he'd decided, before finally busting the busybody's
goddamn nose for him. Jimmy was mistaking himself for the head of
the whole Curtis concern. Miss Becky was sick with a wasting malady

that rendered her too weak to supervise any work; Andy would soon go off to the madhouse; Tom Carter was a fool; and Captain Moore was busy with his own harvest-time affairs. Into the great hole these four left, Jimmy was enlarging day by day. It seemed he'd taken it into his head it was his place, not any mulatto's, to run the farm.

By early fall the birds had finished molting. Pile-Driver's apricot hue brightened; his wings and tail regained their satiny sheen. Buttermilk plumped out to nearly five and a half pounds and got his creamy color back and commenced strutting around the yard on his long legs, snapping at the pullets like a whip. It was time for Hamby to set to work, and he did so with a will, happy to escape Jimmy's condemnations.

First he tested the alertness of the chickens by throwing pieces of cracked corn near them and watching to see how quick they spied and pecked up the kernels. The two proved about equal in this— pretty damn fast, though maybe Buttermilk was the faster by a shade— and Hamby surmised Livingood must've already put them through that program. Pretty quick then he moved on to flying them so as to build up the power in their wings.

Twice a day—morning and evening—he repeatedly took each bird by the neck and bottom and tossed him backwards high in the air so he had to beat his wings hard to come down easy. Hamby did that each time till that stag commenced to pant, then he stopped and took up the other one and flew him. When he flew Buttermilk he found that Pile-Driver, looking on, would get excited and want to fight, so he got in the habit of tying a hood of sacking over Pile-Driver's head to keep him from pitching into Buttermilk. Oddly, when he worked Pile-Driver, Buttermilk paid no mind at all.

At this same time Hamby changed to hard feed. After a spell he found their droppings starting to get dry and white-capped and saw the two popping their heads arrogantly about, so he knew they were near to ready. Then he took a file and sharpened their spurs. He'd heard folk in other places took off the spurs and put steel gaffs on their chickens, but nobody in this country was going to do that on account of the cost and the difficulty of getting hold of such an item. Besides to Hamby a gaff was cruel; it aimed to slice a bird up to no purpose beyond blood.

Next he built two six-foot-high fly-pens of poles and withes, laying down a bed of shucks and straw in the bottom of each. He put the chickens in, so they'd flounder up and down trying to get out and so strengthen themselves even more. After some days of this he weighed them. Pile-Driver came in a bit over four and a quarter pounds—he'd given up fat for hard muscle in the chest and wings—and Buttermilk was just the right weight for fighting at five. Both felt agreeably corky in the breast—light and buoyant—which meant it was nearly time to pit them.

Neither was the equal of Gouger. For one thing they were both far too young—Buttermilk looked to be about thirteen months and Pile-Driver maybe eleven or twelve—and of course they entirely lacked Gouger's hard-won experience. Working with the new birds often brought Gouger sadly to mind; Hamby would recall the way Gouger carried himself, knock-kneed and pigeon-toed, his head aloft; he'd remember Gouger's shrewd and calculating style that made the quick slash of his attack so surprising; sometimes he'd recall the air of melancholy Gouger had worn near the end.

But he knew also that the likes of Gouger came along only once in a great while. These ones were all right; Livingood had done a fair job of work on them. Buttermilk, bulkier but smaller than Pile-Driver, had a stolid disposition that, combined with his stoutness, made you think he'd be slow. But he was fast as a shot when he needed to be. Hamby liked it that he was calm; it showed he knew how to husband his power for the times he'd need it. Pile-Driver was a shuffler, whereas

Buttermilk was a cutter. Pile-Driver was more excitable; his gold eye gleamed with malice; he wanted to do damage; he was always on the lookout for gore and trouble a little like Gouger, but without Gouger's craft and wisdom.

The first of October, Hamby commenced pitting them. He carried them in their wicker cages slung on either side of the jenny's withers, the jenny flinching from them, the two birds raising all hell and glaring eagerly out at the passing world, as if they hoped to coax from it some varmint as mean as they felt so they could give it a licking. That first time, up on Shooting Creek at a hack fight Eli Abernathy put on and Cecil Dobbs judged, Buttermilk killed two birds—a stag Whitehackle and a Nigger Roundhead—and nerve-blinded an old Mug shake; Pile-Driver killed a Black Henny but took a bad cut on his chest from a Shawlneck of Mose Sullivan's, and Hamby pulled him out to nurse him. It was understood he had his birds in training.

He treated Pile-Driver's wound with chimney soot and let a month pass before pitting the both of them again at a hack fight at Luke Truly's place on Greasy Creek. Mose Sullivan was the judge. This time Pile-Driver rattled a Minor Blue and Buttermilk whipped a Red Brown. But Pile-Driver's cut opened up again. Looking on from a nearby stump that day was the Cherokee Longrunner, sent down by Livingood from Hanging Dog to oversee his rented birds. The others knew the Indian's mission. They put up with him for Livingood's sake, but none would speak him a welcoming word or engage him in any talk. Their eyes flicked at him edgewise where he occupied his stump, this dingy savage who sat in a white man's place only because his boss was accorded more respect than they could command. He ignored them, sought no sanction. Nor did he offer any sign he even recognized Hamby. He just sat and took in the fight, and when the match was over he got on his mule and left.

Late in November Hamby decided Pile-Driver needed more time to heal and pitted Buttermilk alone in a match Dobbs put on and Mose Sullivan judged. Longrunner showed up and watched this one, too, not wagering, not talking, just looking on as impassive as a figure carved out of rock. Buttermilk licked a War-Horse stag, and Hamby was satisfied and withdrew him. This time Longrunner stood and came over to him, leading his mule, and addressed him as Hamby was lashing Buttermilk's cage to the McClellan saddle. "Bird look like he coming sharp. Where the shuffler?"

Hamby explained about Pile-Driver. Then he lit his pipe and propped one hand against a pine bole and leaned there puffing. Even though Longrunner had broken his watchful silence, his reticence still stood between them like a wall. Looking into his honey-and-chocolate eyes, Hamby tried in vain to remember why he'd ever thought he and this expressionless redskin had purchase on some common understanding. "You watching over Livingood's share?"

Longrunner folded his arms, shrugged. "You might say." He held the reins of the mule in his right hand. The mule jerked at them and pulled them free, so Longrunner grasped the reins with both hands and jerked back hard, at which the mule gave a doleful grunt. Longrunner said no more but stood unmoving, as if he awaited some initiative of Hamby's, to which he was prepared to respond.

Hamby had no idea what it was Longrunner expected. Behind him on the saddle Buttermilk crowed and banged his wings against the sides of his cage. It occurred to Hamby that maybe Longrunner had come in the function of a collector. So he said, "I got sixty dollar due to Livingood. Won thirty more today. That make eighty-something for him altogether. Only got the thirty on me, though. You want it?"

"Hold on to it awhile yet," Longrunner replied. His mouth curled at one end, and his brown eyes lit with amber went wryly a-glitter.

"You can settle up," he added, "when you get done with the king."

Hamby stared. He'd told no one of his aim; Longrunner had to be guessing. He must know that Hamby and Lige Dollar used to be close, that Webb Darling had done Lige in and Hamby was likely to resent it, that Darling loved to fight chickens—from there Hamby reckoned it wasn't much of a leap to the notion his deal with Livingood gave him the means to inflict on the king some considerable hurt in pride and purse. Leaning against the pine, Hamby took thought, sucked on his pipe, breathed smoke out through his nose in two plumes. Since the Cherokee had divined the truth, he couldn't think of a good reason to deny it. Besides it was Livingood's money that was at hazard, and Hamby supposed he deserved to know. So by his silence he let Longrunner take his confirmation.

Longrunner eyed him mockingly. "You know who Webb Darling *is?*"

"Sure I know," Hamby said. "He the bogeyman. He the goddamn Klux, ride around all night in a mess of bedclothes wearing a pointy hat, scare all the niggers fit to shit." He grinned. "All the niggers but *me.*"

"You shame him, he lynch you."

"He *try.*"

"He got a whole pack about him, and every one a Kluxer." Longrunner stopped himself then, gave another shrug, unfolded the pinkish palm of one hand before him in dismissal. "It your ass, you want it hanging from a noose." Lowering the hand, he wrapped the mule's reins over it, unwrapped them, wrapped them again; gazing down, he watched what he did with such fixity it seemed he regarded the idle act as having a special consequence. "Livingood staked you," he went on. "He got to watch his interest." Longrunner lounged back against his own pine and rested there, seeming to sink deep in study of a topic that partly amused and partly vexed him. Beside him the mule now and then tested his grip on the reins with a twist of the head, as if contemplating mutiny even yet.

Hamby lifted his chin in inquiry. "Livingood know 'bout me and Darling?"

"He know," said Longrunner. Again he resumed his pondering.

Hamby sensed the Indian had more to say and waited on him to say it; from behind, Buttermilk nibbled at Hamby's shirt collar. Now it came to Hamby what it was he and Longrunner secretly agreed about. Neither man spoke much, but what little each did say was true. Both had set the same terms for living their lives; both believed the word they gave was good till blood flowed—their own, if need be. For whatever reasons—good or ill, wise or foolish—Livingood had the Indian's word and the Curtises had Hamby's. They were bound. Maybe Longrunner even wished to be free of Livingood just as Hamby yearned to leave the Curtises, but as long as they stayed in the same country with those they'd pledged themselves to, each would keep that bond, no matter how they might resent it. And that made them the same.

Now Longrunner glanced up and set his gaze squarely on Hamby's face. "Livingood," he said, "got his own grudgement with the king."

Hamby was intrigued. "How so?"

"Remember when Holden called out bushwhacker Kirk to get the Ku Klux?"

Hamby nodded. The Kirk-Holden War, they'd called it. Holden, the Reconstruction governor, had summoned a militia to beat back the Klan and gave command of it to George Kirk, an old Tory guerrilla chief despised in the mountains for his scavenging raids in wartime.

"Livingood, he Cyclops of a den back then," Longrunner continued. "Had a brother was a Night Hawk. Kirk's Lambs"—in derision and scorn, that's what folk had called them—"laid hands on this brother. Fellow never got right afterwards. Drooled and shat like a babe. Still does. Livingood, he go to the pen, quit the Ku Klux." Longrunner faintly smiled. "Ain't forgot the brother, though." Again he dropped his look to his hands and carefully considered the wrapping, unwrapping and rewrapping of the mule's reins. " 'Twas Darling done the beating."

It was more all at once than Hamby'd thought Longrunner had it in him to say in a week. But based on what he knew Hamby was puzzled; by repute Livingood wasn't the sort to let an offense so glaring pass by unrequited. "Why he ain't took the price of that brother out of Darling yet?"

Longrunner pushed away from his tree and straightened his hat. "Nobody but Livingood got an answer to that." He took his mule by the bridle and wrenched the head sharply; it popped its teeth at him, showing itself a mean mule after all. He put the toe of his boot in the stirrup and swung up. "My guess," he offered, gathering the reins, "the right time ain't come."

Hamby scowled. "In ten year?"

Longrunner turned the mule. "Livingood, he a patient man," he said over one shoulder. Then he walked the mule off through the woods toward the wagon road.

At the next fight, at Sandy's Branch a ways up the Tusquittee, Livingood himself attended, with Longrunner and Petrie the brother-in-law. Keenly Livingood watched as Pile-Driver finished off a Roundhead of Donald Youngblood's and a Claret that Cecil Dobbs pitted and as Buttermilk savaged a Butcher of Sonny Funderburk's. As before, Petrie sat and smoked a short-six. Longrunner stood apart, not even glancing Hamby's way. Now and then Livingood would absently touch a knuckle to his birthmark, as if it itched him. Around the place where he stood was a circle of emptiness no man dared enter; reverence or fear or contempt—who knew which?—kept them back. No more than Longrunner did Livingood pay Hamby any heed, except to send him one quick and slanted look in which Hamby thought he saw an approving glint, as of lordly dispensation.

A cold and mizzling rain was falling the day Captain Moore came for Andy Curtis. Mist shrouded the far hills and the course of the river, and tendrils of it drifted across the valley one by one like the veils of ghostly brides drawn toward a serial wedding of the dead. Each train of fog as it came closed off the distances with cottony white, then in going on opened them up again to show the drenched and lightless fields spread wide under a clabbered sky, the next skein of vapor advancing. The rain didn't so much fall as linger in the air, its droplets suspended, lightly blown, wetting your flesh and clothes, making you sodden, chilling the bone, conjuring from your coat a stink like the pelt of a drowned dog.

Hamby sat waiting on the top step under the lip of the first-floor gallery. He felt the cold atoms of rain dancing on his face. Before him in the turnaround glistening with rainwater stood the captain's Moline wagon with its team of white mare-mules in the traces patiently abiding the weather, manes and tails hanging lank as oily rags. Tom Carter's buggy stood yonder, as did the Prices' Studebaker. Thank God the Prices hadn't fetched along their gaggle of younguns to wear out everybody's nerves; Oliver had left them back in care of his step-son Jim. Ves his oldest—the fool—still lurked somewhere in hiding, lest he be cut down for the Revenue Dog everybody in the valley now knew him to be.

Hamby was tired; it was eight o'clock in the morning and he was tired, not from toil or sleeplessness but for a cause that had no name. No, that wasn't so. It had a name, all right—the same name that had been giving him fits of distraction going on nearly twenty years, the goddamn name of Curtis. He hawked up a gob of phlegm and spat.

Curtises. He was tired of nursemaiding Curtises while they failed and faltered on toward the end of their pitiful line. Once they'd ruled the country, basked in renown, enjoyed the esteem of all, possessed goods beyond measure, possessed even Hamby himself and several like him. Now, maybe *because* they'd kept others as slaves—maybe it was their punishment from God, as old Madison used to believe—they were down to the last of them. And what a shabby lot these two were, one headed for the lunatic asylum, and the other—if he was any judge of Miss Becky's cough—on the way to a sanatorium for consumptives or to the grave itself.

He'd known Andy Curtis all his life. And just like Jimmy Cartman, Andy was nearly kin, so Hamby reckoned he owed him a certain deference. Hamby was pledged to Andy, as he'd once been pledged to old Madison and Miz Sarah. Also Hamby had to concede that Andy in his right sense was a kindly soul and over the years had showed him nothing but respect, which was a good deal more than could be said for most whites. But he *was* white, wasn't he? And there wasn't a white in all Creation that didn't harbor a nigger-hate in him like a toad under a rock. So Hamby was scarcely grieving or full of pity; generally he thought the fewer white men able to do mischief in the world, the better. That applied even to the ones that might seem to act decent, as Andy had; underneath they were all the same.

He kept nodding off and then yanking himself back from slumber with a jerk of his head. He scrubbed a damp hand over his face. He couldn't think why he felt so slow. Inside, Andy was hollering, as he'd done more and more of late; he said his cancer was speaking out the unholy rages that would kill him. Together with Andy's screams Hamby heard Miss Becky sob, Captain Moore speak words of solace, Oliver Price's Miz Henslee croon, Oliver himself offer up a prayer, Tom Carter miserably say Miss Becky's name again and again like a chant.

In time the captain came to the door and called to him, and

although he felt a hot spurt of irritation like a match striking on his heart Hamby rose and turned and went in with him. The two Cartmans stood side by side in the dim hallway wearing identical black frock coats and holding their hats before them, as if posing for a likeness. They parted to let Hamby and the captain through; Hamby wondered what in hell good they were doing just standing there useless as a pair of crows roosting on a fence. The captain's boots and Hamby's brogans clumped hollowly on the floor. Andy's halloos echoed through the house; one in particular resonated in the brass of the hallway chandelier and made it faintly ring.

A long time ago Andy, eighteen years old to Hamby's seven, had taken him across the swinging bridge over the river to the Indian mound to show him how after a storm you could pick up the arrowheads and spear points of flint the old redskins had made. Hamby thought of that now—thought of a perfect arrowhead lying in the hollow of Andy's hand, each of its tiny scallops making a cup of hardedged light, a thousand such crisply glowing cups intricately arrayed along its point and edges and shank. Andy was on the settee wearing a traveling suit and greatcoat, his mouth shaped in an **O** as he howled. But when he saw Hamby he hushed and looked on with interest, as if Hamby were a stranger or maybe wore an outfit he thought peculiar. Then when Hamby stepped close Andy reached out and smacked him in the face with the flat of his hand. Hamby didn't flinch, though the blow smarted and made his eyes water; he just took Andy under one arm and lifted him up, as the captain did the same on the other side. "No," Andy said. Then again, "*No!*"

Hamby let him go and stood back frowning. With only the captain to hold him up Andy sank back sideways into the settee. He peered up at Hamby with what looked like hopefulness, or maybe appeal. But Hamby was mad and tired out. "You going to give me shit?" he cried. "Today? You gonna give me shit today? After twenty goddamn year of giving me shit, you gonna give me shit now, too?"

Miss Becky drew near and took Hamby by the arm, and he turned to her, and the sight of her balked some of his anger even before she begged him not to cuss and speak abuse. But enough of his rage still flamed to make his eyes bitterly swim.

Again Andy searched him with that expression of beseeching and expectancy. "I'm sorry," Andy explained. "It's not me, it's my insides. Why, *I'm* at peace. Take me to the library. I'll be all right." He smiled.

So they took him up again, and he neither struggled nor gave voice. With Andy lolling between them they started for the door; the others came behind. Hamby was vaguely aware of some moaning and crying, of another prayer from old Oliver, of Miss Becky grasping the tail of Andy's coat and hanging on as they came through the door onto the gallery. But what was in Hamby's mind was that arrowhead Andy had showed him years and years ago. Till that day Hamby had never thought about persons that used to live long back on the same ground he trod. Looking at that arrowhead made him see how he and a person much like himself living too far off in time to count nevertheless were linked. Bound. Bound as Hamby was bound to the Curtises. Bound by kin. Bound by the land, this land.

Andy was talking some sort of nonsense; his breath stank of tooth rot. Awkwardly they made their way across the gallery and down the steps into the misting rain, Miss Becky still clutching the tail of Andy's coat, Tom Carter trying to fetch her away. "Brother," Miss Becky said. "Brother." Then a fit of coughing took her, and she had to let Andy go. Tom peeled off his suit coat and held it over her while she shrank against his chest hacking and weeping. Hamby and the captain manhandled a murmuring and unresisting Andy into the wagon.

After that Hamby moved back away, stood a moment in the drizzle, then returned to the steps and sat, this time on the lowest step in the rain. His cheek stung where Andy had boxed him. He sat

rubbing the spot with the tips of his fingers. *Damn old white boy prob-*
ably been wanting to do that to me all my life. He made an exasperated face.
He wasn't any part of what had to happen now. He didn't want to
be. Dully he watched as the captain climbed to the box and sorted
the reins, as Miss Becky broke free of Tom Carter and mounted the
muddy hub of the wheel to hug Andy close, as Tom came to steady
her from below with both hands, his face buried sideways in the soiled
and sopping mass of her skirts; nobody remarked what would otherwise have been condemned as an indecent liberty. While Miss Becky
embraced him Andy looked confused but gave a wan smile and put
out his hand to touch the top of her head, even as he kept on with
his senseless mumbling; he didn't even hear when she asked him to
forgive her or when she said she loved him. Oliver Price helped Tom
ease her down; she stumbled away, bowed over coughing; Tom draped
his coat on her again and ushered her up the steps to the gallery,
where the Cartmans—what damn *use* were they?—stood with their
hats still before them; Miz Henslee took her in her arms. Old Oliver
stepped up on the hub then and gravely shook Andy by the hand.
Andy had ceased his maundering, but his face was blank as he
looked down at Oliver and then around at all of them. Then for
an instant his face came alive. He grinned, wigwagged a hand.
"Bye," he said. The captain clucked to the mules, and the wagon
turned in the cul-de-sac.

They all watched the Moline trundle steadily up the drive toward the road. Its tires crunched noisily in the gravel; now and then
they would squirt a pebble out to the side with a tiny flash of sparks.
Under Tom's arm and the makeshift hood of his coat Miss Becky
stood now stiff and puffy-eyed and tearful, so pale she appeared empty
of blood; she might've been Lot's wife turned to a pillar of salt for
gazing on Sodom's ruin. Her mouth was one tight pleat of feeling
bitten back. Hamby mused. In some ways he figured Andy'd been

father and husband to Miss Becky, as well as a brother of the flesh; he'd been everything there was. It was a good deal to lose all at once, and a good deal of pain to feel. Looking at Miss Becky, Hamby concluded he'd done what he came for and now it was time for him to go.

He stood, passed around the corner of the house and through the apple orchard and went quartering up the weedy slope, up and up through brambles that snatched at the legs of his trousers, till he gained the line of the fence that bordered the wagon road. He climbed over the fence just as the span of she-mules and the big Moline came rattling up. When he dropped down on the shoulder of the road the captain gave him a nod; Andy peered at him with a puzzled air. Hamby let the plodding mules and the wagon pass, then, walking behind, unlatched the tailgate, dropped it with a crash, swung himself up and turned and sat on it with his legs hanging down.

He sat there awhile jouncing, soaked by the mist, watching the road unwind behind him, watching the Curtis house finally slide out of sight back of the rain-shiny laurel thickets. He rode along backwards, saying nothing. Nor did Andy or the captain speak to him, though from time to time Andy would turn his head and look keenly back at him through the yoke of the hood. Hamby had never been so tired. Now and then he curled his fists and scrubbed his eyes with them like a drowsy child.

Presently they came to his place, and he dropped off and stood in the yard and watched them go on. When they passed around the bend and he could see them no longer, he went inside and stripped off his wet clothes and laid himself down on his cot and fell fast asleep.

CHAPTER 12

November-December 1881

*V*es Price laid up the better part of a month in the old two-room log house Captain Moore and Miss Hattie had stayed in the first year they came up the Tusquittee to live. The place stood by the Jack Holler close behind the barn, not a hundred paces from the back of the fine two-story gabled mansion Irish Bill had built once he got prosperous and where, Ves coarsely imagined, he now lolled in unjustifiable luxury while his vast herds of sheep and hogs—two hundred head of each, Ves had learned—multiplied themselves into even greater numbers, thus adding criminally to his already enormous wealth, all without need of even his least supervision. Hell, the old man got richer every minute just sitting on his front gallery beating on his goddamn drum. Why, the third day Ves hid out there, he was awakened by the sound of many small bells ringing in the distance. He got curious and arose from his pallet and peeped out the front window of the cabin to see Irish Bill's whole drove of hogs coming down the road all by themselves, each one wearing its bell of tin; they'd been up in the woods on Fires Creek all summer feasting on acorns and chestnuts, but the first frost had stung them up there, and so the goddamn things had started home on their own hook. Here they came in one big bunch, waddling and grunting, bells going *tinktinktink,* looking shortsightedly this way and that from under their long blond lashes, their big ears a-flop. All the captain had to do was watch them go by. It was like they'd come down to be in time for the butchering; Ves half expected to see them cut their own damn throats and save old Moore the trouble.

Not that Ves wasn't grateful. He was. Shit, if it hadn't been for the captain, Ves would surely be worm feed by now. The old jasper had tended his bruises, sent word to his pap that he was safe, looked out for his every want. But even so, Ves's gratitude didn't carry all that far, for the captain professed to be a Christian—maybe even *was* one—so in harboring Ves in time of trouble Irish Bill was only doing as the Scriptures exhorted him. Doing it let him approve of himself and feel satisfied.

This was a trait of Christians Ves had often relied on when in a scrape, especially so in the case of his stupid pap, who'd give over his last meal if he was starving and you came to him looking pitiful, believing Jesus required it of him. *Charity* was a word Ves had heard but whose true meaning eluded him; to him it was a quality one sometimes fortuitously found in others which was to be taken advantage of. So yes, he thanked the captain. But he also knew the captain did what he did so as to believe himself Christlike, not because he wanted to save Ves Price—a rogue and a wretch in his eyes—from the vengeance of the blockaders.

Irish Bill had put the cabin up with his own hands in his younger years, right after the war. He'd laid a good firm rock foundation, hewed and split the wall logs, fit them at the corners with a hogpen notch, chinked them with red clay and then roofed the whole affair on laths of oak he'd chopped by hand. That was a good roof, shingled and boarded, lapped halfway. The place hadn't been used in years, save for a storehouse—one room of it was cluttered with old window frames, singletrees, kingbolts, plowshares, hoe handles, rusty scythe blades, broken harnesses, every kind of castoff miscellany—yet the roof hadn't sprung the first leak, and the cabin itself remained as tight and snug as the day Irish Bill finished it. It had a rock chimney and a fireplace, and although it was running with mice on account of the fall chill Ves slept cozy-warm.

By day he had a view past the mansion across the bosomy hillocks of the valley and the fields of young winter wheat, off toward the mountains, whose low domes—spiked now with the delicate gray-and-black quilling of the leafless trees—seemed slightly to tilt to the west. He supposed it was a pretty scene, but after the first week he grew sick of it.

It wasn't long till he got weary of his benefactor, too. For a time Ves was spared old Moore's attentions, for the captain was absent carrying loony Andy Curtis off to the crazy house. During this time Miss Hattie fetched Ves his eats. Ves supposed many would think of Miss Hattie as some kind of a goddamn angel just because she'd come from quality folk in Henderson County and in linking up with Irish Bill had married beneath herself and then gone off with him into the wilderness to bear him ten live younguns and several dead ones and toil herself near to death, all without a complaint. But hell, that was what a woman was *for*. Ves didn't think anybody ought to expect credit for doing what was natural—though he did make an exception in his own case, when it came to the work commonly accorded to a man.

Anyway he found Miss Hattie annoying. Continually she displayed what he reckoned some would call a sweet smile, though behind it, he was sure, she was secretly judging him, weighing him up, finding him wanting. She gave him the excessive courtesy he recognized from times past as an unfailing sign of the contempt and loathing the high-born always felt for the low-down, but thought they were concealing. The eats were good, though. He dined on smoked venison, deer and hog ham, mutton, pork loin, fried chicken, trout breaded in cornmeal, yams, peas, leatherbritches beans, sweet corn—all the abundance of Irish Bill's wide and fertile domain.

Still he was glad when the captain returned from Raleigh—glad at first, that is. For by then he was altogether fed up with Miss Hattie's pretense of caring for a fellow she obviously wouldn't have deigned to spit on, had she met him on a public road back in her glory days in grand old Henderson. Even if the captain had meddlesome ways and was infected with a degree of sanctimony, at least he spoke what he thought right out, spared no feelings, wasn't above expressing a vulgarity or two—was a *man*, for God's sake. He wasn't a posing smiler like Miss Hattie, keeping back her worst and deepest feelings; he didn't conceive himself higher than anyone.

In fact the captain came of the same kind of low stock Ves himself did, which was several cuts toward the bottom of the scale from where Miss Hattie's people ranked. By Ves's lights the lower end was the preferred one, where folk put on no airs. So if he was going to be tormented by the virtuous Ves wanted Irish Bill to do it, and not his woman. Consequently when he heard old Moore's wagon pull into the barn late one afternoon in November he was gratified to think he was done at last with Miss Hattie's sham goodwill.

Pretty soon, though, Irish Bill started to wear on him, too. The evening of that same day he returned from taking Andy to the madhouse, he came up to the cabin and engaged Ves in a conversation Ves found dreary and dispiriting. "Here's a case," old Moore said, speaking of Andy Curtis, "where you can see what a hard business living is. It's got no pity in it—life, I mean. A fine strapping fellow, forty-two years of age, in his prime, accomplished, churchly, beloved of God, wealthy, respected far and wide—and nearly overnight Providence touches him in his mind, renders him an idiot and an invalid, degrades him, ruins his good name, smashes him down, wrecks his family. Extinguishes his line."

Lordy, thought Ves. *Who in hell cares?* It was Andy that was the lunatic, not Ves or the captain. Ves figured that if a man wanted to feel sorry for somebody, he ought to feel sorry for himself—and thank his lucky stars that disaster had fallen on another and not on him. But Ves made noises of concurrence as old Moore droned on; there was no profit in provoking him and maybe getting thrown out for Webb Darling to find.

"Adversity," the captain was saying, "adversity's not something that comes on us from time to time. No, it's what life *is*. There can't be the one without the other. And for most of us it's how we bear adversity that counts, that proves what we're made of. We either show grace or"—here he slanted a significant look at Ves—"we whine and blame others and commence to scheme out plots to get our own way the next time."

As soon as the captain glanced aside again Ves crimped up his mouth and rolled his eyes in exasperation. Not even back a whole day and old Moore was already in the pulpit.

"But when your wits go you've got no means of drawing on your spirit," said Irish Bill. "You can't show your faith or your dignity or be brave. You can't rise above it. You're just a brute. You befoul yourself. Demean yourself. Them that used to admire and love you, they turn away revolted. You're a dishonor to yourself and everybody around you. And there's no remedy. No remedy beyond shutting you away. Caging you like the beast you've come to be, through no fault of your own."

Ves made a small blowing noise and waited impatiently for old Moore to finish. He wasn't sure where the captain was heading, but if he meant to argue that Ves ought to be grateful he hadn't gone mad like Andy, instead of only falling afoul of the king and so far surviving it, then Ves was ready to agree in hopes of quickly bringing an end to the lecture.

But the captain came out at a different place than Ves expected. "So when we've got our sense and can decide how to be," he mused, "*what* we decide is the measure of us, tells whether we're any account or not. Poor Andy can't decide that kind of question anymore. What was human in him, what was Godly in him, what gave him the power to decide, why, it's gone. He's lost to us. He's gone to be with the beasts." He sat a spell gazing into the fire on the hearth, then raised his head and fixed a steady eye on Ves and said, "But you and me, we've got the will yet. *We* can decide."

Another time he got to talking about Miss Hattie when he wed her. She was well raised and hadn't ever known work, and then he brought her over the mountains and up what was then the howling waste of the Tusquittee to keep house in a log shack with but two windows in it, to cook, to birth a host of younguns, to bury some, to nurse their ills, to learn them their letters, to make their clothes, to knit their mittens and mufflers, to tell them about God and the Devil. Because of being so fine she had tender hands, and the washboard raised up blisters on them, and the blisters would bust, and she'd bleed as she washed, and the wash water would turn red. "I like to died of shame," exclaimed Irish Bill, "when I saw that bloody wash water. Here was this girl used to naught but coddling and refinement, and working her hands to the bone. It was on my head. I felt it heavy on me. I'd have understood if she hated me. But she didn't. She loved me. Loves me still, right to this very day."

He shook his head in reverent wonder at the goodness of his

saintly wife. Listening all unwilling, Ves surmised that the captain wished him to draw from this account a lesson about the rewards of fidelity and hard work, but instead he regarded it all as one great mound of shit. He believed if everything the captain told was true, Miss Hattie was the one at fault. She should've married herself a city swell and lived high, according to her custom, instead of picking old Moore and suffering such rude ways as he offered. Maybe the captain figured she was a saint; Ves thought she was just a fool.

Another evening old Moore told about the time he was captured by bushwhackers—roughriders, he called them—after he'd come back from the war. A gang of them was pillaging through the country and robbed his place while he was away from home. They stole his gold watch and his best saddle horse but fortunately didn't harm Miss Hattie. When he learned of his loss he got on another mount and coursed after them days and days, till he ran on them someplace down in Georgia one blackberry-winter day in May. They took him prisoner and held him there a week. "I argued I was a poor farmer," old Moore explained, "a veteran of the Cause—for the most part they'd been Confederate in the Struggle. Said I'd been ruined by the war, had a wife and younguns to feed. Those were some hard old boys. Vagabonds, murderers, every man's hand against them, nothing to lose. But when I told 'em my story it softened their hearts. Made 'em think of home, I reckon—their own mas and pas. They gave me back my horse and saddle and sent me on my way." Wistfully the captain smiled. "Kept that watch, though."

Ves frowned and wondered what edifying principle he was supposed to parse out from this.

Naturally the captain didn't leave him long in ignorance. "Perseverance," he declared. "If a man will only persevere, nine times out of ten he'll prevail."

Perseverance, yes. Ves subscribed to the notion. While he restively endured the captain's homilies he was studying in secret how best to accomplish the two enterprises now nearest his heart; he aimed to persevere at both. He wanted to lay up in ambush back of some downed tree with his old Springfield muzzleloader and shoot that son of a bitch Tuck Richbourg in the brainpan for whaling on him so that day on Pot Rock Bald and for keeping back his lawful pay and bounty. But even before he essayed that, it was his plan to pay a visit over to Downings Creek, for he was suffering in his loins and dreaming of the moist pleated place a women kept down below, and so he meant to slip away safe from the captain's one of these first nights and go sneaking over to the Shuford place and lend sweet Katie his trouser serpent to play with.

Ves left out of the captain's one crisp night under a waning moon. Old Moore and his kin had been slaughtering and dressing hogs since before sunup that day and had gone to bed early, so nobody suspected Ves had slipped off; he'd never done it before for fear of the king, so it didn't figure he ever would. He was counting on that; it was part of his program; he was using his shrewd head. Going out, he crept past the big hole full of water they'd dug in the ground by the pens and heated with hot rocks to dip the fresh-killed hogs in; fouled now and scummed with hog bristles, the pond as it cooled gave off a stench of cooked hair and scalded pigskin. The ground underfoot was muddy with pigs' blood, and it stunk, too. The fire they'd used to heat the rocks still smoldered, and the tart smell of it hung in the air; a gauzy haze of its smoke lay over everything. Dangling from a pole with sticks run behind their hamstrings were the carcasses themselves, headless and gutted, glowing like old silver; the pale light that came through the bare branches of the trees marbled the silver of them with delicate lines of black.

He hurried through the front gate and set off down the Tusquittee breathing quick and shallow with excitement, glad of the moonlight, which was just bright enough to show him the way. The night sky was clear, and the glittery band of the Milky Way ran overhead like a river of gems. Left and right of him, the walls of the valley were touched with a faint tinny glow. His breath blew white before him; deliciously he shivered in his woollen shirt. He was tickled to get out of the cramped cabin at last, to free himself awhile in the outdoors, to elude Irish Bill's moralizing and go rummaging in the raptures of the flesh before sneaking back to the captain's well before daylight. He saw no risk in the plan. People didn't go abroad much by night; few would spy him or know him if they did, because he'd dodge into the shadows if he saw somebody coming; the king would get no report of him.

As he walked in the rutted road Ves suddenly cringed at the notion of the king. Against his will he remembered that bitter day on Pot Rock Bald, something he'd been trying hard never again to do. Now, unbidden, here it was after all, his degradation. Stumbling up the steep path, blinded by that burlap hood, Richbourg hauling on his arm, screaming in his ear. The gunfire. The nasty whiz of bullets. The fellow that went over the edge. The blows, the gluey taste of blood in his mouth. Him trying to explain—" 'Tain't my fault"; "They changed everything around"; "They got more men this time"; "That wall's raised up higher'n when I was here"—and all the time Richbourg hitting him licks. *Goddamn.* Devoutly Ves wished that day had never dawned, or if it had that he'd never been a part of it, or if he'd been a part of it that his part would've been valiant and not craven. Mostly he just tried to think it hadn't transpired at all. Maybe when he wound up Tuck Richbourg with his Springfield deer-shooter it would all be wiped away at last. He surely hoped so.

Presently he was able to push the whole sour business off by dwelling on the charms Katie Shuford would soon allow him to plunder at his will. Engaged in these agreeable supposings he made his way down to the mouth of Downings Creek, crossed on the footbridge where the moonlit water ran under him like a wrinkled ribbon and in another quarter-hour of brisk walking approached the Shuford place. The gate he knew so well stood open; for an instant he thought Katie might've somehow, improbably, guessed he was coming and left the gate ajar in welcome. Smiling at the thought, he passed through into the grove of maple and ash that shielded the house from the road. His heart was pounding; already his peter had grown hard.

At the edge of the grove he stopped and peeped about to see what was what. His nose told him the Shufords had been butchering hogs this day, too. As he squinted he made out the big cast-iron tub next to the barn where they'd done the scalding. Old Shuford was about as rich as Captain Moore and could afford such a costly article, whereas the miserly Moore preferred to dig a hole in the ground for free; Ves snorted in contempt. Before the black mouth of the barn the hog carcasses hung in a row from a log rack like executed criminals left out as an example. The house stood silent, its rough shingles aglow with moonlight. The barn, the privy, the smokehouse were still, too. Not a light showed.

Stepping out of the grove, he moved quickly across the yard and crossed behind the house. As he did so the Shufords' old black-and-tan bitch emerged from the hole in the foundation where she always slept and came to him whimpering and wagging her tail. She approved of him when most everybody else didn't, and for this he'd always felt grateful. He crouched now to pet her, and eagerly she licked his hands, and then he gave her the two pieces of hog liver he'd fetched along to keep her occupied. Greedily she set to feasting.

Leaving her, Ves went and stood under Katie's second-story window. He picked up several pebbles and threw them against the panes in the old way. But he got no response. Puzzled, he turned and crossed to the privy and pecked lightly on the door. Again only stillness answered him. He opened the privy door and looked in to make sure, but it was empty, its two holes staring up at him like a pair of eyes gone enormous with disbelief to see him there. He shut the privy door and decided—he couldn't say why—to inspect the barn. From where he stood the barn was as dark as a bear's insides, so it was doubtful anybody lurked there. But he still held his fancy that perhaps Katie expected him and was lying in there on the straw with her legs apart, hoping he'd arrive any minute. He hurried past the rack of smelly carcasses and into the maw of the barn. "Katie?" he whispered.

To his infinite delight there was a rustle of straw nearby, almost at his feet. He heard a gasp of surprise. It was Katie's voice; he knew it, knew how it rang when she felt horny. Ves grinned to think she'd known he was coming and had lain down to await him, as in his fantasy. His member got tight as an ax handle as he turned to his left, where he'd heard her. He spoke her name again. But even as he called her he smelt the wet musk of love rising up out of the dark and stood confused. Then to his amazement a male voice suddenly burst out, "You goddamn son of a bitch."

Ves was in the act of frowning in surprise—he knew that voice, too, but couldn't place it; he wondered why the fellow was even here, what he was doing with Katie and she with him—when, as Ves now dimly perceived, his old pard Jared Nutbush, his britches down around his ankles, snatched the big Colt's revolver he'd laid by when he and Katie commenced their sweet business in the straw and jumped up and whomped Ves on the skull with it. Ves dropped like a stone, laying his head between Katie's moist thighs, as he'd so long dreamt but was unable now to revel in.

When Ves recovered his senses it was daylight and he was straddling a mule bareback with his arms wrapped around the mule's neck and his hands bound under its throat with plowline. His head was sore; his clothes were crusted with blood; he felt a little sick to his stomach. His mule was plodding up a mountain path and in front of it was Jared Nutbush on another mule leading Ves's mule by a rope. Ves's mule had a spine like the blade of a butcher knife and was making him fear for the welfare of his manly parts, till he remembered the whole of him was in even more danger yet. He was inclined to presume on the old friendship in hopes of evading what he hardly dared suspect might be his fate; he would even forgive Nut for screwing Katie Shuford. "Nut?" he weakly called.

Nutbush drew rein, turned his mule in the path, gazed scornfully at Ves. "We was pards, remember?" he said. "From the time we was shirttail younguns." He'd been chewing a wad of hickory bark; now he spat it out as if the sight of Ves had turned it bad. "I put you in the business," he complained, "set you up to make good money. Then on account of you being dumber'n a damn rock you pour the slops where any fool atall can see 'em, and Ree and me get picked up by the Revenue, spend a year in the goddamn pen."

Ves tried to look directly at Nut his former chum, which required him to bend his head awkwardly back and rest his chin in the coarse hairs of the mule's mane and strive to see past its long ears. It wasn't easy, but it seemed necessary if he was to appeal somehow to their old connection. "Nut, wait," he pleaded, "wait just a minute . . ."

But Nut wasn't finished yet. There was a catalog to recite. "My mama passed away while I was locked up, you know that?" Ves shook his head and did indeed feel sad, but mostly on his own account. "Then," Nut kept on, "you got the damn gall to turn Dog and give up all the best blockaders in the country, friends and neighbors of yours and your pa's, folk you've known all your goddamn life, that never done nothing but treat you good."

Nut was mad as hell, Ves could see; Nut was a pal no more; Nut was a servant of the king; this Nut—this grim new wrought-up Nut—was a figure not of mercy whom he could implore but of retribution to be dreaded. Nut had gold-brown eyes, usually mild like a setter's, but just now they were snapping with a lethal fire. Ves shuddered. "Where we going?" he somehow found the voice to ask, though he suspected—feared—he knew the answer already.

Nut confirmed the calamitous surmise. "You know where we going," he said. "We going to see the king."

CHAPTER 13

December 1881

*P*hthisis, Dr. Killian said it was. No doubt he used the medical term in the hope it would scare Rebecca less than would consumption, the more common name. But Rebecca was beyond scaring. She sat eerily composed while the doctor spoke; she even felt borne up a little by an implausible, almost hopeful expectancy, as if she found the news not unwelcome, even heartening. She was certainly not surprised. For weeks now she'd known a vile and alien thing was in her; she thought of it as a great loathsome worm wrapping its coils around her lungs; she'd even named it that, The Worm. Of course now that she knew for sure what it portended, she felt a little regret. But while the news that she would very likely pass before her time did not actually please her, it did have about it a sense of comfort, of benison, of balm, which promised to answer the ache she had for rest.

Tom, too, had watched her shrink and weaken, had even reluctantly suspected the worst. Now, as the doctor talked on, the anguish that Rebecca would not allow herself to feel turned in his vitals like a giant screw twisting tight, and although he did not cry out his dismay, a scream ran through his mind like a cold wire drawn suddenly taut. To imagine and even prepare for a calamity was one thing; to face it head-on, to see it for what it was—implacable, irresistible, terribly indifferent—was another altogether. Tom's powers were insufficient for such a test. He could not flatter or cajole the disease as he might a neighbor who bore him ill, or ingratiate himself with it as he hoped he'd done with Rebecca, or propitiate it with some offering of piety as he'd yielded up in his prayers to God of late. Tom was powerless, was stricken; Tom wept.

Later as they rode home in his buggy Rebecca spoke the words they both knew she must. "If I'm a dead duck"—sickness hadn't unbarbed her style of talk—"we got no business marrying, you and me. You heard him. I'll last three, four years at the most."

"But he also said it might go into arrest," Tom hastened to remind her. "If that happens, why, there's no telling how long it would be. Years and years, maybe."

Scornfully Rebecca smiled. "The Curtis luck don't run in that direction anymore, Friend Tom." There was a bleak amusement in the remark, but resignation, too; one could scorn one's fate but not avert it. Truly fortune had turned its face away. The once esteemed and flourishing clan had gone to rot, was ending in the shame of lunacy and consumption. All the luck they had now was bad.

"It makes no difference," Tom insisted. He looked more resolute than she'd ever seen him; his mouth pinched his face in a flat line like a new-healed cut from a razor. "I want to get on with the marrying."

Rebecca scoffed. "You want to marry a lunger? You want to have me around so weak I can't even cook your supper or clean house or see to the younguns? I suppose you'll desire me when I'm greasy and stinking from the fever and the night sweats. I reckon you'll want to clasp me to your bosom while I'm a-coughing up gore all over you. When I blow my bad wind in your face so's you can taste the foulness I got in me." It wasn't proper to speak of such private matters to a man, even to your bespoken, but Rebecca no longer cared; she could talk how she liked now; she was discovering that The Worm of death could give freedoms which life could not.

But Tom had found an anchor in a sea of despair, and he clung fast to it. He nodded, declared, "The sickness will be arrested."

"You're a hopeful cuss," Rebecca dryly remarked. What a dunce he was! Before The Worm he and the aggravations he caused her and all else, too, was diminished. Already she felt a shade drawn between herself and the living world. Already Tom was a stranger simply because he could go on and she could not. She thought of Hamby and the Cartmans and the Prices, and they were all apart from her now, behind that shade. Around her the valley and the mountains and the vault of sky over them all retreated there also. Life was withdrawing; The Worm was coming on. Only Brother was on the drear side with her.

When they got to the farm she bade Tom go along to his own place. She needed time to herself, she told him, to think how she felt; truly she knew this already but made out she didn't, so as to get free of him.

Everything came clear to her now. Creation bristled; spirit was made flesh; notions wrote themselves in the sky like script. She was so much wiser than Tom now that she was dying. She knew things he'd never understand. He embraced the belief that the consumption would abate and spare her to be his wife and the mother of his children, but she understood that even if it did for a time, one day it would come back. It always did. It would come back and finish her off. Why marry, then, and bear young, when in time she must inevitably and all too soon leave behind the family she'd started to make—a lovelorn widower, motherless orphans, all lost and full of woe?

Wrapped in a shawl against the chill of the gray day, she walked down past the barn and then by the smithy, hearing the musical ring of Hamby's hammer at the anvil inside—he was fashioning mule shoes with the help of Jimmy Cartman—and so around a fence corner of the south pasture, where Nephew Andy was fitting in the new locust rails he'd split. He knew nothing of The Worm, knew only that she'd been poorly; she'd said naught to either of the brothers. Nephew Andy straightened, solemnly hailed her, returned earnestly to work. She went on down the lane and came at last to the bank of the river.

It had been raining in the mountains, and the river was running full. Behind the shade drawn between herself and the life of the world, the plaits and braids and winding cords of cocoa-colored water went coursing by intermixed with sharp-edged wavelets and up-bursting spouts that marked where the currents clashed, each swirl and coil wearing a froth of creamy white. Around the few rocks still visible above the flood she saw curved bits of brown spray such as the bow of a fast-moving boat makes. Near the far bank an old oak had fallen in, and its crooked and mossy branches reached up from the moving surface like the supplicating hand of an old man in the act of drowning. The river uttered a soft rumble and smelt like old iron. It was a good smell. She breathed deeply of it.

She sat herself down on the grave under a contorted antique of a weeping willow whose bare tendrils drooped so low that the river dragged at some of them, making them continually sag and lift, sag and lift, as though they wanted to plunge in but at the last moment changed their mind and pulled quickly back. Papa had dug the grave a long time ago, in the war; a Yankee bushwhacker was in it, a boy Papa used to know who'd gone bad and got hanged by the Home Guard. She sat on the bushwhacker's grave watching the river roll, the dead keeping with the dead. Across the way the ranges in Georgia were all beclouded, wreathed with fog except for the nearest, whose summit stood forth like a low pyramid. It was slate-colored with winter but for a small spot on a flank where the clouds opened and let down one wafer of gold light. Against the gray the gold looked warm, and she thought if she could get to it, it might have healing in it. She gazed at it as long as it lasted, till the clouds closed again and snuffed it out.

Presently she sighed and stood and turned to make her way back up. Nephew Jimmy had joined his brother at the fence; as she passed they waved; she waved and went on. At the smithy she stopped. Hamby's hammer still rang at the anvil. A wind had come up from the west, and it was bitter cold, and as it whipped around the corner of the smithy Rebecca shivered and drew the shawl tighter. Yet now she could count it a privilege even to feel the bite of a winter wind; even that was a part of what must soon fade away. Again she shook with chill. She stepped into the searing mouth of the smithy.

In a cloud of ascending sparks Hamby stood over the glowing forge, lifting out with tongs a partly finished shoe that burned whitish red. In the firelight of the forge he was bare of chest under the straps of the scorched leather apron. His arms and shoulders were covered with a shiny oil of sweat. He wore his raggedy-brimmed straw hat, which it was his pride never to remove. His muscles flexed as he turned, laid the shoe on the anvil, struck it a time or two with the hammer, then, grasping it again with the tongs, plunged it with a steaming hiss into the dirty water of the slack tub. As he moved she saw above the bib of the apron the ugly dark pucker of the bullet wound in his chest he'd got so long ago, when he'd taken the Curtises' part against the scalawag that tried to kill them. She remembered hearing the shot, a little girl lying frightened in her bed while dangers circled outside like wolves.

Till now Hamby had given her no notice, probably thinking she'd just come in idly to watch him work, as she sometimes did. They had always shared long silences, unspeaking companionships, and were content in doing so. But now when he took the smoking shoe out of the tub and stood holding it with the tongs, he looked at her with his light eyes and read her face. Then he set the shoe in the coals of the forge and laid by the tongs and stood waiting with his big hands hanging by his sides.

She told him. There was no change in his expression, nor in any part of him; someone who didn't know him as Rebecca did would have thought her tidings concerned a person he'd never known in all his life. He waited there motionless in the crimson wash of the forge coals that deepened his normal hue of copper to tarnished brass.

When she finished he waited another moment, then nodded and said, "I figured it already." He looked at her a good while afterward—ten or twenty seconds, she guessed—but said no more and made no motion. Then presently she nodded back, and he fetched up the tongs and retrieved the shoe from the forge. She stepped out again into the blustery cold. Behind her in the smithy his hammer resumed its clanging.

Rebecca swore Tom to silence. The last thing she wanted was for old Mrs. Hemphill and her ilk to come flocking all a-cluck with pretended sympathy, when in fact their purpose was eagerly to observe every aspect of her decline for evidence or absence of Christian fortitude, upon which they would then critically remark among themselves. Rebecca did not intend to become fare for the gossip of busybodies, as Brother had. But as she might have foreseen, Tom couldn't keep from telling Miz Henslee. And when Rebecca saw the Prices' Studebaker coming down the drive with Miz Henslee on the box cussing the mules like a bullwhacker, she didn't blame Tom, was actually glad he'd tattled.

Rebecca hadn't passed her the word herself because like a wounded old bear she only wanted to lick her hurts and not seek solace from others, especially from Miz Henslee, who had plenty of woes of her own, including the mystery of Mr. Price's rascally boy Ves, whom no one had seen since he vanished on Pot Rock Bald and whom some feared was lying dead in the woods by the hand of the Tusquittee blockaders—as he rightly deserved, Rebecca thought. The one person Rebecca had told was the one she felt needed telling. Hamby had kept them going all these months as Brother's wits dimmed and Rebecca fell more and more sickly; it was Hamby who knew what to do when the worst befell, so he needed notice in order to get ready for the day. That wasn't the whole reason she'd told him, but it was a good part of it.

On the gallery Miz Henslee captured Rebecca in a hug and held her close, enveloping her in the soothing scent of cool earth and damp rocks, of the breath of caves, that was always about her. Miz Henslee kissed her on both cheeks, patted and stroked her back with a consoling touch as Rebecca cried.

Inside, Rebecca made tea, and they sat sipping it and quietly talking as the winter day waned and its pale light slanted through the parlor windows. Presently Rebecca offered up for the first time in words the worry that had commenced to plague her in recent days: "I can't help feeling it's a punishment for what I done to Brother."

"Punishment?" Miz Henslee echoed, but in disbelief. She set aside her teacup and saucer and leaned at Rebecca and colored even ruddier than normal. "From who?" she demanded. "From God?"

Rebecca shrugged. She was a doubter; she knew better. But there it was, the blot of sin. "I expect so," she admitted. For a long time she had not practiced the religion that had sustained Papa in time of trouble. Mama had lost her faith when the war took two of her boys, and after that Rebecca had hewed to Mama's line and not Papa's. But the irony was, once you had the teachings of the Word in you, often there was no escaping them afterward, even if you tried most of your life to forget. And a great part of the teachings had to do with recompense for evil. Rebecca suspected it might have been a sin to put Brother Andy away. Maybe she'd done it not for his own good at all but just so she could find some ease in a grinding life. Maybe instead of wanting to spare him dishonor she'd been selfish and willful and was only tired of the drudgery and humiliation of dealing with him. If so, and if God did live and the teachings were true, God would have to chastise her for it. One of the teachings floated into her consciousness now. "He marks the sparrow's fall," she said.

Miz Henslee snorted. "Maybe He marks it, but He don't go hunting for whatever kilt it to pay it back, I don't think. I reckon God's got bigger things to do than go tracking after every single mortal person in the whole world, checking to see is he's fit or unfit, keeping book like a store clerk on folk that are trying to deal with the hardships of living, doing the best they can, deciding according to their best lights. Why, a God that would do that, what good would He be? We got relatives and neighbors right here on earth to do that for us."

Faintly Rebecca smiled, thinking of Mrs. Hemphill. "What is He then?"

"Well, I don't know that any more'n you do. But I'll tell you what my guess is. My guess is, He's the one holding it together—all the world and the stars, I mean. He can't let go either. He's got to hold on. 'Cause if He lets go it'll all fly apart, and that'll be the end of the whole outfit. So you see it takes all He's got just to hold on. He ain't got the time—and probably not the inclination either—to go snooping hither and yon weighing out penalties one by one for what missteps we humans make. I reckon to Him we're like a mess of ants all a-hurrying around, and He don't pay no more heed to any one of us than we do to a single ant in a hill. He knows we're there, I expect, but that's all."

Still the thought of Brother Andy stung her. Again her tears started, and she dabbed at her eyes with a soggy handkerchief. "But I feel it so—the fault."

"Sure you do," Miz Henslee vigorously nodded. "But it's the preachers done that to you. God never did. What's a preacher but a man a-yelling? Telling about how God hears every soiling notion that comes in your head and charges each one against you, to be read out before you at the Heavenly gates, so's you can be cast into Hell." Miz Henslee pulled a wry face. "If that's so, then I reckon Hell's fuller of preachers than anybody else."

Rebecca couldn't help but laugh, which eased by a jot the blame that was gnawing away at her. Then she pondered Tom. "But I can't be marrying now," she remarked, not sadly, but actually thinking of it as a burden she'd been dreading that she wouldn't have to bear now after all. Not till this moment did she realize how much she disliked the prospect of joining with Tom Carter in wedlock. To say a marriage was no longer possible was another of the unexpected freedoms The Worm had conferred.

Miz Henslee drained her cup and set it aside in its saucer. The gentle sarcasm that had made them laugh before was gone now; she set on Rebecca a flat and somber regard; the hazel eyes that usually smiled had gone gravely dark. "Awhile back we talked on this," she said. "A year or more ago. You weren't puny then. Nobody'd said you must stare death in the face. You were just fagged out with cares and trials. And you said the same thing to me then that you're saying now. And I'm telling you back just what I told you then. You got to marry Mr. Carter."

Bitterly Rebecca burst out, "He'd be taking a corpse for a bride." Then it seemed to her that she should be entirely truthful. Pushing aside the false argument she'd just made, she added harshly, "I don't *want* to marry him. The sickness apart, I don't want to spend my last days—however many they might be—with a man so mulish and dull-headed I can't bear him more'n an hour or two at the time."

Miz Henslee leaned at her. "You said that before, too. But what's *wanting* got to do with anything? Do you reckon any of us *wants* what comes down on us? Precious little we get is welcome. Most of it's bad and cruel. The cruelest trouble of all is coming down on you. D'you actually think you can stand it all by yourself? D'you think it'll be neat and tidy and easy? D'you think you can just take to your bed and pass off a-dreaming?" She sat back, shaking her head in pity. "No, ma'am. It'll be a great deal harder than that, I can promise you. I seen a person or two die of what you got."

Miz Henslee bit her lip, as if she almost repented the coarseness of what she'd said. But then she drew a breath to summon up the power to risk doing injury, so as to make Rebecca glimpse what lay before her. She scowled. "One I seen perish so was Mr. Price's first wife Nancy. She went hard, I can tell you. And even though I was by her 'twasn't enough to give her comfort, for Mr. Price was away. He was up here helping your brother fend off the scalawags. Only got back in time to see her go. How she suffered! Smothering to death from the water rising in her lungs." Rebecca cringed, burst into tears anew. "How he could've eased her way!"

Seeing her cry, Miz Henslee softened her tone a little and reached out a hand to touch Rebecca's. "And here's a good and decent man that loves you past all reason, wanting to help you through the tribulation, and able to." Removing the hand, she sat back sorrowfully smiling. "He may not be no fairy-tale prince, but he's strong and tender of heart, and he's up to nursing you through what's coming. You may not want him, but you sure as shootin' *need* him."

A small dose of self-pity passed through Rebecca; deathly ill and dogged by guilty suspicions, now she must sit in the parlor of her own home and be frightened by accounts of the agony to come and roughly rebuked for her waste of spirit.

Miz Henslee saw her pain but even then didn't let up. "Besides," she continued, "you got more grit to you than this. Why, you speak as if you're ready to crawl in the coffin and pull the lid over on yourself. You don't know if your time's short or long"—clearly Tom had been arguing to her that the consumption would arrest—"but however long you've got, you have to live it. Live it full-up."

Now Miz Henslee's temper lightened; her voice took on its customary tone of compassion. "You don't need me to tell you this neither," she said with a pointed look.

Rebecca saw Miz Henslee was right, knew it was in herself to push on no matter what, no matter how The Worm might squirm and eat her vitals, even if the strength she needed to push on seemed far away now and hard to tap.

"You know how much you love life," Miz Henslee said.

Rebecca nodded, began to sob. Yes, she had loved it, but lately she'd been afraid to love it because of knowing she must lose it. She'd even *wanted* to lose it.

Now Miz Henslee finished up by saying with tears welling in her own eyes, "Right now you're feeling low. But you'll come back from that. You'll see you don't even *have* a choice. You'll come back from losing heart, and you'll take Mr. Carter for your husband, and you'll live whatever amount of life is left to you. The life you'll have will be good. Maybe in living it you and Mr. Carter'll even bring some more life into the world. And then even when you do go you'll be leaving back a life or two to take the place of yours. Then who knows what good the ones you leave behind might do with what you gave them?"

When she was strong enough she would walk the place sometimes, softly weeping in a mood of melancholy farewell. The shade separating her from the world had dissolved by now; everything had come clear again. She looked closely about, as if to brand in memory the images she saw, so as to carry them away with her when it was time. The graceful hemlock at the top of the lane tapering to a point, wearing successive skirts of shapely boughs that got smaller and shorter going up, each one a delicate frond of millions of tiny needles. The fine grain in the split lengths of poplar at the woodpile, heartwood the color of chocolate, the rest a soft yellow that looked so inviting you wanted to sink your teeth in it. The sere stubble of winter grass in the yard, covered each morning with a white rime of frost till it resembled masses of tiny spears held up by soldiers too minute to see. The lines of mountains shading off from indigo to powder-blue to a gray as faint as a dream. The woven balls of dormant mistletoe clustered in the tops of Spanish oaks stripped of leaves. Little doilies of ice on the panes of the window in the winter kitchen. The sky, the clouds. Fog. The way the chimney smoke leveled out in long streamers that ran up the valley like the white pennons of phantom crusaders, through which the morning sun, an old medallion, sometimes dimly glowed blood-red. The scalloped pattern of the molded tin shingles on the roof of the house, overlaid in rows, the silver paint beginning to flake and wear off, mottled now with rust. The house itself. Papa's house.

She remembered once asking herself if a house was a dead thing or a live one. She knew the answer now. Papa's house was alive. He was in it, Mama was in it, they were all in it—herself when young, her brothers cut off by war, her sisters dead and living, their younguns quick and dead, Brother Andy before his madness, Mr. Price a pixilated young man in his butternut uniform as yet uncrippled, Miz Henslee, the Cartmans both young and grown, Hamby impudent as a boy and impudent still, brave old Daniel McFee. All of them were there. They'd be there as long as the house stood. Wistfully, ironically, she smiled; just now the house was more alive than she was. And after she was gone, she knew, it would keep dear a wisp of her that would never leave. And that wisp would mix with the ghosts of the others so they could all commune together in a mystery like the smoke.

⤶

The next time Tom came to visit she eyed him curiously, for he seemed somehow changed. Whatever had happened was very slight but had altered everything about him, as if he stood in a new kind of light that fell on him alone. He looked oddly crisp and fresh; his face made her think of a new-minted coin; his blue eyes gleamed; the two wings of his honey-colored hair swept back from his brow in bountiful curves, each silky strand separately aglow. As always he was as anxious to please as a spaniel that might piddle on the rug with joy if you showed it a kindness. But behind that she began to discern—as day after day he came and sat with her quietly, patiently, undemandingly—how serenely he bore himself. And over time she came to know a thing that had escaped her entirely till now—that the serenity had always been there without her noticing. Then finally she started to understand Tom hadn't changed at all; Tom was just as he'd always been. It was she who'd changed.

Whatever of her had been surly, impatient, fretful, whatever had found fault with him, whatever had scorned or condemned him—all that melted away. She couldn't say why this happened, except to recall that much had seemed different to her in these last weeks with her own death hovering close. However her new sight had come, it let her grasp how settled Tom was in himself, how he knew his own powers and had such confidence in them he needn't boast or brag like others, but could instead stand modestly by and say awkward or silly things or even abase himself to her—play the panting spaniel—without any sacrifice of what she couldn't help thinking of now as the strength that was the core of him.

Because he adored her and unlike many a country man let it guilelessly show, because he was sparse of word and slow of deed, she'd mistaken him for a dullard, when in fact he was a man of parts a good deal beyond the ordinary. She sensed the decency in him, the gentleness, the charity, the long-suffering nature that had withstood her tart tongue and borne her nagging; a good and simple-hearted man was Thomas Carter. She could never love him, but she could see a way to begin to respect him. And wasn't that enough? A woman shouldn't want all—Miz Henslee had taught her that. Instead a woman ought to seek only what was enough. And if she got what was enough she'd be lucky, for most never fetched even as much as that. So on the cusp between dying and living Rebecca resolved at last to commence a new part of life even in the face of her death. She told Tom she'd marry him.

Rebecca was a woman of few illusions. She knew she'd be cut off early. The grim knowledge colored all she thought and did. But inside her, too, was a buoyant hopeful maiden she couldn't control who all of a sudden commenced to dream of marrying, of mothering, of a long full life. At first she tried to suppress the hope she knew to be vain. But in the end it proved too robust, too driven by the force of life; she couldn't hold it down. In spite of herself she wanted it, wanted it too badly to throttle it. Soon in spite of everything it filled her up. And against her will she found herself in love with the life she'd almost looked forward to losing not long before, and which now would end when she was no longer ready. That was hard, she thought—to give up the wish for life and then get it back, only to die untimely, regretful and repining, just as its riches came.

They celebrated a modest Christmas Eve—Rebecca, Tom, the Cartman boys. Tom put up a fir tree in the parlor, and they trimmed it with strings of popcorn and with many small candles in tin holders and with ribbons of gold and red. Jimmy Cartman fashioned a Star of Bethlehem out of foil wrapped around a five-pointed piece of cardboard, and they put it on the peak of the tree and then stood about in a half-circle looking up at it and holding hands and singing the old songs of the Nativity. Outside in the yard Hamby, more than a little drunk, was filling the knotholes of trees with gunpowder and setting them off with lucifer matches. The pops and cracks of the small explosions, the fizzles followed by his fervent swearing when the powder failed to ignite—these punctuated their singing. They exchanged a few simple gifts—for each Cartman a pair of suitably identical store-bought stockings, for Tom a monogrammed hickory shirt that Rebecca had made and the cravat she'd bought for Brother in Asheville that Andy'd never had the chance to wear. There was no use wasting that, she'd thought in a fit of practicality. With a fierce blush Tom slipped on to Rebecca's finger a tiny silver ring wrought to resemble a wreath of twisted ivy, to solemnize their betrothal.

They sang some more, and Tom prayed. Tom thanked God for all His blessings, and for once Rebecca didn't flinch her disapproval; she thought perhaps there were blessings to be counted indeed. During the prayer Hamby's fireworks in the yard died down; he'd set in to do some serious drinking, which Jimmy Cartman would be sure to deplore on the morrow. Awhile longer the little band of them sat talking in the parlor. Then about midnight Rebecca bade Tom goodnight, and he gave her a warm buss on the cheek and went out to the buggy and drove off into the night, and soon the brothers drowsily arose to undertake the mule ride back to Grandma Cartman's.

When she was finally alone Rebecca donned her afghan and took up a package and went out to the gallery. Hamby sat on the top step drinking now and again from his flask. He reeked of whiskey and of the grime in his old coat. She came and sat by him, and together they gazed companionably out across the Hiwassee bottom before them, milky in the light of a moon just past full. They sat like that awhile, saying nothing, not stirring except when Hamby stole a dram, watching into the moonlit distance. Then in time she gave him the package. He opened it. It was a sweater she'd knitted. He nodded, studied it in silence, laid it aside in its bed of tissue, then fished in his pocket and passed to her a small article that rolled loosely in the cup of her hand. She held it up to the wan light, saw what seemed to be a human figure no larger than a walnut carved in wood. It had wings. "That a angel," Hamby said. "Maybe fly you up."

CHAPTER 14

December 1881–January 1882

*W*as it not the right and duty of a king to go a-progress through the realm meting out high justice? It might be true that the region on the north scarp of the Valley River range, where the two clans of blockaders were contending, wasn't strictly a part of Webb Darling's domain. But neither had any other king ever laid claim to it, not even the fabled and now-vanished Bill Berong. In fact no monarch at all reigned along the big ridge called Buckhorn, where the aptly named Vengeance took its head and where the Greybeard and then the Pruett and then a dozen other little brooks and branches joined its plunge into the yellow fields streaked with woods of dark green like verdigris on tarnished brass, thence to the little swift-running river dividing the flat that had always been the best way east through the gap to the Nantahala country and beyond.

Darling had long coveted control of that land of lofty steeps and many springs and fast brooks and high wet coves that looked across to the Snowbirds, at whose foot the bright line of river meandered, giving off a grainy shimmer like a slurry of ground-up mica set loose to make its sparkly way along. Unevenly the river lazed; it wove and unwove; here it fetched the forest close; there it pushed it far off; it went on always easterly in long loops twinkling and shiny; it rounded the small orange-and-brown scab that was the hamlet of Valleytown; it dwindled after that to a flat curl like a thin shaving of iron whose nicked-metal glint the hills around Rhodo and Topton soon shut off.

Blockaders aplenty were stilling in that wilderness, who no doubt counted it a privilege to have cooked brush liquor for generations free of any tribute to a king. But the fuss between the Crosslands and the Broadfoots on the upper Vengeance showed the risks to be run for such freedom as the Valley River moonshiners enjoyed. Without any sovereign to whom all were obliged, none could appeal for justice to a greater power. So when disputes arose, arguments of equity had no place, and force ruled. A consequence—inevitable, in Darling's view—was that a Broadfoot had shot and crippled a Crossland for trying to preempt a stream near where Broadfoots had been making dew since before the Cherokee Removal.

"One of the first duties of a king," Darling instructed the younguns before he left, "is to be a judge, so the people can get a fair deal. You might suppose being king is just being the boss and doing whatever you like, bulldozing folk, trampling 'em down, taxing 'em, making off with their goods and crops. And yes, there've been some kings of that sort in days gone by. But those were bad and selfish kings, and sooner or later the people grew tired of their misrule and cast 'em off." He smiled. "The best kind of king is one that looks out for his people. And the way to do that is to give 'em fair justice."

He reached out fondly to pat the nearest of several towheads arranged in a half-circle about him, and even though the child drew slightly back, still he managed to touch a fringe of hair with the ends of his fingers. "When you hear about a king, you might think because he's the boss the people have to show him loyalty, just for fear of the power he has over 'em. But that ain't the right of it. No, sir. The king's got to show loyalty to the people first, by giving 'em justice. Then they'll give him their loyalty back. But they only do it in return for his. If he don't give it they won't. So you see, the king and the people both got a duty, one to the other."

He meant it, too. He kept close his notion of stewardship. Often he held sentimental thoughts of the folk he owed protection. They were the meek and lowly of the earth, borne down by hardships, who only wished to sweeten the bitterness of life a little by the ancient expedient of making and selling whiskey, as their forefathers had always done—an act honored by time and custom but which a government of strangers in faraway places had now declared illicit, according to no logic a man could understand or condone. It moved Darling to think of his afflicted subjects; sometimes his throat would grow full with sympathy and his eyes blur with tears of pity for their plight. Extending his sway over the Valley River country was as much for the benefit of the poor unfortunate ones striving there—unsupervised, mired in unmediated conflict, abused by the Revenue—as it was for Darling's own.

But he was also sufficiently at ease with his ambitions to admit that he wanted the Valley River country not just for the sake of its people but also to feed his own hunger for power over men. After all, no king worthy of the name was without such a hunger; it was what drove a king, much as the fire at the heart of a steam engine gives out the power to rotate the blades of a timber saw; it was an indispensable trait of royalty; you couldn't have one without the other. Still he was capable of being amused on occasion by the elevated motives he sometimes arrogated to himself, even in the secrecy of his own heart. It was as if he thought some other self in him—some solemn arbiter—even yet needed to be convinced his deeds were beneficent and not born of greed only. He supposed that, too, was a trait of royalty—the ability to delude one's own conscience about the reasons one did what one did.

He took Ree Bolt and the brother—those two only. Too great a show of force, he'd decided, would smack of uncertainty and a want of confidence. Better to arrive with only the Melungeon and the brother—the one so black and grim he might've been a devil forged in Hell and vomited forth for the purpose of doing evil in the world, the other a rangy slow-moving cuss bearing his well-worn Winchester across his knees as he rode along bareback, shaking his one rein of plowline like some raggedy-assed sharecropper, but of whose several killings, done with a speed that belied his languid ways, even the men along Vengeance Creek must've heard by now. Darling took those two, and of course he brought the majesty of his own self. It was all he'd need.

From Fort Darling they followed an old game trail north and west over the flanks of the Tusquittees and by the place where Fires Creek rose. The spring at the stream's head in its bower of now-leafless yellow birch wore a fantastic crown of ice, an inverted chandelier formed of clusters of little shiny bulbs and globes and frozen teardrops, through whose transparent lenses you could see the cold black water within if you bent close. From there they headed west across the snow-whitened spine of Wolf Ridge and over the head of the Rockhouse, unseen below in its thicket of laurel, whose massed leaves were now tightly furled from winter cold. Big Peachtree Bald stood on their right, but they were too near to glimpse its peak, which would anyhow be obscured by mist and cloud; instead they saw only the outcrop of its foot slope, its turrets and towers of gray rock stained with the apricot and rust-red of unnamed minerals and crookedly seamed with frost. The sky was the hue of old lead. It blew a sparse snow sometimes interspersed with pellets of sleet into their faces.

When they crossed the last of the Valley River tops toward Buckhorn Ridge, they were in snow knee-deep to their mounts, and the low growth all about them stood silently encased in glittering rime as fine as cut crystal, each twig and barb and stem and stalk and balsam needle a separate feature of ice, delicate beyond belief. Soon though a wind of searing cold came up. It roiled the already fallen snow, whipped it at them in bone-numbing swirls; it shattered the frozen peace of the woods with a noise like the smashing of a warehouse full of crockery. The gossamer sheathing broke, and they were deluged with shards of ice that stung like a blizzard of sewing needles.

It was hard going, but there was no help for it. Winter was the season for moonshining, and the grudges of Broadfoots and Crosslands would be festering afresh. It couldn't hurt Darling's case to show the Valley River boys he had the sand to cross the two ranges even in the worst of weather, so as to render the justice they needed; a king of conscience, of accountability, of dedication, could do no less. At the brink of the last ridge a shroud of chill mist parted and rose like a curtain in a theater, revealing below the slender valley of pied green and tan, the wayward seam of river winding brightly through it. Rising on the north, the white Snowbirds wore bare black trees that made them resemble a family of snowbound porcupines, quills bristling. Darling stopped his mule and sat awhile feasting his eyes. It was good to be the king.

Once off the tops they had an easier time. Descending the nose of the ridge, they encountered fog and light rain but much more clement air. Having slept out two nights coming, they rode into Valleytown somewhat muddied and besmirched but also looking agreeably fit and possibly dangerous—a salutary impression, Darling thought. By prearrangement he met his informant—Moonlight was what he was called—at the dramshop the fellow owned on the east side of the village. Moonlight had once blockaded for Darling but had moved to the Valley River country because his wife, a native of that place, wanted to live near her sick mama on Beaver Creek.

Affably they drank, thawing the cold that lingered in their joints. They spoke; they laughed. Plans were soon laid. There had been no question of the parties at odds calling on the law; blockaders made it a point of honor to keep their quarrels close. As one of them Darling commanded the respect an officer couldn't. Already Moonlight had secured from the Crosslands and the Broadfoots alike the same binding pledge to abide by whatever judgment the king might hand down. If a shooting war could be avoided, it must be. Every man in the highlands knew how a feud could run wild, what cruelties it could inflict even on the innocent. So tomorrow Darling would meet in Moonlight's tobacco barn with the aggrieved factions. He would hear their arguments. Then, like Solomon of old in the fullness of his power and wisdom, he would give them judgment, and they would have to bow the knee to him.

"But I ain't just judging," he assured Moonlight before draining his schooner of lager beer. "If I'm to hold this place I'll have to enforce the judgment myself." It was his duty and his right; it was the crown of thorns he must wear. He bore not only the glory of kingship but its pain as well. A king needed to fetch to himself the burden of his choices; he must be brave; he must be bold; his blood must move in him as dense and slow as syrup that the winter cold has made stiff.

❧

"I was looking for a place to set up my still-house," old man Crossland explained from his seat on a hogshead turned on its side in the middle of the floor of the old log barn. "I always like to find me a stream going west off a north-facing hill. So I got up on the ridge by this creek feeding into the Vengeance and found me a good little spot."

Outside, a storm of wind had come up and was blowing puffs of snow in through the imperfect chinking of red clay between the wall logs; now and then the whole barn would sway and groan and ease its timbers as the gusts came and passed. The woods gave forth a low rattling murmur that sometimes coarsened to a roar and then to a thunder of clashing boughs whose twigs scraped and clattered at the roof shakes, sounding like some big critter trying to get in with its claws. The barn was full of men standing or sitting or hunkering on their hams, Broadfoots on one side and Crosslands on the other, Darling and Ree Bolt and the brother in between; their breath smoked in the chill, waxing and waning. The air was heavy with the smell of their bodies and their grimy clothes and also with the sweet lingering scent of the tobacco that had recently hung in the barn to cure.

"There was this laurel thicket in the ravine there," Crossland went on, "and some ash saplings a-growing on both sides that a-body could pull over and tie together with withes for a shebang and cover up with evergreen. The next holler over on the east was a wet cove, too, and I had me some two-inch iron piping, so I was a-figuring I might send my smoke over there by way of this pipe and let hit out in that other branch and hide hit."

He had a long line of mouth with a pouch of fat underneath it like a frog's, and now the corners of that mouth formed an upside-down **U** of scorn for the pretensions of the Broadfoots, while the underslung pouch commenced to throb in indignation. "I never thought nobody could claim the whole of a creek and all hits branches from hits head to hits mouth," he sourly declared. Sitting on the barrel, he shifted his bandaged hand conspicuously into view. "Wasn't no other still nowhere close about the place I was a-favoring."

He nodded, as if in agreement with himself. "I knowed where them Broadfoots was. Everybody did." Looking sideways from under his eyebrows, he sent a censorious glance to the half-dozen Broadfoots arrayed nearby. "But they was lower down," he growled. "They had a good run of water, and a log shack there a-hiding the still. They burnt their smoke. They looked mighty well set up to me. And if I went to stilling on that branch of the Vengeance that I liked way up above 'em, why I reckon they wouldn't of hardly knowed I was up there atall. Hit wouldn't harm them none. They'd still have plenty of water."

The head man of the Broadfoots made a show of leaning to one side and dropping a contemptuous line of spit to the ground. Darling was leaning against one of the stanchions of the loft. When Broadfoot spat he revolved his head a fraction of an inch toward him and caught his hard black eye and held it till the man finally stirred and looked away. Then, shoving himself off from the stanchion, Webb began walking slowly up and down the floor of packed dirt before old man Crossland, rubbing his chin in thought. All the Broadfoots watched for some sign of his inclination, but he knew they could discern none. The Crosslands watched him, too; some were nodding to corroborate the old man's account. The bursts of wind outside rattled the shutters, and the twigs scratched at the roof. "So when you moved into the Valley River country from up on the Watauga," Darling mused, "nobody told you the whole of the Vengeance belonged to the Broadfoots?"

Vigorously old man Crossland wagged his head in denial. "They tolt me the Broadfoots had just the stretch of the creek they was a-stilling on. Nobody ever said they owned the whole caboodle, ridge top to mouth and all that drained into hit. I never heard of such a thing when I was in the Watauga country. Why, if a feller can claim a whole goddamn stream, hit's the same as one of these what-you-call monopolies. Ain't hit?"

Darling allowed himself a thin smile but returned no answer. He bade the fellow go on.

"Well," Crossland resumed, "I was just a-poking around there, seeing what I could see. Come on this fair-sized hole in the ground. Looked kindly like a old dropped-in tunnel, like maybe a long time ago there'd been the shaft of a mine down in there somewheres. You always hear about Injun gold, you know. So I got curious. Said to myself, 'Let me look in this hole.' So I knelt down there, a-propping myself agin a deadfall poplar with this here hand"—he brandished the damaged member—"and was just a-craning to look in when, crack-whiz, somebody up and shot me."

Next the chief of the Broadfoots took his place on the hogshead. His rusty beard was cut straight across and lay flat on his chest like a scraggly bib; it had a streak of white growing down the middle. He was lean and sinewy and had a large goiter under his jaw that poked out from the edge of the beard like the head of an infant somehow installed there to peer covertly forth. "My old granddaddy was the first white man to ever come into this country," he declared in an adenoidal whine. "There was a camp of Injuns lived at the top of Vengeance then, and he took his old flintlock rifle-gun and went up there one day and showed 'em how he could shoot the knots out of a pine board, and after that he never had the least trouble with 'em. Sometimes two or three'd come down to his place and eat out of his hominy barrel and set down with him and go to talking. But pretty soon they moved off, and one of 'em—the top one, I reckon—come and tolt my old granddaddy the whole creek was hisn, that they were giving it over to him."

Compliantly Darling nodded, then asked in seeming innocence, "This was all Cherokee land then, wasn't it?"

"There wasn't any white man's government anywhere around, if that's what you mean," Broadfoot smugly replied. He was proud of the pluck of his ancestor, alone in a rude and alien place, unafraid of the savages, making his life anew in a wilderness far from the soft ways of civilization. Briefly and almost lovingly he touched the goiter, as if it were a talisman of that time and owned the power to draw to him the hardy spirit of the patriarch he admired.

Webb had been pacing to and fro, but now he stopped in front of Broadfoot and stood with his arms crossed and his hands cupping his elbows. While he stood gazing another burst of wind smote the barn, and they all heard the place quake and squeal, and then they heard the dry crackle of some of the shakes tearing loose. Oblivious, Darling inclined his head; his face took on what he meant them to infer was a thoughtful expression. "So your forebears didn't get a legal deed then," he said, speaking the words with such careful deliberation it seemed each was occurring to him only on the spur of the moment. "On account of there wasn't any authority to get it from." Then he grinned, and it had an edge like a honed knife. "Your old granddaddy was on the land illegal."

Confused now, Broadfoot squinted; his black eyes shifted, darted toward his fellows, came back, stared no more at Darling's countenance but at the buttons on his shirt instead. He folded his mouth into a little pucker like the bunghole of a cat. "Him and a bunch of others," he conceded. But then in extenuation he burst out in his nasal honk, "That's how this section was settled up, you know. They was all pioneers." Even in the cold of the barn his forehead had begun to show a moist patina of sweat.

Darling smiled down on him with such tenderness it could've been—likely *was*—mistaken for a sign of impending mercy, despite the admission Broadfoot had just made. "When they *did* set up government here, after the Indians left, did your old granddaddy—or anybody else in your family—then go down to the courthouse or to the agents of the state in charge of selling Indian lands and *buy* the whole of Vengeance Creek legal, and file papers on the transaction?"

Broadfoot squirmed on the barrel. Darkly he colored. "No, hit was ourn already," he truculently insisted, "for the Injuns give it." But for all his doggedness he still didn't—or maybe couldn't—meet Webb Darling eye to eye; he put his look there on Darling's chest, and it wasn't about to move; maybe he thought by not seeing Webb he wouldn't hear him either. Again he touched his goiter, but this time with an air almost of entreaty. With the hairy back of a hand he wiped droplets of sweat from his brow and flung them impatiently aside.

Darling changed his mood again, and to the men in the room he seemed even more wistful, sympathetic, suffused with regret; now it looked like he felt a kind of despairing love for the errant Broadfoot, like he pitied him and rued the necessity of vexing him further. With a forefinger he pointed to Crossland. "Mr. Broadfoot, did you shoot this old man here when he was looking for a place to put up a still on a branch of the Vengeance?"

Broadfoot took the ends of his beard in both fists and pulled down two or three times, as though testing to see whether the whole mass were still attached. He frowned. "I done that," he admitted after a second or two of thought. Then he hastened to extenuate: "I got the right, though. I can shoot me a trespasser. *Any* man can protect his land and goods from a trespasser." He made a vague gesture of dismissal. "Warn't nothing noways. I no more'n struck him in the hand. I'm a good shot, too. I hit what I aim at. Meant to sting him some, scare him off. Had no wish to kill him."

Darling nodded, stood back a pace or two, rounded on old man Crossland standing by. "Are you a right-handed man, sir?" he inquired in a mild voice.

"Was," Crossland said, gesturing with his lump of bandage. Then he shrugged, and his froglike mouth gave a wry twist. "Reckon I'm a lefty now, though."

Darling turned back to Broadfoot. "And you, sir. Are you a right-handed man?"

A deep stillness settled over the crowd in the barn. In the silence the howl of the wind seemed to come louder than ever, even though in actual fact the storm was waning; one set of twigs insistently scrabbled at the roof still. In a corner a rat shuffled in a heap of old tobacco stalks. Now at last Broadfoot raised his eyes and looked Darling full in the face. "I am," he said with a slight shiver in his voice. "What of it?"

Webb examined him not unkindly. "Did you freely give your consent to abide by whatever judgment I make here today?"

Broadfoot stood. He was a head taller than Darling—could glare down on him from a height that might otherwise have been commanding—but just now that advantage did nothing for him. He was tall, but in that moment he also commenced to wither to a frail and spindly vestige of himself, to lose all recourse; he was drawing up like a hank of wet buckskin drying on a stob; he shrunk before their eyes; even his goiter hid in his beard. He shrugged. "I did."

Darling smiled in the manner of a schoolmaster whose worst scholar has just offered up a right answer, against the odds. "Did all the men in your party give the same consent?"

"They did."

Webb nodded, leaned to one side, hawked and spat in a parody of Broadfoot's earlier act of disrespect; the small gob of his spit struck the floor and lay there delicately foaming in the velvety brown dust. Sweating, Broadfoot watched him. "Mr. Broadfoot," Darling said, staring calmly up into the black eyes that for all their towering height now wore the empty, flat, unlit gaze of a shot deer, "you don't own the Vengeance. Your pappy didn't own it, nor his pappy before him. Nor the Indians before that. And Mr. Crossland here don't own it either. You know why?"

Dumbly Broadfoot shook his head.

Darling stepped so close that the end of his nose almost touched the tangled pelt of Broadfoot's beard. "Because *I* own it," he said. "I own it, and I say who uses what part of it. And here's my ruling in this case. The Broadfoots get to use the part of the creek they're on, and the Crosslands get to use the part they want. Any man acts otherwise, I'll kill." He vented a small laugh that might've been congenial but that it never reached his china-blue eyes. He moved back, swept the room with a lordly look. "Agreed?"

After an instant's hesitation a ripple of confirming comment circled through the crowd. Darling waved a hand in acknowledgment, then dropped it in a chopping motion toward the center of the room. "Clear me a space there now," he said. The four men standing behind the barrel parted, two one way and two the other. From inside his coat appeared Webb's Richards-conversion Colt's six-shooter. "Now Mr. Broadfoot," he said, cocking the pistol with a sharp double snick of metal, "I want you to spread out that right hand of yours on that hogshead there, so's I can execute the sentence, which is that you must lose the use of it, just as you've deprived Mr. Crossland of the use of his. That's justice. That's the balance in the world that must be restored, which you disturbed by your unlawful act. Creation demands a balance, you see. And I'm the one to set the scales a-right."

Obediently Broadfoot bent, laid his hand palm-down on the side of the barrel. He shook only a little. Just then Darling felt a surge of affection for him—poor fool that he was, gone wrong due to overweening pride, who now must pay the cost of his bluster and folly. Webb came close, pressed the muzzle of the Colt's down vertically against the top of the hand. He saw the freckles and liver spots on the back of it, the curled hairs, the blue tracery of its veins. He pulled the trigger.

❦

Having so easily annexed the Valley River country, Webb Darling was in a mood to reward himself for his initiative. So instead of returning across the mountains to Pot Rock Bald after finishing his business with the Crosslands and Broadfoots, he decided to amble on up the valley to the town of Murphy—less than a day's easy ride from Moonlight's—and fetch up there in Ramseur's Long Hotel, his favorite haunt, for the jollification he thought he'd earned. At Ramseur's he'd eat fine food, drink good wine, steep in the hot baths he loved and slumber in a soft bed between crisp sheets, savoring his dreams of omnipotence.

He took the brother with him. Ree Bolt he sent back over the hills to Fort Darling, confident as always that as Ree traveled he would speak of Webb's destination, and so the word would spread from mouth to mouth throughout the kingdom faster than any telegraph; by this means, perfected by long habit, every man in the domain always knew the king's whereabouts within a few hours of his arrival or departure.

So it was that the morning of the day after Darling settled into his rooms at Ramseur's, Jared Nutbush came knocking on his door to say he'd captured the vile Revenue Dog Ves Price and shut him up in the fort to await Webb's pleasure.

CHAPTER 15

January 1882

*V*es was in such a fix he wanted to offer up a prayer for deliverance, even if calling on the Most High did mean he'd be as bad a hypocrite as Holy Tom Carter or Jesus Jimmy Cartman. He didn't relish being counted in that despised company. And furthermore he recognized—thanks to the moral instruction he'd got, in spite of himself, when young—that after a lifetime of unbelief it was a mighty low thing to ask Divine help just because your ass was all of a sudden in deadly peril. But it was pretty clear to him he wasn't going to last any longer than a June bug in a gang of puddle-ducks once Webb Darling got back to Pot Rock Bald, so he figured if God was going to take pity on anybody, why, He'd have to search right far to find a fellow in worse need than Ves Price.

So it was worth trying. The problem was, he couldn't think how to go about it right. He couldn't get started. He'd invoke the name of the Deity. "Lordy," he'd say. "Oh Lordy." But then he couldn't get much farther along than just saying that, and he figured if he couldn't do any better than just lying there in the corner muttering the title of the Almighty, he wasn't likely to attract much Heavenly attention. Yet try as he might he could summon up no single word of fit entreaty. His brain was scrambled and dull, the way it had felt when he came up to Fort Darling to scout it out for that son of a bitch Tuck Richbourg. His mind wouldn't grasp anything; it kept circling and looping and wandering around, till he was dizzy from its conniptions.

So for whatever good it would do, and for lack of any better plan, he set in to just repeatedly mentioning the Holy Name. Curled up in his damp corner, folding both hands over his crotch, Ves uttered his doubtful incantation—"Lordy, Lordy, Lordy, Lordy, Oh Lordy"—and hoped against his own expectation that some big angel with wings a-whip would come and bust the bolt of that big oak door and bear him off to safety. Of course this gave him pause to think how after he got miraculously delivered he'd be obliged to act pious for the rest of his days by way of thanks. He didn't think he could do that, but neither did he want to share his reservations with the Lord, lest the knowledge turn Jehovah—known to be a harsh judge—against Ves's case. First things first; Ves would wait till he was sprung before he made up his mind whether to give himself over to virtue afterwards.

In addition to beseeching the aid of the Heavenly Father, Ves tried to think how he might propitiate the king when he came in to murder him. After all, he'd heard it said the Lord helped them that helped themselves. And up to now he'd had better luck—not a great deal, to be sure, but some—relying on his own shenanigans, rather than waiting on any angel. It was true Ves had told on all those Tusquittee blockaders and got them arrested. But on the other hand he'd led—in a way—the raid on Fort Darling that had got a deputy killed with none dead or even hurt on the king's side. Ves wondered if he couldn't somehow parlay that to his advantage, maybe arguing it was thanks to him the king had licked the Revenue that time.

But after studying the option awhile Ves concluded it wasn't likely the king would see himself indebted to him in that fashion. It was more probable he'd just take off Ves's head as he'd done with Lige Dollar. Ves shuddered, cupped his groin, drew up his legs, formed himself into a tight ball in his corner. He reckoned he was finished if that angel didn't turn up. Yet even amid his fear he felt a flare of annoyance at how unfair life had been to him; it distressed him to think how often he'd laid careful plans to get hold of gain, only to come out at the small end of the horn time and time again. Wasn't it worthy in a man to want to improve his lot? Why then was Ves's every effort to raise himself up foredoomed? He was as good as anybody else; he was as smart as a great many who'd had far better luck. It was like he had a mark set on him from above, like Cain in the olden time. When he thought of this Ves had to wonder if he wasn't wasting his time beseeching a God that had already cursed him with a mark of shame. For a time he stopped his Lordying on account of the pique this notion aroused. But as time passed he grew more and more afraid, and in his despair he resumed his litany in hopes of convincing God to regard him charitably as a poor repentant sinner and not vengefully as a man He'd marked for past acts of dishonor.

Ves lost track of how long he'd been shut away. He and Nut had got to Fort Darling the afternoon of the day the king left for the Valley River country. Five days ago? Six? Maybe even seven. The first day or so Ves hardly took notice, due to the throbbing of the place on his head where Nut had hit him with that great big six-shooter. But he did know, from listening at the door, that Darling's people had sent the king word of his capture. In the meantime Ves reckoned he was pretty safe. Nobody at the fort was going to touch a hair of his head till Darling came back and claimed the right and evil bliss that was his, of dealing out by his own hand whatever grisly fate he thought Ves had earned.

In consequence, other than being locked up in a dank and drafty little cubbyhole made of stone slabs and having but a single slit of a window too high up to reach, Ves was being treated right decent. They fed him the same rough fare they ate, gave him a flimsy blanket, left him a candle and lucifers, laid him a fire in the little fireplace of an evening. But none would speak to him or address him in any manner. Silently they came and went, sometimes darting narrow looks but never setting a gaze square on him. They acted either like he were some beast too loathsome to look at or like he'd taken the form of a piece of furniture. Yet if they were reticent they were also careful to make him comfortable. And that reminded him, as much as anything did, that they were fattening him up like a veal calf in a pen, awaiting the slaughterer's knife.

A little bat hung upside down from the top of Ves's window. Ves guessed it was sleeping through the winter, for it seldom moved except once a day, when it would slowly turn itself right side up to squeeze out a tiny ball of dung and a single thread of pee, then rotate upside down again and hang as before. Ves didn't know if it went out at night to feed; if so it left and returned while he slept, for every morning when he awoke there it was dangling in the same place. Sometimes in the middle of the night he'd hear a rustle and a flutter up there; he reckoned it was the bat departing or arriving, but he couldn't be sure. Maybe it was just cleaning itself.

At first Ves mistrusted the bat, for he'd heard they sucked your blood by night. The first few mornings when he got up he touched his fingers to his neck to feel whether the bat had been at him in the dark. But he found no wounds, and pretty soon he gave up the notion of its being a bloodsucker. After that he got right fond of the bat. It made him content to see it always hanging there, as if it had decided on its own to take up with him. He thought its little ears were cute, the way they stuck up. Before long he was talking to it and telling it his troubles.

In his conversations with the bat Ves began to reflect on the ones he'd miss once he was dead. Of course the first was Becky Curtis. By now he couldn't recollect her as she actually was, but only as a splendid being, hardly even human, he conjured out of his heartsickness. No more did he coarsely imagine the joys of the flesh he might've pillaged, had she given them up to him. It was true that even now when he thought of her he saw the fullness of her hair, which he'd never touched but had long imagined felt as smooth as new grass, hair whose light brown hue caught beams of sunlight in flashes of gold that made her whole head sparkle like a sun itself. He spoke of her plump mouth, her tiny nose with its nostrils as delicate as a bird's, her honey-colored eyes—all her charms he'd never in life get to pet and hold dear. But now she glowed chastely like a saint; he dwelt on her bodily beauties not in vulgar terms but as the proof her soul was as perfect as her form. It was adoration he felt. For him Becky was like the Madonna he'd heard the Catholics worshiped. Now she was far above his own sullying touch.

To the bat he explained how she'd finally shipped idiot Andy off to the asylum and got engaged to Tom Carter, the bastard. Of course by the time Ves learned this it hardly mattered anymore; he'd long since yielded up any claim on Becky beyond just the yearning he knew would never be fulfilled. Yet the ache of her kept on in his vitals. And the one comfort he'd known—that he and she were in the world together at the same time, so he could see her now and then, even if only from afar—would be lost when Webb Darling arrived and sawed off his head. And the pity was, if Hell did exist, then Ves was pretty damn sure he was destined for it, and he knew for absolute certain there'd be not even a wisp of Becky Curtis down there in the Bad Place to ease his eternal torment.

Another time he was surprised to tell the bat that some of the folk he'd miss most by dying were the very ones that used to aggravate him worst in life. Old Irish Bill Moore, prattling on about how a man's fortune wasn't what he wanted but what he had. Telling Ves all those dumb stories about self-reliance and hard work and how they made for strong character. Beating on his drum. His big stallion Crockett. Walking Crockett alongside Ves as they crossed the bridge at Sanderson Ford. Moore was a meddlesome old fool, but Ves reckoned he'd meant to help. Not many had. He told of Miz Henslee and her bossy ways, and of his sister Martha and his brother James Littleton and his whole gaggle of half-brothers and half-sisters, who were at him all the time about something or other that he wouldn't do or, if he'd done it, had done wrong. Andy Curtis, the Cartman boys, goddamn Tom Carter, Miss Hattie Gash, the sassy nigger Hamby McFee. Even Jared Nutbush and Ree Bolt, that wished him dead. Tuck Richbourg. Whorish Katie Shuford, agent of his downfall. He'd miss them, though he couldn't say why. It had something to do with his being alive and their taking part in that, for good or bad. They were of him and he of them, bound together in the business of his living. So when Darling killed him Ves would lose them along with his life, and he wondered then if more than just him might possibly be lost when he passed on; maybe the others would lose something, too, would die just a little because he'd died all the way. Wistfully he mused whether that had been the whole purpose of his living and dying—to take a piece out of all that knew him, leaving a hole where pity might enter. The notion appealed to him, for just now he felt much in need of pity.

Next the name of his pap came unbidden to his lips. He realized he would miss his pap. Him, too. But then having uttered the name Ves could say no more; he turned from the window and the hanging bat; he sat down in his corner and stared unseeing at the opposite wall.

⌒

One evening while it was still daylight the bat stirred for the first time other than to relieve itself. Ves watched as it commenced to flex its web of wings and turn its head this way and that to lick. After this spell of grooming it used its sticklike front legs with hooks on the ends to creep down the side of the window to the sill, where it lay awhile and did some more licking. Then with a racket that startled Ves it spread its ugly scalloped-looking wings and took flight and vanished, leaving the window empty and Ves looking on in dismay, worrying it might never return. He'd come to see it as a kind of guardian against the worst that might befall, and now that it was gone he felt like anything could happen.

And by God it did. No sooner had the bat flown off than the door behind Ves was unbolted with a crash and in swaggered Webb Darling. As Ves turned to meet him Darling came close and ran the heel of his hand against the bridge of Ves's nose and broke it like a stick of green wood, pop, and Ves sat down on the dirt floor clasping both hands over his nose and starting to choke on his own blood as it poured into his gullet. The king curled both fists on his hips and smiled down on him in a satisfied way. "Hello, slop-dumper."

Ves spat out a quantity of gore. "Hidy," he gurgled as best he could.

Darling had tipped his hat back on his head to expose the widow's peak of his white-gold mat of hair; it gave him a casual, almost negligent look that Ves hoped against odds might perhaps bode well for himself. Maybe despite having walloped him the king was feeling unexpectedly merry after his trip into the Valley River country; maybe he was even in a forgiving vein, however improbable that might seem. It was hard to tell, for Darling's habit was to show a pleasant face no matter the occasion; from the king's expression Ves's prospects might as easily be auspicious as fatal.

Ves thought he might as well probe the question, so as soon as he could rid himself of another gout of blood he inquired, "Are you a-fixing to kill me?"

Darling laughed. "Oh yes, surely."

Ves cowered, coughed up more blood. His doom was sealed; all was lost. He heard himself whine like a kicked pup. "Are you a-going to cut off my head like you done Lige Dollar?"

"You can bet on it," said the king.

Ves burst into tears. "Is this the time?" he wailed. "Is this my very last hour and minute? Have you brung the ax?"

Ves's anguish seemed to amuse the king to no end. He bent down with his hands spread on his knees and gave another laugh of derision directly into Ves's face, and when he did he breathed on Ves the sweet scent of the licorice he'd recently been chewing. "You have an inflated idea of your own importance, slop-dumper," he declared. "You may be a Dog, but you're not the Dog that Lige Dollar was. Lige was not a frivolous Dog." He straightened and shook his head and made a contemptuous clicking noise with his tongue against the roof of his mouth. "Do you even *know* the word *frivolous*?"

"Reckon I've heard of it," Ves quailed.

"If Lige went to give up a blockader to the Revenue," the king explained, "he was scrupulous about it." He leaned down again, grinning in scorn. "Do you know *scrupulous*, slop-dumper?" Ves nodded, holding his nose with both hands. "You turned over moonshiners wholesale, didn't you? Turned 'em over just for the bounty on 'em. Old Lige did it one or two at the time, and only when he thought he had good reason. He might've been a nigger, and maybe I had to White-Cap him on account of it, but I respected that old coon. And when the time came to wind him up I went down there personal to attend to it. It's the king's duty to put out a subject who's a man but has gone wrong. So I was sorry for it even while I was White-Capping him." Now Darling got down on one knee close by Ves and laid what seemed a confiding hand on his shoulder. "And I'll tell you something else, slop-dumper. Because I respected Lige I had him shot dead *before* I took his head."

Unaccountably Ves wanted to sneeze through his smashed nose. He tried to stop himself but failed, and when he did sneeze he blew a spray of blood all over the front of his shirt and a slobbery drool of it into his lap, though thank God he didn't bespatter Webb Darling with his mess. The pain of sneezing made him cry afresh. When he got his voice back he posed the obvious and most terrible question: "Does that mean you aim to cut my head off while I'm yet a-living?"

Darling took his own chin between thumb and forefinger and held it, appearing to indulge in deep thought. "Yes, it does," he replied, and Ves's heart plummeted like a stone dropped in a quarry pond. "But remember, you're not a man like that nig was. You don't deserve such respect as I showed him. You're just a sorry, no-account, dirt-eating squealer. You gave me no loyalty, so I owe you no respect. I'm the king. I can do as I please to them that betray me. So I'm going to play with you, slop-dumper."

Kneeling next to him, Darling looked at Ves with eyes as blue as an Indian-summer sky; like a woman he slowly batted his long yellow lashes. In fear Ves's stomach rolled sluggishly over.

"Ever see a cat with its mouse?" the king asked. "Well, from here on, I'm the cat and you're the mouse. Anytime something happens around here that upsets me or makes me cross or even just mildly irritates me, why, I'm going to come in here and commence to playing with you till I feel better. I think you'll be surprised to learn the kinds of games that'll improve my state of mind. And you might as well know, I get wrathy about *something* at least four or five times every day."

While he talked in such dreadful fashion the king got to his feet and fetched a big stag-handled bowie knife out of the back of his britches and stood flicking the blade with its wicked recurved point to and fro, so it flashed in the light from the one window. It was the biggest and worst-looking knife Ves had ever seen.

"Now," Darling was saying, "it so happens I'm in a pretty mild temper today, because I've just enjoyed a successful business venture and blessed myself with a mess of pussy over Murphy-way, and because I've come home to find you waiting here like a Heaven-sent gift to offer me all the joys of revenge I may want to think up. So this is the only visit I'll make today."

Despite the fearsome sight of that bowie relief swept through Ves like a cool wind in hot weather. He was thinking himself fortunate only to have given up a nose on this his first day of torture when, before he could react, the king reached and caught him by the hair and with the bowie quick as lightning sliced off a part of Ves's left ear about the size of a wedge of lemon a lady might put in her tea. The piece of ear fell to the floor, and to Ves's horror he saw it lying there between them in the grit; he howled in outrage to think himself separated into rashers like a side of bacon; he clapped one hand to the slashed ear that burnt like fire while he held the other on his ruined nose; what a mess he was, he thought with woe. The king stooped, picked up the rind of ear from the ground and held it high. "I think I'll feed this to my roosters," he mused. He wiped the blade of the bowie on Ves's sleeve, stepped back, put the knife away behind him. He stood there awhile smiling and holding that piece of ear to the light to examine it. "But I'll be back tomorrow," he said, "whenever matters start to spite me. And the day after that. And the day after that, too. Every day that comes, for as long as it takes."

That night while he lay in the corner nursing his wounds Ves quit his Lordying altogether. He knew now the angel he'd sought would never descend to set him free; Webb Darling was so full of deathly power not even an emissary out of Paradise could get past him. In his desolation Ves saw Creation in a new and baleful light; what the king had said and done to him had changed his whole notion of the world, which before had seemed a rich feast laid on for him alone, if only he could wangle a way to get to the table; now he saw it as a kind of machine that ran on principles entirely foreign to any doctrine of faith or charity, an engine that was pitiless and indifferent in all its workings, that would grind a man up like so much gravel and not even take note of having done it. In a few short minutes Webb Darling had made Ves nearly forget his fear of dying and replaced it with a fear of maiming and mangling and insupportable pain that in nowise could be warded off. Ves's ordeal was upon him; he could not elude it. He faced this cold truth with a surprising calm that arose not at all out of bravery but instead from a black pit of utter despair. He felt inert; he felt numb. He even thought that, in contrast to what awaited him, the prospect of his dying—even of losing his head to the ax—might take on a sweet guise of mercy.

He knew he couldn't stand what was coming. He knew he'd disgrace himself. He had no courage. He'd holler, sob, scream, beg, soil himself. Darling would laugh at his antics. He remembered a dog he'd once doused with coal oil and set alight; he remembered how it acted, how it sounded; he'd laughed at that dog the same as the king was going to laugh at him. The notion gave him pause. Maybe it was that burnt dog he'd be paying for, and not any arrested blockaders. Maybe the God he hoped would help him would instead set him the selfsame penalty he'd imposed on that poor brute so long ago. God was stern, many said.

For a long time he couldn't sleep. This was partly because he was thinking about the dog but also partly because he was looking for the bat to come back; he didn't want to miss the bat, because even if he'd given up hope he clung to the silly notion the bat bore him some smidgeon of goodwill that might give strength when the king set to work on him. But the bat never came, and finally Ves's weariness overwhelmed his watchfulness and even the discomfort of his hurts, and presently he fell to drowsing under his thin blanket by the fire. He dreamt of his mam. Or maybe it was not a dream but a memory. A memory of a time when he and she were the same, when he rode suspended in her warmth, lit by a ruddy light that came from somewhere outside, her blood coursing in his veins and his in hers, their hearts beating in time—a memory he couldn't possibly have but which felt so real he heard in his ears the deep rumble and pulse not only of his mam's self, in which he so benignly floated, but also of the world beyond which awaited him.

Then came a vision of his mam that was not at all an image of her face and figure but instead only a sense of her presence. Yet somehow this was clearer than any actual sight. So immediate was it that it jolted him awake. He sat bolt upright. "Mam," he said. She was in the room, in its moist air, in him, around him. He lay curled in her arms. He felt her bosom swell with her breath. She sang to him. All his life he'd been unable to recall the words or tunes of any of the songs she used to sing to him. But now as she rocked him in comfort it all came back, and there on the edge of his troubled sleep Ves

heard her fine tremulous alto and instantly recalled the words of her
song—that song and all the others, too:

> I love the Lord for what He's done;
> 'Tis through the merits of His Son
> I feel my sins are all forgiv'n,
> And I've a resting-place in Heav'n.
>
> But oh, when that last conflict is o'er,
> And I am chained to earth no more,
> With what glad accents shall I rise
> To join the music of the skies!

CHAPTER 16

January 1882

*H*amby was in the dooryard adding some pretty blue paregoric bottles to the branches of his spirit tree when he spied Katie
Shuford coming down the road from her pappy's place. She was dragging a stick along his fence, making a dry rattling noise he guessed
was meant to announce her—although Katie didn't need to strike up
any racket to draw notice. The day was unseasonably warm, and she
wore a loose dress of sacking fastened at the waist with twine. She'd
cut the dress low in front and then in tying the twine had pulled the
neck of it even lower to reveal the cleft between her titties; enough
of her bosom showed that you could see the two firm mounds just
starting invitingly to swell out, and what you couldn't see bobbed so
agreeably in that sacking you wouldn't have looked away even if a
mad dog had you by the leg.

She came to his gate and stopped and stood lounging there
hipshot, pecking at the gatepost with her stick. "Hidy," she said. Her

green eyes touched him and flicked away; coltishly she shook her head so her many black locks flicked over one shoulder in a coiled mass.

Holding a bottle in each hand, Hamby said hidy back but made no motion, nor did he smile or in any fashion encourage her. Katie Shuford was one white woman that could get a nigger gelded and hanged and probably burnt, too. Lately she'd been keeping with Jared Nutbush, but before that she'd lain on her back for half the men in the county—on one memorable occasion even for Hamby himself. Katie didn't care what she did or whom she did it with; white or black, brown or red, it made no difference to her; she just loved the feel of a man's best bone in her belly. In consequence she was likely the most feared mortal in the valley, for if Katie ever told all she knew, names good and bad would go smash from Aquone to the Nottely River, and not a few stud niggers would ascend the lynching tree. Still Hamby was defiant enough of fate not to remove his hat or act subservient, although as he faced her a twinge of dread did pluck at his innards.

But today for all her fetching looks Katie seemed subdued. She ceased beating on the gatepost and instead began to amble around in slow circles in the road, flicking the point of her stick at the ruts. She chewed her nether lip; she scowled; she stopped again and stood gazing not at Hamby but past him, along the flat expanse of bottom grizzled with rye stubble, on toward the line of birch and sycamore that marked the river. She took a curl of her hair and wound it about a finger and began twisting and untwisting it. "That Ves Price," she said at last, "the one nobody can find?"

Curious, Hamby nodded. Katie sighed, held up her stick, closely examined its point while continuing to toy with her curl. Hamby remembered exactly how she'd tasted and smelt, but as soon as that memory came he shunted it aside. He was done with such as that; if he was going to have something to do with a woman she'd not be white, not ever again; too much was at risk for the thin reward one was apt to get. He waited while she drew her curl out straight and squinted at it; he could tell she had more to say and decided to let her get at it in her own time. Behind him in the two pens Buttermilk and Pile-Driver chortled, and the hens clucked and scratched in the dirt.

"Them people of yourn, them Curtises," Katie presently commenced.

Hamby broke in, "They ain't *my* people."

Katie's face drew up as if she'd tasted a sour apple. "Why, law, you *work* for 'em, don't you?" He shrugged. Katie paused, took a breath, went on. "I reckon they's good friends with them Prices of Ves's. That Mr. Oliver and Miz Henslee and them."

Hamby sensed Katie was fixing to relate some large piece of news about the vanished Ves. He bent and set down his two paregoric bottles and straightened again and nodded, wary of any tidings to do with Ves Price or the vengeance the king might want to take on him; Hamby didn't wish to be distracted from his own plans for the king.

Katie continued. "I know a secret about that Ves. About what's become of him."

"Why tell me?" Hamby wanted to know. He didn't desire to learn her secret. Ves Price was nothing to him. Hell, he despised the scrawny son of a bitch. Ves had long since earned whatever evil destiny might've overtaken him. Hamby had watched him grow up from a youngun; he'd always been a nasty and hateful cuss, the kind that would pluck the legs off grasshoppers, cut ants in two, put a pair of cats in a poke and then throw it in the river so the cats would drown fighting each other. Hamby suspected Ves was even in a bunch of peckerwoods who'd come at him drunk one night three years ago to amuse themselves pretending to be Ku Klux; they'd made as if to burn Hamby out, till he ran them off with a blast of his sawed-off ten-gauge loaded with turkey shot. Ves was no credit at all to his pap Oliver, who at least acted fair to most, regardless of color, even if he was little better than a trashy white himself. But Hamby figured he oughtn't degrade Ves Price or indeed any white in front of sluttish Katie Shuford, who—if he provoked her by slurring some gent whose long prick she favored—could get him killed in about an hour's time. So he said nothing in that vein.

Katie came to the fence and put both arms between the palings and leaned on the rail with her stick in one hand hanging down. More of her titties were showing, but Hamby paid them small heed now. As if a storm cloud had suddenly blown over him, he was oppressed by a dark foreboding; he felt he was about to become privy to something that would change him against his will once he heard it. He wanted to spurn her, to go away and leave her there, to tend the roosters, groom the jenny, sweep the dooryard, anything. But he didn't. Maybe he couldn't. He stood by the spirit tree watching her.

She tapped the end of her stick against the inside of the fence. "I come to tell you," she said, "on account of maybe you could help, for he's in trouble, you see."

Hamby blurted out a scornful laugh. "Why *I* want to help? I already said I ain't no Curtis, much less no goddamn Price. 'Sides, I the wrong color."

Katie put her head engagingly to one side. He'd never seen her earnest and vexed like this; he had to admit the new feelings looked sublime on her, deepened her eyes from milky jade to moss green, filled out her face so it didn't seem so bony and hard-edged with cravings of the body. He noticed how creamy white and soft her skin looked, how glossy her raven hair.

"Well," she offered in a near-whisper, "ain't Ves close to them Curtises of yourn? Ain't he nearly like . . . family?"

He chose not to bandy words with her anymore about whether

he was part of the Curtises and Prices, which he damn sure wasn't—
at least not in any way that counted. Also he felt uneasy; the longer
they stood there in the open engaged in close conversation the greater
their chance of being seen and of his actions being fatally misconstrued. That time he'd gone to see her he'd snuck into the Shufords'
barn only before moonrise. Whites could afford to flirt in daylight,
but darkies had best keep hid by day and crawl of a night like snakes.
Now that he no longer nourished any hunger for her ready flesh his
whole hope was to escape her. Accordingly he made a quick motion
and growled, "All right, go on, say your piece."

Bashfully Katie swayed one way and then the other, drawing fig-
ures in the dirt of the road with the end of her stick. "Ves, he come
to see me one night when my sweetheart Jared and me was in the
barn," she recounted. She resumed twirling her curl of black hair; she
looked down at her brogans; a flush bloomed redly—and prettily, he
had to concede—on her cheeks. "He was hiding out somewheres ever
since that fuss on the bald. Jared, why he boxed Ves with his pistol,
lashed him to a mule, led him off, took him to the bald." Katie glanced
sideways at Hamby. "The king wants him, you know."

Hamby nodded. "I know." He didn't need to find out any more
than Katie had just told him, and yet in surprise and disbelief he
heard himself ask her a question: "When this all happen?" Maybe, he
thought, the fool was dead already.

"A week ago yesterday." Katie made a regretful face and resumed
her swaying and picture drawing with the stick. "Law, I was scairt to
tell anybody," she murmured, "and scairt not to."

Hamby believed that, felt the fear coming off her the way a horse
can feel the disquiet of a man afraid of riding as soon as he takes the
reins.

"The king aims to keep him a spell up yonder on the bald, to
hurt him till he kills him, says Jared." Katie shivered. "But I had to

tell." She stood in the road holding her stick by her side and commenced to cry. Big beads of tears traveled down her face. Yes, Hamby felt sorry for her. "I don't want Ves to die," she moaned. "He's a scapegrace and a rounder, but he was always sweet to me. He don't deserve to die."

Secretly Hamby begged to differ about that; dying might be too damn good for Ves Price; maybe Webb Darling had got the right idea about the punishment Ves deserved. Aloud, he demanded, "Girl, what you want *me* to do?"

Katie set firmly on him her green eyes brimming with tears. "Can't you save him?" she implored.

Save Ves Price. Now there was the single most crackbrained goddamn notion ever. To start with, why would somebody the whole world considered to be a darky take the part of *any* redneck coonhating po' buckra, not to mention one as rank and scoundrelly as Ves Price? As far as Ves and all his sorry ilk were concerned a nigger was just a beast to hurt and put to shame and beat on, and a high-yellow like Hamby for all his airs was a nigger the same as any blue-gum straight out of Africa. Why then lift a finger on Ves Price's account? Hamby would as soon think of saving a polecat.

Family, Katie'd said. Coarsely Hamby laughed and swore. Why, Ves Price wasn't even good enough to be family with the Curtises— folk his own color, if not his own kind. Hell, he wasn't even family *with* his own, the way he ran down his old crippled-up pappy every chance he got. He sure as hell wasn't any kin to Hamby—not by blood, not by color, not by the spirit, not by nothing. Damn him. Let the cracker suffer; let him die; it would help thin out the supply; one less low-downer was one fewer for the mobbers to stir up to go hanging coloreds whenever the evil mood came. That evening he sat by the fire cleaning and oiling his five-shooter, shaking his head and chuckling at Katie Shuford's folly. Hell, Ves Price had come at him wearing a goddamn sheet over his head, fixing to burn him out. When he finished cleaning the pistol he wrapped it in an oily rag and laid it by.

Next morning he went out to the pens and squatted in the yard looking over Pile-Driver and Buttermilk. They stopped pecking and strutting and stood watching him back with fierce little jerks of their heads. It was only two months since he'd pitted them. Those fights had mostly been light ones meant for conditioning, though it was true some had been right hard. Still it wasn't good to fight a rooster more than twice in a year, allowing at least six months between times. And Pile-Driver had got that bad cut from Mose Sullivan's Shawlneck on Shooting Creek, which, though healed, seemed to have slowed him some, maybe by severing a muscle in his chest that had knit back weak.

Hamby knew little of Darling's birds. He'd heard they were strong and fast and could cut like anything; they were famous in the valley; they were said to be as mean as Rollin Livingood's, and smarter than any. Buttermilk ruffed up his neck feathers and whipped his wings against his legs, sounding like a pheasant beating on a log. Pile-Driver tried the withes of his pen with his beak, tore off some strips, cast them aside with a violent motion. Hamby folded in his upper lip and caught it with his bottom teeth and held it. They were good birds, but they didn't yet have the experience they needed. They weren't ready—wouldn't be ready for weeks yet. He had no business even thinking of putting them in the pit. He meant to wait maybe till late fall before sending the king his challenge. In the meantime he planned to work them and pit them lightly on occasion, till he got them at their peak. If he fought them now he was pretty sure they'd get licked. And if that happened where was his requital for Lige Dollar? Where was the money he aimed to win, that would pay his way out of this dismal leached-out corner of the world?

Katie had urged him to hurry. He turned his head and spat. What did that matter? The king could finish up Ves Price anytime; maybe he'd done it already, and Ves was lying somewhere in the brush this very minute with crows pecking out his eyeballs. Hamby would go when his birds were ready, not a moment before. He had his own designs, and not Katie Shuford and surely not Ves Price entered into them. He was going to be the nigger that went up to Pot Rock Bald and cleaned out King Webb Darling the fearsome White-Capper; losing his bankroll to a darky would wreck the goddamn high-and-mighty Ku Klux son of a bitch; folk would laugh at him for it, and when they laughed it would be the beginning of the end of him.

Hamby might not live to tell of it; he knew that, had known it from the first. Of course if it came down to a fracas he'd scrap with them. But dying wasn't something he much troubled himself about. He could just as easily fall in the river and drown; he could get a fever; a black widow spider could bite him; a bale of hay could drop on his head. As long as he was alive he'd keep on living, and then when his time was up he'd go; that was it.

That evening he stropped the blade of his straight razor till it would cut a hair held between thumb and forefinger. Then he heated a ten-penny nail in the fire till it glowed red and took it up with a pair of pliers and with it burnt a hole through the end of the razor handle. He cut himself a thong of leather twice as long as one arm and threaded an end through the hole in the handle and then tied the ends together to make a lanyard. He dropped the lanyard over his head and slipped the razor down inside the front of his shirt, where it could hang loose. When he reached in his shirt and drew it quickly out, the blade came open with a pop and cut the air an arm's length away, at the lanyard's end.

He knew where there was a bell tree. It was an old hollow poplar near the head of Qualls Creek. Inside the tree was a cowbell. A fellow that wanted to buy a drink could put his money in the hollow place and ring the cowbell, and the blockader would hear the bell and come down and put a dram in the tree. You could use a bell tree for messages, too. Whatever moonshiner got your message would give it to one of the runners that went up and down Pot Rock Bald every day. So Hamby sat straddling his bench and scrawled out a note to the king, saying he wanted to set a chicken fight for noontime Saturday next on the king's own ground. If Ves Price gave up the ghost before then, so much the better; Hamby was determined he wouldn't be rushed. That evening he rode the jenny up the creek to the bell tree and put the note in the hollow and rang the bell.

The following morning he rode up the creek again and found his note there in the hollow, but folded over once and with the word "DONE" written on it. In one corner of the paper was a crude little drawing of a kingly crown.

Hamby took the note and went on to Hayesville. Passing through a gate in the tumble-down fence of chestnut wood that partly ringed the place, he rode around the log courthouse in its treeless square—they'd long since cut the grove of maples the courthouse used to sit in. Arriving in front of the Commercial Hotel, he found the mail hack waiting to make its run to Murphy. He gave the note to the hack driver and asked him to deliver it to Rollin Livingood by Hanging Dog.

Late on Friday Hamby walked along Downings Creek to the Hiwassee and then west along the river to the place by the swinging bridge opposite the old Indian mound, where a long time ago Andy Curtis had showed him the pottery shards and flint arrowheads and spear points the savages had left behind. Because of these memories Hamby sometimes fancied he could sense the spirits of those old Indians stirring amid the trees that grew out of the mound to lean over the river, or hear their voices in the muted rush of the water. He sat in a niche he'd dug out of the clay of the riverbank, on a short log he'd laid in there for a seat. The grassy lip of the bank was above him by a good bit, so he felt closer to the water than to the fields. The cool of the river bathed him; he smelt its coppery tang. The water ran clear as glass, and in the shadows the trees cast on it you could see the flat stones of its bed lying under the running surface, gold and tan and brown like cobbles on a street, a fretwork of sparkles playing over them in places where the sun did come through. Big dark trout hung suspended in it; slowly they waved their tails.

Hamby wondered if it was old-time Cherokees—Longrunner's people—that built the mound or if it was some other tribe entirely, of whom not one descendant remained. He wondered if, whoever they were, they believed the body of a man, even one that had done wrong, ought not be dismembered, as the folk of his grandmam had believed and as Hamby himself had come to think. Did they aver the soul was mutilated if the flesh was? Did they name it a sin to separate the bones? If they did, then they and Hamby were joined across time by one and the same belief. It was a thought too big for his mind. Still he felt he had a place in some huge matter in which the whole world and its story hung.

Long before dawn Hamby awoke. For a time he lay in the dark unmoving, his thin quilt drawn to his chin. Cold seared the skin of his face and seeped in at him from the edges of the quilt and from the parts of his mattress he hadn't slept on. He shuddered; he hated the thought of leaving even such scant comfort as he had. He lay in blackness so thick he half-thought if he reached out he could take up a dab of it on the end of his finger, as if it were a mess of pitch. Somewhere in the loft of the cabin a mouse was gnawing on wood and now and then dashing about on its tiny feet. He smelt the dry odor of the shucks in his mattress and the bitter scent of the ashes cold in the fireplace. At last he spoke an oath and rose.

In his underwear he struck a light and put it to the candle on the table. Venting a spout of vapor with every breath, he waited in the numbing chill while the candle flickered, caught, finally flared, sent the blackness fitfully retreating into the corners, where the birds were stirring now. He'd kept them in to pamper them. In the uneasy glow their eyes gleamed like new coins. They were tethered in opposite corners, too far apart to permit a fight but near enough to aggravate them. They crowed, lunged at one another, pounded their wings, stuck out their necks from big rosettes of feathers. "Easy," Hamby said to them, "easy."

He used the chamber pot rather than venturing out to the privy in the cold. But he elected not to lay a fire because he'd be gone from the place before any blaze could get going good enough to make a difference. Shaking, he looked to the birds. He'd given them dry feed the night before, and now he checked their droppings; he found them agreeably crusty and crowned with the little coils of white that meant the birds' constitutions were set up good to fight. He hefted the pair, liked the buoyant feel of each rooster. He'd done the best he could; now it was up to them. Had they as much grit as he suspected, they might do right well, even young and mostly untried. If they didn't, so be it. He fed and watered them and talked to them in ways he thought might bolster their spirits.

Breaking the crust of ice in the water bucket, he ran a sour washrag over his face and up beneath his undershirt. The roosters eyed him rudely as he ate a breakfast of pone and cold cracklins and yesterday's coffee and then brushed his teeth with a frayed twig and got into his clothes. He took his razor and hung it inside his shirt by its lanyard. Then he sat at the table in the light of the candle and unwrapped his stepdaddy's five-shooter from its oily rag and carefully made up five paper cartridges and rammed one into each chamber and sealed every chamber with wax from the candle. He opened the chamber vents with his little metal pick. He fitted a copper percussion cap to the nipple of each chamber except the one under the hammer and put the fifth cap in the pocket of his coat. He made up no more than just the five. Hell, if five wouldn't do it, nothing would.

With Pile-Driver and Buttermilk balanced in their wicker cages on the jenny's withers, Hamby set out along the wagon road, whose middle was one line of silvered grass stiff with frost. It was good to get moving after padding about barefoot in the chill of the cabin; now the cold that had seemed so malevolent before was refreshing instead. Crisply he felt the throb of his heart and the pulsing of the blood in his veins; he and the jenny blew more clouds of white than they needed to, simply because they enjoyed seeing the bountiful jets and plumes. The roosters fussed and crowed. On his right the sky behind the Nantahalas had begun to take on a faint cast of greenish blue like the light in an opal. In the brightening he could begin to distinguish the dense contour of Chunky Gal set against the paler background of the high tops beyond; soon he could see that a few of the taller peaks wore small tilted caps of snow. He picked up Peckerwood Branch and crossed thence between the Double Knobs and Stamey Knob into the drainage of the Tusquittee.

Here on the creek by the mouth of the Peckerwood he came

across Rollin Livingood and Petrie his brother-in-law and Longrunner breaking camp in a fence corner. The Indian stood and sent Hamby a bob of the head but as usual spoke no word, turning away at once to resume furling the bedrolls as tidily as if that would be his only duty today and he would be graded on how well he did it. Petrie stood in the road relieving himself; in the morning light his stream of piss was a curved wire of brass that smoked in the cool. Livingood came from the smoldering remains of the pit fire, stopped by the jenny's head, looked one way at Pile-Driver and the other at Buttermilk, then said to Hamby without even glancing up at him, "Got your message." He squinted at the birds. "They looking right good." When he'd finished with them he stared off down the valley, still not meeting Hamby's gaze. "Thought I'd come along and look out for my investment," he explained, touching a knuckle to his birthmark.

On they went up the Tusquittee, the four of them, Livingood in front on his roan stallion, then Hamby astride the jenny, followed by Longrunner and Petrie riding their mules. They did not speak. Before them rose the range in a mass of crags whose flanks were darkly pleated with the coves that lay in the lee of the sun. The topmost ones with their mantles of snow took the gilt of the new light and held it, slowly changing from white to rose to gold and back to white as day came on. They crossed the little log bridge spanning Cold Branch and then heard the first horn blow above them from a shank of Piney Top, a long and lonesome-sounding note like the cry of a woman demented with grief.

Just then a strange surmise trailed through Hamby, as light and deft as the tail of a silk scarf wafting past. It made him turn in the saddle, peer inquiringly back along the way they'd come. In the last bend of the trail stood a big slick of laurel, and although he saw no motion, still he apprehended something uncommon about it, even seemed to remember having glimpsed a blur or twitch that did not belong there, but which of course he hadn't seen at all. He frowned, checked the jenny, watched awhile longer as the others went ahead. But whatever it was did not stir again, if it ever had. He shrugged. Maybe it was a bird.

Fording the Tusquittee, they started up the course of Matlock Creek toward the brow of Julie Ridge. They heard another horn, way off in the distance on the crest of Dead Line. A third note sounded from the bald ahead of them when they mounted the spine of Julie Ridge and turned up for the last climb to the fort. Here a skinny man slipped from the ash woods into the path and bade them stop. His face seemed to have grown out of his beard, rather than the reverse; above the thicket of black whiskers his features looked pink, newly formed, tentative, uncertain of their survival amid such a luxuriance of thistly growth as surrounded them. He held crosswise before him a pretty little Whitney-Kennedy carbine with fancy scrollwork on the receiver. "We're expecting the nigger and his birds," he said to Livingood. "Who in hell are you?"

Livingood told his name. "You send on up to Darling," he said. "Tell him I'm here with my brother-in-law and my Indian man to see the match."

The fellow made a flapping gesture of one long hand from a wrist as thin as a stick, and a red-headed boy of about twelve came out of the woods behind him and stood waiting. The other addressed him without once turning his head, and after that the boy whirled and darted on up the path out of sight. Livingood got down off his roan to tighten his cinch. Petrie, who seemed to be afflicted in his kidneys, dismounted to pee once more, and did so grimacing and swearing. Hamby and Longrunner patiently sat their mounts, Hamby crooning a reassuring word now and again to the squabbling birds. The man whose head was growing out of his beard leaned against a rock and eyed them doubtfully, his finger on the trigger of that cute little Whitney-Kennedy.

Pretty soon the boy came back and spoke to the sentinel, who nodded and turned to them and waved them on; as they passed him going up Hamby noticed how he watched them narrowly one by one, slightly smirking, as if he knew a secret he thought they might find disagreeable, were it to be suddenly revealed. They went past a patch of hawthorn and around a steepening bend between two boulders and presently found themselves on the stony snow-speckled expanse of the bald, a blue arch of steely sky over them and the fort standing a hundred yards ahead, sending up a thread of smoke, looking like the ruin of a tabernacle made by a people so primitive they were not yet fully acquainted with the art of building.

Hamby, who'd not been to the bald since the fort was put up but had heard for months how august, how imposing it was, looked on in amazement, trying not to guffaw. Every sort of odd rock had been used to wall it in, but no clay or mortar bound them, and they'd all been laid crazy and cattywampus, not orderly so as to reinforce each other; it looked like the merest touch would topple the whole of it. The roof was made of timbers that were comically aslant, and a parapet of split peeled logs bounded it, but the logs were already warped from the weather, and the warping had pulled out most of the spikes that were supposed to hold them, so the parapet resembled nothing so much as a set of dried-out old slices of celery laid end to end. The entire concern leaned to the left like a tree in a high wind. Before it Webb Darling stood proudly smiling, his arms folded on his chest—the monarch posing at the gate of his castle. Somewhere inside, Hamby knew, the wretch Ves Price must languish—if he yet lived. Observing the king drawn up so grandly at the portal of his ramshackle redoubt, Hamby saw for the first time how small and petty was Webb Darling, how puny his ambitions, how wrong his acts and from what low spite they stemmed. Now he was glad he'd come.

Except for the ragged hulk of Tusquittee Bald rearing high to the northeast, they might've been standing at the zenith of the world. On three sides the summits of mountains fell away from them, steadily diminishing in scale till all melted into one faint pencil line of purple along the skyline. Above, the dome of space and light too immense to measure seemed not only to invite them upward into its vastness but to offer a means of ascent as well; you wanted to rise higher and higher still, and the warming air hinted that you could. Yes, the bald was far too fine a place for who lived on it and what he'd built there.

Darling advanced as Livingood stepped down from his stud. Coyly he fluttered his long eyelashes, exclaimed, "See who's here. Does this mean bygones are bygones?" He beamed, extended a hand. Livingood took the hand but dropped it almost at once; Darling laughed as if in rue and pretended to examine the member to see what might be amiss with it. Around him in the yard stood or sat a number of men— Hamby counted eight—including Darling's brother leaning on a brass-framed Winchester, Ree Bolt with his Sharps, Jared Nutbush and Abner Mullinax apparently unarmed. The others Hamby didn't recognize; he saw that one of these had a pistol shoved in the waistband of his trousers. Two more unknown to him looked down from the parapet, whose rim was jaggedly edged with icicles like the teeth of a meat eater.

"I come for the sport," Livingood declared. From behind, Hamby couldn't see his face but did notice how he stood—straight-backed, slightly bent-kneed, somehow loose and tense at the same time, looking like he was awaiting a signal to make some great leap. He poked a thumb backward over his shoulder in Hamby's direction. "This darky's rented two of my chickens to fight you. Maybe he'll give you a whipping. I'm betting he does."

Darling slit his eyes and thinly smiled. "Then the bygones are with us yet." The smile seemed to warm. "But only in a sporting way, eh?"

Livingood said nothing by way of answer. As the king spoke Petrie stirred; Darling glanced sideways at him and then coldly watched as Petrie swung groaning off his mule to open his britches and go to pissing in a nearby ditch; the look lingered and grew hard with malice, and though Darling uttered no syllable of reproof Hamby could see that the majesty of the king had been sorely insulted and that sooner or later Petrie would be made to pay for his disrespect.

Petrie finished, buttoned himself up. Darling watched him a second longer, then turned to Hamby and spoke not to him but mockingly to Livingood. "When did you start trafficking with coloreds—a man of your convictions?" Yet the look he gave Hamby was bland, was not unkind. He even tipped his head in greeting, and Hamby was obliged to touch the brim of his hat in return.

"My convictions are different now," Livingood rejoined.

Darling laughed. "That's good for McFee here. Ain't it, McFee? Better'n being hanged like some nigs I know Livingood did business with down Rutherford County way."

Livingood refrained from replying, and Hamby dared not comment; a bloody pair of Ku Klux might banter one another as they wished, but a coon had best stay out of any such, whether it be joshing or hostile. He sat the jenny, saying soft words to the roosters and sending quick looks this way and that over the bald to get his bearings. Beside him Longrunner casually lifted a leg, crooked it over his pommel, began to build himself a smoke. In such company a nigger and a redskin were wise to feign a calm they hardly felt.

A pit had been marked off by scoring with a sharpened pole a low place of hard-packed ground set in a half-moon of outcropped rock at the edge of the dooryard. There was a short line drawn down the center of the pit to indicate where the birds that got badly cut would finish up. The whole arrangement gave ample room for birds and handlers and judge; the arc of rock that rimmed it, jutting out as it did, was perfect for folk to squat on and see the match. They'd swept out the snow that settled in the pit overnight, but not before the sunny weather had thawed the surface, leaving a thin skim of mud. Mud was better than the bare rock covering most of the bald, on which a rooster would have had a hard time getting purchase.

It looked all right to Hamby. He gave it a study while Livingood and Darling fussed over who was to be the judge. They settled on a man named Ives, who presently came out of the fort. Darling insisted Ives was not a menial of his, as Livingood suspected, but was instead a farmer from Rattlesnake Branch that sold cool-weather garden truck and was only on the bald making delivery of some carrots and turnips Darling had ordered. Hamby'd seen Ives at hack fights and knew him to be fair and vouched for him. Looking somewhat reluctant, Ives consented to serve. Soon then it was time, and Hamby went to the jenny and opened Buttermilk's cage and lifted him out and blew on his combless head to calm him.

Though littler, Buttermilk was faster and stouter than Pile-Driver, and Hamby thought he was the stronger of the two. And he hadn't been hurt and poorly healed up, as Pile-Driver had. It hardly mattered what kind of fowl Darling pitted against him, since Buttermilk was the best Hamby could offer; if Buttermilk prospered so would the cause. Hamby bore him away while in the other cage Pile-Driver squawked in protest, as if he knew he'd come off second best. Buttermilk struggled to free his legs from Hamby's grasp, writhing like a snake caught by the tail. Again Hamby raised him up, blew on his speckled head, spoke a bracing sentiment into his ruby eye.

Darling had named Ree Bolt his handler. Bolt stood waiting at the pit, holding the king's first bird. Hamby gave a quick appraisal. Between the Melungeon's big hands the thing looked more like a weasel than a chicken—long and sinewy, slim of head, short of leg, showing a quick agate eye. His head was coal-black, but the rest of him was red as Georgia clay. Hamby had no notion what the breed might be—maybe some kind of Roundhead. Unlike Buttermilk he lay quiet, holding his beak partway open, as if testing the air for a scent that might reveal his enemy's temper; the only thing about him that moved was that eye.

There was a wrangle about who was to hold the bets, but finally the parties settled on Abner Mullinax after he pledged to play square with both sides, despite his allegiance to the king. Hamby and Livingood put up with this because here on the bald they had no other good choice. Besides it seemed reasonable to think the king wanted things fair, so the Tusquittee men would respect the outcome, which he naturally assumed would be to his favor.

While Ives commenced weighing out the cocks Darling took a place behind Bolt and stood with his hat pushed back on his head, which showed the point of his low-grown albino hair. He was happy; he grinned in his lightly freckled face. His bullyboys mostly took seats on the crescent of outcropped stone. Some had stripped off their coats in the mild weather so as to soak up the sun. Livingood and Petrie sat close by the pit. Longrunner stood off in the rear by himself. The two on the parapet held their stations. Already the demijohn of corn whiskey that was as essential to a cockfight as the chickens themselves began to make the rounds.

When he was finished Ives reported to the king, "Your chicken's light by a quarter-pound."

Darling pulled a face of mock distress, then broke into laughter and moved one hand in a flourish. "Let it pass. He's got at least a quarter-pound of meanness in him to make up for it." Loyally all his minions laughed.

Ives gave back the birds, and Hamby and the king and the watchers all made their wagers, and then Hamby and Bolt knelt at opposite sides of the pit, and Ives said, "Bill 'em."

Hamby shoved Buttermilk in and held him tight while he and the king's bird stabbed at one another with their beaks. Then all of a sudden that sense of some flimsy thing wafting over him intruded again as it had on the trail coming up, and in spite of himself Hamby let it draw his eye from the pit and away toward the point of the bald, as if to spy out some mystery lurking there. But he saw nothing save the great spread of the blue valley. Then Ives said, "Pit 'em," and that brought Hamby's mind back with a jolt. Caught off guard, he thrust Buttermilk into the pit, knowing with a sink of dread he was a split second late, that his glance toward the rim had fatally delayed him, that now due to his blunder Buttermilk had to suffer. And sure enough, even before Buttermilk got set in the pit, the king's bird shot across at him, snapped his dartlike head—and just that quick Buttermilk was missing an eye. In contempt the weasel-bird slung the eye aside. A cheer went up from Darling's gang; Livingood and Petrie looked grimly on.

Now the king's rooster circled to the right, and a pang went through Hamby as he watched Buttermilk turn with the other, unmindful of his hurt. Buttermilk held his head at a queer angle so as to see with his good side; pluckily he ruffed out his neck feathers, flogged his wings. He aimed to close with the other bird and cut it, but the weaselly thing kept scuttling away, and now it occurred to Hamby that the king's rooster might be a one-stroke clipper that didn't mingle up close at all. No sooner did the thought come than the clipper jumped high with a flurry of wing beats and came down on Buttermilk and hit him hard with both spurs and flew on to the opposite side of the pit, leaving Buttermilk aflutter in the mud.

Amid the shouts of the bettors Hamby crouched sadly watching. There was nothing he could do but regret his own lapse, for which

Buttermilk must now pay the last and greatest penalty. Dancing around the edge of the pit, the clipper stretched out his long neck, displayed a bristly roundel of feathers, crowed his triumph. But amazingly Buttermilk floundered to his feet and pivoted, still flicking his head in that sideways fashion, trying to see with his one eye. His creamy color was soiled now with gore and mud; his beak was open; he'd been rattled; the weasel had cut his lungs; he was choking on a clot of his own blood. Ives pointed down, told Hamby to handle him. Scooping him up, Hamby took the marred head in his mouth and sucked to free the clot; Buttermilk was a tart and rusty flavor that mildly scalded the throat. He seemed to know Hamby meant him well; he didn't struggle; for an instant his hard narrow head lay as if in respite on Hamby's tongue. The clot came free, a hot little nugget that tasted of salt. Hamby spat it out, drew forth Buttermilk's head, looked into his one eye. Fiercely it glinted up at him. Hamby felt ashamed. He pushed Buttermilk back into the pit.

Buttermilk was done for, would bleed to death in minutes. But he meant to get that weasel. The clipper kept scampering around the edge of the pit as if taunting. Buttermilk held the center and wheeled with him, peering at him aslant, waiting for a chance, coughing up more gouts of blood, ridding himself of them with impatient jerks of his head, dying some more with every move. The weasel soared, swooped down in a shower of feathers, clipped Buttermilk twice more; Hamby winced to see it. But despite his several hurts Buttermilk somehow got himself on top and sank a spur deep in the weasel before he could escape, and all of a sudden—was it possible?—the weasel wilted, dropped flat, lay in the pit panting. A fountain of blood as thick as a finger spewed out of him, curled lazily over.

But this time Buttermilk couldn't recover; he'd used all he had. He, too, sank down. Silence fell. The two birds lay gasping in a pool of dark blood that slowly got wider. Now it was a case of which died first. Ives and Mullinax leaned intently in; several of the watchers stood, the better to see; momentarily the whiskey jug ceased its travels; Hamby looked away, not wanting to witness Buttermilk's passing. The weasel went first. Buttermilk died a few seconds after, having bought victory with the coin of his life.

The loss darkened slightly the king's cheery manner, but feigning good grace, he praised Buttermilk's grit and paid off. He told Ree Bolt to fetch another bird. Already the king seemed drunk, and when the jug came to him again he hoisted it high. The next man to get a gulp reeled as he drank, nearly tipped backward off his seat. You could smell the stuff on the air and see its blear in every eye. The peckerwoods were filling up.

Hamby gave them small notice. He was blue; he'd made a silly mistake and got Buttermilk killed. Now there was only Pile-Driver. Pile-Driver with his weak chest. Disaster hung over Hamby and all his works. He drew Buttermilk out of the pit and carried him to the edge of the bald by the legs, his wings dangling down, limply spread; Hamby whirled him into space and stood watching as he spun lightly down and down, a wafer of white soon dwindling to a fleck. Coming back, he crossed to the jenny and unfastened Pile-Driver's cage and fetched him out. Pile-Driver made a feint at his nose. Blowing on his head, Hamby said, "You the boss bird now. It all be on you."

Darling's next rooster was a Whitehackle, pumpkin-colored with yellow legs and ruffles of pale underfeathers that peeped out like the frilly hems of a woman's unmentionables. He, too, had the sleek and finicky air of a single-stroker, and Hamby began to wonder if that was how Darling bred all his fowl. If so he doubted the wisdom of such a policy, breeding birds to fight one way only; pretty soon everybody up the Tusquittee that raised game chickens would know what to expect and would breed against it. The king, he concluded, was powerful but not smart.

As Hamby approached the pit Longrunner fell into step beside him and asked in a hush, "You heeled?" Hamby nodded. "These old drunk boys here," Longrunner said, "they ain't a-letting us off this bald." He was smiling. Hamby smiled, too. Longrunner bore off to the right and resumed his post in the yard behind the ring of watchers. Hamby knelt by the pit cupping Pile-Driver in both hands. He could feel Pile-Driver's heart madly throbbing.

Mindful of the bird's old injury Hamby yielded him up like a sacrifice, figuring Pile-Driver was whipped before he started. But as soon as he hit the pit Pile-Driver showed how he'd got his name. He came down on that Whitehackle like a wheelbarrow load of dumped-out bricks, driving his spurs with big strokes of his heavy wings. Several times impaled, the Whitehackle shrunk, shivered, blew a number of bloody bubbles, died. It was over in a matter of seconds.

Hamby caught Pile-Driver up, blew on him, held him close. Exultantly Pile-Driver popped his head; he crowed, twitched his bobbed black tail feathers; he was a miracle bird; some force beyond this world—some god, some devil who fancied brave roosters—had blessed him far beyond his merits, half-crippled and overmatched as he was. Hamby laughed aloud, but the king was no longer merry. He stood red-faced, glowering. "That was a lucky pass," he remarked.

"Ain't no luck," Hamby corrected him. "This bird just rough as a old cob."

Mullinax reckoned out the bets, and Darling paid off. As this went on Hamby glanced covertly about to test the mood of the yard. Those white boys had been putting away the dew at a pretty good clip, and though they'd started out hopeful and excited and had bet good money on the king's birds, they'd lost twice in a row now. It irked them, and they were getting resentful, and the liquor made them boisterous. Hamby overheard some grumbling about sassy niggers messing in a white man's sport. Longrunner was right; these peckerwoods were a fire fixing to start.

Bolt brought out another cock. "How many more of them things you got?" Hamby joked. Danger might threaten, but he felt giddy and gay; he thought a miracle chicken deserved to be celebrated. "You gonna wear out my rooster a-killing all them sorry-ass old birds."

Bolt stood on the other side of the pit holding his chicken and turned even blacker than he already was—turned the hue of a sooty cooking pot. But Darling answered for him, and the king's tone was flat: "I got one more after this. Do you reckon that little shuffler of yours is good enough to lick three of mine in a row?"

Exuberantly Hamby nodded. "He that good."

Darling's next was a pea-colored rooster of uncertain breed that stood wide like a bulldog. It weighed out heavier than Pile-Driver by nearly a pound, but Hamby glanced it over, found it fat, gander-necked, droop-chested, spindly of leg; he thought his bird could lick it, agreed to fight it in spite of the unequal weights. The bird was a clipper like the other two but seemed slow and a little stupid, and being shrewder, Pile-Driver could best him every time he came down to clip.

They pitted the pair five times—the last one on the short line, the birds were that torn up. Though outclassed the king's rooster showed courage; he did far better than Hamby thought he might; with all the drunk crackers screaming in his behalf he fought a long ten minutes on the short line before Pile-Driver could contrive to finish him, and by the time he did Pile-Driver himself was nearly fagged out from the blood he'd lost.

Darling's aggravation at losing a third time was tempered by Pile-Driver's bedraggled state, which seemed to promise the king a win to come. Grudgingly he paid off. The watchers grumbled and swore, passed the demijohn, cussed some more. Longrunner ambled innocently over to his mule and fished something out of his saddlebag and slipped it under his coat.

But just now Hamby took no account of any peril; his whole self was bent on his dilapidated bird. He smeared some sugar and chimney soot on Pile-Driver's several wounds; he sang hosannas of praise to him for his miracles; he breathed and breathed on his glossy head; he stroked his apricot-colored back; he lifted Pile-Driver and turned him about and blew wind up his vent to refresh him. He didn't know if Pile-Driver had another pitting in him, but he did know that like Buttermilk he'd die before he'd give out. It made Hamby want to cry.

Mullinax approached and delivered the winnings, and Hamby beckoned Longrunner to come and hold them. The Cherokee quickly counted, leaned close, whispered that Hamby had collected something like twelve hundred dollars—plenty enough, even after settling up with Livingood, to get a long way out of the Hiwassee country. Hamby's spirits, so low when he lost Buttermilk, soared now, thanks to the wonder working of Pile-Driver. He disdained the straits he was in, forgot the outlook for his next half-hour of life. He rejoiced.

But then while Ree Bolt was starting up from the pens with the king's last bird—a great whopping old Red Wheel shake that likely had a pound and a half over Pile-Driver—the thought of Ves Price suddenly wedged into Hamby's mind for the first time since the opening of the match; that was exactly how it felt, like an iron shim pounded in with a hammer. He reeled. *Damn my yellow ass*, he thought.

He had to do it, even if he knew no earthly reason why. And he had to do it now. God*damn*. Darling was naming his wager when Hamby, clasping Pile-Driver to his chest, looked straight at the king and cut him off. "You can keep that bet," he said. "This what we do. You win this pitting, you take all I done got off you." He hesitated, wondering if he'd lost his wits like the lunatic Andy Curtis; he felt Livingood and Petrie and Longrunner frowning at him, saw the king's eyes of heavenly blue freeze over like ice on a pond. "I win," he went on, "you give me the money and that white boy, too, that Ves Price you got cooped up."

The demijohn had come to Darling again, and he held it cocked on the top of his elbow as the last trace of goodwill visibly drained out of him. He was swaying a little, and his cheeks were ruddy with drink. The gold lashes fluttered; his face showed hard new angles along the jaw. When he spoke next he used a voice Hamby hadn't heard from him before; it was fragile and crackly, like a dry leaf underfoot. "What's your game, boy?"

Hamby wondered at himself, wondered if he'd die before he knew. But he smiled and said, "Ain't no game. That just my bet."

Darling hiked up the jug and took another swig; everybody in the dooryard watched him swallow, as if the act were some conjuration of things to come. He passed the demijohn, wiped his lips with the back of his hand, turned to Livingood and asked in that same rustle of a voice, "You a part of this?"

Livingood stood with his hands in the hip pockets of his britches. With the toe of his boot he kicked at some loose pebbles lying on the ground before him. His birthmark flared a dark lavender; he raised his head; his little cinderlike eyes shifted from Hamby to Longrunner to the king and back to Hamby. "No," he said. "Never heard nothing about this till now."

"What you think of it?" Darling wanted to know.

Hamby held his breath. There was no telling which way Livingood would jump. Yes, Livingood had his complaint against the king. But the king was white and Hamby wasn't, and in the past Livingood and Darling had both abused many a nigger no doubt far less trying than Hamby McFee. It may have been a long time ago, and Livingood may have since forsworn it, but still Hamby didn't think a white man that ever wore the sheets was apt to go from lynching to nigger-loving even in ten years' time.

But now Livingood surprised them all—Hamby the most—by showing a crimped smile and telling the king, "I think it's a damn good bet."

The breath Hamby had been holding now blissfully escaped him.

Some of the odds were turning his way after all. Clutching Pile-Driver, he watched Darling vigilantly from under the frayed brim of his straw hat. The king glowered at Livingood, shot a quick glance to Longrunner—who stood easily at a distance with both arms hanging limber by his sides—and looked again at Hamby. "What's this Price to you anyways?"

"Ain't nothing to me," Hamby said.

"Then why . . . ?"

Hamby laughed. "Maybe it a . . . what you call it? A whim. Maybe it a whim."

While Livingood and Longrunner and the king stood stonily, some of the peckerwoods laughed, not at Hamby's sally but at the fate he was courting with his impudence. Here for sure was one uppity coon that needed his lesson taught—that's what their laughter said. They wanted to get at him—that was their agreeable and amusing thought. Half of them were wobbly drunk, wet-eyed, tomato-faced, a-swim with the hate the liquor had undammed. Hamby began to sweat the cold and oily sweat that comes when a black man knows the rednecks are going bad. But he felt calm anyway; he felt strong; he was going to be worthy of the valor of Pile-Driver.

Darling took a short step toward him. The king's voice was even smaller now, even drier. "Do you actually think I'd let a goddamn nigger come up here and degrade me before my own?"

"Well," Hamby smiled, "I *hoped* so."

Longrunner chuckled; Petrie laughed right out; otherwise dead stillness reigned. Pile-Driver snapped at the buttons on Hamby's shirt. Ree Bolt leaned over and set the king's Red Wheel shake on the ground, let it run loose, peeped toward his Sharps leaning against the doorjamb of the fort twenty feet away. Poor Ives started backing toward the tree line. Abner Mullinax left the cockpit and strolled across the yard to where he'd left a shotgun propped on a rack of firewood.

Juncos and chickadees fluttered in the low brush roundabout. Hamby saw a tall woman come to the door of the fort holding a skillet. The two on the parapet looked keenly down. A woodpecker drilled in the woods.

Darling grinned, but now it was the grin of a wolf looking for its supper. He came another step closer. "You're a smart-mouth nigger, ain't you?"

"That's right," Hamby said. "I a *mean* one, too."

Darling reached behind him and brought up a big bowie with a blade that looked to be about a foot long; it was a knife for downing trees. At the sight of it Ree Bolt yelled, "Cut him!" and somebody else hollered, "Slash his goddamn balls off!" One of the rowdies broke into a cackle of glee; another ululated a war whoop. Hamby tensed, moved back; under his arm Pile-Driver glared at the king as if the sight of Darling were an offense to his dignity.

Livingood moved, put up a hand. "Leave it be, Webb," he said.

The king turned on him. "Leave it be? Well, I declare. Tell me, Rollin, does that idiot brother of yours whose skull I beat in, does he still eat his own shit and think it's applesauce?" Then before Livingood could speak or act Darling rounded back on Hamby. His knife flashed past Hamby's nose; Pile-Driver's head popped high, turned in the air trailing one thread of blood, bounced on the rocky floor of the bald.

So far Hamby had been drawing on a thing somewhat like duty that had no name, but now a wave of pure rage lifted him; now the memory of every slight and shame ever inflicted on him by a white poured its poison into him. With a motion quicker than the flick of a frog's tongue he whipped his razor at the end of its lanyard in a back-hand pass at Darling's neck, even as the king set himself to make another stroke. Darling threw up an arm to guard his jugular, but Hamby cut a half-circle around his wrist that went bone deep. The king withdrew, making a noise that was half a yelp of surprise and half a roar of fury; he shook that arm, spewed blood broadcast. Now Hamby could lay Pile-Driver's trembling carcass on the ground in honor.

When the king backed away slinging his bloody arm Livingood came at him from behind; that slur against his brother had to be repaid. He took Darling by one shoulder, spun him about, stood face to face with him and, using a pistol nobody'd even seen him draw, shot the king in the lower body. Hamby saw the smoke burst, saw the bullet come out Darling's back, leaving a ragged little bouquet of raw flesh. *Whoa, now,* he thought. *That a big-caliber gun.*

The king swayed like a partly cut tree ready to fall but then instead of toppling made a lunge at Livingood with his bowie. Livingood shot him again, and this time he slumped, dropped, ended by sitting on his rump with the front of his shirt afire from the muzzle flashes. "Treason!" he yelled.

Across the way Ree Bolt had run and grabbed up that Sharps of his and was training it on Livingood. Hamby drew his five-shooter fixing to get him when from the right-hand side Longrunner shot. Longrunner had a big Smith & Wesson Schofield laid across his forearm that he'd put in his clothes when he went to his mule before. When Longrunner shot it was like Ree Bolt was a rug hanging on a clothesline that had got whacked by a carpet beater; a big mushroom of dust jumped off him. Still trying to aim that Sharps, Ree pitched over backwards and hit his head on the rocky ground, making a sound like the splitting of a watermelon, and that was the end of him.

The compound was a scatter of men moving away from where Livingood stood straddling the fallen king—save for Hamby and Longrunner and the brother-in-law Petrie, who was crouched by the cockpit holding a little Bulldog self-cocker up by his ear. Now Darling made as if to rise, but Livingood put a foot on him and shoved him back. Weakly the king resumed trying to cut, but Livingood reached down and took away the bowie as easily as you'd steal a toy from a baby's hand.

In every corner of the yard Darling's men were snatching up arms and going to cover. The fellows on the parapet were nowhere to be seen; maybe they'd ducked inside the fort. Ives was gone in the hazelnut thickets. Darling's Red Wheel rooster dodged about, squawking in confusion. Everybody was yelling. The woman in the door of the fort hadn't moved; she looked on casually, as if the bedlam in her dooryard were as harmless as a game of tag among younguns.

"Treason," the king repeated, fumbling with his smoldering shirt.

Standing over him, Livingood raised both hands, one waving his pistol, the other Darling's bowie. "Hold!" he said to all in hearing. "Hold, now! This thing's done with."

"Not much, Mary Anne," one sang out. This was Darling's brother; he came running at Livingood from a corner of the fort, his yellow Winchester poked out ahead of him. He shot from the hip and missed Livingood but hit Longrunner, and Longrunner keeled over sideways. Before the brother could shoot again—and before Hamby or Petrie or Livingood could shoot either—a bullet came whizzing past Hamby's head from the rear and hit the brother in the side of the jaw and blew a mess of teeth and bone out the other side, and by the time the report of the shot that struck him slammed across the yard he was already wallowing on the ground, giving out gurgles and squeals reminiscent of a hog with its throat slit.

Hamby turned, saw a gangly man in a broad-brimmed hat advancing through a cloud of powder smoke from the rim of the bald—*that* was what he'd sensed, first on the trail and then again just as he was pitting Buttermilk. The cuss had followed them up the mountain; it was his big old hat Hamby had almost glimpsed, pulling back out of sight whenever he'd looked. The gent came on, cranked another round into the chamber of his rifle, walked past Hamby into the middle of the dooryard. Only then did Hamby know him; it was Richbourg, that hard-ass Revenue deputy from Georgia. He opened his coat, thumbed out his badge to prove his authority, asked everybody please to lay down their irons, and they did it.

Next the woman who'd stood in the door of the fort the whole time came out. She was carrying that big iron skillet. She was bony and crookbacked and shriveled-up—no telling how old, thirty or sixty, you couldn't have said. She had a shock of patchy white hair with spots of bald in it and a face as wrinkled as one of those dolls with heads made out of dried apples. Her eyes gave no light. Behind her came a line of younguns, eight of them altogether, stairstepped in age from the least, a toddler, to one that appeared about fifteen, all having a stringy look. When she got to where Darling lay moaning she stopped, and the younguns stopped, too, and spread out in a ring around him to watch. Then that woman took the skillet and beat Webb Darling's head with it till it was no thicker than a cow pie.

Longrunner lay on his back looking up at the sky. That .44 slug had gone in his back under the right shoulder blade and crossed through to come out the pit of his left arm, breaking the arm, too. Where the top of the arm used to be was now an ugly cluster of bone shards poking out every which way. The hole in the armpit was as big as a child's fist; every time Longrunner breathed a black foam came out of it. Longrunner made no complaint except for continually trying to clear his throat. Livingood stood over him with his hands on his hips. "You go easy now," he said. Longrunner blinked, gave a nod.

Hamby was sitting on the ground next to Longrunner. The Indian's smoky eyes rolled over and fixed on Hamby, and he smiled a little, said something Hamby couldn't hear. Hamby bent closer. Longrunner whispered, "Like I said, you a fortunate nigger."

When Longrunner was gone Livingood went over to where

Darling's brother was still rolling around hollering, and he put his boot on the fellow's neck and stood on it with his whole weight till Richbourg came and drew him off.

❧

"I heard a rumor you and Darling was setting up a big chicken fight on the bald," Richbourg explained as he and Hamby approached the fort. "I figured I might see a chance to finally nab the bastard. And if that damn Ves Price was still alive I'd get him out, too, worthless as he is. So I hung around your place. Then when you left I followed you up."

"Good thing," Hamby said. He eyed the shambles in the yard. "Maybe next time you bring a big-ass posse, too."

Richbourg shrugged. "Figured I could handle it better on my own." It was hard to argue with that.

They stepped through the narrow door. The window shutters in the main room were latched shut, but one stub of candle on a table in the middle gave out a flicker of light, so they could see the woman sitting there in the near-dark. The bloody skillet was on the table. Nearby the younguns cowered on the floor all in a bunch; one or two were sniveling. The place smelt moldy and dank and wet like a cave. A big rat sat on its hind legs in a corner eating a bit of bread like a squirrel with its nut.

The woman addressed Richbourg without raising her head to look at him; her voice was reedy and frail; a shout would break it for good. "Are you fixing to take me to town for killing that man?"

Even if she wouldn't, the younguns watched him close till he replied. "Why, nome," he said. "I reckon he died of getting shot." Hamby thought this commendably broad-minded; already Richbourg had told Livingood to consider himself a Revenue deputy who'd gone after Webb Darling in the course of his sworn duty. Even now Livingood and his also presumably deputized brother-in-law were guarding the crackers outside. It was plain Richbourg was one officer who knew how to tidy things up in a hurry. Hamby put aside his normal mistrust of the law; he approved.

At Richbourg's news the younguns stirred and settled some, but the woman wagged her head and made a croaking noise that might've been a laugh. "No, sir," she said. "He never died of getting shot, nor of me a-whanging him, either one. He died of being what he was."

Hamby went over to the rat, which was so tame it didn't move. Holding its crust of bread, it looked questioningly up at him. Drolly he wanted to ask it if it was any kin to Ves Price. Instead he moved past, went through a door, entered a mildewed corridor where no light showed. He put his hands on the walls on either side of him, and they came away with a clammy scum. "Ves Price!" he called, wiping his hands on his trousers, "Ves Price, you piece of trash!"

From behind a wooden door on his left he heard the forlornest wail ever given voice. "Oh mercy," Ves was crying. "Mercy, mercy, they're a-coming. My hour's nigh. Oh Lordy, Lordy, Lordy, take me to my mam."

Richbourg approached with a ring of keys the woman gave him; he tried several till he found the one that fit; he turned the lock, pushed back the heavy door. The smell that blew out on them was that of a stable long uncleaned. Hamby went in. With a whine Ves drew back in a corner. The cell was pieced together with flinders of stone and had a thin scatter of straw on the floor and a slit of a window high in one wall. A dim light from the window fell on Ves. He looked like he'd been roped behind the caboose of a train and dragged all the way from Asheville to Old Fort and back without missing a single crosstie. Both eyes were black like a raccoon's mask; part of an ear was missing; his smashed nose bore a close resemblance to a squashed muffin; there were several new gaps in his teeth. Yellow-

and-purple bruises covered him, old blood crusted his shirt, and he was missing his left little finger.

He cupped his hands around his swollen eyes and tried to see who'd come. Then he made out Hamby and spoke his name in absolute wonder. "Is that you?" he cried. "Lord bless you, Hamby. Oh Lordy, thank you. Bless God. Thank you, Lord." He bounded up and came at Hamby stumbling, his arms thrown wide. "Oh Hamby, you come to save me. Here, let me hug your neck." He did, though Hamby shoved him away with an oath. "Oh Hamby," Ves sobbed, "I'm ashamed. I know I been hateful to you in time past. I know I done you bad." He flopped down in the straw crying. "And oh I repent of it, I do. I'm a sinner. I'm a evildoer. I hope you'll forgive me. I hope Jesus will bless me." Then, wiping away his tears, he looked hopefully up. "Did you happen to see a little bat somewheres outside? And what in hell was all that shooting anyway?"

Richbourg stepped in then, and Ves recoiled from him as from a leper, put his open hands out to ward off the vision. "You leave me be, now," he hollered. "I been beat on enough. I quit the goddamn Revenue. You ain't got no call to whup on me no more. 'Twasn't my fault, not none of it. You can't beat on a man that's quit you." Then with a surge of indignation he drew himself up, demanding, "Where's my goddamn bounty money?"

Outside in the yard Hamby walked over to where Webb Darling's body lay covered with blood. The king's features were mashed all out of shape from the woman's skillet, so his mouth was not exactly where it should be. It had a funny skew to it that made him look like he was pleased to have ended up so, instead of disgusted as he must've been. One eye was shut and one half-open, and the blue of it, once as sweet as a spring violet, was clouded over with a filmy caul. Hamby took from his pocket the note he'd found stuck in the mouth of Lige Dollar's head all those months ago. Getting down on a knee, he rolled the paper into a little tube and pushed it carefully into Darling's warp of mouth.

Kneeling there, he thought about taking the king's head in recompense for Lige's—and for Pile-Driver's, too—but he decided he'd seen and done enough such business for one day. Besides, if his grandmam was right and strange divinities revenged themselves on maimers, he didn't want to call down on himself whatever voodoo they commanded. He rose then and glanced about. Nearby lay Darling's hat with its shiny emblem of a king's crown fixed to the front. Hamby picked it up, removed his battered straw, set the other on his head. It was a perfect fit.

It was too late in the day to think of going down the mountain; there wasn't time for Richbourg to order up the wagon that was needed to carry the woman and the younguns and Darling's wounded brother. So he paroled the crackers all in one big lot, said they were guilty of nothing more than gambling on a cockfight and getting drunk in public, and those weren't federal crimes; the man wasted no motion, it was clear. He did sequester the rednecks' guns, though, to be reclaimed in a week's time at Hiawassee. He ordered Jared Nutbush to go to Hayesville and fetch a rig back up in the morning and told the balance of the peckerwoods to scoot, and right quick they all complied.

Meantime Hamby and Livingood and Petrie scoured the rocky bald till they found a piece of ground that would hold three graves, and with shovels and a pick borrowed from the fort they dug out places for Longrunner and Ree Bolt and the king and rolled them in. They covered up Darling and Bolt first and then, leaning on their tools, waited a few minutes while Livingood stood over Longrunner's hole. After a time Livingood gave a nod and turned aside, and Hamby and Petrie covered Longrunner up, too, while Livingood looked on from a distance.

That night in the main room of the fort Darling's brother kept them all awake with his sobbing and hallooing. They'd laid him on a pallet in a corner. His jaw had swollen out to the size of a mushmelon, and he was burning up with fever. Brusquely Richbourg examined him, told him, "I don't expect you'll make it, old pard. I think you've got the blood poisoning." Weakly the poor fellow whimpered, clutched at Richbourg's arm. Richbourg freed himself of the grasp and spat. "But think about it thisaway," he went on. "If you was to get well with your face all tore up like it is, why, no woman'd ever want to come near you. So it's all for the best, don't you see? Just you lay there and take your medicine."

While they lounged around the fire Hamby cast up accounts with Livingood. Livingood claimed Hamby owed him seven dollars for the two dead birds, but Hamby argued the king, not he, had killed Pile-Driver. Richbourg backed Hamby, so Livingood settled for the three-fifty for Buttermilk. Hamby reckoned out his winnings then, and minus the three-fifty there was twelve hundred seventy-six dollars and some-odd cents in the pot. Three-quarters went to Livingood and the rest to Hamby. They divided it while Ves Price leaned in, gaping with bedazzlement. "Lordy be," Ves declared, "I never seen so much money all at onct. Look at all them shinies." Livingood put his share in his saddlebag, which he used for a pillow. Hamby had a war bag he kept in the pocket of his coat. He shook it out and filled it with the three hundred nineteen that was his—a whole mess of greenbacks, wildcat notes, eagles and quarter-eagles, silver dollars, some coppers, even a soiled limp old Confederate ten-dollar bill.

Ves avidly watched as Hamby fastened the drawstring of the war bag and laid it by. In the morning when they awoke, Ves was gone and so was Hamby's money.

Part IV

Benediction

CHAPTER 17

October 1882

Raleigh, N.C., October 19, 1882

Dear Mrs. Carter,

It may be that my name is known to you altho' I have not
hitherto enjoyed the Privilege & Pleasure of making your personal
acquaintance. As I was a dear friend of your late brother A. J.
Curtis, haply he has mentioned me in letters, tho' I know he wrote
but little & it is far more probable that I thus boldly present myself
to you as an utter stranger. But whether I am an unknown or not I
trust you will credit my avowal of the deepest kindly feelings, not
only for your departed Loved One, but for Yourself, Your husband &
Your Family as well.

Mr. Curtis oft spoke to me of his fine farm on the banks of the
lovely Hiwassee, of the grandeur of the lofty mountains that surround
it & of Yourself, Your husband, Your nephews, Your negro—all the

rapturous Attachments & Affinities which his heart still cherished despite the lamentable effects of his incapacity. You should know, if you do not already, that he enjoyed some occasions of absolute clarity of mind; & it was upon certain of these instances that he was wont to recount to me the Beauties & Pleasures of his Home, Sweet Home. Such lucid intervals were in fact nearly as common as his regrettable periods of Confusion, Melancholia & Despair. Perhaps it will help assuage your pangs of grief to know that he did not descend altogether into the Abyss of Madness but was always, even to the end, able to rally & know again some of the Joys of Life, albeit by necessity much reduced.

The authorities of the Asylum have by now acquainted you with the particulars of his passing on the 8th ult., of Pneumonia, for which I extend my most heartfelt Condolences & offer up the most fervent Prayers for his Eternal Rest. Peace was not much granted him in life; may he find it Hereafter in Heaven.

Doubtless you wonder how I came to form the connection which brought me so close to your brother. I am in fact a retired Minister of the Gospel, of the Baptist Faith, subsisting on a small pension, & as I live very near the State Asylum it has been my custom in recent years to improve my leisure time by visiting there &—insofar as may be possible—giving spiritual solace to such of the inmates as are able to receive it. In the course of these visits I met Mr. Curtis, found him a most estimable gentleman (when not encumbered by the extremes of his disability) & formed a bond with him that quickly ripened into an Affection which I am confident he fully returned. (In which case he may, in fact, have mentioned me & my Several Kindnesses in communications to you.)

My purpose in writing is to give you some account of Mr. Curtis's last days on earth, for as he fell into his *Final Illness* I was constantly by him & he spoke to me at some length, when he could, of matters with which I am sure you will feel a need to become acquainted. Let there be no mistake as to my Motives; I desire no approbation, no meed of gratitude, no earthly recompense for the solicitude I showed your brother as he languished in his poor cell abandoned by all, cut off from everything in the world he held dear. No, my reward—if indeed I have earned one—will be in Paradise. It is true that I am a poor retired man reliant upon the most scant of allowances; but the Lord has provided for me continually though simply throughout Life &, I am confident, will always do so in future. In the case of your esteemed brother I was actuated wholly by Christian charity which is given, not in order to receive some vulgar bauble the world might hold dear, but solely to Glorify the Name of Christ Jesus.

As I have said, some few of the simple pleasures of life remained always accessible to Mr. Curtis; but of course, in truth, he often wrestled with the Devils of his affliction. And although it must needs perturb you to hear it I am bound by a frank good will to relate to you that the sentiment he most often expressed to me in his waning days was a deeply heartfelt Regret that, as he expressed it, he had failed to *Live His Own Life*. He gave the phrase a most particular emphasis. Since such a declaration seemed so Extraordinary & so to defy Logic I pressed him to dilate upon it & by way of reply he exclaimed with some fervor that Circumstances had compelled him to live a life that others demanded of him rather than one he might have preferred & from which he might have taken greater satisfaction. By this I took him to mean that by answering always to the Rigors of Duty he had placed the Needs, Wants & Welfare of others—perhaps of Yourself & his Other Relations, though I am hardly qualified to speculate—above his own.

It will pain you to learn of the woe by which he was plagued on account of the Toils he undertook for your Benefit & for the Benefit of his other Dependents—which after all were no more than the labors which Society has decreed to be the natural responsibility of a Man of Affairs. I regret to be the agent of any least measure of distress to you, nor do I mean to impute to you any guilt, any smallest measure of Accountability for your brother's despair on this account. But Candour compels me to give you as true an account as I may; a Steadfast Friend could do no less. Let me hasten to assure you, however, that I quite naturally reminded Mr. Curtis that as Christians we are *All* bound to Serve others selflessly—as I now hope to Serve you—& that to lead a dutiful life is to Please God and win a Place for us nearby the Throne (whatever reward other we may haply Earn).

Yet his unvarying rejoinder was to assert himself ruined first by war, which coming upon him in the green bud of his happy youth had irreversibly blighted what might otherwise have flowered into a Genial & Optimistic maturity; and second, by the hard duties which so unexpectedly fell to him upon his return from war, when he learned his valiant Brothers had lain down on the Altar of the Cause the supreme sacrifice of Youth & Life, that his Father and Mother upon whom he had always relied were Broken in Spirit therefrom & that You yourself, then but in your girlhood, & your Sisters yet unwed depended for everything upon his Exertions, as did those others for whom he was obliged by his position to provide.

That he did so provide is a testament to his Resolve & Manly Fortitude. But I fear his discharge of these Obligations came at the cost of great agitation of the Mind & Soul & he told me these torments arose from a Certainty that he had proved Unequal to the Demands placed upon him & a Belief that he had mismanaged Affairs most profoundly. Most particularly did he feel that he had failed to come up to the High Mark set by his worthy Father, Squire J. Madison Curtis, the idol of his days. So extreme was this conception that in the very last exchange I had with him your brother in his delirium begged me to seek out his Father—who of course is long deceased, but poor Andrew had forgotten that—& beg the Pardon of that Splendid Personage for having failed in the responsibilities life had assigned him.

Your brother sometimes declared to me that his most secret heart was as tender as a woman's & as fragile as a hummingbird's egg, yet in order to make his way in Life & to fulfill the expectations so many had of him he had been obliged to harden that Heart—*Make It Hard as a Bullet,* he would say. Yet even that had not been sufficient to bring him the prize he believed must be his if he were to emulate his Father. In consequence he believed he had misspent his life by attempting that which was foreign to his own Nature & Inclination, thus at the end betraying his very self. 'Tis not Mine to judge the merits of these sentiments, extreme as they are; as I have said, the Ills he complained of were the universal due of Mankind. Yet had you heard as I did how expressively & with what sorrow & repining he spoke you would have found it as impossible as I to refute his gloomy argument.

He was as you know convinced he was impoverished—at times mistook the Asylum for a poorhouse; believed he suffered from a multiplicity of repugnant & incurable diseases. Furthermore if I may venture to say it he was persuaded that he had been *discarded* (as he called it) by the very same persons for whom he had poured out his Life, that those he had nourished had committed him to his lonely cell & left him to the ravages of sickness in order to consume his fortune at their leisure—which notwithstanding his delusions of poverty I understand to be quite considerable even yet—& to indulge the same inclinations toward personal felicity that he had been forced by his position to eschew. These sad emotions, it should be remembered, were present with him *always,* whatever the state of his wits; at his maddest & at his most sane they remained Steadfast.

Do not misunderstand, I pray you. There can be no question but what You & Yours made the fateful decision to commit your brother only as a Last & Most Bitter Resort, confronted as you were by his increasingly aberrant behavior, & that You did so only with the deepest reluctance & even horror, & that before taking such a dire step you first exhausted every other honorable & practicable course of action. Needless to say by rehearsing here your brother's manifestly deranged, polluted & unfounded reasoning I in no way imply my concurrence with it. Surely I need not point out that no slightest reflection is implied upon the necessity You & Your Family *must have felt* of pursuing the remedy you did. Let not your brother's fevered ravings awaken in your bosom the serpent of guilt to stir forth & sting thine heart with Reproaches which no man of conscience could possibly think justified. You are, I am perfectly sure, without the slightest blame.

But it will surely be to your profit to know finally—& without equivocation—whereof your dear Andrew suffered in his mind, in the same way that the details of the death of his body given you by the authorities have doubtless already lent much to the healing of your sorrows at his loss. For just as we wish to know all we can of the last struggles of our Loved Ones, and just as we long to commit to memory the sight of their features as they lie upon the catafalque ere they are committed to the earth to await the Judgment, so also do we desire to know a thing normally hidden, *viz.*, what was in their hearts at the last. This then is my gift to you in all humility. By this knowledge of your brother's dolorous preoccupations may you come into an Intimacy with him that is indissoluble & everlasting.

Bless him, he is now at Rest! While I was not privileged to be present when he passed I was assured by those who attended him that in the last moment of all he called out several times the name of Salina his former wife, so long ago torn from him by a dreadful death, & to whose loss he had never become reconciled. Further, I was told, in dying he stretched forth his hand in air. Perhaps she took it and led him Across.

Now I must make an end, for I have presumed too long upon your patience. However, I cannot close without admonishing you in the most cordial manner not to feel yourself under any obligation or constraint to me, a perfect foreigner to you, on account of the assiduous care, companionship & love—yes, Christian love—which I gave to Andrew at a time when he felt—wrongly, of course—most forlornly cast aside by his own flesh and blood. You owe me nothing save perhaps a prayer on my poor behalf to the One Above.

If, however, a need should by chance arise to post to me any letter, parcel or other item, please know that I may always be reached at General Delivery, Raleigh, N.C.

> Very respectfully, I am, Madam,
> Your Most Obedient Servant,
>
> J. F. T. Belflower, D.D.
>
> Mrs. W. Thomas Carter
> Carter's Cove
> Brasstown P.O., N.C.

CHAPTER 18

April 1889

*T*oward midmorning Rebecca at last fell into a restless sleep. Her gaunt head lay on the pillow in a tangle of damp hair. Tom Carter sat by the bed holding one of her hands in both of his. Between his horny palms the hand was parched and hot. She'd had a bad night— raging fever, coughing fits that spewed up alarming amounts of blood and tissue. He was relieved to see that she could drowse now, even fitfully. Still from time to time she'd twitch and jerk; spasms would pass roughly through her. Each one gave him a twinge.

Looking into her face, he had the awful sense that he could already see the skull that lurked inside, almost ready now to shed its film of flesh and start terribly forth. He couldn't confront the bony leer, glanced away from it. Opening his grasp, he turned her hand gently over and gazed at it, at its scars and calluses as coarse as his own, at the withered pads of her blunt finger ends. He recalled examining her hand in exactly this same pitying way eight years ago on the porch of the old Curtis manse. Although he'd pledged then to give her a softer time, and although he'd toiled hard to redeem that pledge, the hand he held this morning was worse off—harsher, redder, more deformed—than the one he'd hoped to soothe that long-gone December evening.

It was hard to be alive, he thought. It was far easier to be dead. Going through the gate from the one to the other, though—that was the mystery. For some it was a blessing, like the onset of slumber. For others—for Rebecca—it was the hardest thing of all. And how unfair her suffering, how unearned! Yet it was the will of God that she bear this trial, and the designs of the Most High lay far beyond mortal questioning. Tom sent up a prayer that he knew to be in vain.

From behind, Dr. Killian laid a hand on his shoulder. "Let her be awhile," he said. "Go outside. Take some air."

Tom nodded, released her hand, rose from the chair he'd drawn close beside the bed twelve hours before and not left since. Pain shot through the small of his back. His swollen bladder hurt. He tottered; his legs were numb; his knees abruptly gave way beneath him; he almost toppled. Dr. Killian caught him under one arm, steadied him. Leaning on the doctor, Tom passed a hand over his brow. "Seven years we knew it was going to come," he said. "Now that it's here I can't hardly take it in."

"I know," said the doctor, "I know." He gave Tom a small and tender push. "You go on now."

On unsteady legs Tom crossed the room, put a hand on the door-knob, glanced back. Her jaw had dropped, and an ugly glottal noise issued forth, the burble of her ruined lungs. She shuddered so violently the ropes under the bed thrummed.

He opened the sickroom door and stepped into the crowded parlor, a million pinpricks of feeling coming back into his legs. Faces revolved inquiringly toward him—his own daughter six-year-old Lillie

Dell, several nieces whose names he could never remember, Captain Moore's Miss Hattie Gash, the inevitable Mrs. Hemphill, the Reverend Thomas, the only male in the room. "She's asleep," Tom told them all, closing the door behind him.

The stale odor of the sickroom gave way to the many smells of the food the women had laid out on the table in the dining room— ham, corned beef, fried chicken, pork roast, boiled eggs, sweet potatoes, cabbage, biscuits, cornbread. The smells were both enticing and repellent; Tom's stomach surged with nausea and perversely with hunger, too. He wanted to get outside, wanted to relieve himself, wanted to feel the springtime sun on his face. But the reverend caught him by the elbow and with fruity intonations invited Tom to join him in prayer. Despite his impatience Tom complied. He knelt wincing at the discomfort of his bladder. It wasn't right to begrudge the clergy, but all the time the preacher maundered on in his rich and rounded tones Tom stared unbowed past him out the side window, befuddled with fatigue, sore-eyed, shaky, wanting to be warmed by the light he saw gleaming on the broad fields.

When the prayer was done he stood and once more made for the door, but now Mrs. Hemphill barred his way, blowing over him her sweetish foul breath like an exhalation of rotting flowers. Because he was a good Christian full of forbearance Tom obliged her, too. In a fulsome and somehow admonishing manner much like the reverend's she reminded him of the solace to be got from the certain knowledge of Rebecca's translation into Paradise, where she would await Tom's own ascent. Tom of course did not need Mrs. Hemphill to remind him of the rapture to come; he knew and believed in it. But just now the certainty was of small comfort. He was ashamed of not praising it, of not thanking the Almighty for it, but neither could he help himself. When Rebecca passed he would be bereft in his corporeal body, in the material life; he did not wish to await the Resurrection to be rejoined in spirit at the Latter Day. No, he wanted to go on sharing *this* existence, *this* time, *this* world with the partner he adored and whom he yet owed the ease he'd promised but had not found a way to provide. He was in torment; he hoped God would show him mercy in his anguish and forgive him his lapse of pious gratitude and trust.

Outside he hurried along a lane that opened up before him, as the men waiting in the yard stood aside one by one murmuring condoling words. He entered the privy and stood pissing for a long time into the left-hand hole, whose rim had been worn satiny smooth from much use. His urine gave off a garlicky stink, as if his vitals had begun to fester; he was mildly offended at the noxiousness of his own inward parts. When he finished he came back to the house again through that same lane of murmurous men and stood basking in the hot light at the edge of the front gallery, bending his knees from time to time to restore more feeling in them. Around him at the base of the gallery bloomed Rebecca's flower garden of irises, jonquils, violets, eyebrights and adder's-tongue, untended now and running to weeds. Still the warmth of the morning had awakened the heady scents of the flowers, and he breathed these gratefully in. But then he was struck by the thought that Rebecca couldn't smell her blossoms—that she never would again.

At the far end of the gallery Oliver Price sat rocking in the bentwood chair that used to be Rebecca's favorite. Silently he nodded, and Tom nodded in return without addressing him. Nowadays you didn't come at Oliver unbidden. He'd lost what Tom was about to lose, and more besides. The ache of it was in the deep lines around his mouth and the hollows of his cheeks, in the blankness of his eyes. Tom watched him as if across a gulf of terrible wisdom that Oliver had acquired and Tom hadn't, couldn't—not yet, not in its brutal wholeness. Soon, though, Tom must grow wise in his own turn. He wondered if the wisdom would change him as it had changed Oliver.

Wearing their Sabbath best the neighbors, the Cartman brothers, other kinsmen and elders of the Methodist congregation filled the yard. They gabbed, though in respectfully muted fashion; they smoked and chewed; discreetly they spat. Some who hadn't spoken before came forward to offer Tom a word of sympathy, but many stood shyly off, reticent country fellows not knowing what to say. The space in front of the barn was a jumble of their wagons, buggies, horses, mules. Younguns—some of Miss Hattie's grandbabies, Tom's own tots Homer and Ethel, others Tom didn't recognize—dashed up and down hollering and laughing, playing hide-and-go-seek. Dogs chased after them barking; guinea hens ran indignantly away. Beneath the big Spanish oak at the bottom of the yard a pair of neighbors glided to and fro in the swing Tom had made and hung there for little Freddy, before the lad had died so untimely the year before, after a fall from the very porch where Tom now stood.

. Down the road perched on the top rail of Tom's boundary fence with his back to the house was a slouching Hamby McFee. Wearing his crumpled old blockader's hat, Hamby puffed on his corncob pipe. Beyond his stooped figure the little valley Tom's father had named Carter's Cove opened narrowly between sheltering mountains just now coming green with spring growth. In successive swales and hillocks the cove followed a tiny creek down and down, till ridges on either side intruded to shut off the view toward the Hiwassee bottom, where the creek met the river. Above the ridge tops the blue Tusquittees raised their ragged tops. Hamby, where he perched alone, seemed to rule it all.

A small hand slipped into Tom's, and he glanced down to see Lillie Dell holding on to him. She didn't look up; instead she stood as he stood and stared as he'd stared down the cove into the distance, toward where Hamby held his station on the topmost rail of the fence. The sight of the crown of her head, of the part in her sandy tresses, of the fine strands of hair that stood awry at temple and nape, of the tight braiding of her pigtails—all of this awoke in Tom a nearly unbearable pain. He suppressed a sob. She seemed so susceptible, so dainty and fragile, so helpless before the madness of the earth. What would become of her? Of Homer? Of Ethel?

"Papa," she asked after a time, "will Hamby ever come inside and see Mama?"

"He says he won't," Tom answered. Rebecca herself had not called for Hamby, yet on two or three occasions yesterday others who knew the affection she bore him—Tom was one—had done so. But always when summoned Hamby said no, sat there on his rail crudely swearing till the asker withdrew. Nobody knew what to make of Hamby, least of all Tom, whose heart was open to all and as simple as a dove's, while Hamby's was a riddle the meaning of which no man could read. "Hamby does what he likes," he explained.

"Why won't he go and see her?" Now Lillie did raise to him her deep-set eyes of pearly gray. "Does he hate Mama?"

Tom shook his head. "No, sweetheart. He doesn't hate her, I don't think. Why, they've known each other their whole lives almost."

They stood hand in hand for quite some time, watching the people in the yard, speaking to some who approached. Tom shook several hands left-handed while he held hers.

Presently she asked, "Papa, is Mama really dying?"

His throat thickened; he strove to master his voice and hold it firm. "Yes, sweetheart, she is."

"When do you reckon she'll get done dying?"

He swallowed hard. "Right directly, I expect."

"Then after she dies," Lillie announced wisely, "we'll have to wait a long time till we get to Heaven ourselves, before we can see her again, won't we?"

"That's right," Tom replied.

She squeezed his hand; confidently she smiled.

God will bring it to pass, Tom told himself. *But how can we bear to live till then?*

While they stood talking two riders appeared at the mouth of the cove and turned up the way to the house at a brisk canter. Studying the horses, Tom recognized the one on the right as Captain Moore's Crockett; there was no mistaking the powerful arch of the stallion's neck or the way it flaunted its long tail, flared out like a battle standard. As always Irish Bill rode straight-legged and erect, showing a perfect cavalry seat.

"Oh, it's the captain!" Lillie cried, bounding eagerly up and down. Abruptly she broke free, ran headlong to meet him. Watching her weaving her way across the crowded yard, Tom was beset by a kind of envy. In a child joys are easy to come by, while sorrows are slower and harder to know. One day Lillie might repent having indulged her wish to go and pet Captain Moore's great horse, rather than staying to grieve as her mother lay dying. But not today. Today joy was stronger than a loss whose meaning she couldn't begin to grasp.

The second horse was a small black-footed gray with good lines, although nowhere near as fine as Crockett's. The figure on its back had a skinny neck and a narrow head he carried somewhat to the side. The pair advanced till they reached the fence where Hamby roosted. There they drew rein and sat their horses, and talk passed among the three of them. Tom saw Hamby make an impatient gesture. He thought he heard Hamby's voice raised in fury; no doubt he'd offered the visitors some unmerited insult. They put their horses into the path again and came on.

They reached the wagons by the barn and stood down and were tethering their mounts to the rear wheel of Miss Hattie's rockaway when Lillie came squealing at them. With a whoop Irish Bill scooped her up, whirled her in a circle of billowing petticoats, lifted her high to Crockett, who stood very still except for the tremors that ran along the muscles of his shoulders while she caressed his big head with her tiny petal of a hand. All this time the second man hung back with hands thrust deep in the pockets of his coat.

Oliver Price got up out of Rebecca's rocker, came to the front of the gallery and stood next to Tom. Together they peered keenly at the stranger, who now seemed to feel the weight of the scrutiny and rounded to meet it. And just as he did Tom knew him—it was Ves, Oliver's oldest boy, long vanished, a rascal and a vagabond of whom no report had ever come, whose ignoble death in some far and benighted place many had confidently presumed. Seeing him, Tom knew at once why he'd come.

After a moment's evident confusion Ves ambled toward the house, while behind him Irish Bill and Lillie fussed on with Crockett. The men in the yard fell silent, parted before him as he came, curiously watched him once he'd passed. Despite his sheepish air he bore himself straight and not without a measure of pride. He crossed to the porch and stopped at the bottom of the steps. He'd put on weight; his color was high; his eyes were clear; he wore good clothes of fashionable cut; improbably Ves radiated a glow of prosperity and fine fettle. "Hidy," he said to Oliver. When Oliver failed to speak Ves politely touched the brim of his hat to Tom; Tom nodded back.

Oliver showed no sign of hearing the greeting or even of seeing what he saw. Seven years Ves had been gone. In that time Oliver had lost Miz Henslee to the influenza and his baby Rachel to the whooping cough. All but the last of his one-time mob of younguns had either got wed or run off like Ves, and the one left to him—his youngest girl—was fixing to marry and move away before summer's end. Oliver, who'd had a dozen children and two wives and had reveled in the chaos of a huge and ungovernable family, was now the loneliest man Tom knew. Presently he spoke to Ves in a voice that was as empty as his life: "Have you got the devil out of you yet?"

Ves frowned, shrugged, didn't reply. Sternly Oliver observed him. Tom guessed Oliver knew why his boy had come, just as Tom had known the moment he recognized Ves. It wasn't for forgiveness or repentance or love of kin; it wasn't for vainglory or to parade the goods he'd got in the great world before those who'd once scoffed at him; it wasn't to gloat or seek revenge for the aspersions all had cast. No, it was a pilgrimage. Ves was no prodigal son returned; he was unchanged, unredeemed; he'd come back to honor the only true thing he'd ever felt, that he'd held to even in a life of untruth.

He faced Tom, took off his hat, held it before him in token of respect. "I was down in Ellijay," he said. "Fellow there from Hayesville told me she was sick and like to die." He paused, rotated the hat between his hands; his Adam's apple bobbed in his long neck. "Is it so?"

"It's so," Tom said.

Ves blinked, chewed his bottom lip. Woe swept over him as visibly as if an actual gale had blown; it left him roiled, unsteady. He made a small dry sound at the back of his throat. "Can I go in and see her?"

Tom supposed he should resent the attentions Ves wanted to visit on his wife. He well remembered Ves's low ways in times past and thought it possible that, if admitted to Rebecca's sickroom, he might make some other scene equally unbecoming. Yet what he saw in Ves's eyes was the same torment that ate at his own heart. Maybe the misery Ves felt was even worse, for if Tom had loved Rebecca when she didn't love him, at least she'd come to love him in the end. No such consolation was Ves's. "She's asleep," Tom said, hoping it would be enough to turn him away, even though he knew it wouldn't.

And sure enough Ves shifted his weight from one foot to the other, darted looks hither and yon, said doggedly, "I won't pester her none. Won't even speak. I just want to look at her."

Now Oliver pushed forward, grim-faced. "The best thing you can do is get back on that horse and light out of here and never come back," he declared. He was trembling; the torment that lived behind the cold words was hurtful to see.

"That's just what I aim to do," Ves rejoined, but with none of Oliver's rancor. Then mulishly he added, "Soon as I see her."

Rage—or was it sorrow?—turned Oliver's countenance a shocking shade of purple. He went down two of the steps and stood over Ves shaking a fist in the air, as if he meant to strike him. "D'you even know what's become of your people?"

But Ves stood his ground, calm yet firm, unangered, without apology. "Surely I know," he said mildly, looking up at Oliver with his clear eyes. "I been keeping up, one way and another. I know what passed. I know your trouble, what you lost, how. Maybe I was even sorry when I heard. But I couldn't of helped. Couldn't of changed it or eased it. 'Tain't in me. I ain't that kind." He placed the hat back on his head and straightened it with a whisk of one hand along the brim. "I'm what I always was," he went on. "Ain't no better, ain't no worse." Then he faced Tom again. "I want to go in and see her now," he said.

Tom took him in, led him through the parlor. The few there who recognized him—his smart appearance bespoke nothing of the shop-worn Ves Price of old—looked on in puzzlement, disbelief, outrage. For his part Ves continued to display that queer air of mingled confidence and embarrassment he'd shown in the yard, crossing the room with a mannerly smile. When Tom opened the door of the sickroom Dr. Killian recognized Ves and sprang up to say a reprimand; Tom gave a placating motion, and the doctor relented, though he stood glowering as Ves removed his hat and entered. Tom shut the door at once, rather than waiting to see more.

Returning to the yard—again past that mixed array of stares in the parlor, again not stopping to explain—Tom found Oliver and

Captain Moore at the foot of the steps engaged in earnest conversation, the captain holding Lillie easily in the bend of one arm while she tickled his chin with a daisy she'd plucked. "I'm sorry I brought him," Irish Bill was saying. "We fell in together on the road. Turned out we were both headed here. An unfortunate coincidence." He blew out a regretful sigh. "I never meant to cause you any distress, Brother Price." He turned to Tom. "Or you either, Brother Carter."

Tom dismissed the apology with a wave of his hand. Oliver said, " 'Tain't any fault of yours. A man on the road can't pick his company." He stood a moment pursing and unpursing his lips, then sent Moore an almost covert glance. Pretending idle curiosity, he asked, "Did the boy say where he'd been all this time?"

"Chattanooga, Knoxville, Atlanta—one place and another. Cities. Gambling, mostly. He claimed he was right flush."

The captain's news made Oliver groan. "Well, he's on the straight road to Hell now for sure. And ain't a thing I can do about it." Glumly he seated himself on the top step. "Never could do nothing with that scamp." He hung his head, spread his hands on his knees, appeared to study them, as if the pattern of their lines had the power to explain his life to him, lorn and terrible as it had lately been.

Irish Bill hefted Lillie, took the daisy from her, commenced tickling her in turn. "That time I hid Ves from the blockaders," he mused as Lillie giggled, "we talked a good deal. I felt I got to know him pretty well. I thought him a lonely boy. And mistrustful of the world. Maybe even scared of it. Like he thought he must cut corners to get the things he wanted—that if he didn't the world would never freely give them. Or having given, would soon take them away again."

A husk of a laugh came out of Oliver. "It's funny. He worshiped his mama. As did I. We both loved *her*. But he couldn't abide me, nor me him in the end. Ain't that funny? All that love we had for her, and none left over for each other." He gave up examining his hands and rubbed them briskly together, then sat squinting into the distance while Tom and the captain waited to see if he would say more. In another minute he did. "I think maybe he held it against me, that she died and I lived." Oliver got a faraway look on his face. "Nancy, her name was."

Just then—and to the surprise of the three of them—Ves came out of the house, not having stayed five minutes. Evidently he'd been true to his word; all he'd wanted was to see her. "I'm obliged," he said to Tom as he approached and donned his hat. He looked composed, maybe even relieved, as if he'd successfully finished a task he'd long dreaded undertaking for fear of doing poorly. Though his eyes swam with tears he didn't even seem particularly sad. Oliver got up from the steps and stood nearby frowning as Ves addressed Tom: "I wonder if you'd do me a favor."

Warily Tom shrugged; he wasn't ready just yet to put his trust in this new Ves. "What is it?"

"I owe McFee some money," Ves said. "Been owing it a long time." Tom had heard the tale; the whole county had. "I want to pay him back," Ves said with a rueful grin, "but I don't believe he'll take it from me. I done tried, coming in. Got myself cussed out for it and never even made my speech." He fished from an inside pocket of his coat a plump leather wallet. "Will you hold it, and give it over to Hamby after I'm gone?"

"Of course," Tom said. Quietly amazed, he took the wallet and slipped it into the waistband of his trousers. Ves seemed both changed and not changed, more what he'd been before and less.

Now he squared on Captain Moore, stuck out his hand, said, "I remember what you tried to do for me, way back. I want to thank you for it." Shyly he ducked his head. "I just couldn't do no better'n I done."

The captain passed the daisy back to Lillie, freeing his hand to grasp Ves's; firmly they shook. "I reckon that's about the best any of us can say," smiled Moore. "I wish you continued good fortune."

Ves tipped his hat to Tom, made as if to go. But then Oliver stepped close, said simply, "Son." Ves stopped, turned, faced him. The look on Oliver's face recalled that of a general who has lost a long and bitter war and who, though saddened by defeat, is equally glad to see the strife come to an end at last. Oliver's dainty shoemaker's hand came out. Ves took and held it. Oliver's head moved up and down in a series of very small approving nods. Then they parted, and Ves went on down the steps and across the yard, mounted his gray horse and put it into the path at a walk. Soon, though, the gray struck a canter and carried Ves quickly down the cove. When he passed Hamby sitting on the boundary fence Ves circled wide.

Tom resumed his place by the bed. It was time to eat. In the dining room the others were falling to with a rattle of flatware and a low roar of talk, but Tom was unready for food. He continued to be afflicted by contrary longings both to ease his hunger and to puke up the poison brewing in his gut. He was bone-tired, and the insides of his eyelids felt as if they'd been coated with salt. With drooping head he sat holding Rebecca's burning hand. *Every moment that passes*, he thought, *more and more of her is lost.*

He longed to sleep yet dared not miss a single one of the dwindling seconds of her life. He had to see and know all. He must keep watch; he must continually bend close and observe; he must bear witness to the last of her living; he must memorize her every feature and every aspect of her decline. And having memorized these he must never forget any jot or tittle afterward. His Rebecca was fading, would soon be gone; by holding fast to each fragment of time, in a way he was also holding on to her. Must it be? Did he have to comply? Could he not resist? Could he not impede it, maybe even stop it? Perhaps if he watched closely enough, if he paid the strictest possible attention, if he focused all his mind and all his senses on keeping the minutes from going by, he could actually slow time down, maybe even stop it altogether. More. Could he perhaps reverse it? Turn it back? Save her? Win for himself one more chance to present her the life that drought and hailstorm and freshet and sheer bad luck had kept him from giving her through all the years of want and hardship?

She rolled her head toward him on the sopping pillow. Her eyes in their deep sockets fluttered open, fixed on him. They were brilliant, as if bathed in some clear fine oil. Her breathing was shallow but rapid like a dog's after a long run, and that wet rattle of bad lungs was in it again. She streamed with sweat; the death's-head beneath its thin tissue of flesh was closer now to breaking through; her cheekbones jutted so sharply they looked capable of splitting the skin. He wanted to tell her how sorry he was, but she whispered something he couldn't hear. He bent closer. "Hamby," she said.

❧

Called at last not by emissaries but by Rebecca herself, Hamby came at once. He entered the sickroom wearing the crimp-brimmed hat that none had ever seen him put by, its little brass figure of a king's crown pinned to the front. But as soon as he came to her bedside, slowly and with ceremony he removed the hat to expose a shiny hairless dome singularly dented and misshapen. He then sat on the stool Tom scooted forward for him.

But she proved immune to his intended show of respect. "All this time," she told him in a voice as faint as the crackle of dry straw, "I thought you wore that thing out of pride. Now I see 'twas to hide an ugly head." She gave him a nearly invisible chiding smile.

Hamby looked offended. "Hell," he burst out unseemly loud, "I

299

ain't *bald*, if that what you thinking. I shaves my head. Shaves it every damn morning of my life. Why, shaving beats cutting all to hell."

Tom winced at the swearwords and at the loudness, but Rebecca smiled more and more as Hamby blustered. Then a spell of coughing racked her and cut him off. Dr. Killian leaned in, extending a cloth; she spat into it a sluice of bright crimson; standing by in mute witness to her agony, Tom felt his heart lash in his chest like an eel trying to escape the net; meanwhile Hamby watched coolly, impassively, holding his hat level on his knees. For a time Rebecca fought for breath, filling the room with phlegmy noises, now and then spitting up blood and bits of dark matter which the doctor deftly wiped away with his cloth. Finally she quieted and lay as before, sweat-sodden, pale, panting lightly and quickly, sometimes shaken by spasms.

Hamby waited her out with apparent calm. When she was ready she whispered to him, "Take some advice. Either let it grow. Or keep it covered up."

Hamby swore and put on the hat and gave it a saucy slant. If he had ever laughed before except in derision, no one had noticed it; now he did, and Tom and Dr. Killian remarked it, amazed. "Fact is," Hamby confessed, "I let it grow, I be gray like a old cat."

Mischief shone in her face. "You *are* an old cat."

He nodded, "Yes'm." Then he asked, "You still got that thing?"

She moved her head in assent, opened a hand to show him lying in its wet hollow the little carved angel he'd given her at Christmas years before, dark now from much handling, all its edges rounded, worn smooth. Again he nodded. She closed her fist over the piece and held it to her chest. A stillness fell that lasted a long time, broken only by the ticking of the mantel clock and the rasp and gurgle of her breathing. During this silence she lay intently watching Hamby with her glowing eyes, and he sat watching her right back. Presently she asked, "Why'd you never leave?"

"Never had no goddamn luck," he replied at once. "Any money I got, I pissed away." He frowned, thinking of Ves. "Or it got stole."

"You could've gone. One way or the other."

Hamby's shoulders eloquently rose and fell. "I go, who keep that fool Jimmy Cartman in line?"

This time Rebecca didn't smile. "You're the last of the Curtises," she said. "My last brother."

Hamby waved a hand in denial. "Save you, the Curtises be all gone now. Damn line of slave owners and Legrees, put the foot on the neck of the nigger, done all petered out. Good riddance, I say. *You* the last Curtis." He paused; he grimaced; his mouth went flat and thin. "Best, too." Then he hastened to add, "Though that ain't saying much." For all Hamby's banter Tom noticed he didn't deny or disparage the other thing she'd called him.

Weakly Rebecca rocked her head from side to side. "You," she said. She reached out to him the hand that held the carved angel. The thinnest remnant of her voice said, "Take him. Fly up, too. When it's time."

Hamby made a scornful sound. "You need such as that, not me." He snorted, looked away. "Ain't no goddamn angels where *I* bound."

Rebecca lifted the angel higher toward him. Her hand was shaking. She spoke in a hush hardly to be heard. "He's flown me already. Fly you, too. Take him."

Presently he did.

⤥

From the gross matter of her body Rebecca felt something finer rising. It left the sick and failing flesh and floated up. The feeling reminded her of times when as a child playing in pools in the river she'd filled her lungs with air, leapt into the water, touched bottom with her toes, then allowed the air within to bring her to the surface again. Utterly relaxed and limber, she would ascend in peace. And there was a moment just before breaking the surface when, looking up, she could see the bright of the sun beyond it like another world entirely, into which she must presently burst.

In rising now she felt all her sweetest senses sharpen and the coarser ones recede—the pain in her chest, the choking-off of her breath, the scald of fever. Instead she became delightfully aware of everything about her and oblivious of her ailing self. She smelt the dinner; she heard the clock; outside the window a chickadee piped. Her mind lost its fog of pain; it cleared like sediment settling in a glass. She saw Tom bend close, felt his hands on hers. She read the despair in his eyes. She knew he believed he'd failed her, that the life he'd given her had proved sparse and mean next to what he'd pledged and meant to provide. She wanted to comfort him, wanted to say he'd given her everything that mattered and nothing that didn't. But she was beyond the power of speech now. She couldn't soothe his anguish. All she could do was hope in time he'd come to understand.

Rising still she recalled how once she'd thought of turning away from life, had believed it was better to await death in apathy and lassitude rather than to pursue a course which, once embraced and savored, must too soon end. How wrong she'd been! Dear Miz Henslee had made her see the truth—that one always had to choose life. Rebecca had chosen it; it had been richly full; now it was over, but she did not repent having given herself to it knowing she must lose it before her time. The twinkling surface was just above her now. She rose toward it joyful, thankful. Around her the room was crowded—Tom leaning in, Lillie peeping at her, Homer and Ethel gazing curiously down, the Reverend Thomas and Jimmy Cartman praying aloud in clashing counterpoint, Andy Cartman shaken by sobs, Dr. Killian kneeling at the bedside with his fingers on her wrist, others—all but Hamby, who'd refused to stay. She tilted her head, peered out the window, spied him perched alone on the boundary fence wearing his raggedy hat and gazing off down the green cove. Then as she kept on floating upward the smiling face of a child seemed to appear above, suspended over the glimmer of the surface she must soon pass beyond. Was it her wee Freddy? Was he the first of the many lost to give her welcome? Expectantly she broke through into light.

Afterword

This book rounds out the trilogy begun with *Hiwassee* and carried forward with *Freedom's Altar*. As in those novels many of the people who appear as characters bear the names and identities of my ancestors. Bare-bones genealogical information forms the small factual basis of what I have written. In the absence of any real evidence about the lives they led I have had to imagine what my forebears were like and to invent a story for them to be caught up in.

It may be useful to recount what befell the people behind the characters in this book after the period of the story.

Sylvester "Ves" Price married a Georgia girl in 1882 and fathered a son and daughter; another child died. When his wife passed away six years later Ves gave up the children by means of indentured adoption—some say by abandonment—to the brothers I have called Jimmy and Andy Cartman, who raised them as their own. Ves next wed another Georgia woman and again sired a boy and girl. At some point between 1895 and 1900 he moved with his second family to Arapahoe County, Colorado. But this wife, too, died young, and it appears Ves once more abandoned his children—one of whom, interestingly enough, was named Oliver. Ves's subsequent whereabouts are uncertain until he surfaced in Los Angeles working as a waiter in a restaurant. He died in Los Angeles in November 1951. He was ninety-two.

Hamby McFee was recorded in the 1880 census as a cousin in the household of Andrew J. Curtis and his sister Rebecca. Nothing is known of him after that time.

Tom Carter was murdered on Christmas Day 1930 by a drunken young man who, contrary to Tom's wishes, wanted to pay court to one of his daughters by a later marriage. Tom and Rebecca's daughter Lillie married Ves Price's oldest son Will. They were my grandparents.

In 1901, at the age of sixty-four, Oliver Price married for a third time, in Gilmer County, Georgia. He had no more children. Of his numerous brood from his first and second marriages only his youngest surviving daughter kept in touch with him in his old age. Toward the end he lived near destitution on a small Confederate pension from the state of Georgia. He died in September 1914 in Sugar Valley, Gordon County, Georgia, aged seventy-seven.

William Patton "Irish Bill" Moore and his family were stricken with typhoid during a terrible epidemic that raged through Clay County in 1898. Two sons died; Miss Hattie was the only member of the clan who did not fall ill. Captain Moore died in 1918. Accounts disagree as to the cause; it was either a kick by a mule or a case of pneumonia contracted while riding home in winter weather from a reunion of his old cavalry regiment in Murphy. I prefer to believe the second version, which seems more consistent with what is known of the redoubtable captain. It is easy to visualize the eighty-seven-year-old warrior traveling thirty-odd miles on horseback in the dead of winter to be with his old comrades in arms.

There was no Webb Darling, though the Tusquittee area was famous for blockading in the old days. Darling is a composite of two actual moonshiner kings, Lewis Redmond and Bill Berong, who operated in nearby upland South Carolina and Georgia during the early 1880s. Ree Bolt, Jared Nutbush and the delectable Katie Shuford are all imaginary. So, too—mercifully—is Mrs. Hemphill.

Acknowledgments

I am grateful to my nephew David C. Galloway for his genealogy of the Price family—particularly for uncovering the ultimate fate of Sylvester Price, so long a mystery. Thanks also to my sister Wanda Price Galloway, who first fired my interest in the Curtis clan, and to Frances Curtis Bogy of San Antonio, Texas, genealogist of the Curtises.

Of particular help to me was C. Edwin Smith of Decatur, Georgia, a grandson of Irish Bill Moore who in February 1918, just before his third birthday, rode on the captain's hearse from the Tusquittee down to the Presbyterian Cemetery at Hayesville. Mr. Smith graciously shared with me some delightful stories about the captain from the Civil War and after, including the text of Miss Hattie's Dear John letter.

Thanks also to my cousin Jerry Padgett of Rock Hill, South Carolina, who after reading *Hiwassee* alerted me to the place and circumstances of the death of Andy Curtis, information which our side of the family had lost. Mr. Padgett also provided genealogical information that clarified the antecedents of the brothers I have referred to as the Cartmans. I am also grateful to the staff of Dorothea Dix Hospital in Raleigh, North Carolina, for confirming the location and date of Andy Curtis's death and burial.

I am indebted to the late Morris Craig of Bull Creek, North Carolina, who spoke to me of old-time moonshining ways—based of course entirely on the hearsay of the country, not on any personal knowledge.

Thanks are also due my cousin Bobby Palmer of Hayesville and Margaret Hartman Abbott of Asheville for reading and commenting on the manuscript. I am also grateful beyond measure to the staff of John F. Blair, Publisher, and especially to my editor Stephen Kirk and Carolyn Sakowski, president.

Finally I must express my deepest love and gratitude to Ruth Perschbacher, who is both my inspiration and my chief critic, roles that may seem in conflict yet, when fused, offer the best help any writer—or any man—can hope to get.

A number of published sources were helpful to me. Dr. Kester's horrendous diagnosis of Andy's mental condition is drawn from an article on insanity in the *Americanized Encyclopaedia Britannica* of 1902. The effects of syphilis Andy ponders and the doggerel he quotes to Mrs. Hemphill are set forth in *The Story the Soldiers Wouldn't Tell: Sex in the Civil War* by Thomas P. Lowry, M.D. Material relating to the Kirk-Holden War against the Ku Klux Klan comes from *Reconstruction in North Carolina* by J. G. de Roulhac Hamilton.

I profitably consulted several other works in the preparation of the book. Of special value were *Revenuers & Moonshiners: Enforcing Federal Liquor Law in the Mountain South, 1865–1900* by Wilbur R. Miller; *A History of Clay County, N.C.,* by Guy Padgett; *The Carolina Mountains* by Margaret W. Morley; *Life and Labor in the Old South* by Ulrich B. Phillips; *Western North Carolina: A History from 1730 to 1913* by John Preston Arthur; and *Whispers among the Laurel: A Vanishing Culture*, volumes 1 and 2, edited by Deby Jo Ferguson.

Anyone who has consulted the first nine volumes of the extraordinary *Foxfire* series, edited by Eliot Wigginton and his students, will recognize the debt I owe to that collection for many details of mountain life in days of yore. In particular I drew on *Foxfire 8*'s material on the arcana of chicken fighting and on the excellent piece on William Patton Moore in *Foxfire 9*.

If I have made errors of fact or interpretation in drawing on any of these sources the fault is entirely mine.